BETWEEN THEM WERE THE REMAINS OF THE BEDDING … IT HAD COVERED A BODY, WHICH NOW LAY IN ALL ITS BLACKENED, SINGED HORROR, A TRAVESTY OF A HUMAN FORM, THE HEAD CURVED BACK AGAINST A PILLOW WHICH WAS LITTLE MORE THAN A HEAP OF ASH AND DEBRIS.

'I reckon that's one of the most burned bodies I've ever seen …'

George looked at the floor and the severe damage there, and frowned. If it was worse than that upstairs, then upstairs must be in a bad state. But she couldn't concentrate on that thought, because Knight was speaking …

'I know that scientifically it's never been proven, but if that isn't a form of spontaneous combustion then I'm not here but lying in bed at home and dreaming.'

The author of numerous works of both fiction and non-fiction, Claire Rayner wrote her first novel in 1964. Her successes include the twelve-volume *Performers* series, the six-volume *Poppy Chronicles* and a new series of medical mysteries featuring Dr George Barnabas, of which this is the third. The first two volumes, *First Blood* and *Second Opinion*, are both available in Signet, and *Fourth Attempt* has recently been published by Michael Joseph. Her two historical romances about the Quentin family, *London Lodgings* and *Paying Guests*, are also published in Signet.

Claire Rayner is Britain's best-known advice and medical columnist. Born in 1931 she worked as a nurse for several years before starting her successful career as a medical journalist and agony aunt, writing for several national newspapers and magazines and appearing on national TV and radio. She was awarded an OBE in the 1996 New Year's Honours List. Claire Rayner is married with three grown-up children and lives in Middlesex.

CLAIRE RAYNER

THIRD DEGREE

A SIGNET BOOK

SIGNET

Published by the Penguin Group
Penguin Books Ltd, 27 Wrights Lane, London W8 5TZ, England
Penguin Books USA Inc., 375 Hudson Street, New York, New York 10014, USA
Penguin Books Australia Ltd, Ringwood, Victoria, Australia
Penguin Books Canada Ltd, 10 Alcorn Avenue, Toronto, Ontario, Canada M4V 3B2
Penguin Books (NZ) Ltd, 182–190 Wairau Road, Auckland 10, New Zealand

Penguin Books Ltd, Registered Offices: Harmondsworth, Middlesex, England

First published by Michael Joseph 1995
Published in Signet 1996
1 3 5 7 9 10 8 6 4 2

Thanks for advice and information about death, detection, rags, fires and sundry other topics are due to: Dr Trevor Betteridge, Pathologist of Yeovil, Somerset; Dr Rufus Crompton, Pathologist, St George's Hospital, Tooting, London; Dr Azeel Sattah, Pathologist, Queen Elizabeth II Hospital, Welwyn Garden City, Hertfordshire; Detective Chief Inspector Jackie Malton, Metropolitan Police; Dr Hilary Howells, Anaesthetist of Totteridge, Hertfordshire; Mr Laurence Barry and Mr Leo Collins of L. M. B. Co Ltd, textile recyclers of Canning Town, London; and many others too numerous to mention; and are gratefully tendered by the author.

I

Sounds. The faint splash of oars in fast moving water, the lapping of miniature waves against rough shingle, the rasp of wood against stone as a boat is dragged up above the edge of the water, footsteps crunching up a beach.

And then a whistling gasp as someone catches his breath in surprise and perhaps horror and a faster somewhat erratic rhythm as the footsteps start again, scrabbling urgently through the shingle to disappear into the tangle of streets that line the Thames at Limehouse Reach. Now the river is alone again, flowing peaceably under an opalescent sky that is fast emerging from the deeper blue of the night, offering listening ears only the distant mutter of traffic from the Westferry Road on the north side and even more softly from Grove Street on the south.

It is going to be a blazing day. The coolness in the air and the scent of the sea that the incoming tide is bringing upriver with it are deceptive. Another forty minutes or so and the sun will be well up and warning Londoners of another sweltering June day in which they'll sweat and mutter and shout bad temperedly at each other as the streets fill with engine fumes and the river with pleasure boats loaded with tourists.

When the sounds come back, they are loud and assured, and certainly there is no shock or horror in the matter-of-fact voices which fill the air. First the car draws up at the end of Gaverick Street beside the phone box and doors slam with scant concern for the people sleeping in the front rooms of the fancy new houses that stand in a neat carriage-lamp-trimmed row on each side. Then the voices come closer to the river as footsteps – more of them this time – start on the beach again. One of the voices is different, not loud and assured at all but whining and anxious, conciliatory and blustering by turns. It is not pleasant to hear.

'Why shouldn't I be about this time o' mornin'? Ain't I got a right to make my livin' best way I can? The buggers tell yer to get on yer bike and look for yer keep, so I do. Only my bike's a boat.'

'On night work, then, are you?' One of the loud voices has a distinct jeer in it. 'So's you can see better, eh?'

The old man – for he can be seen now, as the light steadily strengthens – sniffs lusciously and very disagreeably and looks at the other, a bulky man in a dark suit and carefully knotted tie looking even this early as though he's been up and about and fully alert for hours.

'Shows 'ow much you don't know, that does,' the old man says. 'I bin mudlarkin' on this river since I was a nipper – my dad took me out with 'im in the war years, when we bloody nearly 'ad it to ourselves an' 'e learned me 'ow to use me eyes, an' to see what there is to be seen. An' picked up. There ain't much I miss. An' I didn't miss this.'

'Well, let's have a look at it,' grunts the bulky man. 'And make sure you haven't been wasting police time. I'll have your guts for garters if you have – Hmm.' He stops short as the other two men with him, one in a crumpled suit surmounted by a raincoat and looking far less alert than the bulky man, and the other in uniform, come to stand beside him and all four look down at the beach.

The sky now is a pearly blue, and the men can see much more easily. It is even possible to identify colour: the brown shininess of the bulky man's shoes; the dirty red shell-suit top the old man is wearing; and the dark brown shoe and yellow sock, both very soiled, that adorn the object at which they are all looking.

A human leg, cut off just below the knee. The flesh is greyish where there is muscle, dirty yellow where there is fat.

2

Two gleaming pieces of bone stick up neatly from one side of the leg, one smaller than the other, but of an equal length. The thing stinks. Even without bending forwards, the men standing around it are very aware of the reek and are clearly trying to control their revulsion. The old man, however, does not pretend; he sets his hand over his mouth and nose and says in muffled triumph, 'See? Didn't I tell yer? Didn't I just? Just like I said. 'Uman remains, or my name ain't Sid Martin.'

By the time the river police arrived, Sid Martin was in a high old rage. Not only was it already getting warm – and the smell of the leg lying forlornly on the shingle inside its barricade of yellow police tape was becoming heavier in consequence – he was tired, he wanted his breakfast and he knew with every fibre of his being that he was being cheated by the other mudlarks who rowed by, their noses twitching with curiosity, shouting jeers when they recognized him.

'It's a sin an' a crime,' he cried passionately to the lightening sky. 'That all on account of doin' my citizen's duty I go an' get clobbered by you lot. I acts proper, tells you all I know about this bleedin' thing, and will you let me go? Not bloody likely, an' them out there collecting all manner o' stuff as is mine by rights on account of I gets up so early, and my ulcer playin' up an' all.' He clutched his belly piteously and stared venomously at the bulky man.

'Give him a Rennie, Michael,' the bulky man snapped over his shoulder at his companion in the rumpled suit, who had now taken off his raincoat and left it in a bundle at the top of the foreshore, well out of reach of the water. 'Shut him up, whatever else you do.'

'What'll shut me up is being let go,' Martin cried and the bulky man turned and glared at him.

'Listen you, for two pins I'd take you down to the nick and ask you a lot of very difficult questions. Like what the hell were you doing here in the small hours of the morning and what do you know about this and if you're such a busy collector, how come you didn't take off the shoe? It's a pricey one as anyone can see, and I'll bet you're not usually so squeamish about things like this, or finding stuff people haven't realized they've lost till it's in your bloody boat.'

'Don't you go pinnin' nothin' on me!' Martin was alarmed. 'I just did my duty. I told you, I saw this, thought it might be somethin' good, came and looked an' at first I reckoned it was a bit o' meat, a leg o' pork or suchlike, gone off and stinkin'. But then I saw the shoe and I knew that couldn't be no butcher's meat. Fair turned me stomach, it did. As for the shoe' – his voice became suddenly the acme of reason and commonsense – 'what's the bleedin' good of one shoe, for Chrissakes? No one'll buy one bleedin' shoe, will they? Stands to reason. – And as for –'

'Shut up,' advised the younger plainclothesman, as his senior glared at Martin, and gave him a tube of Rennies. 'Inspector Dudley'll let you go soon's he can, you may be certain of that.' He had a soft Scottish burr to his voice. 'And no one's really thinking you had anything to do with it,' he added in a lower voice as Dudley turned away to speak to the river police sergeant who had been crouching beside the leg. 'He's just bamming you. You did fine calling us.'

'Much good it's done me,' Sid Martin said with deep gloom. 'No knowin' how much good stuff I've missed over this bleedin' business.'

'Is there that much around?' The detective constable, Michael Urquhart, sounded genuinely interested. 'I wouldn't have thought –'

'Is there much?' Sid stared up at him from his perch on a piece of driftwood set on edge in the shingle. 'There's wood for a start, an' it's well popular if it's fit to burn. There's geezers in the fancy flats' – he jerked his head downriver – ''oo pay a bomb for firewood for their modern gaffs all done up with Victorian fireplaces.' He laughed, a fat contemptuous sound. 'An' if the wood's all funny shapes there's idiots there – artists, round the studios in Wapping – as'll part with real money for 'em. They polish 'em up and calls 'em objays troovay and sell 'em for a packet.' He shook his head in a ruminative manner. 'Takes all sorts, I suppose.'

'Is that a living?'

4

'Nah, not on its own. It's all the stuff together, see? Bits o' this an' that what falls over the side from the tourist boats. It's amazin' what'll float. I've 'ad binoculars carried along by the air inside the waterproof cases they're in, an' cameras likewise, an' any number o' good jackets an' so forth. A few bob at the cleaners an' they're fine. I sell 'em in Wentworth Street or Watney Street, down the markets. Or if they ain't, I take them to Connie over at St Saviour and get a bit there.'

'And who might Connie be when she's at home?' the policeman said and Sid quirked his head at him.

'Blimey, you ain't bin on the job long, 'ave you? Everyone in these parts knows Connie.'

'Well, so they may.' Mike was nettled. 'But I don't. And I've been at Ratcliffe Street nick for the last four years. If your Connie's at St Saviour's, which is over the other shore, she's outside my patch. I couldn't be expected to –'

The old man snickered. 'Connie's a fella. Constantine Georgio-somethin'-or-other. 'E buys a lot o' my stuff what I finds – when I'm allowed to be about me business, that is.' And he turned and glowered at the man in charge, who was still in colloquy with the river police.

'I'll see what's happening,' the other said good naturedly. 'Just you shut your bletherin', there's a good chap. It upsets him.'

'Well, 'e upsets me,' Sid said darkly. 'You're all right, but 'e's a right bugger.'

'Tell me about it,' the young man said.

Sid looked at him sharply and then laughed, his almost toothless mouth opening into an unlovely gape. 'You're all right, ain't you?' he said. 'What's yer moniker?'

'Michael Urquhart. If it's any of your business. Now be quiet, and I'll see what I can do to get you on your way.'

Sid watched him join his colleagues as he sat there gloomily sucking one of his few remaining teeth and occasionally muttering as flies, attracted by the all-pervading stink of the putrid leg, zoomed at him.

At last Mike came back and Sid looked up hopefully. 'No joy,' the policeman said. 'Sorry. We've sent for the Soco and once he's cleared things you can be on your way. I'm hoping it'll not be too long. I'd gladly get away from that thing . . .' And he looked over his shoulder at the focus of everyone's attention.

'Soco?' said Sid, looking alarmed.

'Scene-of-crime officer,' Mike said. 'Has to check it all, do the pics and so forth. An hour or so should see you free to go.'

'Ah, shit,' said Sid and went on to more comprehensive and explicit swearing that seemed to give him some comfort as Mike went back to Dudley's side to wait for instructions.

Dudley was snapping the aerial back into his mobile phone and as he stowed it away in his pocket he looked pleased with himself.

Mike looked at him, his head quirked. 'Anything I can do?'

'Not a thing,' Dudley said, almost cheerfully. 'We just have to wait till they get here.' He chuckled then, an odd sound from someone usually so dour, thought Mike. 'That'll show 'em.'

'Show what?' It was the river sergeant, who had joined them, and Inspector Dudley looked at him and grinned.

'Well, her, really,' he said. 'The doctor.'

'Oh, yes.' The river sergeant, a tall thin man with a young face and an almost completely bald head, whose name was Slavin, looked interested. 'That'll be Dr Barnabas? I've heard about her. Bit of a goer, 'n't she?'

'You could say that,' Dudley said a little grimly. 'Bit full of herself, the way these feminist women are, is how I'd put it. Drives you barmy if you let it.'

'Dyke, is she?' Slavin said with a sympathetic but slightly avid air.

Mike opened his mouth to protest, caught Dudley's eye and decided to be more cautious than valorous. But he scowled.

'Might be easier if she was,' Dudley said. 'You know where you are with them. No, not this one.' He slid his glance sideways at Mike's disapproving expression. 'Well, you'll see for yourself soon enough, Slavin. Called her, didn't I? That'll get her out of bed. Or out of someone else's.' He looked at Mike again and said sharply, 'See if anyone in those houses up there is willing to make a cuppa for a few tired coppers, will you?'

Mike scowled even more. 'It's barely six in the morning. Won't be up yet, will they?'

'It's worth a try,' Dudley said and Mike turned and stomped away, every inch of his back showing his distaste for his errand. Dudley turned back to the sergeant.

'Can't say too much,' he said. 'Not in front of the children.'

'What, that DC?' Slavin looked surprised. 'Looks a good enough bloke to me.'

'Yeah, but the Guv'nor's best mate, if you ask me. A bit too pally, seein' he's just a DC. Mind you, the same goes for the Guv'nor with the doc, too pally by half.'

'No!' The other man was clearly fascinated. 'Is that a fact?'

'Yeah,' Dudley said. 'It's a fact. I swear she spends as much time in his bed as her own.'

'Are they married? To other people, I mean?' Slavin settled to a good gossip.

'No,' Dudley said, almost regretfully. 'No, they're footloose enough. The Guv'nor's always been too busy with the job and his fish-and-chip shops to get himself caught, as far as I can tell, and as for her ...' He shrugged. 'I dunno. She seems to like blokes well enough. Maybe a bit too well. I remember from her first case – well, I'll tell you over a drink some time. It's a long story.' He scowled. 'And then there was a case she really did meddle in. Made me look a right berk, she did. An' how can I say anythin' about it to the Guv'nor when they're cuddled up all cosy like that?'

'I'm not sure it's proper, is it?' The river sergeant looked dubious. 'Could it make trouble at the nick, like, the doc and a senior officer?'

'Listen, they meddle with our private lives enough, we all know that, but they don't actually check where you puts your ding-a-lings, not to the best of my knowledge. As long as it's not with one of the villains' women, or another copper's wife, you're all right.' Dudley looked pugnacious. 'I don't want no more fuss than we have to. But I get right fed up with this bloody woman.'

'Well, that's women for you,' the other said with an air of having said something very perceptive. 'Look, do you need us here any longer? There's not a lot more we can do. We've noted the leg, done a bit of checking on the way it lies so we can make a stab at where it might have entered the water. We can go and look for the rest of the poor bugger now, if you're finished.'

'I've sent for Soco as well as the doc,' Dudley said. 'You might be needed. To explain about tides and so forth.'

'Then we'll wait,' Slavin said. Then he raised his voice as Mike came crunching back over the foreshore. 'Hey, did you get that tea?'

'No. As I thought, people are still asleep,' Mike said.

Dudley glared at him. 'Yeah, I know. You didn't knock too hard in case you woke 'em.'

'That's right, *sir*,' Mike said, looking at him very directly. 'Don't like to get complaints about the way we deal with the public, do we?'

Dudley, remembering a recent pep talk on that very subject by Superintendent Whitman at Ratcliffe Street, looked blacker than ever and the river sergeant, picking up the vibes, grinned.

'Tell you what,' he said. 'I might have the makings on the launch. I'll just go and see what we can do.' He took himself off to the edge of the water where the shallow-bottomed police launch rocked on the tide, which was still running upriver and was well towards the full. 'I hope they hurry up,' he said over his shoulder. 'Your Soco and the doctor. Another couple of hours and all this foreshore'll be covered. High tide's just after nine at London Bridge and it's well after six now. Another ... well ...' He squinted at the water and then at the leg lying untended and ignored in the middle of its patch of shingle. 'Another hour and that'll have to be bagged and removed, if it isn't to go back into the water.' And he climbed into his launch and went forward to talk to his companion who was waiting for him.

'You see what I mean?' Dudley said loudly to Mike. 'That bloody woman always makes life awkward. Now she might be too late, the time she's taking to get here.'

8

'You've only just called her,' Mike said in a colourless voice. 'And the Soco. I doubt they'll be that long. Dr Barnabas is usually very fast, as you well know.'

'Is she so? Well, not fast enough for –' He stopped as a car turned into the road behind him and drew up at the end of the tiny street. They could see it from where they stood, a small battered green Citroën, and Mike lifted one hand in greeting as the driver got out and stood for a moment peering down at the foreshore, her head up and some of her dark hair blowing round her ears in the slight breeze that was still coming up the river with the tide.

She squinted at the glitter that was beginning to show on the water's ripples as the sun strengthened, lifted her own hand in recognition, and then dived back into her car to pull out a bag. She was wearing a pair of jeans and a loose white shirt tied into a knot by its tails at the waist, over bare tanned feet thrust into denim espadrilles.

'Look at her,' Dudley said in disgust. 'Thinks she's on a bleedin' holiday, does she?'

'Watch it, sir,' Mike said, knowing he was sailing close to the wind. 'Your fangs are showing.' And he went up the foreshore to meet Dr George Barnabas and bring her to the piece of body they had waiting for her.

2

George Barnabas came down the little beach, her small site bag tucked under one arm and her hands in her jeans pockets, looking as cheerful and relaxed as though she were meeting friends for a holiday drink. Her hair, which was thick, curly and abundant, was pulled into a dark knot on top of her head, but there was enough of it loose to fly around her face and make her look very young, an effect increased by her big round dark-rimmed glasses. Sometimes she wore contact lenses, but this morning she hadn't stopped to fiddle with them; trying to get herself dressed and out of her Bermondsey flat as fast as she could had been too important. The last thing she wanted was Dudley complaining about having to wait for her.

'Morning, Roop,' she said sunnily. She was rewarded with a black glare from Rupert Dudley, who loathed this diminution of his given name almost as much as he hated the way some of his junior colleagues referred to him behind his back as Rupert Bear. He was as powerless to stop George's use of the nickname as he was to control the juniors' private conversation and that did little to soothe his temper this morning.

'Over there,' he said, offering no other greeting, and led the way. Sergeant Slavin followed, as did Michael Urquhart, the uniformed constable and Sid Martin, and they all stood solemnly watching as she stopped beside the leg and looked at it.

'Not a pretty sight,' she said cheerfully and opened her bag to pull out her camera. The Soco would take pictures too, but she liked to collect her own as much as possible. One of these days, she had been promising herself for some time now, she would write a definitive textbook on forensic pathology and make her fortune. The nastier the illustrations the more value the text would have; even academics and students enjoyed having their withers wrung, as she told Gus Hathaway whenever he commented (as he often did) on her photographic efforts.

'No need,' Dudley said, falling into the trap as she set the focus and lifted the camera to her eyes. 'Soco'll have to do that – and watch out what you touch before he does get here. Can't have the scene disturbed.'

'You go teach your grandma,' George said, but without rancour. 'I'll just use my eyes till he gets here, scout's honour.' And she winked swiftly at Michael, not caring at all that Dudley saw her do it. 'Taking my own pictures won't do any harm. I like to have them.' She concentrated, snapped the shutter, focused again, taking half a dozen pictures in rapid succession. 'My God, this is a really smelly one, isn't it? Just the job before breakfast. I'd recommend you order the eggs rather than bacon when you get back to the canteen – all this dead meat around can put you right off your chow.'

Sid Martin sniggered but Dudley chose to look affronted. 'We try to show decent respect to human remains,' he said woodenly. 'If you'll just do the necessary, doctor, we'll get it bagged up and sent to the nick as soon as Soco gives the go-ahead.'

'I'll have it in my own mortuary, if you don't mind,' George said. She was now peering at the severed surface of the leg without touching it in any way and the young constable averted his eyes. 'Now, there's an odd thing . . .'

'What?' Michael said and crouched down with her, braving the stink. It couldn't be much worse close up than it was standing a few feet away. 'Something useful?'

'It's so clean,' George said. 'The cut. The leg muscles are thick, you know, hellishly hard to get through in one swipe, but this swipe not only cut the muscles and fat off clean, it sheared the bone. Hardly a splinter there.' She was squinting through a large magnifier now, leaning so close that her nose was almost in the muscle, much to Mike's admiration of her cool. Didn't the woman have a nose like other people? Or was she just hardened to it by her job?

'Christ, that's disgusting.' She leaned back and waved her hand in front of her face. 'I've dealt with a few nasties in my time but this really is ... Well, there you are. It's an oddity in that it's been severed clean. I can't say more at this stage, not till I examine it more carefully. Doesn't look like a propeller injury to me, though.' She looked up then. 'Anyone here from the river police?'

Slavin stepped forward a little self-importantly. 'Morning, doctor.'

'Morning,' she said. 'Have there been any vessels big enough to have a propeller that could do this? It would have to be one hell of a big one, I suppose, to make a cut like this and not be fouled in the process. Any reports?'

Slavin shook his head. 'The river's been a bit thin of heavy stuff upstream. Tourist vessels, of course, lots of them, but they don't carry that big a screw – and anyway, we'd have heard sure as sure if they'd hit anything really big, like a body. I mean, they'd have known it if they had.'

'I would have thought so.' George was looking at the leg again, and frowned. 'Do they always report accidents and so forth? I mean, if a vessel does have propeller trouble and they think they might have hit something, would you know?'

'Not always – but we're around all the time. There isn't much that gets past us.' He preened a little. 'Like I say, we'd have known if anything big upstream had hit a body, I reckon.'

'What about downstream?'

'Most of the stuff that comes ashore like this goes in the water upstream,' Sid said unexpectedly, pushing himself forward with an air of great superiority, clearly regarding himself as the expert witness on the issue. 'You 'ave to go right down the estuary to get the stuff what goes in down there.' He jerked his left thumb eastwards. 'I start well downstream when I goes out on me trips for that very reason.'

Slavin looked at him, sniffed and nodded. 'He's right,' he

said grudgingly to George. 'This fella was most likely thrown in somewhere upstream of here. Of course, wind speed and the height of the tide come into it, but it's odds on this went in on an ebb tide and came back up with the next turn of the water.'

'Hmm,' George said and looked again at the leg. 'Where's Soco? I want to take the shoe and sock off.'

'I'm here,' someone muttered and the little group opened up to make way for the new arrival, a tall thin man with a quiff of hair that stood up in a surprised sort of fashion over a slightly pockmarked face. 'Sorry to keep you. Bit o' trouble starting the car.'

Mike grinned, knowing a lame excuse for falling asleep again after being called when he heard it, and Dudley just stared hard at him.

'I'll get on then,' the man muttered, sliding his eyes away from Dudley, and they all stood back and let him go to work. There wasn't a great deal to do: photographs to take, samples of the shingle underneath the leg to collect, and a few measurements of such things as the distance from the leg to the water's edge, as well as to the embankment to be taken. ('Not much point in that,' Sid said loudly. 'Seein' as 'ow the tide's still runnin' up. Must be a foot or more 'igher'n what it was when that there thing landed 'ere an' I spotted it.' No one paid him any attention.) Less than fifteen minutes later, Soco indicated George could do as she chose with the leg.

Perversely, she chose to remove the sock and shoe there and then. She had the necessary equipment – the mat to catch any detritus that fell from them and bags to seal away any findings – so although it might have been just as easy to let the Soco bag up the leg and have it sent up to Old East, the hospital where her mortuary was, Dudley's even more obvious than usual hostility had hardened her. He was looking a touch green at the putrid nature of the leg, and she knew it would be even more unpleasant when it was moved. So move it she would, and if it made Dudley throw up, it would serve him right. She wanted to grin at herself for being so childish, but all the same went ahead, kneeling on the rough shingle comfortably, and spreading her gear.

Within a few minutes, though, she had forgotten that she wanted to discomfit Dudley and was absorbed in what she found. 'The sock's made of silk, I think,' she said. 'Expensive, certainly. Very damaged and holey but –'

'Fish,' said Dudley loudly to no one in particular. 'Water rats. There are plenty of scavengers that do that sort of damage.'

'Yes,' George said equably. 'You're probably right. I just mentioned it for the record.' She lifted her brows at the little tape recorder she had set up and which was collecting her comments. 'Now,' she went on. 'The shoe. Let's see . . .'

She peered inside, handling the sodden leather gingerly, her rubber-gloved finger probing gently. 'I think . . . Yes, that's it. Harrods. Pricey fella. Gets his shoes at Harrods.' She turned it over and looked at the design judiciously. 'It's a fancy design, for all that. What say you?'

'Flashy,' said Mike.

'Flashy it is,' she agreed, shutting the shoe into its own plastic bag and sealing and labelling it. She turned then to the now bare leg. It looked forlorn in its nakedness.

'Nails.' She peered closer. 'Well, well, manicured, no less. Soft skin, if a bit macerated in the water. A rich man's foot, I'd say, then.' She added more details about the skin to the little tape machine and then concentrated her attention on the severed end.

Now she could actually touch the flesh she was able to see it more clearly, using instruments delicately to explore the edges of the wound. She asked Michael to hold her magnifying glass while she did it, and was oblivious of the greenish tinge that showed round his lips and the rims of his nostrils as he gripped it close to the cut side.

'It *was* one swipe,' she said after a while. 'I'll double check with the big magnifier and get good pictures at the mortuary but it's pretty clear to me. The skin and the edges of the subcutaneous tissue are folded in here on the calf. I'd say he was lying face down when the whatever it was attacked his leg, and it went through from above. See?'

No one responded and she went on, directing Mike how to turn the glass to improve her vision with little jerks of her chin. He watched her face with gritted teeth and managed to control his nausea. He didn't miss a single one of her signals, either, which made her grin up approvingly at him before she went on.

'He had to be lying on his front when it happened, or the wound would be different. It must have gone through very fast – that degree of power implies speed, of course – so he wouldn't have moved. If he'd been in a state that made movement possible, that is. We can't know that till we find the rest of him. Or some of him.'

She straightened. 'I'll need to see the bones under a higher magnification, but I'll bet they'll tell the same story. OK, Roop. Get it back to the mortuary, will you? I'll have a report for you as fast as I can. We're not too busy this morning, to the best of my knowledge, so unless something horrendous happened in the night – and you'd know if it had, wouldn't you – I can see to this this morning.'

'Not all your bodies come through us,' Dudley said. 'Do they? And I wish you'd remember I'm to be addressed as Inspector, *doctor*.'

'Oh, you can call me George!' she said, smiling. 'Or Dr B., the way Gus does. I don't mind a bit.'

Dudley snapped an order at the uniformed constable to call back to the station for the van to remove the remains to Old East. The young policeman crunched gratefully up the beach, clearly glad to get away from the scene. He didn't come back, but waited in the street for the van to arrive. No one else seemed to have much to do until it got there, and they stood watching the Soco finally pack his gear away and depart, at which point Sid could remain patient no longer.

'Yer gotta let me go now,' he said pugnaciously. 'Ain't yer? Don't I 'ave no rights? 'Ere it is well on to seven and the river as busy as bleedin' 'yde Park Corner and not a penny of business likely to be done this mornin' in consequence. You gotta let me go now or it amounts to whatsit, don't it?

15

Harassment.' He said it with a marked American twang and George grinned at him.

'You've seen too many episodes of *NYPD Blue*,' she said. 'English police never harass anyone, do they, Roop? Inspector Roop?'

'No,' Dudley spat. 'They just get harassed, that's all. Hey, Urquhart!'

Mike, who knew that Dudley only used surnames like that when he was livid with rage, sighed and turned to look at his senior officer. 'Sir?'

'Get a written statement from this man, and then check every detail in it. You hear me? Every single bloody detail. I want to know exactly what he was doing on this foreshore at five a.m. I want to know that every single thing he's told us is true.'

'By my life!' Sid Martin cried shrilly. 'By my bleedin' life –'

'It will be if you've lied,' Dudley said. 'Right, Urquhart. Get on with it.'

'I'll do it here,' Michael said after glancing at Sid Martin. 'Quicker than taking him back to the nick.'

'You can't check his statement from here, you bloody fool! Take him to the nick and get on with it! And check with the Missing Persons Register for any leads as soon as you get there. On your way.' And he turned and stamped back to Sergeant Slavin, whom he clearly regarded as the only person on the scene with whom he could bear to have any conversation.

While Michael Urquhart managed to persuade the still loudly protesting Sid that he might as well give in and helped him draw his boat safely up the little beach to be tied to a great iron ring set in the concrete stanchion at the foot of Gaverick Street, George followed Dudley. She wasn't going to be put down by him, she told herself. Not this morning or any other morning.

His hostility, it seemed to her, had grown over the time she had been in her post as Forensic Pathologist, Home Office approved, working at Old East, the large district hospital which, despite severe shabbiness and a chronic lack of resources, managed to look after the health needs of most of the local population. It was a hard patch to work, as she had discovered. Was that what made Rupert Dudley so unpleasant and so dismissive of her? She doubted it. His boss, Gus Hathaway, hadn't become unpleasant. Rude sometimes, bloody-minded usually, difficult undoubtedly, but plain nasty? No.

Her lips curved a little as she thought of him. Gus, the absurdest policeman she could imagine. Detective Chief Inspector at Ratcliffe Street nick, and as near a millionaire as made no matter. None of his colleagues had been able to comprehend why he hadn't retired from the Force when his old dad had died and left him the very lucrative chain of fish-and-chip shops and restaurants that dotted the East End, but he hadn't. He liked the job too much, he had told them – and George – and that was that. So he stayed in it, while running the business in whatever time he could salvage round the edges of his police day, and living life as fully as he could.

That full life included George. They'd been an item for – she thought about that as she made her way across the beach towards Slavin – eighteen months. A year ago last Christmas, after the affair of the dead babies on which they'd worked together so hard. And in which, she now remembered, Dudley had been involved. It had not gained him much glory. She'd scooped what glory there was going from under his nose, and Dudley, she told herself, has a long memory.

Ah well, why should she worry? She had won that round, and more. To have Gus Hathaway as her lover was much the most satisfying part of the outcome of that case; Dudley would get over his loathing of her in time. She'd just have to let him get on with it. 'Horse's ass, Roop,' she murmured to herself and beamed sweetly at the man as she reached the place where he was standing talking in low tones to Slavin.

'Sergeant,' she said winningly to Slavin. 'Tell me about the tides hereabout. I've lived here a while now and I have to say I've not paid as much attention as I might to the timings. I've only noticed that they happen.'

Slavin grinned. 'It'd be hard to miss it, living right by the river as we do. Old Thames is a busy river. Right, the tides. Twelve and a half hours apart they are, roughly. Creep up a bit over the year, like. Right now ... let's see.' He reached into his pocket, pulled out a battered notebook and riffled through the pages. 'High tide today at London Bridge this morning'll be nine-fifteen a.m. Low tide three-fifteen this afternoon. The water turns around – oh, tennish, I dare say. And then again this afternoon around four o'clock, to go back upstream again. So, high water tonight at the Bridge'll be at nine-thirty p.m. and –'

'I see,' she said hastily, afraid he was about to recite all the tide times from now till Armageddon. 'It's pretty stable, then.'

'Pretty stable.' He closed his notebook and stowed it back in his pocket. 'You have to take into account the winds and the changes in the clocks and so forth, but overall, that's the shape of it.'

'I can't be sure, but going by the state of the putrefaction of the leg – first sight you understand – that limb was in the water about a week. So it could have gone in –'

'No need for you to worry yourself over that, Doctor.' Dudley could keep silent no longer. 'That's our business. No need for you to –'

'Go on, say it!' George said and laughed. 'No need for you to worry your pretty little head.'

'I'd be hard pushed to get the words out,' he snapped. He stared at her witheringly, then turned and went away up the beach to the car to bawl at the constable for standing around doing bugger all.

Slavin watched him go and laughed. 'He missed his morning coffee, didn't he? Well, there it is. Some blokes in the Bill are like that. Hardened. We're all right in the river force, of course.'

'Of course you are,' she said and patted his shoulder. Then she wondered if she had been the one to be patronizing, but he only grinned back at her. 'Do something for me,' she said. 'I know I'm only the doctor, but I like to get involved in these tricky cases, you know. It's kinda more fun. So will you watch out for any other pieces of body? I'd really like to be sure I get my hands on anything that turns up as soon as it does, even before the coroner hears of it. Leave it to Dudley and he might even try to get the whole job handed over to McCulloch at the forensic unit further down the river, in Greenwich.'

'I get you,' Slavin said. Now it was his turn to pat her shoulder, which he did with obvious pleasure. 'I'll tip you off. At Old East, are you?'

'That's it,' she said. 'And even if I'm not there someone reliable'll take messages. Just ask for the Path. Department direct. Not Appointments, but Path. Department, got it?'

'I've got it,' he promised and then looked up at her slyly. 'You'd better ask the Guv though, as well, hadn't you? It's not as if he'd treat you as unkindly as our inspector here.'

She looked at him sharply but he gazed back artlessly. 'No,' she said after a moment. 'I get on very well with the DCI. But he's tied up on other cases and Dudley'll be in charge of this. Which is why I'd like you to help me. Will you?'

'Well ...' he said and then glanced over her shoulder, to where Dudley was waving at him and shouting that they were leaving. The van had arrived, and already the leg had been double-bagged, labelled and was being borne off to the back of the vehicle for transporting the couple of miles upriver to George's mortuary. 'Glad to help. I'll be in touch.'

'I know you will,' George said and winked at him. Then she followed him back up the beach to climb into her own little Citroën to go rattling back to the hospital for a shower, breakfast and the day's work.

And behind them the little beach lay quietly, waiting for the last efforts of the tide to swallow it up and wash away the evidence that they, or their find, had ever been on it.

3

George liked best the first hour or so of the day at Old East. The hospital, an ill-matched conglomeration of buildings sprawling over a cramped piece of Shadwell ground between the Highway and the river, looked at its neatest and cleanest before the day's detritus of discarded Coke cans and sweet wrappers and worse built up in the courtyards and the waiting area in A & E and the linking corridors, and while the staff and patients still looked reasonably fresh. By mid afternoon, especially on these hot summer days, everyone was frazzled and ill tempered and tired and it showed in the way patients moved sluggishly between the long corridors and the clinics, with either aggressive or shuffling steps, and in the staff's pallid oily skins and baggy eyes, even the young ones. The place smelled tolerable in the mornings too; of all hospital food breakfast was undoubtedly the best, so the scent of toast and bacon and even coffee would wander through the wards and cheer everyone; it certainly was easier on the nose than the steamed fish and mince and puréed Brussels sprouts that seemed to dominate the lunch menus. There was in addition a faint scent of the disinfectants used overnight to wash the floors and walls, and though it could have a slightly ominous effect on patients who found hospitals alarming places, it was a great deal more agreeable than the reek of sweating sick bodies and blood and medication that filled the air as the day progressed.

This morning, since she was particularly early, it was even

pleasanter than usual in George's estimation. The night staff were busy on the wards, so the corridors and the courtyards were quiet. On the straggling bushes in the flower-bed supposed to adorn the centre of the main courtyard, which was the hospital's main thoroughfare, and which the Estates Department struggled to look after, there were even a couple of new pink roses. George stopped to touch one and try to smell it. It was still in too tight a bud to offer any scent, and by lunchtime, when she would come this way again, it would, of course, have gone. Visitors seemed unable to prevent themselves from snatching every flower that appeared. Well, she thought, I might as well have it myself. At least I work here. She twisted it off and took it to her own rather drab little office in the Pathology Department where she stuck it in a specimen glass on her desk.

The desk was blessedly clear and she contemplated it with lively pleasure. The amount of paperwork her job created was awesome, she would tell Gus, who would merely snort at her and point out how much more burdened with bumf he was, which was of small comfort. Most days started with a struggle to clear the most urgent material and ended with an attempt to finish the rest, which rarely succeeded. Usually there was a backlog screaming out to be done; but not this morning, and she was grateful. She was due in court at two this afternoon, to give evidence at the Old Bailey about a man who had died of injuries sustained in a fight outside a Leman Street pub last weekend, which would, if there was any justice, result in all three of the men who had attacked him going down for long stretches, but she doubted it. She had become almost as cynical as Gus and his colleagues about the lightness of the sentencing of the villains their work uncovered. That would leave her enough time to do a full work-up on the leg she had just seen at the riverside, and she stretched and went to put on her little coffee machine to get the first brew of the day ready.

Roop, she thought and grinned as she spooned the grounds into the filter and scrabbled in her cupboard for biscuits and a mug. Thought he'd scored one over on me. But not this time.

She knew perfectly well how much Rupert Dudley disliked

her and resented her relationship with Gus, how suspicious and shut-out it made him feel. There was nothing at all sexually ambivalent about the man – he had a lively wife and three teenage children living in Romford to attest to that – but he didn't like women as work colleagues. He was distant and unfriendly towards any women police who drifted into the team, an attitude that ensured that they often drifted out again as fast as they could put in for a transfer. And he had certainly been unfriendly to George when she had replaced her male predecessor in her job. It had been bad enough for him that she had not allowed herself to be dismayed by his attitude (it was some time before she actually noticed it, to tell the truth) but when she had become emotionally involved with his boss, Gus Hathaway, Dudley had been almost in despair. She knew it and he knew she knew it; and that somehow made it worse for him. What was it that plagued him? Simple inability to realize that women could do any job a man could do? Confused jealousy based on some deep and (to George) incomprehensible male bond? Or just an old-fashioned he's-my-mate-and-I-was-here-first? She didn't know, and frankly she didn't care. His behaviour was just silly, as far as she was concerned, occasionally tiresome, and always a tedious waste of time.

Anyway, his tricks hadn't worked this morning. He'd phoned Gus's number to reach her. The screech of the bell had woken her suddenly, but not so suddenly that she hadn't had her wits about her. Gus had already left his flat, due to join a stake-out set up by the team he was using to deal with a series of high-profile robberies that had afflicted the whole of East London in the past few months, and she knew everyone involved would know that. If they'd wanted Gus while he was *en route* they'd have called him on his mobile phone, not his home. This had to be someone prying, trying to find out if she was there.

She had lain there once the phone stopped ringing, waiting, and sure enough within a few moments her own mobile had rung and she had answered it, sounding suitably sleepy, told Rupert Dudley she'd be with him as soon as she could, and broken the connection in great satisfaction. He'd clearly wanted to catch us out, she thought. Bastard.

Not that it mattered, that was the silly thing. There was no reason why she and Gus shouldn't have the steamiest of love affairs if they chose. Neither was attached to anyone else, and it did no harm to the job, so why worry? And this time in fact, what Dudley had tried to catch them in was a piece of very unsteamy cosiness.

She'd gone to Gus's flat last night to make him dinner, something she did occasionally when neither of them wanted to go to one of his restaurants, and she'd fallen asleep on the sofa, waiting for him to get home so that she could grill his steak. He'd come in at midnight, almost dead on his feet, and wanted no more than an omelette, and by the time she'd made them and they'd eaten, it hardly seemed worth getting into her little car and driving back over the river to her own flat in Bermondsey.

So they'd curled up and slept like an old married couple without an atom of passion between them. Just the sheer comfort of being together. It had been, she thought now as she settled at her desk and sipped her coffee gratefully, really rather nice. It wouldn't set the world alight with excitement but it was very *nice*.

But whether it would go on being so nice was another issue. He'd been working these crazy hours, seven days a week, for almost a month now and it was really getting rather much. He looked thinner and more pinched with fatigue (though it would take a lot to extinguish the humour in that square face or to flatten the exuberance of the dark curly hair that covered his skull) and certainly was abstracted in his manner. They hadn't worked together on a case in all that time and had hardly talked at all; she missed that: sharing the digging out of facts in tricky cases was the best fun she knew, even more fun than sex; though that was there too when they worked together. Somehow there had always seemed enough time and energy left over for themselves. But at the moment there was no slack at all for him in which to live his own life, or to share hers. All she could do was make sure she went to the flat, as she had last night, to remind him of her existence and herself of her need of him.

It would be worth it though, eventually. She knew that. Gus, despite the financial security provided by the nine fish-and-chip-shops-cum-restaurants that had spread themselves right across the East End of London, and which were threatening to move northwards into more upmarket areas like Islington and Dalston where trendy young media types were colonizing, remained as ambitious a copper as he'd ever been. And now he was about to become a superintendent. It was just a matter of time.

She thought about that as she finished her coffee. Gus, in charge of an Area Major Investigation Team, responsible for all the big cases that came into ten nicks. It was so heady a prospect for him. And perhaps for George too. If she could become the forensic pathologist permanently attached to Gus's AMIT, wouldn't life be fun? No longer to have any responsibility for Old East's pathology services, to be able to concentrate entirely on being with and working with Gus. She stretched as luxuriously as a cat as she thought about it. Lovely.

Just a matter of time, he had told her, when it had all started. 'Get this case sorted, get the whole bloody lot of 'em in the dock and I'll be free to go on my assessment course and then way-hay, just watch me!'

'Assessment course?' she said, surprised. 'Ye Gods, Gus, how much more do they have to know about you? Haven't you been a cop long enough?'

'A coupla years,' conceded Gus. 'Twenty or more. But this is different. A hundred of us go off to Hendon assessment centre for two really intensive days, and after that you know eventually, yes or no, whether you're in or you're out. I'll be in, no question, and then it's just a case of waiting for a berth.'

'You mean they don't just give you a super's job right away? That doesn't seem fair. Once you're ready for it and have passed their crazy assessment, surely –'

He'd shaken his head. 'I don't want any old job, darlin'. I want this one. AMIT taking in this patch. I don't want to

24

leave my manor! But no sweat, not a bit of it. Old Cumberland'll retire once he knows I'm ready, willin' and able. He's dying to get out to his garden and spend all day fiddling with his asparagus. And artichokes and antirrhinums. He's got this plan to have an alphabetical garden, see? All the way to zinnias. But the job's kept him stuck at A for the past ten years. So, like I said, it's just a matter of time. I'll get this case sorted in time for the assessment and then just you wait! By Christmas it'll be a new life for yours truly. And maybe for you . . .'

She'd thrown a sharp glance at him at that point but he'd merely grinned back with an expression as open and innocent as a child's, so she hadn't pursued the point. The number of times they'd come close to talking of the future were matched by an equal number when they'd both hurriedly skated away from any such discussion.

'Well,' she said. 'I hope you're right about getting this one sorted out in time. When's this assessment thing?'

'October,' he said. 'Middle of October.'

'And what's this case?'

He had become vague then, waving his hands in the air with a sort of flapping motion. 'Oh, do me a favour, ducks! I've got fifteen bulging files and Gawd knows how many floppy discs, and you want me to explain what it's all about, just like that? All I can tell you is it involves not only armed robberies but insurance scams and protection rackets and a good bit of money laundering. There's even a fella pushing out Ecstasy to half the country's kids – but that's not all. It's the way the whole lot of 'em interconnect – they've turned it into a network thing. A lot of villains gettin' the notion that they can operate like a legit business. And I won't have it. Business plans and long-term strategies, for Chrissakes!' With which gnomic utterance she had had to be content, because the phone had rung to disturb their rare treat of a shared lunch on his desk at Ratcliffe Street nick and he'd had to go. So she wasn't much the wiser about what the case was than she had been when he started on it.

But that it was important to both of them she did realize.

Maybe when he was a super running an Area Major Investigation Team he'd have a little more time for a normal life? Maybe he'd have enough inspectors and so forth working for him that he'd be less overworked? And in addition, there was the matter of George's own involvement: maybe he'd be able to put even more interesting cases her way? That would be great.

'Great,' she said aloud, rolling the R so that she sounded like a cat with an unusually loud purr, and then laughed as a startled face appeared at her door.

'Hullo, Sheila,' she said, choosing to ignore the puzzled expression the face bore. 'You're in early. It isn't half-past eight yet.'

'Got a lot to do,' Sheila said importantly and with an air of being hard done by. She inserted the rest of herself into the room, glancing across at the coffee pot, still bubbling on its little hotplate.

'Help yourself,' George said amiably.

Sheila did and came to perch on the edge of her desk. 'I don't want to fuss, Dr B.,' she said, 'but I really must say –'

'Here it comes!' George said. 'As soon as you say that I know there's going to be one.'

'What?'

'A fuss.'

'I'm not the one making it,' Sheila said virtuously and drank her coffee, looking over the rim of her mug with wide doleful eyes. 'I do my best to keep the peace but –'

'What has he done now?' George interrupted in a resigned tone.

'It's not him,' Sheila said and lowered her cup. 'It's Jane.'

'Jane?' George said, and frowned. 'But Jane's a marvellous technician. One of our best. You've always said so!'

'I dare say she still would be,' Sheila said tartly. 'If she wasn't so cow eyed over Dr Short. I really do think we ought to keep them apart somehow. She works better when she doesn't have to work with him, if you see what I mean. We could put her on the forensic stuff that Jerry usually does and then –'

'Now hang about a bit!' George was angry now. 'This is nonsense, Sheila, and you know it. It's been fixed for almost six months now that Jerry Swann is on the forensic budget, so he does all the forensic work. He's a good chap, and mucks in with the path. lab work when you're pushed, and does a great job, but that doesn't mean he's entirely interchangeable. Jane is officially employed by the Old East Trust without any input from my forensic budget. Although they both work here, you know as well as I do that I have to keep an eye on the way various staff are deployed. I'm not having that damned Archer woman down on my back for misuse of Trust budget moneys. She's a pest, but she's also a bloody good Director and manager and she'll spot it the minute you try doing things like that. So it won't work, ducky. You'll have to send up another bird.'

'You're beginning to talk like ChiefInspector Hathaway,' Sheila said with a flash of spirit. 'It sounds very peculiar with an American accent. You ought to watch out.' She slid off George's desk and flounced to the door. 'Don't blame me if none of the work gets done because Jane Rose and Alan Short are canoodling at each other all day. I've done my best. I wash my hands of the pair of them.' And she went out, only just not slamming the door behind her.

George sighed. Life was complicated enough just doing her job without having to worry over Sheila Keen's airs and flounces. She'd thought when she at last squeezed agreement out of Professor Hunnisett and Matthew Herne, the Chief Executive Officer, that if she could have a senior houseman-cum-registrar on the path. lab strength life would be easier, but had it hell. She should have remembered Sheila's well-known tendency to make a grab for any likely-looking man who came her way. She'd taken one look at young Alan Short, a New Zealander with a wide innocent face that made him look like a Norman Rockwell cover for the *Saturday Evening Post*, complete with shock of untidy fair hair, freckles and huge white teeth under an upturned nose, and that had been that. Sheila had been in full cry even though he was a good dozen years her junior.

It mightn't have been so bad, George thought mournfully as

she got to her feet to follow Sheila out into the lab to see what she could do to mend fences (because life was never easy when her senior technician was miserable), if only Short hadn't taken such a fancy to Jane Rose! George herself had seen the way he wasted time staring at her across the lab when he was supposed to be doing the reports for the patients' notes, and had known trouble was coming. Well, now it had, and she would have to tell Alan to lay off. 'If he wants to chat up Jane, he can do it outside working hours,' she told herself. 'I'll promise Sheila I'll sort it all out and maybe, just maybe, I'll be able to convince her and then get on with that leg so that I can get the job finished before I have to go to court.'

And she hurried out of her office, into the lab beyond where the separating machines and the agitators hummed and clattered and the glint of glass and chrome waited for her.

4

Her peacemaking efforts were not aided by the fact that both Jane and Jerry were perfectly aware of what it was she was trying to do and were highly amused by it. Jerry, of course, laughed at everything, but most of all at Sheila, and George couldn't blame him. Her ever more frantic attempts to snare herself a man – almost any man – were ludicrous; but George was beginning to find it harder and harder to laugh at them. It was too easy to despise women who felt incomplete unless they had a man in tow, especially as she herself had Gus. Sheila was a bright, capable and highly successful woman in her own sphere who had no need of a man to validate her, but she clearly didn't think so. Hence the antics that Jerry found so funny. Now Jane too was amused, where once she had been sympathetic, showing a sort of fellow feeling. But since she'd had Alan Short trailing after her, it seemed that her self-satisfaction had overcome her kinder side. George began to feel pity mixing with her irritation when she contemplated her senior technician.

So, she spent the next hour sorting out staff rotas in a way that would make Sheila happy and ensure that both Jane and Alan Short were able to get on with work without being too much together, for Sheila had a point: when they did work together their output plunged and that was the last thing George wanted. Ellen Archer, the Business Manager of the Investigations Directorate of which George's path. lab was part (together with the X-Ray department and ECG and

Cardiography and similar sections), was a tough lady and determined to shave at least three per cent off her budget in the current financial year. Crossing swords with Ellen was far more trouble than spending time rearranging her department so that work ran more smoothly.

'Nice work, Dr B.,' Jerry murmured when he came in and found on his work station the sheet of paper detailing the new arrangements in the lab. 'You've managed to come up with a system that'll keep Sheila quiet and won't leave Alan moping like an abandoned puppy. Let's see how long this lasts before Sheila hits the roof again.'

'I wish you fancied her,' George muttered. 'That'd solve a lot of problems.'

'For you, maybe,' Jerry said tartly. 'Do I deserve it, though? That's the question.'

'Your tongue's so sharp, you don't deserve anyone,' she said lightly and he made a face.

'You could be right,' he said and George could have bitten off her tongue. Jerry had, she knew, had his share of personal problems in the past. She hadn't meant to twist a knife in old scars.

He looked up as he settled himself on his stool and grinned. 'No need to look so woebegone,' he said. 'Believe me, I'm in clover these days. I've got just the sort of work I like and not a debt to disturb my sweet slumbers. What's on the agenda?'

She was grateful for the change of tack and let it take her further than she meant it to. 'I've got a nasty little job in the morgue you can come and help with if you like,' she offered, and explained about the leg. Jerry listened, fascinated, and made a loud smacking sound with his lips when she'd finished.

'O frabjous day!' he said. 'Lots of lovely digging around in the nasties. What more can a man ask for? When are you starting?'

'Give me half an hour,' she said. 'The coroner's officer won't be here till then. I imagine Harold Constant will come – though maybe, as it's only a piece of a body, he might not. The coroner's officer is supposed to be present if there's going to be an inquest.'

'Can there be an inquest on just a leg?' Jerry asked.

George stopped to think and then made a face. 'Not unless there's an identification of the fragment, I think.'

'So, why the coroner's officer?' Jerry asked reasonably. 'Or have you said you can identify the leg?'

'Of course I haven't. But there's always the possibility, I suppose, if they find a lead via Mispers – the Missing Persons Register. Anyway, I can't know till I've looked and even then I doubt I'll be able to. Maybe he won't come. Anyway, it doesn't matter. See you down there in half an hour, OK?'

'Very OK,' he said and leered across the lab at Sheila who had just come back in. 'Aren't I the lucky one, Shee? I'm going to help dig around in a lovely luminous lump of dead leg. Want to come and help as well?'

'You're disgusting,' Sheila said, and George escaped before they could settle into their usual squabbling, finding the prospect of dealing with the leg rather more attractive.

She found Danny Roscoe, her mortuary porter and general assistant, tucked into his cubby hole with a pot of tea and a plate of sandwiches, which he'd clearly scrounged from someone special since they were delicate things with the crusts cut off. He peered up at her as she came in and offered the plate.

'No thanks,' she said, even though she had not had breakfast, apart from the cup of coffee in her office. One of Danny's more remarkable gifts was his ability to enjoy food and drink in the mortuary, quite unperturbed by the sights and smells around him. However long she was in this job she would never achieve that degree of nonchalance, she was sure.

'Please yourself,' Danny said. 'All the more for me. An' they're smoked salmon'n all. Do themselves well, they do, over on the Admin. Block.'

'Tell me about it,' George said. 'Listen, has my –'

'– leg arrived. Yers.' Danny pursed his lips. 'Nasty one, 'n't it?'

'It must be if you say so,' she said lightly. 'I didn't think anything ever seemed nasty to you.'

'Oh, I 'as me feelin's same as anyone else,' Danny said a

little huffily and got to his feet as footsteps came down the corridor behind George. 'Mornin', 'arold.'

'Morning, Danny. Morning, Dr B. So, we've got a funny one, eh? Makes a change, having just part of a bod, doesn't it?' Harold Constant, large, benign, always a little breathless and as reliable as sunrise, beamed at Danny. 'Would those be sarnies you've got there, Danny? Well, well.'

''Elp yourself.' Danny was generous. 'An' there's still a cup in the pot, though it'll be a bit stewed by now. Still, you should manage it all right if you use lots of milk. Dr B.'s not dressed yet, right Dr B.? We'll be ready when you are.'

She changed quickly, tying her hair up in a theatre cap to protect it from the smells which tended to cling, if she wasn't very careful. It was the smell of Festival, the thick, cloying, vaguely fruity disinfectant that she found most disagreeable; a little honest decomposition seemed much more human, some-how, than that chemical reek.

The leg lay in solitary splendour in the middle of its slab, covered with a green cloth because Danny had a delicacy about some things, and Harold, his tongue exploring his teeth for any remnants of his snack, was leaning against the wall waiting for her. Beside him Michael Urquhart was standing with arms folded as he concentrated on not noticing the unpleasantness in the air.

'Two of you, for just one leg?' George said. 'Well, well.'

'The Inspector said he wanted me to come,' Michael said a little grimly. 'For my part I'd have been happy to have left you to it, especially as you removed the clothing there on the scene, but there it is. Ye canna argue with Roop in one of his moods.' Then he relaxed and grinned at her amiably.

She grinned back but said nothing, turning her attention to the leg. Once it was revealed in the hard white light over the slab it was much more a pathetic object than a fearsome one. There was a staining of the skin below the severed surface, and she described that into the microphone dangling over the table before she touched anything, standing with her gloved hands folded under her arms and just talking.

Then she measured, and tried to do the sums in her head,

remembering the proportions of the human body as best she could without a written reference, and measuring the foot, too, to help her calculations.

Jerry, who had arrived while she was dictating the first appearance of the leg, leaned forwards, clearly fascinated and quite unfazed. 'I've checked the shoe and sock,' he said. 'Only briefly of course – I'll do the more microscopic investigation after this – but the shoe's a size eleven. Big feet.'

'Mmm,' she said and re-measured the foot. 'I'd say about six foot two or even three. Not too heavy a man: the joints don't show the sort of distortion you see on the feet of overweight people. And as you can see, not a lot of fat on the leg . . . So he was on the thin side. Certainly not too bulky. Now as to his age . . .' She pondered a while and leaned over the leg to peer more closely at the foot. 'I'll have to check the epiphyses on the tibia, but I have a hunch that he's a mature adult but not an aged one. Somewhere between, oh, twenty-five and forty-five, say –'

'That's a hell of a between, Dr B.' Michael said and she threw a glance at him.

'Fortune telling might be quicker,' she said dryly. 'I've only got science. And at this stage I'm only using my eyes anyway. Let's see what we find with a knife and fork.'

She worked delicately and steadily with her instruments, first shaving some of the edges of the skin at the severed surface to provide a sample for more detailed investigation of the punched-in edge, and next separating the different muscles so that she could inspect the fascia that lay between them. Then she stopped, peered more closely and said to Jerry, 'A slide, please.'

Jerry brought a box of the slips of glass and she slid the point of her smallest forceps into the wound and then, moving very slowly, extracted something and lay it on the slide. All of the watchers craned to see more closely.

'Fibres,' she said with great satisfaction. 'There's some fibres here that have been driven into the wound.'

'From his clothing?' Michael said, his eyes sharp and intelligent.

George nodded. 'That's possible, of course. But we can't be sure. We'll have to look more closely at the material; see what it is.'

'If it's a piece of good wool, showing signs of pinstriping, then it's natty gentlemen's suiting to match the Harrods shoe and the silk sock. If it's a scrap of rubber then he was up to something naughty when whoever or whatever it was got him,' Jerry said. He leered at Michael who snorted with laughter. Harold Constant ignored them both. He was looking puzzled.

'Dr B.,' he said slowly. 'How can you be sure you've got fabric fibres there? It looks the same as the muscle from here.'

'Because I'm experienced in looking,' she said a touch sharply. 'Of course it looks like muscle to your eyes – it's covered with blood! But this *isn't* muscle fibre. I know.' She poked the glass slide towards Jerry who covered it and slid it into a tray with a label on which he wrote swiftly.

'I didn't mean that you didn't know what it was, exactly.' Harold had gone a little pink, which made his round face look somewhat like a strawberry blancmange. 'I just meant that, well, if it looks so like muscle couldn't there be lots more that you haven't spotted? If you see what I mean.'

She looked at him for a long time and then nodded slowly. 'Yes, Harold, I see what you mean,' she said. 'You think I spotted that scrap of fibre by luck.'

He went even more pink and made noises of denial as she shook her head at him.

'You have a point. I did just happen to spot this bit. Now I'm going to look. Much more carefully. So that you're completely reassured. OK?'

Harold looked miserable as she returned to her work and the PM room sank into a relative silence, though they could hear the hiss of the water that was running into the tiled gulleys and the faint hum of refrigeration. After a while they could hear themselves breathing, too.

She could not have been more painstaking. She explored every area of the exposed muscle, inch by inch, slowly stripping it further and further down the leg so that the bone emerged to stand pallid and glistening in the harsh light; and still they were silent. Because she was pulling from the muscles of the upper part of the leg piece after piece of fibre. The number of slides increased, and Jerry's face seemed to brighten a little with each of them. In the end he couldn't keep quiet any longer.

'Listen, was he stuffed or something? Or are you just taking anything that might be fibrous? I mean, could some of it be roughened connective tissue or something?'

She shook her head, never lifting her eyes from her work. 'No, Jerry. These are foreign fibres. It's a ridiculous amount, isn't it? If all this is stuff from his trousers they must have been ripped to shreds, and the cut must have been even more violent than I first thought, to have driven the scraps in so deeply. It's extraordinary.'

As she went lower into the leg towards the ankle the amount of fibres she found diminished and finally stopped. When she reached the ankle proper, exposing the medial malleolus, it ceased altogether and Jerry took away the remainder of the slides and finished the labelling.

She completed the examination an hour and a half later. Each and every muscle in the leg was carefully separated out – what remained of popliteus gastrocnemius, soleus, tibialis – and the narrower bone, the fibula, had been exposed more clearly so that detailed photographs could be taken. She took samples of the skin too, though she suspected they would be of little value after a week's immersion in the Thames, and also of the toenails. Investigation of them might, she thought, reveal something of the owner of the leg's past uses of heavy metals. Jerry watched her and then snickered softly.

'Seeing you do that reminds me of that awful joke about the fireman who poisoned his wife with a chopper,' he said. 'He gave her arsenic.'

She looked at him witheringly but the two men watching laughed, Harold with a particularly loud bray. 'Oh, very funny, very funny,' he said. 'Gave her arse a nick ... Are you saying this fellow might have been given arsenic?'

'You never know,' George said. 'Or antimony or thallium.

They all finish up in hair and nails eventually. Well, we've got no hair, but we've got these.' And she dropped the last crescent of large toenail into the specimen box that Jerry was holding out for her. 'The fact that we have this section doesn't necessarily mean he's dead, you know.'

There was another silence and then Michael said carefully, 'Not dead? But...'

George grinned. 'Oh, I'm pretty sure he is. There's been heavy blood loss, and no sign that the major blood vessels clamped down to reduce the loss, as they do if an injury like this happens in life. I'm pretty clear this was cut from a dead body, but you can never be totally sure, can you? If a tourniquet's used above the line of the incision, then that can mimic the look of an injury to a body in which the circulation has already stopped – a dead one in other words. I'll know more when we've inspected the samples in detail. But if he was dead when his leg was cut off, what did he die of? We have to investigate every possibility, right?'

'Right,' said Michael.

'OK. We'll clean up now.' She began to push the tissues back into some sort of shape and then indicated she wanted a wrapper. Danny brought her one and carefully she wrapped the now almost unrecognizable leg into a neat parcel, ready to be put into one of the cold drawers.

'Right, gentlemen,' she said briskly. 'That's it. We'll get a report to you as soon as we can, but there's a lot of work to be done on the samples. I have to tell you, though, that until you find me a bit more of this chap's anatomy, the chances of my being able to say who he is, or when or how he died, are as slim as a skeleton. So, Michael, it's over to you and that chap from the river police – Slavin, was it? You have to hunt around for a bit more material for me to work on. I hope you find some. I'd really like to get to the bottom of this one.'

Again Jerry snickered and murmured in mock cockney. 'Oh, Dr B., you are a one!' But she ignored him. She was so used to Jerry's scatological sense of humour that she hardly noticed it any more.

'I'll talk to Slavin as soon as I get back to the nick,' Michael promised, also ignoring Jerry. 'Between us we ought to be able to get a few more pieces to this little puzzle. I hope so. The Guv doesn't like bits of dead people turning up on his patch, I don't suppose. And we have to keep the Guv'nor happy, don't we?

'Yes,' George said brightly. 'We certainly do.'

5

She woke early next morning and lay for a few moments disoriented, trying to think where she was. For one mad moment she thought she was still in her bedroom at her mother's house in Buffalo. How many years was it since she had slept there, for pity's sake? Then she thought she was in Gus's flat in Docklands and sat up sharply to look round for him, and at last knew that she was in her own Bermondsey bedroom.

She peered at her clock and swore: only a half after six. Much too early to get up, and not safe to try to get to sleep again (even if she could, which was doubtful; she felt very wide awake) because she'd be sure to oversleep and be late at the hospital. So she bunched her pillows up behind her head, stretched out and stared at the window where the net curtains flapped lazily in the most minor of morning breezes.

It was not surprising she had thought herself at home in Buffalo. She had dreamed, she now recalled, that she was in America again, doing the shopping for her mother the way she had used to. She had been going home with a big brown bag of groceries under each arm to unload them on the kitchen table and argue with Vanny who complained she'd brought all the wrong things. And when she looked at the things they were all rotten and damaged and stinking like that dead leg . . .

She made a little face at the flapping curtains. How Freudian could you get? Vanny, her mother, needing her to help her, and she saying she would and doing it all wrong. Giving her decomposed flesh in place of food. She closed her eyes against the growing light of the morning and tried to think of something else, but it was impossible. She had talked to Bridget for too long last night, had worried too much to be able to empty her mind of it all now.

The afternoon had been irritating anyway because the case on which she was to be an expert witness started late, so she had to kick her heels at the court when she had much more useful things she could have been doing back at Old East; and when the case had come into court the defence had managed to obtain an adjournment on some technicality even before she had been called; so she had gone back to the hospital having wasted several hours to no purpose at all, and with another date in her diary for the trial.

All of which had meant she couldn't leave her department till after eight, by which time she was hot and more tired than she would have expected even after being called out of bed so early in the morning, and certainly past eating any dinner. Now, lying in bed, she became aware of the hunger that was tightening her belly and promised herself a proper breakfast when she got up. Eggs, even.

But now she went on remembering. Last night. The phone ringing while she was in the shower trying to wash away her irritability and fatigue and she as usual being totally unable to let it just ring – for she had forgotten to set her answerphone – and then standing there by the phone in the living room, dripping wet and wearing just a skimpy towel because she'd grabbed for the small one instead of a large one, and hearing the faint ting that meant it was a transatlantic call. And that meant she wouldn't be able to tell whoever it was to hold on while she dried herself and put on a wrap, for that would be expensive for them.

She felt the lurch of fear that such calls always caused in her. Her elderly mother, back home in Buffalo, living with her old friend Bridget Connors, was a constant anxiety deep in her mind. Was she ailing even more? Dead even? She caught her breath as she heard Bridget's voice, but slowly the fear subsided. There were problems, yes, but nothing dramatic had happened.

'She's not been at all well, George,' Bridget had said fretfully. 'It's a real pain sometimes to listen to her. She goes all over the place and when I go after her, I find her in the craziest places, looking for you and your father. It'd break your heart to see it, truly it would. She cries because she's so glad to see me, and when I tell her her husband's dead and you're in England, she says she knows. But then a few minutes later and she's forgotten it all and asks for him again. And for you –'

'Oh, my God,' George said. 'Should I come?'

'What for?' Bridget said. 'What on earth for? She doesn't know you're not there, not really. And if you were, she'd forget within a minute of you going away again that you'd been there. You're better off where you are –'

George hadn't been able to help it. 'Christ, Bridget!' she'd cried. 'Why do you call to tell me all this if you don't want me to come to her? Just to make me feel bad? I –'

'Just so you know,' Bridget had cut in. There had been a little silence. 'Just so you know.'

'I – Thanks Bridget. Sorry. I didn't mean to bawl you out. It's just that sitting here I feel so –'

'Sitting here I feel the same,' Bridget had said dryly. 'And so would you. Only it'd be worse for you if you were here because sooner or later you'd have to go back to England and that'd be terrible. How is he, that gorgeous guy of yours?'

George had caught her breath and wanted to cry. The old lady was trying so hard. There had been times she had found her mother's best friend as irritating as a woman could be, but now her gratitude towards her for her unswerving devotion to Vanny overflowed.

'He's fine,' she said. 'Just fine. Says you and Ma gave him the best Christmas ever when you were here. He sent you his love.'

'Ah, bullshit, George! He doesn't know I'm talking to you now, and he sure as hell doesn't think about me when I'm not.'

George had grinned into the phone. 'OK, you old bat! So he would if he was here. I'm acting as his go-between.'

Bridget had laughed fatly then, sounding happier. 'That's

better. No need to go all stiff on me. Hey, George, I guess I shouldn't have called you, at that. But –'

'No, no,' George said quickly. 'I shouldn't have said what I did. It was great. It's good of you to. I don't know what I'd do if you weren't there and –'

'Like I said, I shouldn't have bothered you.' Bridget went on as though George hadn't spoken. 'But I guess it was for me more'n for Vanny. When I think of how much longer either of us has and it's no time at all, I just get so *mad*. Inside I'm as young as a spring chicken and twice as sprightly and here's time playing these lousy tricks on us. My only comfort is that Vanny isn't here to see what's happened to her.'

There had been a little silence and then she had laughed again, a soft chuckle. 'Hey, did you ever hear anything so crazy as that? What a thing to say! Look, George, thanks for listening.'

'What?'

'I said thanks. I don't want you here and neither does Vanny. It'd upset her a hell of a lot, one way or another, if you were. She wouldn't understand why she wasn't in her own home. And why screw up your life for no reason? Vanny'd hate that. The real Vanny, I mean, not this crazy one we're stuck with now. But it helps me a lot to be able to bend your ear, you know? I feel great now. In fact, I'll go get a coupla packs of chop suey and egg rolls and Vanny and I'll eat lunch in the garden together. She likes Chinese food and she's as nippy with a pair of chopsticks as she ever was. So long, honey. Take care of yourself.'

'And you take care of yourself, Bridget,' George had said, and then did what she used to when she was a small child and her aunts and uncles had called from distant places like Boston. She blew a loud smacking kiss down the phone and Bridget, three thousand miles away, laughed softly and said, 'That was nice. I really felt that. Goodbye, hon.'

George had sat there for a long time, wearing only her skimpy towel as her skin slowly lost its gooseflesh, staring at the blankness of her dead fireplace trying to imagine Vanny, her dear, maddening, plain-speaking, difficult but always beloved old Ma, in the state Bridget had described; and when at last the image fixed itself in her mind she began to cry. She wept silently and bitterly for a few minutes; then, feeling better, not happy about the situation but resigned, she had gone to get into the shower again and finish her preparations for bed.

Now, she sat up sharply and looked again at the clock. A quarter to seven. Now she would get up; another shower, for the night had been a restless one and she was aware of the clamminess of sweat on her skin as the weather settled to another day of blazing sunshine and some humidity, and then scrambled eggs and toast and work. Everything'd be fine once she got to the hospital. There'd be too much to do to worry about Vanny. Or to miss Gus. Because she had to admit that some of her low feelings were due to that. Maybe, after she was at the hospital and had got the day properly started, she'd be able to track him down on the phone. A comfortable gossip with Gus would cheer her up wonderfully.

And she swung her legs out of bed and headed for the bathroom.

It wasn't till late afternoon that she got her phone call. The morning was busy in its usual way and in the afternoon she had a PM to do on a man who'd died in the A & E department from a massive myocardial infarction and whose family wanted the coroner's inquest over as soon as possible, because they were Jewish and didn't want the funeral delayed beyond the next day if it could be avoided. She had done her best to oblige them, hurrying to finish quickly enough for Harold Constant to process the paperwork and send them on their way to Golders Green crematorium in good time. But the rushing had unsettled Danny and made him bad tempered and therefore obstructive, so she had to spend some minutes mollifying him. One way and another she was thoroughly stirred up when at last she had a chance to get to her phone.

Which didn't help. She used his mobile number and the first time she got through he barked, 'Oh, hell. I was just about to make a call. Give me a few minutes, George, will you? I'll talk to you later.' She waited, dialled again and again and not until half an hour had gone by managed to get a ringing tone. This time he did talk to her, but he was clearly not thinking of her while he did so.

'What?' he said when she asked him why he hadn't called. 'Listen, ducks, you should see what's going on here! There's more to do than sweep Brighton Beach. I'm up to my arse and over my hocks –'

'Yeah, well, me too, but a minute to phone, for Chrissakes!' she snapped back, and then simmered down. 'Sorry, Gus. It's just that I miss you.'

That had been his cue. If he'd just said, 'Me too,' and then hung up she'd have been comforted. As it was, he said nothing and she said sharply, 'Gus?'

'Mmm?'

'Did you hear me?'

'What? Oh, yes. You missed me. Sorry, ducks, I was thinking about something – Listen, I'll try to call you tonight, OK? Depends on how this all works out. I've got a pile of paperwork that has to be done – without it we'll never get the case to stick and even with it I'm not sure. I've got a long way to go yet to crack this bugger. I'm sorry if I'm not much fun at the moment.'

'That's better,' she said, managing a grin, important even if he couldn't see it. 'Sorry I was such a pest. I should know better. Look, hon, what about supper? I could bring it to the nick tonight. Just call me when you're ready and I'll be over.'

There was a little silence and then he said quickly, 'Supper? I like it. Yeah, sure. I'll call you at the flat, hmm? Or on your mobile.'

'Either.'

'Well, I'll call and see you at the nick. But God knows what time. So long, ducks.'

'So long,' she said. But he'd already broken the connection.

Ellen Archer put her head round George's door ten minutes later, as she sat there glowering at her pile of paperwork and feeling hard done by.

'Can you spare a moment?' she asked.

'Of course,' George said with false heartiness. She reached over to the extra chair and removed the pile of notes on it while Ellen came in and sat down.

'Problems?' George quirked her head at her.

'Just look at the effect I have on people!' Ellen said in mock misery. 'And here am I just trying to be everyone's friend.'

'Well, you're not the most likely candidate to bring friendly messages,' George said frankly. 'Usually when you turn up it means I have to make more budget cuts and I'm already counting the paper clips.'

'Well, I don't have much choice in the matter either,' Ellen said. 'But believe me, I'm on your side. That's why I'm here, in fact.'

'Oh.' George looked at her a little more closely. Ellen was always neat in a classic sort of way: cream silk blouse that never looked creased or stained with make-up round the collar; crisp blue skirts and jackets to match in the winter; but she had an agreeable expression that wilted the starch a little.

'It may seem like bad news, but with each other's help we can, I think, make sure it isn't.' Ellen became businesslike. 'As you know, since we took Trust status there's been a hell of a cost-cutting exercise going on.'

'What, really? And me never noticed!' George said, open-eyed and innocent.

'Well, all right, I know, I know! But it's more than that. We're in competition with other hospitals and we've been lucky to escape Tomlinson. I was afraid they might close us down altogether, like Bart's.'

George's eyes widened. 'Could they? They couldn't!'

'It's all right, now. We're safe enough. Not too close to the Royal London, nor to Guy's either – and they're on the way out, of course. But we do have to rationalize. They're talking of putting some of the hospital's services out to tender. It could save a lot of money, they say.'

George frowned. 'You mean catering and cleaning and so forth?'

'That's already been done,' Ellen said sardonically. 'Haven't you noticed how much longer it takes to get the corridors swept these days? And the food . . .'

George shuddered. 'Well, yes. All right, then, things out to tender. But what has that –'

'Got to do with you? A lot. They've been considering doing the same with pathology services.'

George stared and then shook her head. 'They couldn't!'

'You keep saying that, but I'm afraid they could. Someone on the Board – one of the non-executive directors – has heard of a place in Leeds or somewhere where they've saved around a quarter of a million on the path. services costs by doing so. I wanted to warn you that this sort of thing is happening all over the country. If it's cheaper to rationalize a service on one site, getting nearby Units to subscribe to it, they'll do it. That's why so many accident and emergency departments have been downgraded into minor-injury treatment units. It's cheaper to concentrate expensive gear and personnel in one place. If it works for A & E it can work for path. services, is the thinking. They can get specimens from here to another site in a matter of minutes, and with good computer back-up, they say they won't need a path. lab here, except at a very basic level.'

George was sitting up very straight now and her jaw was tight. 'They can't,' she said. 'I won't let them.'

'That's what I'd hoped you'd say. I don't want us to lose our own path. services any more than you do. What worries me is not so much the suggestion we get a private sector service – it's the alternative that another of the non-execs came up with. He reckons we should share with St Dymphna's.'

'St Dymphna's? But they're a specialist psychiatric hospital! How can they deal with our path. work?'

'They're so close getting stuff over to them would be easy, and they've got the space. They're offering a chance to use their accommodation in exchange for a share of the income. It's a complicated scheme. They'd tender for GP work, too, of course –'

'It's a crazy scheme,' George said firmly. 'We can't let them do it!'

'I agree with you. That's why I'm here. There's a Board meeting on Monday. Can you come with me to talk to them?'

'Try and stop me,' George said. 'Of course I will! I can't let them close this unit down. How would the hospital manage?'

'Oh, it would manage well enough,' Ellen said, getting to her feet. 'That's the trouble. But I just don't think it's on. It smells wrong to me, and I need your help to make sure Old East doesn't lose out. One way or another, we'll sort it out, you and I together, hmm?'

'Count on me,' George said, her forehead creased and tight, and watched her go.

6

The streets smelled oily and sour and brassy as though they had been doubling as a steel foundry all afternoon, and the heat hung overhead almost as palpable as a blanket; but as the evening progressed and the sky deepened in colour, the air became a little fresher and it wasn't as difficult to walk quickly as it had been earlier. George didn't sweat so heavily, for a start, and that was a comfort. She'd actually put on a little make-up before leaving the flat; not a lot because that wasn't her style and as far as she knew Gus didn't particularly like it (not that they ever actually discussed it – she just knew), but she had felt the need to make an effort. She had pulled on one of her newest outfits too, one she'd bought on a rushed visit to the West End last month when she'd had the time to go all female and shop. A long blue and white striped heavy linen skirt, split to the knee, with a matching top tied at the waist, it made her look even taller and longer legged than she was, showing a regular flash of brown thigh as she went loping through Watney Street Market on the way to the nick.

The stalls were already almost all gone, for it was now well past seven-thirty, but she stopped at one of the few that were left to buy a mango from a cheerful West Indian in an orange and black shirt, exceedingly skimpy and shiny black shorts, which had a group of watching girls giggling almost hysterically every time he moved, and luxuriant dreadlocks. The mango was large and scented the air even in the middle of the stink of the market, with its overtones of rotting fish from the whelk stall at the far end, and she turned the lovely coloured thing in her hands and wondered what it would be like to sit on a Caribbean beach with Gus and eat mangoes all day.

'Only fifty pence to you, doctor!' the man said, grinning at her, his teeth absurdly brilliant in his cheerful face, and she shook her head at him as she dug out her money.

'Are there no secrets in this town?' she asked with mock despair. 'If I ever went out on a toot I'd never get away with it. There'd always be someone who knew me, dammit all.'

'You took some blood from me once,' he said as he palmed the pound she gave him and looked for change. 'They tried to get it from me in the Sickle Cell Unit but they couldn't and Dr Choopani was on holiday so they sent for you. I'm Gregory St Clair.'

She remembered then. He'd been in a sickle cell crisis, in obvious pain, and she had seen to it that he was admitted and treated. She grinned at him. 'You look great now.'

'I'm always great even when I feel like hell,' he said and then, as one of the girls in the group watching him said something in the West Indian patois, turned and shouted back at them, so George went on her way, marvelling not for the first time at the many different languages that could be heard in these streets. How would they cope if there was some major emergency that involved them all, the way it had been in the war when the whole area was blitzed night after night? Would they hold together now as they had done fifty years ago?

It was an odd idea and she set it aside, amused at herself in a wry sort of way. The trouble was, she'd rather think about things like mangoes and language and community cohesion than about what she was doing. She had waited for Gus to call, as he had said he would, but the phone hadn't rung and in sudden irritation she had gone ahead anyway: made some supper – all very healthy stuff, Tupperware containers of salad and barbecued chicken wings from her fridge, some good Stilton cheese and wholemeal bread and a bottle of Australian Chardonnay – and just marched out. Now she had added the mango. With a bit of luck he'd be hungry and glad to see her.

Or not. As she reached the steps that led up to the entrance to Ratcliffe Street police station, she quailed for a moment. The last thing she wanted was to be seen as pushy, dependent, clinging, but wasn't she being all three in not waiting till he did as he had said he would and called her before bobbing up on his doorstep?

The double doors swung and someone came out to run quickly down the steps and then stopped at the sight of her.

'Dr B.? How are you? Got over your early call yet?'

'I've caught up on my sleep,' she said, looking up at Michael Urquhart, who had stopped on the step above her. It was rare that she could look up to a man, tall as she was. There was something rather comforting about doing so, she thought inconsequentially. 'How about you?'

'Och, I'm used to it, the way they run me ragged. Here to see the Guv, are you?'

'Uh, yes.' She hesitated and then mentally shrugged. She'd known Michael Urquhart almost as long as she'd known Gus, after all. They were good friends, had worked together on a couple of dicey cases. No need to be shy of being honest with him. 'How are things with him? Are the storm cones hoisted?'

Michael shook his head. 'I couldna say, Dr B.! We hardly see him these days. He's dealing with some great big case and he's playin' his cards unco' close to his chest. I can tell you that much, but no more, for he's got a sergeant from over Canning Town way on his team, and a DC from Bow and only one of our DCs and it's no' me.' He looked sore for a moment. 'And I'll not pretend to you that my nose isna a bit out of joint. I'd as soon be with the Guv as dealing all the time wi' Inspector Dudley, but there y'are! The Guv's got this big case an' we're out in the cold, puir wee us!'

'Hmm.' George looked over her shoulder. 'And is – um – is Roop in at the moment?'

Michael laughed. 'It's great when you call him that! He hates it so. He's gone home to the family, left me to clear up the bits and bobs. But what's a DC for, I ask m'sel'? You go away in, Dr B. He's in the big suite towards the rear of the top

49

floor, you know the way.' And he nodded at her and went on down the steps and away.

Inside, she showed her ID and pass to the desk clerk and went up the stairs slowly, relishing the coolness. Ratcliffe Street was one of the older police stations, and still had a good deal of green and cream paint and dark green tiles about, but the doors had been replaced with flat modern ones and in some areas the rooms had been knocked together to make a big open-plan workspace. The one Gus was in was on the third floor overlooking the scrubby recreation ground, which contained more wrecked children's toys, old prams, garbage and drunken street people than trees and grass. She stood in the doorway, hesitating, and looked around.

There were half a dozen desks and each was piled with paperwork as well as having its own computer screen and keyboard. The walls were covered with charts of all sorts and on one board were pinned series of photographs, all mug shots clearly taken of living people, which made an agreeable change from the sort of photo board she was used to in incident rooms, on which explicit pictures of very dead and damaged bodies were the norm. At three of the desks there were people with their heads down, all men, all clearly very busy.

The one nearest the door, a bulky man with a thick neck and very sleek dark hair, looked up as she came in and tilted his head in enquiry.

'I'm looking for Gu – Inspector Hathaway,' she said and the man stared consideringly at her for a long moment.

'Perhaps I can help you,' he said smoothly. 'I'm Sergeant Salmon.'

'And I'm Dr Barnabas,' she said. 'Pathologist.'

'Ah!' said Sergeant Salmon with a faintly knowing air. 'Then it *is* the Guv you want. He's in his office. I'll show you the way.'

'I can manage,' she said, irritated by the smoothness of the man and the clear implication that her relationship with Gus had been the subject of nick gossip. She looked across the big room to the far side where she could see a separate office behind a partition. There was a light on behind the half-glassed door, and she moved towards it with more assurance than she felt. She was aware of Sergeant Salmon watching her go, and was equally aware of the eyes of the other two on her. She knew neither of them, though by now she was on tolerably familiar terms with most of the Ratcliffe Street nick's personnel, and she wondered briefly why Gus was working with strangers. It wasn't like him; he was always happier with a team he knew well and whom he had trained to his own little ways.

She didn't wait at his door; just opened it and walked in. He didn't look up, but continued scrolling something on his own computer terminal. As she stood there and looked at him she was very aware of the lines on his face, for they showed particularly clearly in the bluish light thrown by the monitor screen. He looked tired and not too well and she felt a momentary pang of anxiety.

'Well, what is it?' he snapped, not taking his eyes from the screen. Her anxiety vanished; he sounded so much his usual self.

'Supper,' she said, closing the door behind her and coming over to his desk. 'I doubt you had any lunch, so it'll do you no harm to stop and eat now.'

'George!' he said and blinked at her. 'I thought you were Salmon.'

'Thanks a bunch,' she said tartly. 'That makes me feel really great. I'm not that big! Do I have his sort of fishy-eyed look?'

'Oh, very funny,' Gus said, and went back to his screen, as though his eyes had been dragged back to it. 'Do me a favour — no fish jokes in his hearing. He gets bored with 'em and when he's bored he's ratty.'

George, who had not intended any pun, made a face. 'I wasn't referring to his name. It's the way he stared at me when I came in. I suppose they've gossiped. Are you going to eat or aren't you?'

'In a minute,' he said, clearly abstracted. 'Let me get through this lot first, while it's still clear in my mind . . .'

She sighed and sat down and the room settled to silence

broken only by the sound of the keys as he hit them, and she studied his face. Why was it this man had such an effect on her? All her previous attachments had been to classically good-looking types. She remembered Ian, the over-ambitious Scottish surgeon who had all unwittingly been the reason for her taking her job at Old East in the first place, and the physician Toby Bellamy who had been a most splendid piece of male beauty who had attached himself to her in her first months at Old East, and sighed again. Gus was not a beauty by any stretch of the imagination. His hair was thick and curly but receding a little over his forehead, and he made no attempt to keep it brushed and neat or to use it to enhance his looks in any way. He had a pleasant face, modified by a considerable number of lines and pouches, and a solid squarish body that no one could call elegant, though it was a strong and clearly functional one; he liked jogging and when he had the time spent an hour in a gym making the most of his muscles. But none of it added up to beauty. So where did the charm come from, the pull of the man?

And then he looked up and smiled at her and she stopped thinking about it at all. He was Gus and that was enough.

'Bob,' he bawled, still grinning, and there was a sound of movement from the big room outside. 'Bob. Put a bloody move on, will you!'

'I can't fly,' Sergeant Salmon said from the door which had opened behind George. 'What's the matter?'

'It's enough already. It's nearly eight o'clock.' Gus glanced at the clock on the wall facing him. 'Why didn't you tell me?'

'I thought you could tell the time,' Salmon said and Gus laughed.

'Go home, you cheeky bugger,' he said amiably. 'Enough's enough. We'll go on with all this tomorrow. Any joy yet?'

'I've got a couple of possibles we can start on in the morning. There must be a tie-in between Hampden and whatsit and the Harlow set-up. They're both registered at Companies House, but I did a run on some of their directors and there are a few names that come up in both.'

'I like it,' Gus said. 'Even if they're both as legit as the

House of Lords it could be a lead in. Checked the McCann directors as well, did you?'

'Not yet. I'm being alphabetical. I've done as far as half way through the aitches – that was how I spotted the link-up between Hampden and Harlow. Give me a coupla days.'

'This is goin' to take a bleedin' lifetime at this rate.' Gus stretched and yawned. 'OK, Bob. Take the others with you. See you in the morning.'

As soon as Bob Salmon had closed the door behind him, Gus pushed his monitor and computer keyboard back and flicked his thumb and forefinger at his forehead as though tipping an invisible hat. 'Cleared the decks for you, Mum. Over to you, *if* you please.'

'So you are hungry,' she said, reaching down for the basket she'd brought.

'Bloody starving.' He watched her greedily as she unpacked the food. 'Ah, now, there's a bit of all right! Did you do the chicken with that barbecue stuff you use? Good. I love it. And is that your own mayonnaise or the bottled sort? Well, you can't have everything – All right, I know. You're busy. Me too. And what's that? A mango? You sexy object, you!'

'What's sexy got to do with it?' George was cutting bread and Gus reached for a slice, buttered it thickly and started eating a leg of chicken held in his other hand.

'Mangoes are famous for it,' he said. 'Eat a mango together and soon you'll be splashing in even sweeter juices. Everyone says that. Here, what are we drinking?'

She ignored the mango pointedly and gave him some wine, still cool from the insulation envelope into which she'd stuffed it as soon as she'd taken it from her fridge, and the cluttered little office settled to contented greedy silence. After a while he sighed happily and reached for the mango and started to slice it, crisscrossing it with his penknife with finicky precision.

'There's a special way of doing this,' he said. 'We had a DC Patel once who showed me. Like this, see?' He presented her with the open mango, the cubes rolling neatly apart on the rind and she took one. 'So, how is it with you, sweetheart? I'm sorry I'm so buried in all this stuff. I miss our evenings together.' He leered wickedly. 'And nights.'

'It's your choice,' she said, mopping her sticky fingers dry on a paper napkin. 'It's been like this for weeks. Months, even.'

'And likely to be weeks more,' he said. The laughter had gone. 'It's one hell of a case, George. I thought I was after just a bunch of robbers – the villains who cleared out the bonded warehouse towards Millwall as well as the whisky warehouse and the big supermarket and the safe deposit, but then it turns out they're linked with a bookmaking scam here in my own patch. And then there's some sort of protection rubbish going on that one of the local market traders is involved in, and though it looks like he's just a trader it turns out that he owns the lease on the whole market site and is cleaning up. On top of that it looks as though there're links with other businesses – they have Board meetings, I swear to you! I tell you, it's like a bleedin' octopus, only it's got more'n eight legs. If I clean up this lot, I reckon I've got one of the biggest scams in London sorted. But I've only got a few weeks because of October, you know?' He brooded for a moment, staring blankly at the opposite wall. 'If I miss the next assessment, there's a risk old Cumberland'll take his cards and go before I'm ready for his job at AMIT, and that means someone else'll get it, and I'll have to wait another twenty years – and I want it now!'

'Can't you hand this job over to someone else?' She was sympathetic. 'Do your best but when it comes to the assessment course tell them you have to go.'

'Oh, that'll make a great impression.' He was sardonic. 'You can't just dump a job in someone else's lap because you want to move up a rung. I doubt it'd be possible, anyway. I'm so embroiled. A lot of this has to be in my head. You can keep records till you're blue' – he jerked his head at the monitor screen – 'but when it comes down to it, it's what's in human skulls that cracks cases of human villainy.'

'Well, I suppose you know your own business best,' she said. 'But take care you don't get too involved, Gus. You've got your own health to think about and you look . . .'

'Awful, hmm? Come here, wench. I'll show you how awful I am.'

'Oh, sure.' It was her turn to be sardonic. 'I can just see me settling down to a bit of nookie on the middle of your desk. Very nice and I don't think. Help me clear up and we'll go home.'

'Now there,' he said, 'is an offer I couldn't possibly refuse.'

The phone woke her at four a.m., shrilling furiously in her ear, and she emerged from sleep bemused and somehow frightened, which was unusual. She was so used to middle-of-the-night calls that they never alarmed her; annoyed her maybe, but they were part of the job. Why feel so bothered now?

She picked up the phone, listened and said tersely, 'OK. Repeat the address ... Oh, I know. The new flats ... Uhuh. Give me five minutes. What? A car? No, I'll drive myself.' And she hung up.

Gus hadn't stirred. He lay sprawled flat on his back, his pillow on the floor beside him as usual, and she bent over and kissed him; but he still didn't move so she went and dressed, grabbed her emergency bag and scribbled a note for him in the usual way, with soap on the bathroom mirror. *Gone to work. A fire. See you when I see you. Luv G.*

7

Barely ten minutes later, since there was no traffic on the roads, she was pushing up Narrow Street towards Limehouse. Ahead of her the sky was showing the opal light of early morning, though behind her, westwards, it was still as dark as ever. But there was more than dawn lifting away from the deep blue; there was a faint orange glow in the sky, and her belly tightened at the sight of it. No intelligent person, in her view, could fail to be alarmed by fire. The sight of it, the smell of it – and she could already fancy she smelled the reek of burning on the cool air streaming in through her open car window – had terror built into them.

The block of flats she was looking for was in Ropemakers' Fields, just where Narrow Street turned northeasterly away from the river to curve round the dock before Limehouse Pier, and as she reached the end of the road she saw it clearly, the cluster of police vehicles with their blue lights rotating and the fire engines and the ambulances similarly alight. A big one, she registered, as she thumped her window to point out her police pass in the corner of the windscreen to the uniformed constable who tried to stop her, before taking her car up the street as close as she could get to the action.

Rupert Dudley was standing talking to a senior fireman, his face red in the glow from the fire. As George made her way towards the two of them, picking her way carefully over the tangled snakes of water hoses and cables, she looked up at the building.

It was one of the more stylish of the blocks of flats that had sprung up all over Docklands in the piping days of the Eighties, when money had seemed to come from a bottomless well and no one ever dreamed things would change. The flats had sold well then, but now she could see to one side the row of *For Sale* boards adorned with the names of various well-known local estate agents, tilting forlornly against the light. So, plenty of empty flats here, like everywhere else in the district. But at least one of them must have been occupied, because the phone call had been quite specific.

'A body, burned badly as far as we can see,' the anonymous policeman had clacked in her ear. 'Inspector Dudley's called out the Soco and the Fire Investigation Team because the firemen reckon it's a dicey one, and he wants you too, if you please, doctor.'

Only one half of the building seemed to be burning, and the firemen were working as hard to stop the thus far unaffected part from being caught up in the conflagration as they were at putting out the part where it had taken hold. And it had taken a very firm hold; George could see that clearly. Windows gaped blackly through frames of fringed charcoal, and the front of the walls seemed to be dissolving as paint and assorted other finishes melted and slid down the underlying brickwork. At one point she could see through the window apertures to the interior, where a burned-out room was displayed in all its piteousness to anyone who cared to look. There was a fireman in there picking over the debris on the floor and George, from her vantage point standing on a low wall at the front of the building, both to keep out of the way and to see over the milling heads of neighbours and onlookers, could just see the wreck of a sideboard, a dining table and, miraculously, a scrap of blue curtain to one side of the window which had somehow escaped the flames. Her throat tightened again.

Rupert Dudley saw her and came across at once, the fireman on his heels. 'Dr Barnabas, we've got a body upstairs, severely burned, dead of course. We thought it a fire death but Mr Knight here thinks it might be more than that.'

The fireman pushed forwards. He had a snub nose rather ludicrously tipped with soot between round cheeks similarly adorned. He looked more like a child dressed up for Halloween than a senior fire officer, George thought. Until he spoke. Then his clear authority removed any hint of immaturity from his appearance. This was a man who knew his job and all its ramifications.

'Morning, doctor,' he said. 'Sorry we had to get you out so early but it seemed a good idea, seeing as the observations I've made don't tally with the situation we'd expect. You see, we found –'

'If I might interrupt,' Dudley said. 'It'll be easier to explain if we go up. Doctor?' And he stepped back and indicated that George should lead the way.

'You go first,' she said. 'You know where we're going.' She fell into step behind him as he led the way to the main entrance of the flats, which had not, so far, been burned. He was being remarkably polite, she thought; last time he called me out early he was tickled to death with himself, thought he'd caught me out. Why is he being so charming? Well, charming on his terms, if not on anyone else's . . .

'We can use the staircase safely,' Knight said. 'The upper floors aren't so good, the stairs are badly affected there. But this flight's OK. The fire went upwards.'

'Isn't that what you'd expect?'

'Not entirely,' Knight said and she looked at him over her shoulder, for there was a grim note in his voice.

'How do you mean?'

'It will be better if we look first, talk later,' he said and obediently she followed Dudley up the stairs, with Knight walking close behind her as though to catch her if she fell.

The smell of charring was stronger and now there was the reek of dirty water too. The first floor, when they reached it, was awash; what had once possibly been costly carpet was now a thick squelching colourless mess, and water splashed around her shoes as she moved along the corridor, still sand-wiched between the two watchful men.

She was glad of them when her foot slipped on a particularly sodden patch and she nearly lost her balance. She found herself hanging on to Rupert Dudley's shoulders with both hands, her bag swinging from one of them so wildly that it caught Dudley a sharp blow on the ear. He swore and grabbed for his ear and almost toppled her, but fortunately Knight was hanging on to her by now, so they all remained upright. Dudley threw her a furious glare over his shoulder and perversely she felt better; he hadn't been behaving charmingly to her at all. Roop in a rage was one of the comforting things in life; made you feel you knew where you were.

The flat they reached had been almost burned out. The floor near the door was safe enough, but Knight set her aside and insisted on going first. Someone had set long thick planks over the remainder of the floor (which was severely charred, so much so that in places the joists, or what remained of them, could be clearly seen) using an unburned area on the far side to hold them, and he made his way gingerly on to one of them and held out his hand.

'You'll be safe on this, but don't set foot on the floor whatever you do. It's as strong as paper, only crumblier,' he warned. 'This way.'

She followed him carefully, not taking her eyes from her feet as she set them one in front of the other, until Knight said, 'OK. Here we are. Can you see from here?'

The plank had brought her to the bottom of a bed, which tilted dangerously on the wrecked floor. It had been, she suspected, brass; she could still see the balls on each corner and the lattice work of metal rails that had made the head and footboards, but they were cruelly twisted and blackened. Between them were the remains of the bedding, a very thick mattress and what had been a large duvet. It must have been its thickness that prevented it being entirely consumed; certainly she could still see its shape. It had covered a body, which now lay in all its blackened, singed horror, a travesty of a human form, the head curved back against a pillow which was little more than a heap of ash and debris.

'I reckon that's one of the most burned bodies I've ever seen,' Rupert Dudley said after a moment in a low voice, but

Knight laughed and his commonplace voice was a comfort in the thick atmosphere of the room.

'Oh, I've seen 'em worse'n that!' he said. 'At least you can see this was a bod. Sometimes it's worse than if they've been through the crematorium ovens. No shape at all, really. You'd be amazed.'

'What is it you want to point out to me?' George said crisply, wanting to get on with the job.

'Well, she's there, do you see,' Knight said, and George looked at him sharply.

'How do you know it's a she?' she demanded.

'Ah, no pulling of any wool over your eyes, right?' Knight sounded jovial. 'I don't know, I'm guessing. But it's an informed guess. The tenant of this flat is listed as a Miss Lisa Zizi, aged thirty-seven, exotic dancer.' He glanced at George then. 'And possibly a bit of a part-time lady on the side, if you get my meaning. The same sort of – you know . . .'

'A Tom,' Dudley said flatly. 'Expensive one, if she was.'

'How can you be sure that's who that is?' George said, tilting her chin at the body. 'Or that she was a prostitute?'

'I said, we can't. But it seems a fair guess. Anyway, you don't often get men around five foot three, give or take a few centimetres, sleeping in rooms with pink satin curtains. See? There's a scrap left over there.'

'That is amazing,' Dudley said, looking from the shred of curtain at the window to the bed. 'That there should be this much damage here but curtains at the windows should be . . .'

'Oh!' George said, and stared again at the body!

'Exactly!' Knight sounded like an approving schoolteacher. 'You've spotted it, doctor, right?'

'Why should this bed and the person in it be so badly burned and there still be curtains at the window?' She looked over her shoulder at them, then around the rest of the room, which was illuminated by the police photographer's Tilley lamps as he gingerly photographed where he could. 'It's a bit odd.'

'Odder than a bit. It's as odd as Dick's hatband – which went round three times and never met.' Knight looked smug.

'I'm glad you spotted it, doctor. Shall I tell you what I think? Before you look at the body? It might help you.'

'Try and stop him,' Dudley said.

Knight grinned at him. 'Well, you could be right. When I get on to something I really do ... look, doctor, when there's a fire what do the people caught in it usually do?'

'Try to get out,' George said. 'But just tell me, please. Let's not have any quiz games.'

'Who's playing games?' Knight said. 'Just look at this. Here's someone who had to be woken, surely, by a fire as fierce as this was, but lay there in bed and let herself get frizzled up. Not one of your hide-in-the-corners-and-try-to-escape-it, hmm? Not one of your leap-out-of-the-window-and-take-your-chance, eh? Just lay there.'

'So you think she – he – might have died before the fire,' George said. 'It's not uncommon. We've seen it before. A body set on fire to hide a murder.'

'I'm sure you have,' Knight said. 'So have I, lotsa times. But this one's different. I've had a good look here, and I have to tell you that I think the fire started in the body itself.'

'Started where?' Dudley said. 'Are you saying this was arson?'

'You can never be sure,' Knight said. 'But I'll tell you this much. This wasn't electrical, because we've been able to check right back to the fuse board which hasn't been touched. There's been no overloads or short circuits. I'll stake my pension on it and I'm going to be top of the Brigade before I retire, so it'll be a hell of a pension!' He laughed, happily relaxed in spite of his surroundings and for a moment George marvelled, until she remembered that this was the man's daily work. He was as comfortable here as she was doing one of her post-mortems, and most people found that extraordinary.

'I'll tell you something else,' Knight said. 'This fire spread *upwards* almost entirely. Hardly down at all. Generally a fire in a building like this will go both ways – out from the centre, if you see what I mean. This seemed not to affect the flats beneath – or very little. Our water's done more harm downstairs than the flames did. It all adds up to a very unusual fire.'

She looked at the floor and the severe damage there, and frowned. If it was worse than that upstairs, then upstairs must be in a bad state. But she couldn't concentrate on that thought, because Knight was speaking again.

'I'll tell you what I think. You can pooh pooh it if you like, and I dare say you will. I know that scientifically it's never been proven, but if that isn't a form of spontaneous combustion then I'm not here but lying in bed at home and dreaming.'

There was a long silence and then George said carefully, 'Spontaneous combustion.' Dudley said nothing. He just stared.

Knight looked a little pugnacious. 'Well, it's something I've read about. Amazing cases, few and far between, I'll grant you, but not unheard of.'

George blinked. 'Um,' she said, trying not to sound as dismissive as she felt about the idea. 'The only proven case I've read of involved the build-up of flammable gases in a decomposing corpse, and then there had to be an igniting spark of some kind. There's no sign here that this body had started that process. I have to say I think spontaneous combustion unlikely. There has to be some other reason, surely . . .'

There was another silence as the three of them contemplated the body on the bed, and behind them the flashes of the Soco's camera started again. Then he came over to Dudley and said, 'I think that's it, sir. You can take over now.'

'Thanks,' said Dudley abstractedly. Soco picked his way back over the planks and went, leaving just the three of them and another uniformed policeman waiting for instructions.

'I'll take a look,' George said, and moving carefully crossed to the adjoining plank, so that she could get nearer to the head of the bed, and stood staring down at the skull.

There was a bulge on one side of the crown and, amazingly, remnants of black hair low on the other side. Very little, but it was there; as though the fire that had attacked this body had been as one-sided as the fire that had attacked the buildings. For a moment she wondered, though only briefly, if the fire officer's idea could have any basis in fact. It certainly looked as though one part of the body had flared into flame suddenly, consuming the face and part of the skull, but leaving only less severe marks on the rest of the body.

She reached for her bag to see if she could make some sort of preliminary examination before the body was moved; Dudley handed it to her and then leaned over the body himself.

'That lump on the head,' he said shortly. 'Could she have been bashed?'

George had her bag open by now and had pulled out some of her instruments. She reached over and carefully probed the lump. 'I don't think so,' she said. 'I can't be sure till I get her back to the mortuary, but I would have thought not. This is likely to be a heat haematoma.'

'A what?' Dudley was fascinated. He had come round to the other side of the charred bed to watch her.

'It's nasty,' she said. 'If the scalp is burned as this one is, it's possible for blood to boil out of the diploë and the venous sinuses.'

'Diploë?' Dudley said and George, not thinking about the effect of her words, nodded.

'Uh huh. The red-marrow-bearing material between the inner and outer tables of the skull. And the venous sinuses are the –' She stopped as she saw Dudley's face pale. 'Are you all right?'

'The blood boils out, did you say?'

'Something like that,' she said hastily. 'Anyway it isn't due to a blow, though it looks like a contusion. So if she was dead before the fire it wasn't likely to be because of a hit on the head. But as I say, I can tell better back at the mortuary when I do the PM.'

'But you don't think it's this spontaneous combustion, then?' Knight asked.

'I doubt it,' George said, wanting to be diplomatic. 'It's pretty rare, if it's ever happened – we've no proof of it, I'm afraid. Sorry, Mr Knight. But I do take your point that this woman was perhaps dead before the fire started. It certainly would seem so. She stayed in bed and her damage from the fire is ... Well, I really can't say much more, though I can't deny it's a little bizarre. The PM, that's the thing. I'll do a few simple things here just for the report, Roop, and then if you'll arrange to get the body to the mortuary first thing in the morning, I'll make the PM a priority.'

Dudley didn't seem to have noticed she had used his hated diminutive, and indeed she'd hardly noticed herself. 'OK, doc, I'll get the rest cleared here. There's another body in the flat above and –'

'Another?' She looked up sharply. 'You didn't say!'

'Didn't get the chance,' Dudley said. 'Old man, found in the corner, no fire damage that we can see, but he's very dead. Have a look when you're ready, OK? We've had to bring the body downstairs. Couldn't leave it in situ. The floor's likely to fall in.'

'Now he tells me!' George said. She looked up a little fearfully. Above her head the ceiling sagged alarmingly and in places she could see light above where the floor had burned through. 'I'll get going.'

She did what she could swiftly, taking her usual pictures and making notes about the position of the body and confirming the fact that it was indeed female. The other men hadn't disturbed the covering enough to check, but their guesses had been right. Below the duvet it was still possible to see the shape of her external genital cleft and though her breasts had gone, there was the evidence of the bones. George would confirm that when she got the body under her lights at the mortuary. She closed her bag at last and made her way back over the planks to the door, ready to go and look at the other body from upstairs, puzzling as she went. It was one thing to dismiss, albeit kindly, Fireman Knight's absurd notion that this was a case of spontaneous combustion, quite another to account for what were undoubtedly some of the oddest fire injuries she had ever seen.

8

It was Danny who came up with a more rational explanation for the injuries on the woman when he first saw her on the PM table, and heard what Knight had had to say about the cause of the fire. George, wearing a mask – something she often didn't bother with, but felt the need for this morning – was carefully separating the small lock of remaining hair from the scalp so that it could be examined; Danny looked at it once she had it in its sample envelope, and then squinted at what remained of the woman's face.

'Indian, is she?' he said. George lifted her head and looked at him. Across the room, Norman Vale, the young man from the coroner's office standing in today for Harold Constant, who – luckily for him – had a migraine, looked at him too. DC Wheeler, who had been sent from Dudley's team to observe, remained as he was, his head down and his eyes fixed on the floor. It was the only way he could ever cope with post-mortems, pretending he wasn't there.

'What makes you think that?' George asked.

'Oh, we 'ad a little spate o' them a few years back. I remember it well. One after another, like it was in fashion.' He carried the sample carefully to the tray at the side which he had prepared for the reception of such items. 'Old Dr Royle, 'e got quite expert at 'em.'

'Oh, did he?' George said, bristling a little at the mention of the predecessor who had caused her some problems in her first months at Old East. 'Tracked down an arsonist, I suppose.'

Norman Vale, an ambitious man, perked up considerably. Reporting arson would make him a man of some note at the coroner's office, he reckoned. He sidled a little closer.

'There wasn't no arsonist.' Danny was dismissive. 'It was a lot of dowry battles. Nasty, they was. The local Race Relations lot stepped in, sorted it out.'

'I beg your pardon?' the coroner's officer asked.

'It was a big scandal at the time.' Danny settled to a luxurious gossip of the sort he liked best. 'Indian girls from poor families, see, brought here for their arranged marriages. Their parents had to pay dowries to the husbands, didn't they? Then if there wasn't enough money or the husbands' families got greedy, the wives burned themselves. Or got burned. Self-immolation, Dr Royle used to put on the certificates.'

There was a long silence and then George said, 'Mr Wheeler, could you check on this with Inspector Dudley? I was told the woman who rented the flat was called ... I think I wrote it down somewhere. Show me the notes, Danny. Yes, here it is, Lisa Zizi. I thought that was a stage name but, well, see what you can find out.'

Wheeler departed with alacrity, and the room settled to quietness as George went on with the job. It wasn't an easy one. The severe burning was all in the top half of the body, where the damage was bone deep in many places; the teeth, which were in good condition, and the jaw could be clearly seen as far back as the mandibular joint on the left, and the neck on that side was also destroyed down to the vertebral column. On the other side, however, it was not so severe, and she dictated her notes very carefully indeed, putting in all the details she could.

Further down the body the damage petered out. The legs were hardly burned at all in comparison though there were several patches of second-degree burns, as well as wide areas of first-degree damage with great red flares in the tanned skin and on the edges of the more severely affected areas, where the burns were more clearly third degree.

When she checked the lungs and trachea she decided that this woman had definitely been dead before the fire. Had she made any attempt to breathe once the fabric of her bedroom had flared, there would have been carbon particles in the nose and larynx, trachea and bronchii, but there weren't. George would have to check blood – if she could get any – for carboxy-haemoglobin, which would indicate the woman had inhaled carbon monoxide before death, a gas that was produced by fires, but she had a strong conviction she would find none.

She stopped to think at that point. What was it her professorial lecturer had said? 'Never assume that the absence of soot and monoxide means that the victim must have been dead before the fire started. In flash fires due to substances such as petrol very little of either is produced.'

But there had been lots of soot around at that fire, she reminded herself, conjuring up a memory of the charred wood of the floor. No, she was sure. The absence of soot in the breathing tubes had to mean that this woman had died before the fire started. Or so soon after that the fire could not have been the cause of death, however much damage it had done afterwards. And she dictated as much for her notes.

For the rest, the woman was, she estimated, in her middle thirties, going by her bone age, but there was no way she could identify her racial origin, for although she was dark-skinned, she was well within the range of Caucasian colouring. There would have to be other evidence for that aspect of the identification and she was eager to know whether Wheeler had managed to find any.

When she had finished and showered and changed, scrubbing herself even more thoroughly than usual, she hurried up to her office. Wheeler was there, sitting at her desk using the phone, and she waved her hands when he attempted to get up, to encourage him to continue. So he listened and nodded, spoke a little and then hung up.

'All that we've managed to find out is that the tenant of the flat was seen going in at midnight, which was a bit on the early side for her, apparently. She had a man with her, but the neighbours were used to that. They all knew what she was up to – one or two of the others in the block are on the game too and they're mostly a tolerant lot. Bohemian, you know?' He said it like a rude word. 'No one saw the man go. But it seems likely to have been the woman we found. The name we've got they all say – the neighbours – is the only one they know for her. But we've checked with banks and GPs and so forth and found out a bit about her. Her full name was Zivkonek, Isabella Zivkonek. She was a British national with a Yugoslav father. Said to be part gypsy, according to her doctor. He's given us her dentist's name, so we can get a firm ID from him.'

'Yes, that'll settle it. And she used this other name –'

'For business. Yes. Not badly off, it turns out. You know what banks are like, not keen on handing over info unless they've got a warrant starin' at 'em, but it seems she was pretty well off. Lived in an expensive block, that's for sure. But then, these women can earn big money, I'm told.' He looked down his nose a little and George smiled. She'd heard DC Wheeler was a lay preacher of some small and ardent sect, and could see that he would find the lifestyles of some of the more colourful characters on the Ratcliffe nick patch not entirely to his taste.

'So they say,' she said demurely. 'Well, there it is. It's not a self-immolation of the sort Danny meant. Wrong ethnic group. You've got a murder on your hands, haven't you?'

'We have?' He looked a little startled.

'Oh, of course, you didn't hear what I said down there. She died before the fire got to her.'

'I thought you told Dudley the lump on her head was due to – due to . . .' He swallowed.

'Post-mortem . . . um, movement of blood,' she said diplomatically. 'Due to the fire. Not due to being walloped on the head to be killed. It was done some other way.'

'Were you able to find out how?'

She shook her head. 'Sorry, no. I've still got to do the tests for various poisons and so on, and we'll be checking the blood, but at present I don't have any cause of death.'

'I'll tell the Guv,' Wheeler said, reaching for his coat, which he'd left draped over her desk. 'He'll want to get an incident room set up.'

She lit up. 'Inspector Hathaway'll be back to do this one? They'll let him leave his big case?'

He looked surprised. 'Oh, no. Inspector Dudley'll do this. He's acting DCI at present, till we get another pair of hands, I suppose, but everyone's a bit pushed at the Met at the moment, seemingly.'

'Oh,' she said, flattened, and then brightened. 'Still, I imagine when Gus – Chief Inspector Hathaway hears about this he'll want to take over? It could be a big one and it's just the sort of case he likes. I'll talk to him about it.'

'Well, that's up to you, of course.' Wheeler was at the door. 'But Inspector Dudley's likely to be ... Well, it's up to you.' And he went.

Inspector Dudley's likely to be unhappy about that, she finished inside her own head. Well, up yours, Inspector Dudley. I'm still going to tell Gus. He's sure to want to take over, and then won't we have fun! And she pushed aside the guilt that came up at once when she realized she was pleased to have a body for Gus to come back to and wasn't thinking of the woman whose body it had been.

She had to go over to A & E almost immediately she had finished dealing with the last details in the post-mortem room, remembering just in time that she'd promised to go to a meeting about the way urgent path. requests would be handled there in the future. The A & E department was to be reorganized and she'd promised Hattie Clements, the sister in charge and one of her best friends, that she'd be there to help her in her ongoing feud with her consultant Margaret Hill-Sykes.

'She's hell bent,' Hattie had told her with feeling, 'on running down the A & E department till it gets itself closed by the Department of Health, I swear it. She's doing it on purpose for the benefit of David Delaney. He used to be her favourite junior here, but now that he's been appointed consultant to A & E over at St Chad's and she's retiring in a couple of years, she's more interested in building up St Chad's for him than protecting Old East's interests. She always fancied that chap Delaney – half her age, too!'

'I'll do all I can to help,' George had promised. 'They're trying to do something similar with the Path. Department and I won't have it either! I'll be there. Eleven o'clock, you say?'

Now, at five minutes past eleven, she went rushing through the walkways, across the courtyard, her white coat-tails flying and her head down as she tried to organize her thoughts. What with the post-mortem she'd just done and the ideas that had thrown up and her continuing preoccupation with getting Gus back on the case, it was going to be hard to think of A & E and its problems.

But it wasn't as hard as it might have been, because she walked into an atmosphere of bedlam that immediately banished her own concerns. There had been a major row at a pub a little further upriver, she was told breathlessly by one of the A & E clerks as she stood just inside the department, staring hard at the hubbub that greeted her startled eyes, and two men with knife wounds had been brought in.

'The copper what brung them in said it was a row over some sort of racket they was running,' the clerk said, breathless with excitement. 'So I thought drugs as usual, but he said not. It's all over who drinks where and who gangs with who and so forth –'

A bell pealed suddenly and then continued to ring with an insistent pulse. At once George started forwards. It was a long time since she had been in a cardiac response team, but her reactions were still in place and she headed across the waiting hall behind the other doctors and nurses who appeared from every corner, equally galvanized, as though she were still a junior doctor in her first year in A & E.

The far treatment room, which was where the call came from, was full of people but somehow George found herself almost at the foot of the couch on which the patient was stretched and she caught her breath at the sight of him.

He'd been stabbed in the belly and blood was pulsing from it, bright scarlet and almost sparkling in the blaze of overhead lights. As she arrived, Hattie, who was beside the head of the couch, dived for the site of the bleed and pushed down hard with both hands, so that the pulsing was held back. 'It just blew,' she shouted as the new arrivals, expecting a cardiac collapse case and finding something very different, hesitated, not sure what to do. 'There must have been a nick into the aorta. Get a sample and some packed cells fast and then call the vascular team and the theatre. I can hang on here a little longer – George!'

Her eyes lit up as she caught sight of George, who now moved round closer as the various people who had come into the room with her scattered to do Hattie's bidding. 'I think I've got this but can you try? Grab some gloves and see if you can take over here. It's a surgeon this needs . . .'

George had already registered what was needed; she had been an A & E registrar herself for a while before moving permanently into pathology and she remembered cases very like this one. She reached for the gown a nurse had pulled out of a sterile pack for her, and then for gloves. There wasn't time to scrub properly but there was a second to pull on two pairs of gloves to improve the degree of asepsis; she did just that, then came and stood behind Hattie and reached over her shoulder.

'OK,' she said. 'Hold on there, Hatt. I'll slide my hand down alongside yours . . . Where is it? Left or right . . .?'

Hattie closed her eyes, concentrating on the sensations from her fingers. 'To the left,' she said. 'I can feel the pressure – yes – you're in the right place. Now hold on hard there . . . Got it!'

George had. Her gloved hand was now firmly closed around the area where the blood was pulsing. She could feel the strength of it against her fingers, weak as it was, and now for the first time the man it belonged to turned his head and made a thick sound in his throat. He had a ventilation mask over his mouth and nose and the frightened-looking young doctor who was holding it in place and using his other hand to pump air into the patient with regular clutches of the bag widened his eyes in horror.

'He's beginning to come round,' he said. 'Isn't he? I didn't give him more than nitrous oxide. Can he feel what –'

'It's all right.' Hattie was round the other side now, drawing up a syringe with the help of one of the other nurses. 'He's had a good deal of analgesia already – they did that in the ambulance. I doubt he has awareness. He'll be lucky if he ever does again. Oh, great, the packed cells at last.'

The treatment room filled up with people again. Someone shot round to the far side to set a new bag of blood up to drip into the flaccid arm that was stretched there and someone behind George said, 'I'll take him now,' and reached over her shoulder just as she'd reached over Hattie's.

'Thanks,' she managed and gratefully let go in reaction to the signal she was given as very expert hands took over from her. She recognized the elegant features of the tall Nigerian who was Old East's vascular surgeon and smiled at him in deep relief. 'I've never been so glad to see anyone in my whole life.'

'I'll bet,' he said. 'I'll get a temporary tie into this just so that we can transport him to theatres.' Several people closed around him busily as George slid away from the side of the couch and made for the door. 'Thanks, George!' he called then, just as she was about to close it behind her. 'I'll let you know how he gets on.'

'Please do,' she said and escaped to stand outside and pull off the gloves and gown and stare down at her bloodied white coat. She'd have to borrow one to see her through the rest of the day, dammit, and other people's were never long enough. She'd look like Little Orphan Annie, and she swore out loud.

Hattie touched her on the shoulder and gently urged her to one side as the door opened again and the trolley came out, with so many people clustered round it that it looked like a piece of meat surrounded by tadpoles in a feeding frenzy, and went hurtling out to the far corridor on its way to main theatres.

'Ta,' Hattie said. 'Ta ever so very ta. Jesus, that was a nasty one!'

'Tell me about it,' George said. 'And I thought life in pathology was tough.'

'It isn't always like this,' Hattie said. 'Only enough to make

72

it obvious we have to keep this unit going. If that poor bugger had had to go to St Chad's he'd never have made it. Another ten minutes, even under blue lights, in the sort of traffic there is between here and there, would have killed him. Even Hill-Sykes'll have to see that.' She shook her head and then looked round her department with a practised eye. 'Well, things seem to have settled. Come and sit in the office. I'll see if Hill-Sykes is still here – it was amazing how absent she was when that blew, wasn't it? Some bloody A & E consultant she is!'

'Well, you said she was retiring soon,' George murmured. She had heard Hattie go on at length in the past about her much hated medical boss and wasn't in the mood for more. 'Just hang on in there.'

'Oh, I will,' Hattie promised grimly. 'I will! Look, ducks, I'm sorry to have wasted your time. I'd have thought the bloody woman would hang around and wait to do the meeting when the fuss was over, but obviously she hasn't.' She glared at her watch. 'It's getting on for twelve – maybe she's gone to lunch. I'll try to fix the meeting for another time, then? Meanwhile, shall we go and eat lunch ourselves? Things seem to be under control here.'

And indeed the department had quieted down suddenly in the way that was so often the case in A & E, which could swoop from total peace to bewildering activity and vice versa in a matter of minutes. George grinned at Hattie and nodded.

'Lunch would be nice. So would gossip,' she said. 'Lead on.' And for the next hour she sat head to head with Hattie in the canteen as they talked of the various people in their lives and exchanged the most interesting details of what was happening around Old East. It was a refreshing time for George and she relaxed a little, but not completely. Certainly not completely enough to talk about Gus, and how much she was missing seeing him at present. Somehow she just wasn't in the mood for that.

Because somewhere deep inside she was becoming alarmed for Gus. The knifing she had seen in A & E had been so vicious, so deliberately designed to kill that it had been chilling to look at; and hearing a little more about the background to it from Hattie – and she told George that indeed, as the clerk had suggested, the man had been involved in a protection racket – it occurred to her that it was possible that this was one of the cases Gus was investigating. It was a thought that chilled her even more. Could these people attack Gus in the same way? She felt sick as she considered the possibility.

But then she was annoyed with herself. Gus had been a policeman long enough to know how to take care of himself. He'd dealt with violent criminals before safely. He could again. Couldn't he?

By the time she got back to her own department at almost two o'clock, she had convinced herself he could and felt a little better: more than ready to make and carry out a few plans of her own. She'd track Gus down and talk to him and after that, once she'd told him of her new case and the problems it threw up, then the problems would be over. He'd come and take over this case and be safer doing so – a great remedy for both her anxieties. So she promised herself as she walked into her office; and found Sheila there, agog, waiting to deliver a message.

'Dr B, remember that leg you had the other day? Well, there was a call from Sergeant Slavin of the river police. He says he's got another part of it. He's on his way – How's that?'

'Great!' George picked up Sheila's excitement. 'How long will he be?'

'He said ten minutes – and that was about fifteen minutes ago,' Sheila said, looking at her watch. 'I'll go down and check, see if he went straight to the mortuary?'

'No,' George said. 'I'm on my way down.' But she stopped as she got to her desk to check for other messages. DC Wheeler had called to make an arrangement for the police dentist to come and take casts and examine the body, and she stood, tapping her finger on the message, thinking, and then picked up her phone.

'Inspector Dudley?' she said, once she'd managed to get to him past the switchboard, which had a tendency to protect him from outside callers unless they knew exactly who they were. 'At last. Listen. I think we might have another case for you –'

'Another?' He sounded bored more than anything else. 'Is that a fact. What is it this time?'

'The leg, remember? I think we've got another piece of that body. Sergeant Slavin's bringing it in. I'm not sure what it is or where he found it, but it could help us to get an ID and that'll mean you've got –'

'What I had before. A difficult case with an unidentified victim.'

She felt herself flush at the faint sneer in his voice. 'My point is that having more of the body could get us an ID – and that means you've got two cases on. The Zizi woman and this one. Too much for you on your own, isn't it?'

'Are you trying to tell me how to do my job, Doctor?' He was very quiet and she didn't at first register how angry he was and blundered on.

'Oh, of course not, Roop. I just thought maybe you'll need Gus to –'

'Dr Barnabas,' he said and now his voice was almost shaking with rage. 'I would prefer you to address me by my full name and rank *if* you please, as I do you. And I will thank you furthermore to do your own job and leave me to mine, all right? I'll decide, together with my superior officers here, whether or not I need more help on this case and I'll thank you to mind your own business!'

'Oh, shit,' she said. 'I've really put my foot in it, haven't I? Hell, Roo– Inspector Dudley, give me a break, will you? I didn't mean to step on your toes, for Chrissakes. I guess I did go off half cocked at that. It was just that – well, I thought maybe once we had an ID on this leg case that, well –'

'I know what you thought,' he said and again his voice was small and hard. 'You thought I'm not up to dealing with this on my own. Well, doctor, that really is no concern of yours. I'll look forward to getting your reports when they're ready. That's all I need from you. Good afternoon.' And the phone clicked, even as she said despairingly. 'It's nothing against you, I just thought that maybe Gus –' But she stopped when the burr in her ear became too persistent to ignore and slowly cradled the phone.

You fool, she hissed at herself. Stupid goddamned fool! Why do you keep on rubbing him up the wrong way? Sure he's annoying. Sure he's a pain in the butt, but you don't have to aggravate the guy!

But she'd done it and all she could do now was make the best of the situation. Maybe, she thought hopefully as she clattered down the stairs towards her PM room, maybe I'll get a fix on this latest piece of body. That should settle him – show him I meant no harm. Or at least I don't think I did, I just want to get Gus back on the job, that's all . . .

Sergeant Slavin was sitting awkwardly on a stool in the PM room when she came in ready changed and thumping along in her heavy green waterproof boots. She grinned at him.

'Tell me you've got the guy's head,' she begged. 'Go on, tell me. That way we have a much better hope of getting an ID. Is it the head?'

He made a face and shook his head all at the same time. 'Sorry, doc. Nothing of the sort. Just a lump of flesh. I'm afraid. Hasn't even got a skin on it, and –'

Her face fell. 'Oh. That makes it almost impossible!'

'I said that to the woman I talked to when I rang,' he said, as she padded across the PM room to the slab where the object he had brought in lay waiting for her. 'I said it was just a big piece of flesh and no guarantee that it was any use, but I thought you'd want to see it, just to be sure it wasn't significant.'

'You said that to her?' George said, staring down at the slab and remembering Sheila's excited words. She could almost hear her fluting breathy little voice. *Remember that leg? Sergeant Slavin says he's got another part of it.* She bit her lip. 'Are you sure that's all you said?'

He looked puzzled. 'Well, yes. What else could I have said?'

'I thought you might have said it was definitely part of the same body as the leg, and that you had some reason for saying it.'

76

He shook his head, mystified. 'How could I? Look at it!'

She was looking and now she sighed. 'I'm afraid my assistant got a bit excited there, Sergeant,' she said. 'She had the impression that you said there was a definite link.'

'Oh? Oh!' His face lightened. 'I see. No, what I said was did she know about the case of the leg that was washed up, and she said she did, so I said it was in connection with that that I wanted to come in, and she said fine and I –'

'It's all right,' George said dully, horribly aware of what she had said to Rupert Dudley on the phone. If only she hadn't done her usual thing of getting over-excited and not stopping to think or even to see what was what before rushing to the phone. It was all because of Gus, of course. She wanted to get him away from that big case so much she'd try anything. That was the truth of it and she had to face it. She didn't want him to be so wrapped up in his work that he had no time for others. She didn't want him to risk being knifed like the case in hand. And she wanted him where she could see him. Goddamn it, she was turning into exactly the sort of woman she most hated. Possessive and –

'I meant no harm bringing it in,' Sergeant Slavin broke into her thoughts. 'I just looked at it when we got it – it was fouling an anchor down by Limehouse Reach – and I thought, there are things here that might interest Dr Barnabas. I remembered the things you said about the leg, you see, and it seemed to me that there were sort of similarities. I mean, the sort of clean cut the thing shows. It's not something you see all that often, is it? And yet here it is again, cut clean through the bone and everything.'

'Yes,' she said and became a little more interested, though she still made no attempt to examine the flesh with her hands or instruments. It was a sizeable piece, a block from across a haunch, and the cut that had severed it from the main body was indeed a clean one, very like that on the leg in the Harrods shoe. But that was as far as the similarity ran.

'Well,' she said. 'Thank you for showing me. I'm not sure what it's supposed to prove but –'

'That what cut the leg off cut this up and all,' Sergeant

Slavin said patiently. 'And who the hell is doing things like this to living creatures? That's what's interesting.'

She turned back. 'Well, I'll grant you that it's odd. But I'm a pathologist that deals with human remains, Sergeant Slavin. This is a dog. Or maybe something more exotic that escaped from a zoo. Human it isn't.'

'I know that,' Sergeant Slavin said, looking disgusted. 'You don't think I brought it in because I thought it was *human* remains, do you? Of course not. It's just that the same method of chopping might have been used. I thought that was important.'

There was a silence and then she said, 'You're right. And I'm sorry, Sergeant. Of course you're right. It's just that I went off half cocked when I got the message and –'

He tilted his head at her. 'That woman who took the message – got it wrong, did she?'

'Did she ever,' George said with feeling.

'Sorry about that.'

'Not your fault.'

'I know, but all the same … Well, I'll get rid of it now. Unless you can? Got an incinerator here, perhaps?'

'Of course. We'll get rid of it for you. And you're right, Sergeant. I'd like to look at any other pieces like this you find. It could lead us back to whatever it was that did the cutting and that could be a link to the owner of the leg. So, I'll get some photographs done. Sorry I was so, well …'

'No need for another word,' he said handsomely as he made for the door. 'Ta, Dr Barnabas. We'll keep on looking out. See you soon, I hope. And next time, maybe I'll have the head that goes with the leg, hmm?'

'I wish,' she called after him, and then turned and shouted for Danny. This unpleasant canine leftover had to be dealt with and she, heaven help her, had to call Dudley and apologize and explain. Oh, life could be a bitch sometimes.

9

It was one of the most uncomfortable conversations she had ever had. It took Dudley a few moments to comprehend what she was saying and when he did, he started to laugh. He was not normally a man given to laughter and she had to stand there holding the phone and listening to him indulge himself in it. If she hadn't known herself to be as totally in the wrong as it was possible for a person to be, she would have hung up on him, but as it was she couldn't. She just had to let him get on with it. It was extremely painful.

It was even worse after he'd stopped his chortling. He became amazingly forgiving, kind even, and she could have ground her teeth with frustration as he talked on and on. But at last he stopped to take breath and she was able to cut in.

'It's still interesting, though,' she said. 'And worth investigating. The way the body has been cut is exactly the same way as that leg was. I've arranged to compare the photographs I've taken of the cut edge with those on the leg. It should point us towards the way the body was dealt with and once we've got that, maybe we'll be in a better position to work out who the man was —'

The laughter went from Dudley's voice. 'There's no need for all this *we* stuff, doctor,' he said. 'You've done your job and I'm glad to have your reports. Anything you notice will be taken into account, of course. But the investigation of this case, like the fire death, is my affair, not yours. You understand? Not yours.'

'Well, of course,' she said, trying to be diplomatic. 'But usually with these difficult cases, Gus encourages me to –'

'This is my case.' Dudley's voice had gone small and hard again. 'Not the Chief Inspector's.'

'But, surely,' she cried, almost despairingly. 'He'll be back to deal with this? It's a big case, a very big one. They both are. You must want him to –'

'All I want, doctor, is to do the job I'm paid to do and ensure that other people involved do the jobs *they're* paid to do. No less and definitely no more. So, thanks for your call, doctor. I have work to do.' And her phone buzzed in her ear as he hung up and she indulged herself in some pretty comprehensive swearing.

To be shut out of these cases was more than she could bear, it really was, she told herself passionately, once she had discharged some of her rage at Inspector Dudley. She wasn't going to let him do it to her. She always worked closely with Gus when there were cases like this, and even if they were quite small ones, he was glad of her input. Who did this tinpot general of an inspector think he was, to change such excellent working practices? There was only one thing for it. She'd have to talk to Gus directly about it. Maybe, once he knew what was happening (and she had a shrewd suspicion that he did not) he would override Dudley himself, and take over these two cases?

She brightened at the thought. Tonight, then, she would go over to flat and see if she could sort this out. However late he got home she'd be there to wait for him. She began to plan a simple meal she could cook for him whatever time he came in, and worked out when she could do the necessary shopping at Bloom's delicatessen in Aldgate which, happily, was open till late. Gus loved deli food, especially when he was too tired to eat properly; Bloom's was undoubtedly the answer. Soothed by salt beef, he would be more than ready to take on Rupert Dudley and defeat him. Tinpot general, she thought again, and was comforted.

So much so that she did not do more than point out to Sheila in a mild sort of way that she had delivered rather more message than she had been given. Sheila looked affronted for a moment and then shrugged. 'Well,' she said. 'I got it from him, that river sergeant, so if it was wrong tell him about it,' and George didn't even bother to argue with her. It wasn't worth it.

One of the reasons for Sheila's sulkiness was soon apparent. Alan Short was in the lab when she went in, sitting next to Jane Rose, and though they both seemed to be busy over the slides Jane was working on, there could be no doubt in any onlooker's mind that both were deeply content to be in such proximity. George sighed as she saw them, noticing the mulish set of Sheila's mouth, and she asked Alan with a little sharpness in her tone to come into her office to sort out some cases with her.

He came happily, and grinned at her as she closed the office door behind him. 'You've had some really nasty ones lately, haven't you?' he said. His fair hair flopped over his forehead in sympathy and his wide toothy grin filled the room with its shimmer. 'I wish I could have come down and seen 'em but I was up to my neck in the routine stuff.'

'As long as that was all you were up to your neck in,' George said a shade harshly. 'You seem to be a bit too busy around Jane Rose's station for my liking. I organized the new rotas so that there'd be less – shall we say – overlap in activities. I need to keep the work flow rapid here, Alan, and it doesn't help if you spend too much time with one of the staff and upset the others.'

He flushed a vivid scarlet so suddenly that she was taken aback and was at once ashamed of herself. She didn't have to make the man feel that bad, for heaven's sake, just because she herself had been embarrassed by Dudley.

'Oh hell,' she said. 'I've upset you. Listen, I didn't mean to, but I've got Sheila Keen on my back because she says you're wasting Jane's time and, well, I'm having trouble with the Inspector running the cases I've been working on so I guess I kicked the cat. I should know better.'

Slowly his flush faded. 'That's all right,' he muttered. 'Doesn't matter.'

'Yes, it does. I mean, it matters that I was unnecessarily tough.' She made a grimace, hoping to elicit some sort of smile from him, but he didn't react. He just looked a little sulky now that his first reaction had settled down.

'Actually,' he said, 'I was trying to cover for Jerry. He's been up to his eyes in forensic stuff, so he couldn't help Jane as he usually does for part of his time and all I was doing was helping out. It wouldn't have been so bad – Jerry's pressure of work, I mean – if you hadn't got him to help you with that PM on the severed leg that you did, instead of me. I mean, I am your registrar . . .'

He let the comment hang in the air and she bit her lip. He was quite right, of course. As the other doctor in the lab he had the right to assist on interesting cases, if she needed such assistance; to have asked Jerry rather than him was a bit of an insult. She hadn't intended it that way; it was just that she hadn't yet become accustomed to having another doctor with her and considering such matters as his feelings and status.

She said as much and he, a sunny-tempered individual, cheered up, and became his usual agreeable self again. 'It's all right, Dr B.,' he said. 'I know how it is, and I can't lie – I do like working with Jane.' The flush threatened to rise again and drown his freckles. 'And I'll be more careful. It's tricky, though, when you – when you like someone, isn't it? You can't not think about them and being with them gets to be – well, rather important.'

She thought of herself and Gus and felt a wave of affection for her junior colleague. 'Yes,' she said. 'It is tricky. And thanks for being aware of it. Now . . .' She needed to change the subject. 'How are things going in general for you? Are you managing to keep up with everything?'

They settled to talking about the flow of work through the lab and the various tasks he had taken off her hands. Most of her time in the past had been swallowed up in minor jobs that really did not require a consultant's attention. To have a junior registrar to relieve her of them was a major asset, and she told him as much.

He went away ten minutes later, a much happier young

man, and left her feeling a little better too. And more determined not to let her concern with Gus get in the way of work any more. She'd allowed her concentration to slip and that would never do.

She still intended to go and see Gus that evening, however, but only because she truly didn't believe that Roop was up to handling these cases. The more she thought about the way the fire victim might actually have died, the more certain she was that this was a very difficult one, and needed Gus's superior skills; however able a man Dudley might be, Gus, she thought with some pride, was even more able. The case needed him.

She was ready to leave the lab at about half past six when Jerry put his head round her door.

'Dr B., I've done some work on those fibres,' he announced. 'Not a lot, but enough to tell you it's all a bit odd.'

'Odd?' She lifted her chin sharply. There was nothing she liked better than unexpected findings. They could point the way to all sorts of important conclusions. 'How odd?'

He inserted the rest of himself into the office and came and perched on the edge of her desk. She'd been dealing with the last of her day's dictation and as he talked she stacked her letters neatly and unclicked the cassette from the dictation handpiece ready to send it over to the typing pool.

'It's the variation that gets to me,' he said. 'I've found – let's see ...' He pulled a sheet of scrap paper from his pocket. 'I've made a few notes. I'll get the rest of it properly dictated tomorrow and then we can get it typed up. But so far I've found ... um wool. Well, fair enough. I dare say a chap who'd wear shoes and socks like that'd also wear a hundred per cent good wool. These are very fine lightweight fibres, so I'd say they came from his trousers. Look to be a sort of brown but it's hard to be sure. There's a good deal of blood staining. But then there's all these others. Polyester. Cotton. Some felted stuff that looks like really cheap – well – felt. There's some rayon too. I mean, you'd think he was wearing two layers of long underpants there, all in different fabrics and some of 'em *very* cheap and nasty. Crazy, hmm?'

She stopped tidying her papers and folded her hands on her

desk, thinking hard. 'Well, it's certainly not what you'd expect,' she said slowly. 'What did you say? Wool, polyester –'

'Cotton, felt and rayon,' Jerry finished. 'The felt is the hardest to be sure of. It could be compressed wool, but there's some tow in there too – you know, rough hemp fibres.'

'Could it be rope?'

'I wondered about that, but the fibres are so short it must have been pretty crummy rope if it was.' He giggled. 'Ropey rope.'

'Still, maybe he was tied up and the cut when it came went through the rope and pushed fibres into the tissues?' She was thinking aloud. 'Or maybe the leg was tied up in some way afterwards and collected the fibres then?' Her face fell after a moment. 'In the water. Bumping around the sides of boats with ropes dangling from them. That's the most likely.'

'That still doesn't account for the other things, though,' Jerry said. 'The wool is explicable. So is the cotton, I suppose. Underwear – though who'd wear full length underwear in the summer I can't imagine. But the rayon and polyester? And there may be more yet. I haven't completely finished. Like I said, this is a sort of interim report. The rayon and polyester make no sense to me at all.'

'Mmm,' she said. She sat there thinking and he too said nothing, just watched her. After a full minute had gone by he slid off the desk to go to the door.

'Well, there it is. I'll let you have a proper written report as soon as I can twist a typist's arm. But I'll be dying to get my hands on something pulled out of other chopped-up stuff like that leg. It'll make it a hell of a lot easier if I can do some comparatives, won't it?'

'What?' she said, lifting her head to focus her eyes on him. 'What did you say?'

'I said,' he repeated patiently, 'I'll get my notes typed as soon as possible.'

'No. After that.'

'What?' He gaped at her, for suddenly she was very excited.

'It's all right,' she said and jumped up. 'I did hear you. You said you wanted to get your hands on fibres from more chopped-up stuff – oh my God!' She stared at him in horror. 'I told Danny to get rid of it!'

'Get rid of what?' he cried almost despairingly, but it was thrown at her departing back. She had shot from the room and was heading for the stairs to the mortuary and the PM room as fast as she could move. He followed her.

'Danny!' she bawled as she reached the basement. 'Danny, where are you? Don't say you've gone already, dammit! I need you. Danny? Danny!'

There was a moment's silence and then slowly the door to the men's lavatory at the far end of the corridor opened and Danny came out, still buttoning his flies. 'Cor, Dr B. you don't give a bloke a chance, you don't,' he said, glaring at her. 'I meantersay, if a bloke can't even –'

'Danny! That piece of animal. The piece Sergeant Slavin brought in. What's happened to it?'

'You said to shove it,' Danny said. 'Incinerate, that's what I thought best. No need for no undertakers for that, thank Gawd. More trouble'n they're worth, they are.' He had spent half the day having one of his battles with a couple of severe undertakers who disapproved of Danny's cavalier attitude to bodies as much as Danny despised what he regarded as their sentimental claptrap.

'Oh, shit!' George said and put both hands up to her head. 'Oh, shit and damnation and –'

'Well, you said.' Danny was aggrieved. 'So I got it all set ready to go. First thing in the morning.'

George lit up like a sodium flare. 'You – you haven't done it yet?'

'I bin busy,' Danny said, more aggrieved than ever. 'I can't be everywhere, can I? You said to take them photographs and I did. And then I set the thing aside to get on with more important things.' He brooded for a moment. 'Like dealin' with those bleedin' undertakers, God rot 'em.'

'Danny,' George said fervently. 'You're a wonder. Come on, Jerry, we'll go and find it. Where is it exactly, Danny?'

Danny watched her go belting down the corridor towards the big cold store room. 'Drawer seventeen,' he shouted. 'The one on the end. I wish you'd make up your bleedin' mind.' But he said that so quietly she could not have heard it. For all his bravado, Danny knew how far he could go and get away with it, and more importantly, when to take care.

George was oblivious. She had found the relevant drawer and was staring down at the wrapped bundle in it with relief.

'Thank God for polythene,' she said. 'There shouldn't have been any interference with any fibres that might be there.'

'I wish you'd explain,' Jerry said a little plaintively. 'Is this another bit of the body the leg came from? If it is, you've kept it very quiet.'

'No,' she said almost absently. 'It's a dog. Probably. Could be a wolf escaped from a zoo, but I wouldn't like to swear. It's skinned, you see.'

Jerry gawped at her. 'Oh, yes, I see,' he said weakly. 'It's as clear as flipping mud.'

She laughed, and then explained. As Jerry listened, his face slowly lifted.

'Another cut surface,' he said. 'Somewhere to look for more fibres.'

'You got it.' She was almost bubbling with pleasure. 'More fibres. We can do some comparing.'

'Well, let's get 'em,' Jerry said. 'I'll change,' and turned to go.

'Now?' She stared at him.

'Well, I thought –' He stopped. 'I dare say you've got a date.' He sounded flat suddenly.

'Not till around midnight, I haven't,' she said. 'If then. You're right. We'll do it now. Danny! Can you spare us another hour or so? Overtime, Danny! How about that!'

She reached Gus's flat at half past eleven. The bag of hot salt beef and pickled cucumbers and rye bread was warm in her hands, and she felt more cheerful than she had for a long time. She had never worked late to such good purpose, she told herself, thinking affectionately of Jerry as she ran up the stairs to the third floor, rather than waiting for the lift. If Jerry hadn't insisted she'd have had nothing better to do all evening

86

than sit about and glower over Dudley's blocking of her and her schemes for getting hold of Gus. Instead, she had found plenty of fibres in the cut surface of the dog's carcase, enough to make Jerry's eyes gleam as he collected them, and announce greedily, 'These'll keep me going for days yet. But you watch me! I'll have 'em sorted and reported and the case half solved for you in a quarter of the time it'd take anyone else.'

She had laughed at that, but let him burble on. It was a real pleasure to work with him, she decided. She'd have to deal with Alan Short's probably hurt feelings, because she had once again set him aside in favour of a technician's help, but that was something she could soon sort out, she'd told herself optimistically. And it was worth the effort of soothing a few ruffled feathers to get stuff like this about the case. She whistled softly through her teeth as she slid her key into Gus's front-door lock and went in to wait for him. He'd hear all this, and see at once that it was a case that needed top-rate skills to be solved. Skills far in excess of Rupert Dudley's.

She felt very content as she went round the flat doing a little tidying and then organized his supper, ready to heat as soon as he walked in the door. Thank heavens for little microwaves, she sang softly, glancing at her watch. He'd be here soon after midnight, sure to be. Lovely.

IO

Not only did he not return at twelve o'clock; he did not return at all. She woke stiff, fully dressed and deeply weary on his sofa, and blinked at her watch. Eight-thirty a.m. The flat looked tired and dusty in the morning sunlight, as bedraggled and unwanted as she felt herself to be, and she dragged her aching muscles to the shower and spent ten vigorous minutes there trying to restore some of her sense of wellbeing.

It wasn't any use. She was irritated with Gus for not coming home, even though she knew she had no right to take it for granted that he would: on difficult cases it was not all that unusual for him to stay at the nick all night. He had a sofa in his office that he could use for catnaps when he was working full tilt. Maybe he had one in the incident room on the top floor, and had used it last night; why shouldn't he? It was his right after all.

But it's the weekend, she thought mulishly as she rubbed herself dry and then had to climb back into the creased and tired clothes she had worn all day yesterday. He ought to have been able to get away on Friday night; and suddenly she remembered his description of Fridays as Poet's day. 'Piss Off Early, Tomorrow's Saturday,' he'd cried joyously one Friday last year and they'd gone off to spend two blissful days in Brighton, shopping and sleeping and swimming and making love. She could have wept now at the memory of it.

She spent the morning in a ridiculously housewifely fashion. She cleaned his flat thoroughly, doing her best to restore his bedraggled houseplants by soaking them in the bath (and they did perk up remarkably well, to her surprise) and hoovering everywhere before going home to her own flat to do exactly the same jobs all afternoon. She showered again, bone weary, at nine o'clock, and went to bed early after one of the dullest Saturdays she could remember, but at least with the faint glow that comes from knowing that everything around her was squeaky clean. That made her remember her mother talking of the sheer pleasure that housework could bring, and she felt bad again. Vanny in Buffalo, and she here. Shouldn't she be there with her mother? But if she were, what difference would it make? Bridget had been clear on that point. None at all.

She slept tolerably well, to her surprise, and promised herself she would do nothing about contacting Gus. When he did come home he'd see the clean flat, know at once who was responsible and would surely want to call her. So, she went to the swimming pool in Grange Road, just this side of the Old Kent Road, and swam a vigorous half-mile; ate lunch in a cheerful Afro-Caribbean restaurant she found in Jamaica Road and then went home to watch an old black-and-white film on Channel Four. And still he didn't phone, and somehow she managed not to ring him.

But come eight o'clock she could bear it no longer, and dialled his number. All she got was the answerphone and she didn't say anything, just hung up and sat and stared into the street outside her shiny clean windows, which no longer gave her any pleasure whatsoever. She felt sorry for herself. It wasn't much fun.

Monday came as a relief. She went in early to find that Jerry was already there, his head bent over his favourite old microscope and with a pile of textbooks beside him, all of them open at pages showing enlarged pictures of different types of fibre. She brought him coffee and leaned over to see how he was getting on.

'Can't you do the identification without these?' she said looking at the top textbook. 'I always thought you were rather a whizz on fibres, could spot them at twenty paces for what they are.'

89

'I can,' he said shortly. 'I'm just making sure because these are such a mishmash.'

'Such a what?'

He straightened his back and stretched and she looked at him with sudden anxiety; his face was drawn and his eyes bloodshot. She had never seen him looking so tired. 'Jerry, for heaven's sake, are you sickening for something?' she asked. 'You look lousy.'

'Oh, ta ever so,' he said. 'Makes a guy feel really great, that does. Of course I look lousy. Been working all the hours God sends, haven't I?'

She frowned. 'Not over the weekend, surely?'

'Over the weekend very surely,' he said, yawning. 'I was on duty officially on Saturday anyway, for the usual morning sessions, and then Jane asked me to swap with her – she had the weekend on call for emergencies, but she wanted to do something special, and I didn't mind. Gave me a chance to work on this stuff. There weren't any emergencies – maybe someone up there actually does like me after all – and I've done very well.' He managed one of his familiar leers at her, and looked rather better. 'Wanna hear?'

'Does the cat want the kippers?' she retorted. 'What have you got?'

'Well!' he said, gesturing with both hands, like a child about to tell a very important story to his teacher. 'I've found a positive rag bag of stuff.'

'In the dog's carcase?'

'In the dog's carcase, yes. Look at this list.' He pushed a sheet of paper over to her.

She read it with increasing bewilderment. 'Wool,' she said aloud. 'Cotton, silk, felt, hemp, rayon, nylon, terylene, flax ... What is this? A list of all the fibres there are?'

'Do me a favour, that'd be miles long. No, that's what I found in the stuff we dug out of that carcase on Friday night.'

'All of them?'

'Every flaming one, cobber!' he said with a sudden access of gaiety and a richly phony Australian accent. 'Beats the search for the amber nectar, this does. I've found a draper's shop in a dead dog. Magic? Course it is!'

She shook her head in bewilderment. 'What on earth should they be doing – Hey, have you compared them with the stuff we found in the leg?'

He looked at her owlishly. 'This'll really get you,' he said. 'I have and not a one of them matches.'

'Not one?' She gaped. 'You must be kidding.'

'I kid you not. Not one matches. Like a shop girl's trousseau, hmm? Nothing matches ...' And he began to hum softly beneath his breath.

'It's time you got some rest,' she said. 'You're behaving as though you're punch drunk. You must have missed one. There has to be some overlap, for pity's sake, with all this stuff ...'

He sobered and shook his head. 'Honestly, Dr B., I checked and checked. No two fibres are quite the same. I mean, one bit of hundred per cent cotton can look very different from another bit, even though they're both pure cotton. When it comes to the artificial fibres – nylon and terylene and rayons and so forth – it's even more tricky. If there was a match, I'd have spotted it. Not one of the fibres in the human leg matches the fibres in the animal carcase.'

They were silent and she shook her head. 'I can't work out what this means,' she said slowly. 'There has to be an explanation.'

'Maybe the carcase was wrapped in something before it was chucked in the river,' Jerry offered.

'Like what?'

'A patchwork quilt, maybe? You know the sort of thing. Made out of odds and ends. Or a rag rug. We used to have one on the kitchen floor when I was a kid. Made out of old dresses of my mum's, and Dad's gardening trousers and so forth. Very tasteful, they were.'

'I suppose it's possible,' she said. 'But it's not really much help, is it?'

'Well, I dare say the boys in blue'll find an answer,' Jerry said and stretched. 'Look, if it's all right with you, now you're here, I'll pop home for a while, get some sleep, have a shower and a bite. I'll be back around – shall we say, two? Can you cope if I do that?'

'Yes, of course,' she said absently, and then more strongly, 'Yes, yes, yes. And you needn't worry about getting back at all today. Not if you've worked the whole weekend, for pity's sake. We can manage.'

'Oh, no. I want to come back.' He began to clear his work station, tucking his slides and books away carefully. 'I'm enjoying this job. Thanks for letting me do it.' And he grinned at her and turned to go. 'Oh! Good morning, Alan.'

Alan Short was standing beside his desk in the corner of the lab, pulling on his white coat. His jacket he had already set over the back of his chair.

'Morning, Alan,' George said. 'I didn't hear you come in.'

'No,' Alan said. 'You were so busy talking. I didn't want to disturb you. Good weekend?'

'Very nice, thanks,' they both said, and then laughed, again together. It was as though they were doing everything in chorus.

'Mine was very dull, actually,' George said. 'I spent it doing housework and watching rubbish on the box.'

'And I was working,' Jerry said. 'I'll be off then. 'Bye, both.' He grinned at Alan, winked at George and went stumping away.

'Working all weekend, was he?' Alan said casually. 'Was there something really urgent, then, after I went?'

George shook her head. 'It was forensic, Alan. It's all right. Not your department at all.'

'Oh, I just wondered.' He was looking down at the papers on his desk in a very casual way as he spoke, fingering the pens in his breast pocket. 'You do a lot more of that here than I'd have thought. I mean, forensic stuff on fibres ... I was always told that that sort of detailed examination is done in police forensic labs.'

'It is usually,' she said. 'But I made a sort of special deal.' She laughed softly as she remembered. 'I was supposed to send all the samples to the police lab, but I'm a Home Office pathologist in my own right so there's no reason, legally, why I shouldn't do the work I want to do myself. And I've trained Jerry over the past few months to do more of it – so I made a deal, as I say, to do more of it here. It makes life more interesting and the work more solid, if you know what I mean.'

'Makes the department busier, too, I suppose,' Alan murmured.

She looked at him sharply. 'I hope you're not suggesting that I put the forensic work before the hospital's.'

He opened his eyes wide. 'Of course not! It was just a statement of fact. Most hospital labs don't do any forensic work, that's all.'

She relaxed. 'That's true. It was just that when I came here, Gu – the DCI I work with most, Inspector Hathaway, and I agreed that doing some of the forensic detail here would save time. And money. It's cheaper than when they send it to the big police lab. We only do that for really major stuff for which we haven't enough gear.' She waved her hand comprehensively at the lab, its agitators and centrifuges, ovens and fridges. 'Not that we're too badly off. I get some extra money for Old East because we use the premises and the police get a better job on account of they've got me.' She grinned at him. 'But don't fret you, Alan. No hospital patient suffers at all. Because they've got you as well as me, right?'

'Right,' Alan said. He nodded and sat down.

'I'll make coffee,' George said handsomely as the door opened and Jane came in, carefully not looking at Alan. He equally carefully didn't look at her, and George was amused. Poor kids, she thought indulgently as she went out to make the coffee in her own office instead of in the little kitchen area behind the lab, so as to give them a few moments of privacy. This is a hell of a place to run a courtship. Not easy for them.

Any more than it is for me, she thought, and made a face. That was not a subject to be thought about, and she wouldn't. So she made the coffee, took it to the lab, making a rattling sound with her tray before opening the door to give them fair warning, and then went back to her own office to settle to her day's work.

Ellen Archer found her there at eleven o'clock. 'Nearly ready?' she carolled as she came in. 'We'd better get a move on. They said they'd probably reach us by about eleven-fifteen.'

George stared. 'Who said they'd reach us for what?'

Ellen almost tutted. 'You haven't forgotten, Dr B.? The Board! We're going to talk them out of hiving off our path. services in favour of St Dymphna's.'

George's face cleared and she got up with alacrity. 'Of course! It's this morning. I *had* forgotten, but I've sure as hell remembered now. Lead me to the fray.'

They walked over to the main part of the hospital through the courtyard, dodging other staff and patients as they went and talking hard all the way.

'Don't let yourself be cowed,' Ellen advised. 'Some of these people think they're God Almighty, and they'll try to push you. Don't you let them.'

'Look at me,' George said. 'Is it likely?'

Ellen chuckled. 'That's why I wanted you to help. If I'd thought you couldn't stand up to whatever they throw, I wouldn't have risked bringing you in.'

George looked at her curiously. 'There's more to you than I thought there was,' she said candidly. 'I just thought you were a meddling – Well, I don't mean to be unkind, but –'

'I know.' Ellen was serene. 'A boring old fart, really. Well, I'm not. I care a lot about this hospital and the patients in it. And I'm here to make sure no one comes along and ruins it. That's why I took the job. I could be earning a lot more in industry. I've got a hell of a training in economics, you know.'

'I didn't,' George said as they reached the Admin. building, which was the remains of the original Victorian foundation lying in the middle of the tangle of additions and battered buildings which was today's Old East. 'I was beginning to suspect it, though.'

Ellen laughed and led the way up the flight of well-polished mahogany stairs, her neat navy blue shoes twinkling as they went, and George followed her, for the first time feeling a little apprehensive. The place smelled of beeswax floor polish and flowers and authority. There was none of the comforting reek of the main hospital, with its overtones of disinfectant and unwashed humanity and urgency; here all was quiet and controlled. She wasn't sure she liked it. She rarely came here – there was seldom any cause – and never before had she found it as intimidating as it felt today. But she swallowed and lifted her chin and looked at Ellen's back, straight and self-confident, as she led the way along the first-floor corridor towards the Board Room. She'd be all right. She had an ally.

The meeting was a tough one. First she had to absorb the names that were thrown at her. Some of the people she knew. The Chairman, Sir Jonathan Sprue, a tall bulky man of around sixty who had a background in banking and scant knowledge of the way hospitals ran, though he was a wizard, she had been told, on such things as business strategies, she had met at one or two of the more formal hospital events. He nodded amiably at her as she and Ellen came into the room with the minutes secretary, a harassed-looking man in his fifties with an expression that suggested he knew everything and was already bored by it, and then introduced his colleagues.

'Matthew Herne, of course, your CEO, you know.' George smiled and nodded and remembered suddenly how high he'd been on her list of suspects in a previous case, and wanted to giggle. 'Professor Hunnisett, our Dean and Clinical Director,' Sprue went on, 'and Margaret Cotton, our Finance Director and of course Business Manager . . .'

She let his voice roll over her as she covertly studied the faces of the people she had never met before. There were five of them and she thought: they're the non-executives. They don't have jobs here, not proper jobs, but they're brought in from outside businesses to run the place like a business. Just like an American hospital, really. And she felt a sudden pang as she realized just how much she preferred the old NHS system here to the more commercial approach she had grown up with.

Sir Jonathan interrupted her thoughts. 'Now our non-executives, Dr Barnabas. Mr McCann, Mr Harlow, Mr Lester, Mrs Broad, Miss Hammond.'

They smiled and nodded and she returned the salutes. The three men, she estimated, were somewhere between fifty and sixty, give or take a few years on each side. They looked what she would have expected; prosperous and self-assured. The women seemed more interesting. Mrs Broad was a classically middle-aged woman, grey haired, large and uncompromisingly neat in a navy suit and George thought: I'll bet she's a medical type. She just looks it. The other woman was much younger, very elegant and neat and with a sharpness about her that George found a little alarming.

'Now, Dr Barnabas,' Sir Jonathan said. 'We've asked you and Miss Archer to talk to us about the pathology service. The hospital service, that is. I understand that you are also contracted to work with the police as a forensic pathologist.'

'Yes,' George said guardedly. 'That was agreed when I first came here.'

'And very happy we are about it,' one of the non-executives said suddenly, and she shifted her gaze to see who. Mr Harlow, was it? A large man, rather oily skinned, with sleek hair that was a very unlikely black, and a tendency to wheeze. 'I 'eard the talk about the work you done down my market, doctor, and I'll tell you this much. The local people think 'ighly of you. You've done some good jobs and been in the papers.' He nodded sagely. 'And they notice, indeed they do.' He looked sharply at the man on his left, Mr McCann. 'As the local representative on this 'ere Board let me say I admire the reputation you've given the 'ospital, I do indeed.'

'Well, thank you,' she said, a little startled. A local reputation? She'd never really considered the possibility.

'Indeed,' Sir Jonathan said. He looked at McCann, who smiled.

McCann was a thin man with a few wisps of hair on an otherwise naked head, and was very expensively dressed. 'I am sure that there is no need for us to disturb your forensic work, Dr Barnabas,' he said. His voice was a high thin one, a little surprising from a man of such presence. 'But we are considering the possibility of removing the hospital part of your responsibilities. Would the police service extend their use of your time, do you think?'

'I can't say,' she said. 'But that isn't the point at issue, is it?'

'What is, then?' This was the middle-aged woman in navy, Mrs Broad. She sounded incisive and sensible, George thought.

'The service the hospital gets. My police work is nothing to do with that.' George was very definite. 'What matters as far as Old East is concerned is that the patients here get the best possible pathology service. That means getting what tests need doing done as soon as they need doing and that the medical staff – and therefore the patients – get rapid results. Clinicians can then plan their patients' care much more successfully.'

The ideas she had been rehearsing with Ellen Archer on the way over began to crystallize into passionate words. 'I know that there is a plan to remove the path. work here and centralize it at St Dymphna's, where they have spare capacity, but that seems to me a very dangerous step. First of all, the staff there have a different sort of expertise. My technicians are highly trained, very much part of the lab and work unbelievably hard to ensure the top-rate service you get here.'

She looked accusingly at Professor Hunnisett. 'Have there ever been any complaints about the quality of path. work and reporting among the clinical staff, Professor?'

'No,' said the Professor, 'absolutely not,' and smiled benignly. He's on my side, she thought, elated. That makes two.

She looked at Matthew Herne, a little sternly.

'And have our costs been excessive, Mr Herne?' He shook his head and at once she switched her gaze to Margaret Cotton, the Director of Finance for the hospital. 'Miss Cotton?'

'Not at all,' Margaret said. 'Far from it. I've done some comparisons with other hospital units and, as I told you all before, I –'

'Yes,' Sir Jonathan said. 'Thank you, Miss Cotton. We have indeed heard that already.'

Great, thought George. That's another couple on my side. She warmed to her theme. 'I think I have been delivering, with Ellen's help, a top-rate service at cut price,' she said firmly and looked at Ellen, who showed no emotion at all. That was a good sign, George thought.

'But St Dymphna's might do even better.' This was McCann again. 'I have figures here that . . .'

The next half-hour was tough. They batted figures at her and she replied as best she could, knocking down their hypotheses with all the skill she had, defending her position hard, and slowly became aware that she was winning more of them over. Harlow was definitely uninterested in McCann's figures; Mrs Broad – who, it appeared, had once been a hospital matron, so George had been right about her – was interested, but suspicious. Miss Hammond, like Mr Lester, a small round man in a magnificently cut Italian-style suit, said nothing, but listened carefully. And the executive directors, especially Margaret Cotton and Andrew Pickles, who was the head of Marketing (and what a job for a hospital to have on its staff, George thought disgustedly at one point, listening to him speak passionately about the savings he was sure they could make if they went to St Dymphna's) showed their colours clearly. Much to Sir Jonathan's unease, for at length he held up his hand.

'I think we have used enough of Dr Barnabas's valuable time, colleagues,' he said. 'I do feel we must let her go and continue this discussion among ourselves. Dr Barnabas, thank you so much.'

She lingered for a moment, sitting tight even though Ellen had got to her feet. 'Will I be thrown out at a moment's notice, then?' she said with a degree of flippancy she didn't feel.

They tittered in an embarrassed sort of way and smiled widely at her in their different ways. 'Of course not, Dr Barnabas,' Sir Jonathan said in what was meant to be a hearty voice. 'Of course not! These things take a long time to implement, if we implement them at all. We are just at the exploratory stage, no more. Don't give it another thought. Just you go on and continue with your excellent work and stop fretting. There really isn't a thing to worry about.'

'Not a thing to worry about,' George said to the closed door, when the minutes secretary had ushered them out into the corridor. 'Go and get on with your work and don't worry your little head about it, is that it? Ye Gods, Ellen, how do I manage to do that, tell me?'

II

———

'A fat lot of good that was!' she said to Ellen as they emerged into the sunshine of the courtyard. 'Do I start looking for another job then? And where do I find one that suits me as well as this?' Gus, she thought. Aren't we ever to work together again?

'Oh, I wouldn't start panicking yet,' Ellen said matter of factly. 'Sir Jonathan was right in saying these are early days – even if they vote to go for the St Dymphna's plan, it'll take months of talk before they come up with a scheme and then it has to be agreed by the centre.'

'The centre?'

'The Department of Health. Maybe even the Minister. And there can be protests and all sorts to delay it. This is a long-term plan, believe me.'

'It's a horrible plan,' George said with some violence.

'I agree. That's why I wheeled you out to argue against it. You can't start the battle too soon. You did awfully well. There's a very good chance that Lester will be outvoted and we'll hear no more of this, thanks to you.'

'Lester? Who was he? The little man in the ultra-trendy suit?'

Ellen laughed. 'That's the one.'

'But he hardly said a word, any more than the younger woman and that other man – McCann? – did. I wondered why they were there.'

'Oh, don't underestimate them! They mayn't talk much but

they carry a lot of weight. Reggie Lester is a bookmaker — you've seen his shops everywhere, surely. *Leg it with Lester* and so forth.'

'Oh, those!' George said. 'I know them. But how on earth does a bookmaker get to be on a hospital Board? What does he know about –'

'He knows all there is to know about running businesses on a tight budget,' Ellen said. 'Apparently it's a multi-million business, sixty betting shops. And he's a powerhouse. Got excellent political contacts too. This St Dymphna's thing was his idea, or rather he suggested it.'

'Oh?' George was puzzled. 'Why? What's in it for him?'

'Nothing. There can't be. If they have a personal or company interest in any of the hospital's dealings they have to declare them. No, it's just that he met someone who talked him into the idea. Or so I gather.' She grinned. 'I listen hard to all I can and pick up what there is to pick up in the way of talk. But I can't know everything! I do know, though, that this notion came in via Lester.'

'He can't be that keen or he'd have said something, surely,' George objected.

'Not he. He puts up these things and leaves it to everyone else to talk their heads off and then comes in at the end and sorts 'em all out, or as much as he can. Cynthia Hammond usually does all she can to block him.'

'Hammond? Another strong silent one?'

'That's her,' Ellen said. 'She's very good news for us. I like her a lot. Lawyer, a senior partner in a big practice in the City, seconded for a couple of years by her firm to the Board as part of their social development commitment. They're one of those left-wing groups that are more interested in their pro bono work than in making a fortune. Not that they do so badly! Anyway, she's not at all keen on our Reggie – doesn't like his political friends – so she tends to be suspicious of almost everything he says. Fights him every inch of the way. It's fun in there sometimes.' She looked amused.

They had reached the far side of the courtyard now, and their paths were about to separate. George stopped and looked at her curiously. 'How do you know know so much about what goes on in Board meetings?' she asked. 'Do you sit in with them or something?'

Ellen became a little flustered. 'I? Oh. No. No, not at all.'

'Then how do you know all this?'

'Um ... Well, between ourselves ...' Ellen looked more uncomfortable than ever, yet at the same time curiously pleased with herself. 'I – er – It's Tony. Tony Bentall. He's, um, a friend.'

'Tony Bentall? Which one was he?'

'The secretary. Showed us in and showed us out. Does the minutes and so forth.'

George dragged him out of her memory: a thin man, a little stooped, who looked rather bored.

She grinned. 'He's your guy,' she said almost accusingly. 'Jeez, Ellen, you keep on pulling these surprises on me. I thought you were so proper and schoolmarmish, and here you are in a torrid affair!'

'Hardly a torrid affair,' Ellen said and laughed herself. 'But why not? We've been close for about three months now. His wife went off with his son to live in Australia when the boy got married there and she won't come back, and Tony gets lonely. So do I. So, we're – well, why not? And it's interesting to get all the news!'

'Pillow talk,' George said.

'Like you and your policeman,' Ellen said, and now it was George who became a little flustered.

'Well, why not? I'm not –'

'Precisely,' Ellen said. 'Anyway, I have to get back to my office. I'll keep you posted on all that happens, but try not to worry. There'll be no locking of the path. lab doors in the next year or so, believe me.'

'I'll try not to,' George said a little gloomily. 'But it won't be easy.' She turned to go.

'Dr B.,' Ellen called her back. 'One detail. I wouldn't talk about this too much to your staff. It will only unsettle them.'

'I'll think about that,' George said. 'Maybe getting them upset'll be no bad thing. Encourage them to protest too.'

'Not too soon,' Ellen warned. 'You might harden the Board's will. They're not the sort to be happy if they think they're a dog that's being wagged by the tail.'

'OK,' George said non-committally. 'I'll keep that in mind.'

She went back to the lab, thinking hard. She wouldn't say anything to her staff yet — Ellen had a point that talking too soon could cause more trouble than it prevented. They'd fuss now about possible closures in a year or two, maybe go jobhunting so as to be safe before the threatened axe fell, and that would make life in the lab very difficult indeed. They were a good team, and she had them all pretty well trained to her liking, except perhaps for Alan who still needed some pushing. Going off half cocked now could blow the whole group up in her face. But she had better be aware. If they heard from any other source what was in the wind, they'd be very unhappy that she had not told them herself. It isn't easy, she thought as she slammed her office door behind her, to run a department and do the work she wanted to do while playing politics at the same time.

Sheila came in with her messages as George pulled the first file of paperwork towards her. 'A PM this afternoon from Cloudesley Ward,' Sheila reported. 'Man admitted last night after a fall at home, died seven hours after admission. Not seen his GP in the last week.'

'Tell Alan I'd like a word, will you?' George said. 'That can be one for him.'

'Right.' Sheila looked happy at that. 'Then there were calls from the coroner's office and from that barrister about the case that was adjourned — you remember, the Fletcher affair. And some stuff from the other solicitors about that child's death. And then there's this one.'

George was leafing through the little pile of notes Sheila had given her and didn't look up. 'What's that?'

'I didn't want to be accused of getting anything wrong,' Sheila said with a triumphant edge to her voice. 'So I took it down word for word. Verbatim. Here it is. Would you like some coffee?'

'Mmm? Please,' George said absently as she looked down at

the sheet of paper and the carefully written lines on it, and Sheila went. Rather quickly.

CALLER [George read]: Is that you, Sheila? How are you, ducky?

SHEILA: Fine, thank you. Who's that?

CALLER: Who do you think it is, you daft 'aporth? Gus Hathaway, that's who!

SHEILA: Oh, good morning, Chief Inspector.

CALLER: Is her nibs there, love?

SHEILA: Sorry, Chief Inspector, no. She's gone to a Board meeting with Miss Archer.

CALLER: Bugger it. Sorry, ducks. But it's – Oh well, I've been trying to get a chance to call her and this is the first one I've had and now she's – Oh, well. How long will she be?

SHEILA: I really can't say, Chief Inspector.

CALLER: Well, tell her I called, will you? That I'm sorry I missed her and I'll try again when I'm able. (Laughter.) 'Tell her I came, and no one answered, that I kept my word,' he said.

SHEILA: Sorry?

CALLER: A quotation, more or less, my duck. Walter de la Mare, but why should a child like you know of an old codger like him? Listen, tell Dr B. for me that she's not to bother to call me back, I'm on the move most of the time. I have to keep the phone switched off for fear of frightening the pigeons. It's going well, tell her, but it's still a long haul, OK? Got all that?

SHEILA: Every word, Chief Inspector.

CALLER: You're a great girl. See you around. (He hangs up).

Message ends.

George sat and stared at the paper and then crumpled it in her hand in a fury. Sheila could be the most maddening creature who ever breathed; insolent and yet in a way that made it impossible to complain. George had told her to be more careful with the way she delivered messages, and what she got was this. Sheila Keen, she told herself, was sailing a great deal closer to the wind than she knew.

Sheila returned with the coffee and a smug expression on her face. 'I hope that's all right,' she said sweetly. 'I don't think I missed anything.'

'Not a word,' George said grimly. 'Thank you. Tell Alan I want him now, will you? And then do get a move on with the cardiac clinic material. They'll be complaining again if you don't.' And she bent her head to her own work so smartly that Sheila could not protest, and felt a little better.

When she had gone, almost slamming the door behind her, George smoothed out the message note again and re-read it. Don't call me, he'd said. He'd call back if he could. Oh, dammit all to hell and back. Would she never get the chance to talk to him? The longer the cases went on in Dudley's hands, the harder it would be to wrest them from him, even for Gus.

Then Alan came in and she managed to cover her irritation with a smile. 'There's a PM this afternoon –' she said. 'Death after a fall, admitted to Cloudesley Ward. I doubt it's anything dicey but I thought you wouldn't mind doing it.'

Alan brightened. 'Great! It's been a while since I did the last one. It'll make a pleasant change from all those bloods.'

She nodded at that. 'But don't tell the people outside that's how you feel about doing PMs. They think we're ghouls as it is. OK, I'll sign your notes when you're ready. Enjoy yourself!'

By the time she went to lunch it was almost two o'clock. At first she wasn't going to bother, but her belly made loud protesting grumbles so she went loping over to the dining room to grab a sandwich. She was heading for the way out with it when a voice called her from a corner table tucked away behind fronds of artificial ivy.

'Dr B. Come and have your lunch with us!'

She peered and hesitated. She hated the idea of being far from her phone for too long; after all, Gus might find a moment to try again and she certainly didn't want another of

Sheila's insolent messages. But then she saw who had called her, and thought again. She had her bleep in her pocket; if he called, Sheila would bleep her, of course she would.

'Hello Mr – uh –' she said, and the man smiled.

'Mickey Harlow,' he said. 'From the Board. You can't have forgotten me already!' He sounded roguish.

'No, of course I haven't. It's just that . . .' She looked across the table. 'Oh! Good afternoon Mr McCann.' The man with the almost totally bald head looked up, startled, and she was pleased with herself for matching the name and the face in her memory.

'Good afternoon,' he said, and again George was struck by the thin high note of his voice. He was drinking coffee with an air of disdain.

'We was just 'aving a quiet little chinwag, like,' Mickey Harlow said, and nodded at the third person at the table, Reggie Lester. 'Eh, Reggie?'

The man glanced up at George and nodded. Odd, she thought, I still haven't heard his voice.

She sat down and Harlow, who had a large plate of spaghetti in front of him, fussed over making space for her. He caught her glance at his plate and said almost defensively, 'Got to try the sort of grub they give them 'ere. I don't reckon to do a job like this if I don't do it right. What do you think of the food 'ere, Dr B.?'

She looked at him sideways, a little irritated. 'How did you know to address me by my initial?' She tried to sound light but he wasn't fooled.

'Whoops! Overstepped the mark, 'ave I? Sorry an' all that. It was that Miss Archer – nice girl, Ellen Archer – she called you that, so I did. There you go. Sorry if it offends.'

He was too cheerful a creature to allow herself to nourish any offence and she smiled at his disarming grin.

'No, I'm not offended. When did she call me that?'

'Eh? Last month, wasn't it?' He appealed to the other two men. 'At the last Board meeting? When you first talked about the St Dymphna's idea, Reggie?'

Reggie Lester stirred his coffee, which seemed an odd thing

to do, George thought, since the cup was half empty. 'Mmm?' he said. 'I can't remember.'

His voice was another surprising one, this time because it was deep and rough in tone and also because he had what the British regarded as a cultured accent. He was very unlike his colleagues, whoever he was.

'And what is your special skill, Mr Lester?' she said. 'Mrs Broad's an ex-hospital matron and Miss Hammond's a lawyer, and' – she looked at Harlow – 'you're a market trader, right?' He laughed.

'I'm a bit more'n that,' Harlow said comfortably. 'Got so many stalls and so many market sites you couldn't count 'em, I'll betcha! But yeah, that's a fair enough description.'

'And you, Mr Lester, are the . . .?'

'Turf accountant,' he said. 'Managing director of the biggest turf accountancy business in this part of London.'

'Yes,' she said, amused. It seemed such a fancy way of saying 'bookie'. 'And you, Mr McCann?'

'Engineer,' Reggie Lester said before McCann could speak. 'Builds roads and bridges. More practical than the rest of us. Harlow and I just . . . deal in money.'

There was a sardonic note in his voice, George thought, and she looked at him even more closely. There was nothing she could get hold of at first, but then slowly she began to think more carefully. The way remains of fast-vanishing hair had been pulled across the bare scalp – like McCann he was nearly bald – the subdued silk tie with its wide careful knot, the matching silk handkerchief in the breast pocket, the broad gold ring on a little finger, and – he moved his hand to reach for his coffee cup and she saw his wrist – a very pricey Rolex Oyster watch. A vain man, and rich enough to indulge himself.

Mickey Harlow was chattering. 'So, 'ow do you enjoy the new regime, Dr B.? The reforms, like?'

'Not very much,' she said. 'More upheaval than reform as far as I can see.'

'But something has to be done.' Lester looked up at her quickly and then away again. 'Money was being wasted all through the NHS in the most appalling fashion. We – the taxpayers – can't afford that.'

She looked at the sheen on his suit and said dryly, 'No, I can see that.'

'Had to put that right,' McCann cut in and blinked at her. His bald head seemed to shimmer in the afternoon sunlight. 'You have to admit we had to put that right.'

'I find money rather boring,' she said. 'I deal with patients and –'

'That's what all the doctors say,' Lester said, and his careful accent gave him a disdainful air, 'but someone has to pay your salary. Someone has to make sure you get your staff's salaries paid too, hmm? What about that?'

She made a little face. 'Listen, you shouldn't ask doctors about the way money is spent in the NHS. I've worked in it for more than ten years now and it's a great thing. Coming from the States the way I do, I've seen what happens in a money-centred hospital service. Lots of money and damn all service. I'd hate to see that happening here –'

'It won't,' McCann said. 'Not if you co-operate with us.'

'Co-operate?' She frowned, irritated at the patronizing tone of his voice.

'Don't argue when we get good ideas.'

'Like moving out all the pathology to St Dymphna's?' She was angry now. 'How's that supposed to help the patients here? Who does it do anything for except the money men and –'

'Better to find out first before you jump to the conclusion it's a bad idea, surely.' Lester lifted his head and she saw the sharpness glinting in the surprisingly dark eyes. 'That's what we mean. The way you all tend to refuse even to listen to an idea is ... not wise. This one may be no good, but at least listen to it.'

She looked at the man and then tried to laugh lightly. 'I'm beginning to feel you were lying in wait for me. One Riding Hood, three wolves.'

Mickey tutted. 'No such thing. Accident, I swear to you. It's not on, you two, to go on at 'er like this. She done a good job at the Board meeting. Leave it at that. Eat your lunch, Dr B.' He leaned over and patted her hand. 'An' I 'ope it's better than this spaghetti what's over-cooked and under-sauced. I'll 'ave to 'ave a word about that, I will.'

'I really must get back to my department,' she said, getting to her feet. 'Lots of work to do. Must make sure we get our money's worth at Old East, mustn't we?'

'There now, we've annoyed you,' Mickey said. 'It wasn't our intention, was it, chaps?' He looked at the other two and laughed.

There was a brief silence and then Lester said, 'Of course not. Never dreamt of it. I just wanted to refer to matters in general, you know.'

McCann looked up at her and smiled and for the first time George felt a glimmer of liking for the man. It was an almost shy smile. 'Mustn't mind me,' he said. 'I'm not one of the world's best talkers. Read a good balance sheet though. Know what I'm doing with balance sheets.'

'That's why he's here,' Mickey said, seeming eager to show his colleagues in the best possible light. 'That's why we're all here. To keep the ship afloat and leave you doctors and nurses, bless you, to take the best possible care of the patients.' He beamed happily at her. 'Where would we be without you all?'

'Richer, perhaps,' she said. 'Forgive me. I really must be off. I have a lot to do and –'

'As long as you aren't angry with us.' It was McCann again. 'I certainly meant no offence.'

'There, you see?' Mickey was triumphant. 'So sit down again.'

'No, I really do have to go,' But she hesitated a moment longer. 'But don't worry about me. I've too much to do to sulk. Good afternoon, gentlemen.'

And this time she did go, her pockets bulging with her now squashed sandwich and pastry bumping against her legs as she walked. She'd gone into medicine, she told herself, to look after people and to find out what made them ill and why they died, not to get hung up over money. That had been one of the reasons she had chosen to leave the US in the first place; to work here, because the NHS had seemed to her to be one of the most beautiful things she had ever heard of. And now look at what was happening to it. She was less than cheerful by the time she got back to her department, a mood that was to hang over her all afternoon, which she spent putting the finishing touches to her reports on the two cases for Dudley, complete with greatly enlarged photographs of the various fibres Jerry had identified, ready to send over to Ratcliffe Street by messenger. She had considered taking them over herself, just to see if she could find out what was going on, but decided against it. There was a very real risk that Dudley would snub her in front of everyone, refusing to let her into the incident room, or something of that sort; and that could lead to all sorts of rows and problems. And Gus wasn't in his own office so there'd be no chance of seeing him.

She went home at six, leaving behind Alan who was happily writing up his notes: the case had been a good one, with just enough oddity about it to make it interesting, but not enough to make it anything other than a straightforward natural death from the coroner's point of view. She ate a scratch meal of pasta, collected from an Italian deli on her way home, though there seemed less pleasure in eating when there was no one else to share a meal with, and then settled to watching television for the evening. But that depressed her too. There was little worth watching and she found herself nodding off in her corner of the sofa and that made her feel dreadfully old and staid.

On an impulse, she phoned Bridget in Buffalo, working out that it was mid-afternoon there and hoping to catch her, but the voice that answered said she was out.

George asked after Vanny. 'Oh, she's doing well enough,' the little voice – the home help probably, George thought – clacked. 'Oh, she's doing well enough, Considering . . .'

'Considering what?' George was sharp.

'Well, she's not well, you know.' The voice was cautious, clearly uncomfortable at dealing with a transatlantic call. 'It's kinda hard to explain on the phone.'

'I'm her daughter,' George said crisply. 'And a doctor.'

'Oh,' There was relief in the voice. 'Well, OK then. You understand about Alzheimer's. Miz Connors told me. And she's having a bad day. Wandering a lot. Keeps crying.'

George's throat tightened. 'May I speak with her?'

The voice was dubious. 'Well, we can try,' it said. 'But I wouldn't be too hopeful.'

Vanny came on the line. George sat in her little flat in Bermondsey and spoke as brightly and happily as she could, and Vanny sat in Buffalo three thousand miles away and just breathed heavily at her and said nothing.

'Hi, Vanny. Are you OK?' George heard herself say and knew it was idiotic. How could Vanny be OK, for God's sake? 'Is Bridget taking good care of you? You'll tell her I called, hmm? Mom, I wish I could be there with you.'

There was a little clatter as Vanny dropped the phone at her end and George clearly heard her querulous voice: 'Who's that? Who's that? Who's that?' repeated over and over and her eyes stung with tears.

'I'm sorry,' the little voice came back on the line sounding apologetic. 'Like I said, a bad day.'

'Yes,' George said. 'Yes. Well, thanks anyway. When Mrs Connors returns, tell her I called, will you? Dr Barnabas. Yes, that's right. Her daughter.'

She cradled the phone and then wept, as she had the last time she had talked to Bridget and with the same sense of guilt and hopelessness. She was in a trap and whichever way she turned she would be in the wrong. Staying in London seemed selfish, going to Buffalo would be pointless. What else could she do but weep?

Inevitably, she slept badly, waking with a startled jerk time and again. She was so used to it by the small hours that when the phone rang and she opened her eyes she didn't at first answer it; she thought the sound was inside her own head. But when she did at last pick up the insistent phone, her bad feelings were at last pushed to the back of her mind. She had something else to think about.

There had been another fire and someone had been burned,

reported the policeman at the other end of the line. Burned in precisely the same way as Lisa Zizi had been burned and could she come at once, please.

12

The sense of *déjà vu* was powerful. The same feeling of being not quite in the real world when she drove to the address the policeman had given her over the phone; the same glow in the dark sky ahead of her as she left her flat behind and came closer to her destination; the same smell of burning wood and paint mixed with the familiar reek of the river.

She shivered a little as she came along Narrow Street towards the opening of the Grand Union Canal. She could see now the building that was burning: not a block of flats but one of a row of neat pretty terraced houses, built no more than half a dozen years ago, well bedecked with window boxes of scarlet geraniums and trailing lobelia. But the house that was burning showed its colour not in flowers but in the flames that were licking the frame of a first-floor window, and that made her shiver. There was a great deal of smoke, and the same police cars and ambulances as well as fire engines, all with their emergency lights rotating excitedly. Wouldn't it be better if just one of them had its lights on? she thought briefly as she pulled her car over to the kerb. Or are they like children who all want to have a go?

This time, as she made her way through the staring knots of people, she wasn't stopped by a policeman, and that helped her to feel this was a different occasion rather than a dream of the last one. She found Dudley talking to one of his men in a dark patch out of the well-lit centre of activity as they watched the firemen struggling to get close enough to the burning section of the building to deal with the flames, and to get in to seek for whoever might be in there. Other firemen were herding dressing-gowned and blanketed people out of the adjoining houses, coaxing them along to places well out of range of the shooting flames; they looked like creatures from a mad disco, George thought absurdly, their faces grimacing and lit by alternate pulses of blue from the vehicles and orange and crimson from the fire.

'Oh, there you are,' Dudley said as he caught sight of her. 'Good and quick this time.'

She ignored the jibe and stared at the burning building. 'Very much like the last one,' she said.

'Yeah,' he grunted. He turned to the man at his side who was, as George could now see with gratitude, Michael Urquhart. 'Mike, go and see how it's doing – how soon we can get in there and give it the once-over. Looks too much like the last job for it to be an accident but we can't be sure till we get inside.'

Michael went loping over the mess of hoses and cables and water on the ground towards the building and was held back by a senior fireman who talked to him for some time before he returned to Dudley's side.

'They've sent in a couple of their own blokes in the special gear. They're in radio communication. It seems there's someone in bed – the bed's where the seat of the fire is – and they're trying to get them out. Not easy, it seems.'

'What did I say?' Dudley said as though the idea was a brand-new one that had occurred only to him. 'Another like that last time. Got to be arson and worse'n that. It's murder by fire. Same MO, you'll see.'

George opened her mouth to say something, and then thought better of it. Insulting Dudley would only rebound on her; better to bite her tongue and look at Michael, which she did. He grinned at her and she felt better.

'It's not funny,' snapped Dudley, intercepting the exchange. 'Some of those bloody people have no decency – Treating people like so much butcher's meat ...' With which shot hurled directly at George, he went away to stand beside the fireman conducting operations and to get an update on what he had discovered.

'Couldn't you just kill him?' George murmured. 'Pompous . . .'

'Och, he's just tired,' Michael said. 'He's been at work most of the day, you know, and went home in time for his supper and a bit of wifely comfort and what happens? They get him out at four ack emma. Can't blame the poor wee man for being a bit cranky.'

'I can,' she said shortly. 'Listen, Mike –'

But she could say no more for there was a sudden surge among the watchers, and some shouting too, as the dark, gaping doorway of the house shimmered and seemed to move. One of the firemen, swathed in protective gear, staggered out, carrying a figure across his back.

The ambulance people were there at once, and between them they carried the shape away from the house. Two of them moved in a smooth synchrony to work on it, checking for life and reaching for their breathing apparatus, while another set to work on the fireman. George hurried over.

'Is she still alive?'

The ambulance man peered up at her, saw her identity badge and said, 'Mornin', doctor. Are you here to take over?'

'No, no,' she said. 'I'm the pathologist. I think they thought there'd be bodies.'

'They were right.' The other ambulance man, who had been working over the figure on the stretcher, straightened his back. 'This one's a goner.'

'My department, then,' George said, coming closer. 'Let me get to her.'

'Beats me how you know it's a woman,' he said, peering at the stretcher. 'Unless you actually know her? Do you?'

'No, I don't know her,' George said, sitting back on her haunches beside the stretcher. 'I was just assuming . . . There was another fire a bit like this, a few days ago. That was a woman, so I suppose I . . . Let's see, anyway. Shield me, will you? We don't need these gawpers.'

The ambulance man got to his feet and began to urge the

watchers from the other houses to move away, while his partner came and stood behind George so that his bulk hid her and the dead figure on the stretcher from view.

The body had been brought out draped in a duvet, or what remained of it. Singed and blackened in a great many places, and sodden with the water from the firemen's hoses, it sagged across the body like a sheet of slimy weed. George picked gently at the edge with a gloved finger – for she had already opened her bag and started to prepare for her examination – and peeled it back carefully.

The head, she could now see, was pulled right back so that the chin – or what was left of it – pointed to the blotchy sky overhead, the teeth glinting horribly through retracted lips which had been pulled back by the heat. The nose, like Lisa Zizi's, had vanished, the neck was severely damaged too and the sinews looked like ropes. Below that there was less damage; the skin was smooth and, even in this fitful light, looked pale and young.

George lifted the duvet further and saw the breasts and sighed. She returned the covering to its original place and said, unnecessarily, 'It's a woman. A fairly young one at that. Check with the Inspector and then take her to Old East, will you? To the mortuary. I'll do the full examination tomorrow. She's been moved already so there's no need to do anything more here, although ...' She stopped, looked down on the body again and shook her head. 'Actually, I think I'd like to get in there and look at the bed if I can. Cover her up. Then she can go –'

'Not till I say so,' growled a voice behind her. George looked up and saw the annoyance on the man's face. It was up to him, of course, to say whether the body could go. She had overstepped her line of authority in giving such an instruction.

'Oh, Inspector Dudley,' she said quickly. 'I asked them to check with you first, right, fellas?' The ambulance men nodded like a pair of mandarin dolls in the back of a car. 'I mean that I can't do any more here. It looks similar to the other one. The seat of the fire was the head and face, I can't tell you more than that until I do a proper job in the mortuary. There's no light here and, anyway, what's the hurry? We'll get the facts soon enough.' She scrambled to her feet and looked very directly at Dudley and, almost without taking breath, went on: 'May I take a look inside yet? I may be able to pick up some information for the lab from the bedding – before it's totally lost to the water and the fire. What are the chances?'

He was distracted and looked over his shoulder at the leading fire officer. 'Doc wants to come in and look round,' he bawled. 'OK?'

The fire officer looked dubious. 'Bit hot in there, doc,' he said. 'Mind you, the flames are down.' And indeed in the short time that George's attention had been distracted the fire fighters had won their battle. The house had stopped spouting flames and now sat sulky and wet and blackened in the light from the support vehicles.

'May I have an outfit?' she asked and he grinned.

'There's one on number three vehicle,' he said. 'Harry!' Another fireman came up to him. 'Get the doc a heat-protecting outfit, will you? And take her with you into the house. She needs to look round.' He looked at Dudley then. 'You too, Inspector?'

Dudley blinked and almost took a step backwards, but, outfaced, he could do no more than agree, and the fireman yelled at Harry again, who came back with two sets of protective clothing.

George pulled it over her jeans and shirt, leaving her coat draped over the door of the ambulance, and pushed her feet into the heavy heat-resistant boots. Too big but tolerable, like the helmet they insisted she put on. That seemed heavy at first but once on it was comfortable enough if a little hot. She began to sweat.

The bedroom on the first floor of the little house was a pitiful sight. It had once clearly been very frilly; rags and tatters of *broderie anglaise*, in what had been crisp white, seemed to hang from every corner, and there were curtains draping one wall, where the dressing table was, that were of striped apple-green silk. 'Gawd,' said Harry the fireman, at her side. 'Some people do go in for the fancy touch, don't they?'

'Yes,' George said absently, moving carefully across the sodden floor to the side of the bed. She could see now that this room wasn't nearly as badly damaged as the one they had dealt with in the small hours of last Friday morning. There the ceiling had been about to fall in and the floor had gone except for the joists. Here the floor felt solid and intact beneath her feet and the ceiling above seemed to be untouched, except for the large black smudge immediately above the bed. She glanced up at it as she arrived at the bedside and tried to measure with her eye the angle between the smudge and the head of the bed. It seemed to be immediately above it. She bit her lip, and then turned her attention to the bed itself.

This too had been heavily trimmed with *broderie anglaise* (and now she thought of it, there had been remnants of it on the soaked duvet over the dead woman in the ambulance outside). The lower sheet was taut and the corners were still tightly fitted over the mattress. Beneath the mattress a flounce of thicker and even more profuse embroidery stuck out in a sad parody of the way it must normally have looked, though now it was badly bedraggled.

The pillow at the head of the bed was little more than a shape of ash and half-burned fabric. The unburned parts were at the edges and in the very centre. Looking at it, George said aloud, 'Under the head.'

'What?' She had forgotten Dudley was behind her and she jumped slightly.

'I said, the unburned part of the pillow was beneath the head. See? It burned badly all round where the head wasn't — if you see what I mean — and then started to lose its power as it got to the edges. It's my guess that when I get to look at the body properly, I'll see that there's the same pattern of injury, if less severe, that there was in Lisa Zizi. Burned shoulders, upper arms, upper chest, running down to the trunk in rivulets. The legs will be hardly damaged.'

'So?' Dudley said.

'So,' she said. 'This woman's head was deliberately set on fire. I can't verify that till I've done the PM, but that's how it looks to me. Something inflammatory poured over her face and head and then set alight.'

George decided to go straight back to the hospital from the scene of the fire. There seemed little point in going home to catch up on the remainder of her sleep. It was almost five o'clock now and she could always sleep later. Maybe.

Working alone, without Danny, had its drawbacks. No one to fetch and carry, no one to set up the necessary equipment. But she could manage, she was sure, although she told Dudley she had to have a police witness. No one could be expected to be there from the coroner's office. Not at five a.m.

'Can't you do it later?' Dudley asked as they stood in the cool air outside and climbed out of the protective gear. 'When I've got more people on duty?'

'I could,' she said. 'But wouldn't you rather get the facts fast, and get to work on 'em?'

'Hmm,' he said. 'I suppose so.' He looked at Michael. 'All right with you, Mike?'

'Sure. If you dinna mind the overtime, sir,' he said cheerfully. Dudley grunted again and marched off, and Michael laughed. He told her quietly that for once she'd managed to put the Inspector in his place.

'You shamed him into going into that room,' he told her as she drove them both back to the hospital. 'He'd never have gone otherwise – the last one got under his skin too much. Really upset him, it did. After that, he can't come the acid with you. I enjoyed that.' And he sat and chuckled to himself all the way back.

It took her an hour and a half, probing the woman's burns, outlining the areas that had third-degree burns and those that were second degree, and mapping the wide flamed areas on the rest of the body that had been merely reddened, burns of the first degree. In general, the injuries were a great deal less horrific than Lisa's had been, but in one respect they were the same. Both faces had been almost totally destroyed.

'You know what this adds up to, Mike?' she said as at last she put a cover over the cadaver, leaving it for Danny to put away in a cold drawer when he came in. She collected up her samples and slides and then yawned, a great cracking yawn that startled her in its suddenness. 'Have you worked it out?'

'It's not so difficult,' Mike said. He had become more and more quiet as the work had gone on, listening to the description that George dictated of the woman and her injuries. *Aged between twenty and twenty-five, judging by the epiphyses, notably in the neck of the femur. Non gravid. Pubic hair auburn. No other body hair. Legs and axillae shaved. No scalp hair remaining. Eyes green...*

She had clearly been a pretty young woman, and seeing her lying here like this did not encourage Mike to feel as relaxed as he usually was. But he tried to join in her conversation as though he weren't at all bothered by what he had seen.

'It's not so difficult,' he repeated. 'Someone's got it in for well-off women. Women who live alone. Maybe they're on the game – the other one was – but we don't know about this one. This one's much younger, of course. Anyway, someone has it in for them and he – he pours something flammable over their faces and sets them alight? I suppose they're dead or certainly deeply unconscious when he does it. Any sign of a cause of death apart from the fire?'

'None,' she said. 'Like last time. Just a dead girl with a lot of burns and nothing in her lungs or available breathing passages to show she breathed after the fire started. I'll check for drugs and so forth when we do the body fluids testing, and that may show something – a cause for the victim's acquiescence in being set alight? There wasn't anything in the other one apart from a fairly high blood alcohol. Not enough to cause coma, though, I'd have thought. We'll have to wait to see if this one had been drinking too. But even if she had ...' She shook her head. 'I have no evidence of any cause of death apart from the burns in either of these cases so far. It's a total mystery.'

'So,' Michael said. 'Maybe the work of a serial killer with a particularly nasty modus operandi? Could it be possible?'

'Yes,' George said. She stood looking down at the anonymous body under its cover on the slab. 'I think it is. Very possible.'

13

George sent her report into Dudley at Ratcliffe Street before ten, and then sat in her office and thought. There would be no point, she knew, in trying to get herself any further involved in this case, or in the two earlier ones. She'd done as much as Dudley would allow her to do.

But that didn't mean, she told herself, that she had to give up. There must be some way of getting Gus away from his big case now. What could be bigger than a possible serial killer? It had to beat whatever he was doing, hands down. The job he was on involved money, she knew that much, but this one – or rather, these two – involved lives. If they could find the man who had set fire to these two women soon they'd prevent him from doing it to any others. There was no question, George decided, but she would have to take matters into her own hands and see to it that Gus was given all the facts. Once he knew, of course he'd take over.

That was her thinking, and she was exhilarated by it. Until she began to think about how she would tell him. His phone was indeed switched off; she tried the number several times and got the maddening robotic voice that told her 'the Vodaphone you have called may be switched off – please try later' and without knowing more about where he was likely to be, how could she find him?

It was Michael Urquhart who gave her the answer. He phoned from the nick at half past ten to check on a section of her report on Lisa Zizi's post-mortem which had been smudged in the photocopier, and when she'd sorted that out she said on a sudden impulse, 'Mike, have you any idea where the Guv might be?'

'Here, in the office,' Mike said. 'Leave him alone, Dr B. He's in as nasty a mood as ever I've seen him.'

'I don't mean Dudley,' she said, her voice thick with scorn. 'I mean *our* Guv.'

'Ah!' Mike was amused. 'Not spending his nights at home, then?'

'Mike, don't you start!' she said wrathfully.

'Och, I'm sorry. I mean no harm, you know that. Look, all I can say is that he's on a major situation over in Poplar and all points east. From what I'm picking up here, it seems there's a network of different villains all got together, taking over the patch. Doing a new Krays scenario, you understand. It's bookies and garages and car dealers and all sorts. From what Salmon said in the canteen yesterday to one of his fellas –'

'Who?' she interrupted.

'Sergeant Salmon. He's the senior bloke working with the Guv'nor, remember? Odd sort of chap. I can't quite make him out. But he seems to know what he's doing. He's very busy on these cases, I'll tell you that!'

'I remember,' she said. 'Big. Smooth sort of guy. Bit full of himself. I wasn't crazy about him, either.'

'Well, as I say, he was telling one of his blokes that they're having trouble working out who's straight on the whole damned patch. Let alone bent.'

'Poplar?' she said. 'A big area?'

'Big enough,' Mike said. 'Mind you, lots of it's docks.'

'Where's he most likely to be in Poplar? In one of the nicks?'

'Not if he can help it,' Mike said. 'Not when he can come to Ratcliffe Street to do his proper work. He's verra attached to his own place and things around him, is the Chief Inspector, you know.'

'Yes,' she said, smiling involuntarily. Indeed he was; normally he would never have let his flat get as unkempt as it had. That was why she had cleaned up: not because the mess offended her personally but because she knew how much he'd appreciate her care of his bits and pieces, as he always called his expensive and well-chosen furniture. And plants, of course.

'So he's on the streets somewhere,' she said. 'Driving around in that old car of his. Or will it be a police car?'

'Mebbe,' Mike said. 'Or in a restaurant or a pub, more like. From what Salmon was saying he's used them a lot as meeting places for the various snouts he's got. He's got a great list of informers, has the Guv'nor.' He shook his head admiringly. 'He'll be out eatin' or drinkin' with some of them, that's where he'll be.'

'Will he?' George said and a thought began to form. 'Listen, Michael, when are you off duty?'

'About four hours ago,' Mike said cheerfully. 'I'm into overtime at the present. But I'll no' get much more. I'll have to be away soon, anyway, to get a bit o' sleep. I'm dead on my feet after last night.'

'Well, I'll tell you what we'll do, Mike,' George said, letting her voice become a touch wheedling. 'Dear Mike, you'll help me find him, won't you? Go home, get some sleep and this evening we'll have a wander around Poplar – the restaurants and so forth – see if we can find out where Gus is. What do you say?'

'Just wander around looking for – Dr B., it's a great patch o' ground wi' a gey great number of eatin' places and such like to cover!' His Scottish burr had deepened in his horror at the suggestion. 'It'll take us a fair month o' Sundays to do that! And he'll no' be pleased to be interrupted, I'm thinking.'

'I'll deal with that,' she said with sublime confidence. 'I'll tell you what we'll do, Mike. You just come with me, and if we see him someplace, then you disappear and I'll do the rest on my own. Then he won't even know you helped me. How's that? It's just that I want him to come back and help find this serial killer before he does it again.'

'We dinna ken for sure it's a serial –'

'I know that!' she said, almost irritably. 'But Gus doesn't! And you must surely want to work with Gus rather than that goddamned Roop!' As Mike didn't answer she felt he was wavering. She pushed her advantage home. 'You come to the hospital at – what, six or so? I'll be ready, and we'll go see what we can find. Is it a deal?'

'I don't –' he began but she gave him no chance.

'Och, you're a really great man, Michael Urquhart,' she said in a thick Scottish accent. 'And Gus'll be as pleased with you as I am once he knows. See you at six then.' She hung up, crossed her fingers on both hands and made a thumping action in the air. Please, she prayed in a vague way inside her head, please make him come. And then please let me find Gus. I really must find Gus.

To her great relief, Mike came. He was wearing black jeans and a silk bomber jacket in dark green over an open-necked shirt and looked extremely attractive. She beamed at him and said so, and he went a little pink.

'Och, nothing of the sort,' he muttered. 'I just didna want to look like a policeman. Not when I'm wandering around pushing my nose where I've no' been invited. Not in Poplar.'

'Is it such a bad area?' She was busy locking up and leading the way out to where her car was parked behind the main Admin. Block, hurrying him through the courtyard.

'It can be,' he said. 'And most of the fellas who work from the nicks there know their locals well. They see someone from another nick prowling and they'll want to know the reason why. I dinna fancy that. I wanted to look like – Well, ordinary.'

She glanced at the dark green jacket and chuckled. 'You're a bit snazzy to disappear into the wallpaper.'

'You're no slouch yourself,' he said. 'Now I've seen you I feel a bit better. There'll be no one looking at me with you got up like that.'

'What's wrong with it?' she demanded, looking down at her outfit; a big dark blue shirt over white cotton leggings and trainers. 'I thought it ordinary enough for a hot evening.'

He grinned. 'It makes it very obvious you've got legs that go on a long time after most women's stop,' he said.

It was her turn to redden and she was glad to be able to keep her head down as she unlocked the car and got in.

'Aw, shucks!' she said as lightly as she could and pulled the car out towards the main road. 'Which way, mister?'

He directed her and the little car moved easily through the clotted early evening traffic going eastwards. She was glad to have the sun at her back; it was still very bright as it moved down towards the horizon and there were times when it was reflected back painfully into her eyes from the tall glass-fronted buildings that now dotted Docklands.

'We'll stay in Poplar High Street,' Michael said. 'It's as good a place as any. I hope you've a good bladder.'

'Hey, what?' she peered at him sideways. 'What's that got to do with anything?'

'We'll be getting through a lot of fluid, I'm thinking,' he said. 'I'll certainly need some comfort stops mysel' if you don't.'

'I'll worry about that when I have to.'

'Never pass up a free lunch or a chance to pee,' he murmured sententiously, and leaned forwards. 'It's a good motto. This is the way to Poplar High Street. There's a pizza place very near. The Guv likes pizza.'

'I remember,' she said. 'If I pull up can you go and ask for change for the phone or something? See if he's in there?'

'Something tells me I'm going to collect an awful lot of change,' he complained, but he got out of the car as soon as she slid to the kerb and went into the pizza parlour, leaving her to stare at the street around her.

It was busy, shop lined, full of people wandering and gossiping, or hurrying, head down and purposeful, towards the bus stops. She tried to peer among them to see if Gus was there, simply walking, and realized how difficult it was to focus on individuals in a crowd. Her heart sank. Was this the stupidest expedition she had ever embarked upon? She began to suspect so.

Her suspicions were confirmed as the evening wore on. Mike emerged from the first pizza parlour with a pocket full of change for the phone and an accusation of being a bleedin' nuisance from the man behind the counter. He got a similar response at the next three places they went to, and after that they took it in turns. Hamburger places, Chinese restaurants (their ploy there was to collect a takeaway menu and promise to call back when they were ready to order) and in each of them they scanned the customers as fast as they could to see if their quarry was there.

By eight o'clock Mike had become very quiet. By nine he was irritable and by nine-thirty they were both snapping at each other. They had covered all the possible places south of Poplar High Street to start with, and there were very few there, for the area was mostly India and Millwall Docks, and then had turned their attention to the long slice of buildings that lay between Poplar High Street to the south, the East India Dock Road on the north, and the West India Dock Road and Cotton Street on each side.

George had insisted they went up and down every little street, even those that were clearly empty houses, in case in one of them there was an eating place tucked away in which Gus might be, and secretly because she had a hope of seeing his car parked somewhere.

But when they'd drawn a blank and were back at the end of Bazely Street, the last one before they would be back in Cotton Street, Mike went on strike.

'This isn't working, Dr B.,' he said plaintively. 'I'm goin' no further, and that's the truth of it.'

'Oh, Mike, we've done so much, we can't give up now. He has to be here somewhere. You said yourself he was in Poplar.' She almost wailed it.

'Indeed I did not.' He was indignant. 'I agreed it was one of the places he might be, but there's a lot more possibles further east, and south. Blackwall and Millwall or even as far as Canning Town. You can't search the whole East End for him.'

'I know that, but I have a hunch. Let me at least try a bit more. Just another – oh, half an hour. Please?' She knew she was being childish but she couldn't bear the thought of just driving home and admitting failure. She couldn't. 'Just another half-hour.'

'Oh, Dr B. what's the point?'

They argued for a few moments more and in the end he gave in, of course. He was a nice young man and not used to overcoming powerful women, as he finally said with some resignation. 'My mother's just such another as you. When will I learn to do as I'm bid and not waste my efforts in arguing?'

She laughed and, reaching over, squeezed his knee. Then she let in the clutch. 'Where next, then?'

'Other side of the High Street, I suppose,' he said. 'Go right over at the end of this street. That'll lead you into – let me think – Ida Street, I think. There's a nice pub up there, on the far side – corner of Follett Street, is it, and Susanna? Anyway, we can try there.'

It was, she later decided, as though her guardian angel had relented. She had come so close to giving in to Mike's obvious unwillingness to continue and if she had – well, she preferred not to think about it. As it was, her persistence paid a dividend. It was of mixed value, but an undoubted dividend.

The pub was pleasantly old-fashioned; engraved glass windows, a lot of dark polished wood, a loud band of limited talent and a big crowd of customers of even more limited taste and judgement. At first sight she quailed; to push through a crowd like this would be intimidating indeed, she thought. Then she took a deep breath. Not to push, feeling as she did, would be to be a complete nerd.

'This time I want a drink,' Mike said plaintively in her ear. 'We've been wandering around all this time and all I've got out of it is a pocket full of more change than I'll ever be able to use, an empty belly and a dry throat. So much for worrying about bladders.'

'My round,' George said at once.

'You're on.' He grinned and led her to the bar.

It took a lot of shoving to get the attention of the barman and order their modest half of lager for Mike and bitter lemon for George. ('I'm driving,' she said with a mock self-congratulatory primming of her lips, and he laughed.) Then they turned to lean their backs against the small section of the bar they'd managed to get to themselves, and looked around.

It was, she decided, the usual East End sort of crowd. Girls in very tight low-cut sweaters covered in glittery sequins, downy jumpers equally plunging but appliquéd with satin rabbits and bows, and skirts so short and tight that they looked like oversized garters, with their hair frizzed wildly and their make-up impeccable and highly unlikely. There was a sprinkling of old-fashioned punks and a great many shaved male scalps, one of which, she saw with an academic interest, had a tattoo that looked like a barcode, and copious amounts of male earrings, neck medallions and heavy aftershave.

'Look at 'em,' Mike said in her ear. 'As likely a bunch of villains as you'll ever see under one roof. If I could lock 'em all up and really get to work on them we'd clear up half the crime on Poplar's books, I swear. In one night.'

'Why don't they, then? The local guys, I mean?'

'PACE,' Mike said sourly. 'The Police and Criminal Evidence Act has tied our hands as tight as it's possible to without actually using handcuffs, as well you know. Mind you' – he took a deep draught out of his glass and then looked at its almost empty state consideringly – 'there's a few bent coppers here and there who'd do well if we didn't have PACE, so maybe it's as well.' He emptied his glass completely. 'My turn, I think.'

'Go ahead,' she said. 'I'm happy with this.' And she sipped her almost untouched bitter lemon and went on looking around.

When it happened, it was so sudden that she found her heart literally missed a beat. Her medical mind registered the fact and then monitored her pulse rate afterwards. It thumped along rapidly for some time and she felt the sick lurch in her belly that goes with that sort of adrenaline surge, so made herself breathe more deeply to recover.

Gus had appeared at her left side just as Mike was murmuring something insulting about the woman standing close in front of them, a very short, painfully thin woman, with legs like sticks and a ribcage that looked like a prison cell in a Western movie, yet who wore the same swooping décolletage and pelmet skirt of the much younger girls. George giggled at

Mike's whispering and was turning her head to say something back to him when Gus's voice came loud in her other ear.

'And what are you two doing here?' he said. His voice was icy. Even in the hubbub all around them she could hear that.

'Gus,' she said and turned on him with a grin as wide and radiant as she could make it. 'Gus, I've been looking for you everywhere! It's taken absolutely ages and –'

'Has it now? But not too boring, I trust.' He was looking at Mike with a very straight face, and there was a glint in his eye she'd never seen before. He looked as angry as it was possible for a man to look. She pulled on his elbow, hard.

'Gus? Of course it's been boring, you daft 'aporth!' She used his own idiom deliberately. 'But it was worth it. We've found you. Listen, Gus, there's something I really must talk to you about –'

'I might as well be on my way,' Mike said, looking at her and at Gus and then at his half-empty glass. He turned, set it down on the counter very deliberately and began to push his way out of the crowd.

'Yes. I think you might as well be on your way, indeed I do,' Gus said. 'I'll deal with you some other time.' Mike went without looking back, leaving George staring at Gus with her brows railway-lined and a certain amount of anger lifting inside her as well.

'Gus, what on earth's the matter with you? He spent all this time helping me find you and then you go and treat him like that! Are you mad?'

'What?' He turned and stared at her and again his eyes were flinty. 'Mad? No. Not mad. Unless you mean in the sense of being bloody angry. Because I'm certainly that.'

'But why?' She was bewildered. 'Because I came looking for you?'

'Looking for me? Go and pull someone else's. Maybe theirs will have bells on. Neither of mine have,' he said, and then, quite suddenly, seemed no longer able to prevent his anger exploding. 'Goddamn it, George, I no sooner turn my back than you're out with some other geezer – and one of my own bloody DCs at that. You might at least have made sure you went somewhere where I wouldn't be – and had a better tale than that you were *looking for me*! How bloody stupid do you think I am, for Chrissakes?'

She stared at him still, but her own anger was slithering away, melting and undergoing a sea change. A sense of warmth took over, and became sheer delight that could only have one sort of expression. And she expressed it.

She lifted her chin to point it at the grim smoke-filled ceiling above her head and burst into a peal of delighted laughter.

14

'Oh, Gus,' she managed to say when at last her laughter had spluttered to an end. 'Oh, Gus, you are sweet!'

'Sweet?' He bawled it so loudly that even in a pub famous for keeping its decibel level so high it was painful people heard him and turned to stare. 'Sweet, do you call it? I never heard such bloody –'

'Jealous,' she crooned. 'You're jealous.' And beamed at him, a deeply happy woman. 'I do like it. It makes me feel all warm inside.'

'I don't know why I even bother to talk to you,' he roared. 'You've got the understanding of a bloody flea.'

'And you've got the manners of a louse,' she said, glaring at him. Funny was one thing, but it was possible to take a joke too far. 'Leave it alone, Gus. I came looking for you, with Mike's help. You got jealous for no reason. End of argument, OK?'

'Just like that? Why should I say yes, just like that?'

'Because I've told you,' she said. 'I've explained the situation and you believe me, because I don't lie to you. Do I?'

'Oh, yes you do,' he snapped. 'You lied to me over that business of your so-called birthday party in the Oxford case, and –'

'That was not a lie,' she said disgustedly. 'That was a necessary piece of – of subterfuge designed to solve a tricky case. And it did, didn't it? So what are you beefing about?'

'*You*. You come on like Miss Purely White, utterly honest

in word and deed, when you can be the most manipulative, devious –'

'Me!' She was furious now. 'Me, devious? The straightest and most –'

'So what happened to that bottle you promised me, Gus?' The voice was a thick oily one, sounding as though it reached the open air through a thick lather of peanut butter, the crunchy sort, so that now and again it cracked as well as oozed. George turned her head to stare and saw a large man standing behind her and grinning at Gus.

He was more than large. He was almost square, and since he was about – she estimated it fast, using her own five foot ten as the measure – about six feet three inches tall, that meant he carried a lot of bulk. It was almost more than she could take in at first, the amazingly broad shoulders, clad in perfect smooth dark brown silk and mohair, the glittering white shirt, the jauntily tied bow tie in yellow and brown paisley, and above it a face that was very broad, very pale, very smooth and supported by three chins. The eyes were large and a lustrous green made rather odd by the thick colourless lashes and brows above them. He had a good head of hair, but it was so fine and pale it was almost invisible, so that at first instance he seemed bald. He was one of the oddest men George had ever seen.

'So, where is it, Gus? Won't the buggers serve you? Jim! A bottle of Bolly and quick about it!'

He had not raised his voice to give the order, nor turned his head, but at once there was a flurry behind the bar as one of the barmen rushed to do as he was told. By the time the large man turned his head to look, it was there, a cold bottle wrapped in a white cloth, set on a tray with a large dish of nuts and glasses alongside it.

'Here we are, Mr Ledbetter,' the barman said and Gus lifted his head sharply.

'This is my shout,' he said and put his hand in his pocket, but the man called Ledbetter laughed and shook his head.

'Shove it on my slate, Jim,' he said. 'Bring it along, Gus. And your little friend.' He smiled at Gus widely but still didn't look at George. Then he turned and went and the crowd seemed to open ahead of him without being told or pushed.

'Come on,' Gus muttered. 'And don't say a bleedin' word without checkin' with me. Listen and learn. I'll explain later. Maybe.' He picked up the tray and followed the big man, and perforce George followed him.

By the time they reached him, he was sitting at the table in the corner, leaning back in the space made by the wall and the curve of the engraved glass window. Someone was leaning over the table to talk to him as Gus approached. Ledbetter said something in a low voice and the man looked over his shoulder, then melted away into the crowd. Gus put the tray on the table, pulled out a stool for George and took another for himself. It was, George decided, like being a child, sitting at the feet of a storyteller. Even sitting down he seemed to tower over them.

'So, an introduction, Gus?' the man said.

'This is an old friend of mine, George Barnabas,' Gus said. 'Dr Barnabas, this is Mr Monty Ledbetter, an old friend of mine.'

'George?' Monty said. 'Is that all of it or is it a shortening for something prettier?' He was looking at her now, a very straight shrewd gaze, and George felt herself tightening under his regard.

'There's no shortening,' she said crisply. 'It's just George.'

'Why?' She blinked at the directness of the question.

'Her grandfather didn't like women much,' Gus said. 'Only had one daughter. Got fed up, left all his money to the daughter's child as long as it was named after him. He died before the baby was born. It was a girl and here she is. George.'

Monty Ledbetter grinned slowly. He had very expensive-looking teeth. 'A feminist, hey? Is that why you're a doctor?'

'Yes,' George said. 'And no. Yes to the first. Not entirely to the second.'

'Aha!' Ledbetter beamed at his own perspicacity. 'But partly right? I guessed as much. Women doctors – they like to prove how good they are.' He nodded with a sort of pride in his own knowledge. 'I understand doctors. They're in the family.'

'Oh?' George did not invite further information, but he was clearly determined to give it.

'Two of my nephews are doctors. One's a consultant physician.' He said it very clearly, enunciating every syllable proudly. 'In America. The other' – he beamed – 'is in Harley Street.'

'Oh,' George said again, managing not to point out, as she usually did when people threw the address at her as though it were a qualification, that any quack could rent a room there. 'Really?'

'Yup.' Mr Ledbetter clearly took that as a form of congratulation. 'Not bad, hey? A surgeon. So.' He stared at her. 'You're one of these feminists. One of the burn-a-bra types.'

'No,' George said and felt tighter than ever. 'Just a practical woman. Like my mother.'

'I like practical women. Even when they do burn their bras,' Monty said. 'Maybe especially when they do.' He leaned towards the bottle. 'A little champagne, Dr George? It's very good for you. Clears the system.'

'There's no evidence that –' George began, irritated as ever by silly statements about what was and what was not healthy, but this time even more than usual, but Gus interrupted.

'Lovely idea. I'll do the honours. Now, look, ignore George, will you? She's a friend, like I said. A good friend.' He leered slightly. 'So we can talk in front of her. She won't say nothing she shouldn't, right, George?' He looked at her with an appeal as well as command in his glance and, irritated though she was, and still with some anger in her from their unresolved argument, she responded. This was obviously something to do with his case, and that meant she had to co-operate.

'Yeah, right,' she said, putting on a look of boredom. She leaned back on her stool and accepted the glass of champagne Gus gave her with an even more lack-lustre air.

'So, Monty,' Gus said. 'How likely is it that they'll do it? Your opinion'll be very useful on this.'

'How likely I can't say.' Monty sounded judicious. 'I can do my best to guide 'em, you understand, but I'm only one member.'

'The Chairman,' Gus murmured.

'Well, all right, the Chairman, but me, I'm a democratic Chairman. Would I be sitting on the side of the Council I do if I wasn't democratic, I ask you? All I can tell you is that the committee is a sensible one. I won't work with no lemons, and they know it, so they make sure I chair the best people there are for the job. And they'll look at the whole scheme carefully, decide whether it's a goer.'

He sighed and held out his glass for a refill. He likes his champagne, George thought. Drinks it like lemonade.

'For my part, Gus, I just want to see the poor little kids properly looked after, know what I mean? It's bad enough they are what they are, only elevenpence ha'penny to the bob, without us making the lives they do have a misery.'

'And if it does go through, will you check on —' Gus said and Monty held up his hand.

'No names, no pack drill, Gus, you know that. Would I keep a thing like that from you? Of course I wouldn't. If it goes through, then believe me, I'll be checking hard on who gets what out of it. *Cui bono*, eh? *Cui bono*.'

George was startled and then ashamed of herself for being so. Why shouldn't this man, whoever he was, quote a Latin tag if it was apposite? And it seemed so in this case, though it was difficult to follow the conversation. *Cui bono*: for whose benefit? Gus wanted to know about some Council committee that this man chaired, and which could agree to something that Gus wasn't too happy about. *Cui bono*? She understood that much.

Monty was talking again and now George was able to make a little more sense out of what was going on.

'Building contractors,' Monty was saying earnestly, 'are straight from hell, you know that, Gus. They'll do anything for work, especially when there's so little legit stuff around. If this deal goes through then there'll be a lot of very nice refurbishing to be done and not a little extra building. It stands to reason there'll be people dyin' to get their hands on the contracts. I do all I can at the Council to make sure that there's no dirty work when it comes to tenders or awarding of contracts, but even I can't be everywhere. So I'll make a deal with you, Gus. I'll go on takin' my life in my hands being a snout for you if you'll keep your eyes peeled for some of these villains who're trying to buy out some of my clerks and so forth. Is it a fair exchange?'

Gus gave a little snort of disbelieving laughter. 'I'm trying to see anyone daring to threaten you,' he said. 'Your life's in your hands? Do me a favour, Monty!'

'Don't you be so sure!' Monty opened his eyes wide and looked hurt. 'I'm vulnerable, you know.'

'Monty, you've got all the vulnerability of a crack Panzer division,' Gus said. 'How many fellas'd dare hang around for you on a dark night, do you suppose? You'd squash 'em with one foot. What size do you take, for Chrissakes?'

'Fifteens, specially made for me at Lobb's,' Monty said and grinned at George. 'I'm a fair specimen, eh, Dr George? I weigh close on twenty-two stone, you know, and not an ounce of it is fat. It's all muscle, every bit. I'm as light on me feet as any of the boxers down at Christo's gym, you ask him. I can't even get a friendly these days because there's no one to stand up to me. I was a heavyweight boxer, you know, in my army days!'

'I'm sure you were,' George murmured, looking sideways at the large arm Monty had pushed towards her.

'Go on, feel my biceps,' he invited. She obliged, pinching his upper arm gingerly. It was rock hard. 'See what I mean? Tough, hmm? And big. But I'm still vulnerable.' He turned back to look at Gus. 'Some of these buggers'll stop at nothing if you get in their way. I spend some time on building sites remember – it only takes a medium-sized crane and a demolition ball to do a nasty on me.'

'You're doing it up a bit too brown, Monty,' Gus said bracingly. 'But it's a deal. You keep me informed about the committee's decisions about – the committee's decisions,' he repeated as Monty threw him a sharp glance and lifted an eyebrow towards George. 'And I'll keep a well-open eye and ear on the contracts inside. There'll be no accidents to you while I'm around. Don't you worry.'

'I'm not the worrying sort,' Monty said as he got to his feet. He towered over them and George, almost as a reflex, stood up too. 'I got to go. Finish the Bolly, you two, and make up whatever the row was. It's never any use fighting with your fella, Dr George, is it? Spoils all the fun. You ought to ask my missus how to handle a man. She's a wonder. Does all her charity work, running the old clothes shop, you know, and keeps the family happy, cooking and all that, and keeps me contented' – he looked sideways at Gus and produced a man-to-man lascivious grin that made George want to hit them both – 'and never argues with me. Wonderful woman. Really wonderful. Well, I'll be on my way. Keep in touch, Gus. And don't forget. I won't.' He went out of the pub, the crowd making room for him as before, and George watched him, her brows creased.

'My God,' she said when the door had closed behind him and the crowd had tightened up again to continue its roaring conversations. 'What the hell was that?'

'A bright spark,' Gus said absently. He sat down again and reached for the bottle. 'We might as well finish this, I suppose. Have you eaten? We could go and find something –'

George waved away the bottle. 'No. Not for me. I'm driving. Listen, what was all that about? And why did he give me such a dirty look when you were saying –'

'I was about to say too much,' Gus said, turning to look at her. 'Listen, George, this hasn't been a good time. I mean, I'm trying to work on the toughest job of my whole bloody career, and you turn up here with Mike Urquhart and make me –'

'Make you come on like a character in a melodrama?' she interrupted sweetly. 'Where do you get off, Gus, coming on to me like that? Suggesting I was two-timing you with Mike – I mean, really! Is it likely?'

'Oh, all right, all right! I was wrong, OK? It was just that I was so – I didn't expect to see you here. It rattled me.'

'And you rattled everything for miles around,' she said.

'You can trust me, for God's sake, Gus! Not only not to play around with other fellas when you're not around, especially fellas who work for you, but also not to interfere when you're dealing with a business matter. I've worked with you long enough now, surely, to know when to keep my mouth shut. You can trust me – but you didn't trust me enough to tell your Monty the Giant-killer that I'm your pathologist. Why not? Would it have done any harm?'

'I didn't want him to think you were from the police as well,' Gus said. 'It was hard enough to get him to agree to talk to me – he's a big noise around here, and not the usual sort to go in for being a snout.'

'A snout –' George began.

'An informer. I thought you knew that.'

'I do,' George said witheringly. 'I was about to say, a snout is a good label for him. He looks piggy – those pale eyelashes and the size of him.'

'No need to be nasty. I told you, he's a big noise. Been on the Council here for donkey's years – deputy leader of his group and got his fingers in more pies than you can imagine. He's a real local bloke, you see. His old mum still lives in the street she was born in – she must be over ninety now – with Monty's youngest sister, and she's in her sixties, to look after her. There's a great raft of other sisters and brothers and nieces and nephews, and he looks after all of them. Hell, he employs half of them.'

'What does he do for a living?'

Gus shook his head. 'What *doesn't* he do. Owns a chain of tobacconist's shops. Has an estate agency too, for offices and factories. Owns a couple of factories himself. He's a remarkably successful businessman.'

'Is he straight?' George asked. 'Or is he one of your villains?'

Gus managed a smile. 'He's been checked up on from here to Christmas and back again. He's the cleanest character on the patch. There's never been a hint of bad dealing attached to him. No, Monty's OK. Really one of the old Londoners. Salt of the earth.'

'Is that why you're so scared of him?' George asked.

Gus stared. 'Me? Scared of – Do me a favour, ducks! Why should I be?'

'I don't know. I just thought you were. Hissing at me to be quiet and so forth.'

He sighed in an exaggerated fashion. 'Look, I don't like mixing pleasure and business, see? We're both taking chances, Monty and me. We don't want to alert the people we're after. No need to get you involved too'.

'Then why arrange to meet here?' George said. 'If he's not comfortable to be seen talking to a copper, and you're not comfortable being seen talking to him for some reason, why –'

'Because it can be clever to be seen in public,' he said. 'Think it out, George. If we meet in secret – which is pretty well impossible on this patch, because there's always somebody who twigs what's up and puts the word around – the local villains get suspicious. We meet in public like this, then it's obviously nothing for anyone to worry about. See? But all the same, I wish you hadn't been here. It'd have been easier to – well, I'm sorry I got mad at you, too. It was just such a surprise. Here I was, at a meeting I've spent ages trying to set up and then you turn up giggling into Mike Urquhart's ear. I felt – I don't know. Awful.'

She leaned towards him. 'Have you been missing me, Gus?'

'Like hell,' he said. 'It's been dreadful. Every time I've tried to get home and call you something else has boiled over. It's been a bugger, honestly.'

She reached out and took his wrist between her fingers. 'Can you get home now? Tonight, I mean?'

He shook his head. 'I've got another meet fixed up. Over towards Canning Town. There's someone there knows all about this ...'. He looked at her swiftly. 'This thing Monty's committee is involved with. I might get some sense out of him. I wish I could come home. I do miss you, George.'

'That's all right, then,' she said. 'As long as you do. Listen, Gus, I have to tell you why I came looking for you, right?'

'I've got to go.' He looked at the pub clock and made a face. 'I should have gone when Monty did.'

'Give me five minutes, for God's sake!' she said. And that

was about all it took. She told him all she had found out, little as it was: about Lisa Zizi and the so-far unidentified body from the second fire, and about the leg and the dog carcase and the odd findings that linked them. He listened, his eyes on her face all the time, and did not interrupt once. She was pleased with herself; she'd told her story succinctly and clearly.

'Please, Gus, can't you take it on now? It's too big for Dudley.'

'He's not on his own, you know,' Gus said. 'An inspector, however good and however close to promotion to chief inspector – and he is – would never handle a case like this on his own. Superintendent Whitman's in over-all charge and –'

'Whitman?' she said. 'But he's not the same as you, is he? I mean, he's uniformed.'

Gus nodded. 'You're right. He's not part of the detective branch, but that doesn't mean that he can't supervise the people who are. And he does. The case is in good hands, George. I can't just walk away from all the work I've done here all these weeks just because you want me to!'

'Not just because I want you to! I can't deny I miss your company, but it's more than that. This could be a serial killer with more to come – and though I know you're working on a huge case and you've put a lot into it, doesn't murder take precedence over crime involving money and –'

'I'm sorry, doll,' he said. 'But on this you're out on a limb. I'm not the only one who can handle murder, serial or otherwise. Just make sure Roop has all this information and he'll get on the job. I know he can be a bit bloody at times, but he'll take it all on board, never you doubt it. There's no way he'd be vindictive just because he doesn't like you.'

She pounced on that. 'Then you admit he doesn't like me?'

'He's jealous,' Gus said briefly. 'Wants me all to himself.'

George frowned. 'But Gus, do you mean he's – I mean . . .'

'Oh, George, for heaven's sake!' Gus said, shaking his head irritably. 'What are you going all coy on me for? If you're asking is he gay and does he fancy me, the answer is not on your bloody Nelly. The man's happy with his wife and kids.

But in a professional sense, he's my fella. I trained him, taught him all he knows. He's going through a bad time on account of he's up for promotion, just as I am, and if I get mine and he doesn't get his, then we don't work together any more, and he's got to cope on his own. He gets scared, believe it or not. Especially as you've come along and shown you're sometimes better at his job than he is. Of course he doesn't like you! Even more so when he finds out you and me don't only work together but play together. See? Be your age, ducky.'

She was silent for a moment and then nodded. 'Sorry, Gus,' she said in a small voice. She looked at him unhappily. 'I take it this means that you definitely won't be coming to help, then?' she said.

'It has to mean that. I could spit that the two cases should come up at the same time but that's the way it goes. You can't have it all your own way. I can only do one thing. Roop's got to get on with yours.'

'Well, at least tell him to let me in on what's happening,' she said almost despairingly. 'It's killing me to be kept on the outside looking in!'

'I'll bet it is, you nosy old bag,' he said fondly, leaning over and kissing her. 'All right, ducks, I'll have a word first chance I get. But do me a favour, try not to step on his toes. And don't jump in. Explain first. Don't just go waving your arms about, all impatient. It upsets quiet types like Roop.'

'And he upsets me,' she said sourly.

'Tell me about it. Listen, I've got to go. I'll try and get home in a day or so. The way things are, though, I'm at full tilt. I sleep when I get the chance at Canning Town nick. Leave messages there for me, if it's important, and my phone's switched off. But only if it is important, you hear me? And wish me luck.'

She opened her mouth to do just that, but he'd already gone.

15

Mike phoned her at her office the following week. 'We've got an ID on that second fire victim,' he said. 'Did anyone tell you?'

'No.' She was bitter. 'I just collect the evidence for 'em. They don't bother to let me know the outcome.'

'Well, I will. Sorry about Dudley, but he has been busy one way and another.'

'I'll bet,' she said. 'I'd hoped that Gus would have spoken to him by now.'

'Um,' said Mike. 'The Guv. Yes. Is he – er – is he still mad at me?'

'Oh, he's not mad at you. I told you that the day after we found him. No need to worry.'

'I do all the same though,' Mike said gloomily. 'I dinna like being in the Guv's bad books.'

'Who says you are?'

'He hasna said I'm not.'

'For heaven's sake, Mike, how could he? He hasn't been anywhere near you this past week!' She sharpened then. 'Has he?'

Mike sighed so gustily at the other end of the phone that she almost felt his breath on her ear. 'No,' he admitted. 'But –'

'No buts about it.' George was bracing. 'Take it from me. He's not blaming you for anything. And I'm grateful to you for helping me out the way you did. I told you that. Listen, Mike, enough of that. Tell me about this ID.'

'Ah, yes. Well, those fingerprints we collected in the mortuary paid off. She was on record.'

'She had form?'

'Sort of,' Mike said. 'Nothing much. There was a nasty affair about three years ago – a Tom had her throat cut in the Whitechapel Road area. They did a sweep on a lot of them and this girl got caught up in that. Not that she was an ordinary Tom. She was an uptowner, worked the big hotels. Very expensive.'

'Tell me more.'

'Her name was Shirley Candrell. Aged twenty-nine, or so her documents said.'

'That would be about right.' George narrowed her eyes, remembering. 'Going by what I saw at the PM.'

'OK. Well, she came from Burnley in Lancashire, about fifteen years ago. Runaway teenager. But she did well for herself. Left considerable assets, I'll say that. The father, who's her next of kin and not too well off, is sitting looking at an inheritance of close on a hundred thousand – not counting the house. She owned that, or would have done once the mortgage was paid off. That'll bring in another bit of cash, what with her insurance.'

George sharpened. 'Is that still valid? In a case of arson?'

'Good question. Well, at the very least he's inherited a hundred K from her. Those are her cash assets.'

'It sounds as though we're in the wrong business, Mike.'

'It wasna all the wages of sin, you understand. Or not precisely. She played in a lot of hard porn videos. That was how she got caught up in that sweep a few years ago when she was fingerprinted. The girl who had been killed was in the cast as well. Our Shirley was by way of being the star, though. She could do tricks with her – Well, never mind. But apparently she's a major loss to the industry.' His tone had become very dry. 'She did well as a producer as well as a performer. Was on royalties and all sorts. That's where the money came from.'

'How did you get all this stuff?' she said. 'There's a lot of detail in this, more than you'd expect to get from a fingerprint match, surely?'

He chuckled. 'Inspector Dudley's done well. Actually it was he had the notion of interviewing every girl who was finger-printed in that sweep. That's why this has taken so long – we had to find them. And some of them were glad enough to talk, times being as hard as they are. We learned a lot from them. So there you are. She's a Tom in a decent line of business, made a lot of money on the side in videos, and I dare say that could be one of the reasons she got her fingers burned.'

'Roop thought of doing that?' George said. 'He's not so . . . Well, well.'

'Not so daft, you'd be thinking? You'd be thinking right. Listen, Dr B., I have to go. Got places to visit and questions to ask. I'll keep in touch, since no one else is. As long as you don't drop me in it . . .'

'Would I do that?' she said. 'Thanks, Mike.' She hung up and sat staring into space for a while.

The frustration of not being part of the enquiry was biting hard again. The last week had been hectically busy on hospital business; Ellen Archer had brought her a draft document to work on, which made a strong plea for all pathological services for St Dymphna's and any other small specialist hospitals in the area, such as St Morwenna's Foot Hospital and the dental place over at Hackney, to be based at Old East, and she spent a large part of two days on that. It cheered Ellen greatly when she read George's new version and she congratulated her warmly on it.

'If the devils don't accept this, then they've no right to be called a Trust Board,' she said firmly. 'It's the most sensible thing I've seen. The next meeting is in a couple of weeks, I gather – they've changed the date because of summer holidays or something. I'll let you know, and try to see if they'll let us present this ourselves so that we can argue our corner. I'm determined they're not going to strip us of our lab.' And she went away busily to engage in even more of her wheelings and dealings, leaving George to cope with her exhausted, lack-lustre staff and their heavy workload.

The weather was part of the problem. It became hot and stayed hot and the humidity in the department rose steadily.

Everything they touched felt sticky and they themselves were clammy and miserable. They fixed gimcrack air-cooling systems involving fans blowing in front of bowls of ice filched from the mortuary refrigerators, but that just resulted in papers blowing about and getting into the wrong order and even more bad temper. By the end of the week George was in no mood to think of anything but the possibility of turning her back on the whole boiling lot of them; the lab, the staff and even Gus (who had been totally silent) and legging it away to some distant beach where she could sleep and swim and sleep again. All day.

But that was out of the question for her as the holiday season descended on Old East. One by one key people vanished on their summer breaks and running the place became much more complicated than usual. Consultants in virtually all departments chose to run twice their usual clinics 'because I'll be away for the next three weeks' and dumped a vastly increased amount of work in the path. lab in consequence. The lab staff were having their own holidays now of course, and that meant she was chronically shorthanded.

Sheila, whose own holiday wasn't due until September, worked at twice her usual rate, yet without any loss of efficiency which should have helped George but in fact made matters worse because she became particularly fractious. She never stopped complaining to anyone who would listen and particularly to George, who had to use every atom of self-control she had not to lose her temper and send her off in a huff for ever. The last person George could afford to lose was Sheila and the person she least wanted to have around was Sheila. It was not a comfortable situation.

It was Alan who saved the day, and she warmed to him greatly as a result. He took Sheila out to dinner one night, much to everyone's surprise (and not a little gossip) but clearly with Jane's full consent, for she was serene about it. The next day, when they came in, separately, everyone was agog to know what the enemy had been like, but neither would say. All anyone could see was that Sheila was happy and very gracious to both Alan and Jane, and Alan was treated by everyone with added respect and approval in consequence. So the department became a little less fraught than it had been, though still under great pressure.

But still at the back of George's mind, as she went through her busy days of post-mortems, court appearances and the eternity of heavy paperwork that accompanied her activities whatever they were, was Gus. His silence was understandable, but it hurt, and she would go home each day to her little flat, which was as stifling and uncomfortable in summer as it was cosy in the winter, and sit there in a thin shift desultorily watching repeats on television and reading back copies of the medical journals that she had allowed to pile up all through the spring and even as far back as March. By the end of the week she felt as though her head had been freshly stuffed with the most up-to-date information on her speciality, and a lot more besides, yet had none of the comfortable smugness she usually felt when she managed to catch up on her reading. She just felt lonely and uneasy and irritable.

But then, one Saturday evening almost two weeks after she had seen him in Poplar, he phoned. She had been sitting in her bath, in cold water, considering whether it was worth making the effort to get out, dry herself and dress so that she could go over to the swimming pool and get some exercise. But the place would be alive with children, she thought, on so hot an evening, and did she really want to make the effort just to have them get in her way? The phone shrilled in the living room and she thought of letting it ring, but couldn't. Whenever had she been able to ignore a ringing telephone, dammit? So she climbed out of the bath and with her wet hair streaming down her back and without bothering to wrap herself in a towel, went to answer it, leaving wet prints on the carpet all the way.

'George?' Gus was jubilant. He sounded like his old self and she caught her breath in excitement. 'George, me old darlin'. I've bin and gorn and cracked it, I swear I have! How's that for a turn-up for the books? I can see just what's going on and how. I don't know all the who's yet, but just you watch me. I'll get 'em, see if I don't!'

'Gus, really?' she said and laughed with sheer pleasure. 'Gus, that is fabulous news. It means I might *see* something of you?'

'Every damned bit there is, sweetheart!' he crowed. 'In full working order, too. Oh, George, isn't it the business, though? It all sort of – well, I'll have to explain it when I've got a week to do it in. Right now, dolly chops, get your best bib and tucker out. I'm on my way!'

'Honestly? You're free tonight?'

'I'm back in the world of the living, right now, glory be. I'll file my notes on Monday – that'll be soon enough. I can afford to take the weekend. And take it I shall. Look, I have to drop in at the nick but I'll go home first and duffy myself up for you and pack a toothbrush – if I may?'

She chuckled. 'Oh, sir,' she said with all the shock she could put in her voice. 'How forward you are!'

'Yeah, but at least I'll have clean teeth when I get there. Like I say, I'll go home and get cleaned up, pop in the nick and I'll be with you – oh, around eight. How does that sound?'

'Marvellous,' she said. 'Terrific. Great. I'll tell you what else when you get here.'

'I can hardly wait,' he said. 'Pant pant, my fangs are showing. Cor, but what a night lies ahead!'

She spent a lot of time getting ready. It was just half past six now and she had the chance to do something special for him. So she dried her hair and pinned it up into a fetching heap on top of her head – and for once it was obedient and went into exactly the place she wanted it to, without any protest – and chose her clothes with care. The oatmeal linen with the split skirt and the tunic top was both cool and sexy, she decided, and preened a little in front of the mirror when she put it on. The weather had been so hot and the sun so strong that she had somehow got a tan without realizing it, just on her walks to and from work on the days when the buses were too full and too smelly to be tolerated. She looked good and she knew it.

She busied herself in the kitchen then, setting out little

nonsenses for them to eat with the bottle of champagne that had been lying forlornly in the fridge for weeks now, waiting for just such an opportunity, and arranged it all on a big platter: prawn wontons; smoked salmon rouleaux stuffed with cream cheese (thank heaven for Marks & Spencer, she thought), and strips of carrot and celery to use with her own dips – blue cheese using the recipe Vanny had given her when she had first left home, and guacamole and aïoli.

She even had time before eight to run around the flat, tidying and dusting it, to please his fastidious eye, and to the Busy Lizzie plant that obediently perked up within ten minutes in its usual amazing way, and then, eager and ready, sat down on her sofa to wait for him. Ten to eight. It wouldn't be long now.

At half past eight she was angry. By nine she was frightened He had been so sure he would be with her by eight and he'd just made a breakthrough in a difficult case. Could it be that whatever he had identified was making trouble for him? Could someone have tried to hurt him? Her mind ran away with her: she saw Gus in a quiet alley, saw people creeping up on him, beating him up; saw herself called to the scene unwittingly as the pathologist; and then saw herself at his funeral. The whole thing moved across her mind in a matter of a fraction of a second, but it left her shaking and almost in tears. Where was he? She had been walking to the window to stare down into the street over and over again ever since quarter past eight; now, after forty-five minutes, she was glued there.

'Another five minutes and I go to the nick to find him,' she thought. 'I'll have to.'

She shrank from phoning the police station. If he had been held up by consultations with the Superintendent or something of that sort (and her logical mind told her, despite her emotional responses, that that was the most likely reason for his delay) he would be mortified if she chased him like an anxious mother hen. But if she happened to be waiting for him outside when he came out perhaps that wouldn't be so bad?

But she dismissed that too. He'd hate to find her there. He

had said he was on his way to her, and he'd arrive. This wouldn't be the first time he'd been held up by work, after all. It was the essence of a copper's life, she told herself. Just as is mine, really. She made herself sit down on the sofa again.

It was ten past nine when at last she heard his key in her lock. She shot to her feet and ran out to the miniscule hallway to greet him, all her fear forgotten. It was dark out there – it always was, for there were only doors that led off it, no windows, so she couldn't quite see his face as she seized his arm and lifted her face to kiss him.

'Oh, Gus, I've been so silly and frantic! I'm so glad you're here. Come on through, honey. I'll get you a drink and –'

She stopped. Now that they were in the living room she could see him more clearly in the last of the golden light of the summer evening. He looked neat enough; he had clearly, as he said he would, gone home and changed. He was wearing one of his light summer suits and a sparkling white shirt and had tied a neat if insouciant bow tie at the neck. But now the knot was untied and the ends of the tie dangled forlornly against his shirt, which was open against his thick neck. She could see a pulse beating there, rapidly and heavily, and she stared at it and then at his face. He was white and drawn and she caught her breath.

'Gus, whatever is it? What happened? Honey, you look – Gus?'

He was staring at her with eyes so wide he was almost showing a rim of white above the iris, and that gave him a slightly demented air. She wanted to shake him to make him talk, to look less agitated. But she stood very still, only setting her hands on his upper arms to hold him, and looking at him closely. 'Gus?' she said more gently.

His voice was shaky and he had to cough before he could speak properly. 'I've been suspended.'

She blinked, startled, and shook her head.

'What do you mean?'

'Just that. I've been sent off duty, not to return until – until –' His face crumpled and she let go of his arm and pulled him close, holding him tightly with her own hands interlaced across his shoulder blades.

'Until what, sweetheart?'

'Until they investigate the charges against me,' he said huskily. 'I'm supposed to have been acting corruptly in the matter of fifteen thousand pounds paid into my account last week. Oh, George, what on earth shall I do?'

16

She managed to settle him to something approaching his usual commonsensical self by means of plying him with food and drink; not the champagne and nibbles, both of which languished unwanted in the kitchen, but a big pot of tea, made strong and dark the way he liked it, and a plate of hot buttered toast. He had told her once that for him tea and toast were the most abiding memories of his childhood when he'd been happy and secure, and she, acting almost instinctively, didn't ask him now, but just provided it.

At first he waved it away, but she was insistent so he took some and then seemed to discover his appetite and wolfed the lot. She watched him in silence and, when he leaned back on the sofa again, replete, took the tray away and then came to sit beside him again.

'OK, honey,' she said. 'Let's get the story clear. What happened at the nick?'

He sighed and set his head back on the sofa. It was getting dim in the little room now; the light outside had dwindled to a dark duck-egg blue as the sun disappeared behind her little block of flats. 'I was just leaving my notes on my desk when the Super came in. He had someone with him, bloke I didn't know. Then another one arrived. I did know him – Dave Anderson, used to be with us, went off to Tintagel House.'

'Tintagel?'

He sighed again. 'It's the headquarters building where the CIB operates. In Vauxhall Bridge Road. I'll be seeing a fair bit of them now, I reckon.' He was silent for a while and she left him to it. He started to speak again of his own volition after a few moments.

'Anyway, Dave had gone on to the Complaints Investigation Bureau at Tintagel House and when I saw him I didn't even twig then. I mean, why should I, for Christ's sake? I've done nothing I shouldn't – no one knows that better than I do. I've got the cleanest conscience a man can have.' He laughed then, an ugly little sound. 'Like I told them afterwards, it's easy for me to be a good clean boy. I don't make judgements about other blokes, because it's easy for me. I've got enough money already, thanks very much. I don't have to pull any strokes to get gelt, do I? But they didn't see it my way.'

Again he brooded for a while and then seemed to burst into words. 'I just couldn't believe it! I told 'em if it was a joke it was a bloody bad one, and even slapped old whatsaname on the back. Thought they'd set me up for a laugh on account of I've done so well so far – and then I remembered they couldn't know how well I'd done. I hadn't put my report in and wouldn't till Monday. I'd only just brought my notes in. And what with Whitman looking like a week-old codfish and Dave not able to look me in the eye and the other bloke all icy and – Well, I knew then it wasn't a joke. But I couldn't think what else it could be.'

This time she had to break the silence. 'What happened then?' she asked gently.

'Mmm? Oh, the usual drill for these things. They gave me a form one six three. An official complaint had been levelled at me. That I'd demanded money with menaces from a fish dealer and taken the cash from him in nothing bigger than twenty-pound notes, old ones, and paid them into my own bank. That I was suspended until such time as the complaint could be fully investigated, and I was to keep myself available for interrogation as and when they wanted me. Somethin' like that.'

'But . . .' she frowned. 'But Gus, what are you worried about? Surely you can prove that it isn't true? I mean, paying fifteen thousand in – you've only got to show them your bank books and so on and –'

'That's just the trouble.' He said it savagely, biting off the words. 'I did pay an extra seventeen thousand in cash into the bank last week. Not an extra, exactly, so much as a build-up. I've been so bloody busy this past month and more, I've neglected the business. The shops and restaurants have been carrying on all right, they're all good staff and know what to do. They handle their own weekly take, pay it in, sign their own cheques, keep their own books, the whole bit. Why shouldn't they? They've worked for me for years – worked for my dad before me. I can trust 'em. I just deal with overall things – like this seventeen thousand.'

'I thought you said fifteen,' she said.

'That's what's so bloody clever. They know – whoever set me up with this complaint – they know somehow how much it was and they've gone for a bit less in their accusation. But it was seventeen.' He sighed. 'I'd loaned it to Lenny Greeson, who's got a fish shop over at Canning Town, to get himself out of trouble. It's a long story . . .'

'Well, tell it,' she said. 'All of it.'

He took a deep breath. 'It's hard to know where to begin. Lenny's dad and my dad were mates. Good mates. Went to school together. My dad did well, old Ernie Greeson didn't. Never had more than one little place. When Ernie died ten years ago, he asked Dad to keep an eye on his boys. Dad's dead now, so I do.'

'But how can you be responsible for –' she began, but he shook his head.

'You're not an East-Ender. That's how we are in these parts. Look out for each other, you know? Anyway, Lenny's a – not a mate of mine, exactly, but I take an interest in him. But Lenny's not the only one. He's got a brother, Don, who's a right layabout. He works in the shop too, and getting him to keep his hands out of the till is murder. So I lent Lenny the cash, and he used it to pay some debts he had. He wanted to clear his books so he can sell the business, you see. I told him I'd be interested, that I'd buy and pay his debts, but he wouldn't have that. He reckoned if he paid his debts, then showed me what a good business it was by paying me back in cash, week by week, he could ask for more for the business. As things were he couldn't prove the value of the goodwill he had because of Don. That silly bugger just helped himself before the take went through the books.'

'It's a bit complicated,' she ventured.

'Of course it is! And it sounds such a lame duck sort of story, for God's sake. But it happens to be true and it does make sense once you know the people involved. And understand the way my Dad and Ernie were. Lenny begged me to help him prove he had a business worth his asking price. He doesn't want to fall out with his brother – he's the only relative he's got – so this was his idea. If I'd lend him the money he could repay it from the business in cash before Don could get his sticky fingers on it. The amount of time it would take him to pay it back would show me just how much the business took. Like he said, he couldn't do what other businesses do and sell the place and the goodwill on the basis of bookkeeping because he'd never been good at it and it was a right dog's dinner. And the banks wouldn't lend for the same reason. No hard evidence of turnover, or business value. So I did it. And he paid me back over the last four weeks, to the tune of seventeen thousand. He's got a nice little business there in Canning Town. He'll have the whole debt paid off in another couple of months at this rate. It's impressive for a small set-up. Like I said, I should have paid it in weekly as I got it, in cash, only I didn't have time to pay it in till last Tuesday. And it was that payment which was the basis of the complaint.'

Suddenly he got to his feet as though he was unable to stay still any longer. He began to prowl around the room, stamping his feet down hard at each turn as though to burn off his rage.

'I'm so straight, it's bloody ridiculous. There was nothing in this for me. I don't even get any of the usual interest you get when you lend money. I just wanted to help the fella sort out the mess his business was in so he could sell it. Lenny swore to me that every penny he paid me came straight out of the till – or rather his apron pocket. On account of that's where he put all the cash he had so Don couldn't get hold of it. He paid me back, he showed me his business is a safe one so he can sell it and keep his head high – and now look at the mess I'm in.'

'But I don't understand the problem!' she said. 'Why don't you take these Complaints Investigators to see Lenny and talk to him?'

'I tried!' he said almost savagely. 'But you don't know how their minds work. They'll think I've fitted Lenny up to tell the story – if I'm guilty, that is. And they'll assume I am, believe me! Maybe they will talk to him – but in their own time. And I certainly won't be allowed to be there when they do.'

She was silent for a while, then said, 'But how could anyone know . . .' She bit her lip and thought again. 'Could this Lenny be the one who – who dropped you in it?'

He stopped and stared down at her. 'Lenny? I can't imagine it,' he said slowly. 'Why should he? Oh, shit!' He began to walk the room again. 'That's the trouble with this sort of thing. He could have done, I suppose. I know him. I like him. I've always trusted him since he was a little kid, but what does that add up to? Maybe he told someone what I was doing? There was no reason why he shouldn't. It was no secret that Don couldn't be trusted with cash. Dammit all to hell and back, *Don* knows he can't be trusted with money! He knew Lenny was doing this and was glad enough – he wants his share of the money when Lenny sells up.'

'What's Lenny planning to do once his shop is sold?' she asked. 'Could there be a reason there?'

Gus shook his head. 'He's going to start again on his own. Without Don. Don's going to use his share to go into a bookie business as a partner. Lenny's going to buy a frying van, and travel to sell his fish and chips. Off my patch, of course. That would be part of the deal. Then, in time, maybe he'll make enough to start a proper shop again. Somewhere south of the water where we wouldn't be in competition and could stay friends. Christ, friends! Have I *got* any friends? How can I know, after this?'

'Gus, come and sit down,' she said, holding out her arms. 'You're wearing yourself out. Please, come and sit down here.' She indicated the sofa beside her and slowly he obeyed. She knelt beside him and began to knead the muscles at the back of his neck and across his shoulders. Slowly she felt the knotted muscles loosen and relax.

'That's nice,' he said. He sounded a little sleepy and she was glad of it. 'Thanks.'

'I can help,' she said. 'I can do some investigating of what's going on here –'

At once the muscles tightened again and he hurled himself round to glare at her, grabbing her shoulders with fingers so hard she almost winced. 'You'll do nothing of the bloody sort, lady. Do you hear me?'

'Why not?' She was angry. 'Am I so stupid that I can't –'

'It's nothing to do with stupid or clever! You're as clever as they come – the trouble is you might be too clever by half. There are rules about things. Like not tampering with witnesses. If you go digging around before the CIB does, you could be accused of trying to interfere with police investigations and I could be accused of urging you to do it. Since it would all be on my behalf they'd be sure to believe it was my idea.'

'But it would be me who –'

'I know that and you know that. *They* wouldn't know that. When they investigate a complaint they do it very thoroughly indeed. And if they keep coming across my girlfriend's tracks wherever they go they'll get very suspicious indeed.'

'Yes,' she said. 'I can see that.' But then she brightened. 'Suppose I went after them?'

'After?'

'Mmm. Suppose I wait till they've talked to people and then follow them and do my own digging around. Would that be a problem?'

'But what could you find out that they couldn't? There'd be no point.'

'There'd be all the point in the world. They'd just be

looking for evidence. I'd be looking for evidence in your favour.'

He sat very still, staring at her, and she spoke gently, because she knew she could hurt him so easily. 'Sweetheart, just look at what's happened so far. They found out about this money in your bank account, right? As far as they're concerned, it's evidence. Will they accept your explanation of what that money is, the way I have? I love you, you see. They don't.'

His hands slid down her arms, for he had still been holding them, and drooped, curled and lax, at his side. His eyes became unfocused as he thought, and then he shook his head.

'It's hopeless, George. They'll throw me out, you know that? I'll be out on my ear.'

She bit her lip, still aware of walking on the most fragile of eggshells. 'Gus, let's look at the worst that can happen. So you leave the Force, but you won't be in – I mean you'll still have your business. You've done nothing criminal and they won't be able to prove you have, surely? You won't go to prison or anything. That has to be impossible.'

'I'm not so sure,' he said harshly. 'I wish I were. If it's proven that I took money from people after threatening them, I could very well go to prison. It's not just an offence on the job, you know. It's a crime. But that's not the worst part. If I had to leave the Force –' He closed his eyes for a moment and then snapped them open to glare at her. 'Oh, God, George, it's such a mess!'

'Then all the more reason why I should try to do some hunting out of facts myself. Look, Gus, I'm not that bad at it, am I? I've found out things before for you. Let me try again.'

He sighed, a helpless sort of sound that made her want to weep. 'I don't see how you can,' he said at length. 'How will you know who they've been to see? Who they're going to see? What they're discovering? You can't sort out refuting evidence unless you know what it is they've collected. And they won't be letting the world know that till they've got the case ready.'

'But some of the people in the nick will know, surely?' she said softly. 'However close they play their cards to their chest, there'll be someone at the nick who'll find out. That place, as far as I can tell, is a minefield of gossip. It's always blowing up.'

Oddly he managed a smile. 'That's true. By God, that's very true.' He began to lift his mood a little. 'So you'd talk to people there. Who?'

She had an idea of her own, someone who'd already proven himself her ally on previous cases. But the suggestion had to come from him. 'You tell me,' she said.

'Roop,' he said after a moment. 'He'd do anything he could to help me.'

She was silent and he looked up at her and grinned, a twisted sort of grimace but at least it was there. 'He's all right, you know. I wish you could see that.'

'Yeah,' she said. 'If you could see him through my eyes.'

'Something like that. OK. There's no way you could work with Roop.' He brooded for a while and then seemed to brighten once more. 'I could, though.'

'What?'

'For Christ's sake. I'm sitting here like the world's coming to an end and I can't do anything about it. But that's a load of codswallop, right?'

She looked at him more closely and her own spirits began to rise. He looked better. Not a great deal, but better. 'Right,' she said.

'I can get a bit of work on my own case seen to, can't I? Roop'll do what he can for me, even though he's got a tough one in this burning business.'

'It mightn't be so tough if he accepted a bit of co-operation from someone who could be useful,' she said tartly.

'George, ducks, do shut up,' he said. 'I'm thinkin'. I'll talk to Roop. Tonight. At home. That'll be OK. See what he can dig out for me. And then you needn't –'

'Like hell I needn't,' she said vigorously. 'If you think I'm just going to sit around and let them throw buckets of crap at you, you've got another think coming.'

'You're all right, George, you know that?' he said after a moment. He reached out and took both her hands in his. 'All right, that's what you are. OK. Go ahead and do what you can. So long as you don't go falling over Dave Anderson and the other guy – whatsisname, Richard Shore, the Super said he was.'

'I won't,' she promised.

'How?'

'How what?'

'How won't you?' he said with exaggerated patience. 'If you won't take any inside help from Roop, how are you going to find out where the CIB goes and who they talk to?'

She hesitated. 'Mike Urquhart,' she said at length. 'He thinks the world of you. He'll help me.'

'Hmph,' Gus said. 'As long as it's only me he thinks the world of.'

'Listen Gus,' she snapped. 'This jealousy or whatever it is of Mike is stupid. He's nothing to me apart from a buddy and he helps me a lot. Is that such a crime? Lay off, will you?'

'I don't see I have any choice,' he said, and leaned back in his place on the sofa, letting go of her hands. 'Oh, George, what a bloody mess! The job's the only thing I've ever really cared about, you know. I enjoy fiddling around with the business, of course I do. I like the money it brings in. I like the elbow room it gives me to do what I like in my own time without expecting too much of me. Dad set the business up so it damn near runs itself – I've got the best workers east of Aldgate pump. But I'd turn my back on the lot tomorrow, if I had to choose. The job's the only thing that really matters. Ever since I was a nipper, I drove my old man barmy the way I went on about it – there's never been a copper in the family and as far as he was concerned it was a real let down. But he put up with it because he knew I'd never do anything else and be happy. And now this ...'

'It's all right, Gus,' she said. She came close to him and pulled his arm around her neck so that she could lie very close to him, her head on his shoulder. 'The job'll still be there for you. We'll make sure of it. Trust me.'

'Oh, George,' he said, 'I wish it was as easy as that.' He pulled her round, bent his head and kissed her, hard and with increasing need, and though she responded hungrily, all she could think of was: suppose I can't? Suppose they do throw him out? Then what? What sort of a person will Gus become? It was a horrible thought and a dreadful responsibility, but she'd taken it on and she had to carry it.

He went on kissing her and the worry about her responsibility dwindled and slid deep to the back of her mind, out of the way. She had much more immediate things to think of.

17

If it had to happen at all, George thought, at least we can be grateful it happened on a Saturday. That gives us Sunday, a whole day, to be together unhampered by work or thoughts of work – or, she amended, unhampered by any need to go at once to do anything about work. The shadow of it, however, hung over the day like a morning mist in autumn.

He spent the night in her flat but woke early and made sure she did too; and then later, as they lay in a post-coital half-doze, he muttered about needing to get some exercise. She forbore to make any comments about how much private exercise they had already taken and agreed at once to do whatever he wanted.

So they swam at the local pool and then drove into the middle of town to breakfast on croissants and hot chocolate in the Covent Garden piazza. After that they wandered over to Hyde Park to jog lazily round the track and then to lie on the grass and talk in a desultory sort of fashion about the people who strolled by them. He got restless then, and suggested a concert somewhere. Obediently she followed him back to the car and they travelled eastwards again, though this time they stopped at the Barbican and sat through a couple of hours of music. Not the most cheerful of music, George felt, with the main work being the Verdi *Requiem*, but he seemed to enjoy it. At least he sat quietly through the whole performance and seemed reasonably relaxed at the end of it.

He opted for dinner in Covent Garden again, so back they

went to Joe Allen's where he sat and didn't eat a pile of barbecued ribs with black-eyed peas; and she knew that he could no longer hold at bay his anxiety.

'But you've done bloody well,' she murmured and he looked at her, perplexed.

'Eh?'

'I said, "You've done bloody well." You've enjoyed quite a lot of today.'

He managed a smile. 'With you? Love, it's been great.'

'Until now?'

'No . . .' he said and then let his shoulders slump. 'Well, yes, I suppose so. I managed not to think of it when we were swimming and in the park, but it started to come back in the concert and now . . . Well, you can't blame me.'

'I don't,' she said. 'And like I said, you've been great. Shall we go back to your place or mine?'

He hesitated. 'Both. Do you mind, ducks? It'll be better. I have to get my head together, make a few notes. I'll be lousy company anyway.'

'I wouldn't mind, all the same,' she said. 'But I do understand. Take me home, then, and let me give you some coffee there. You're not enjoying this.' She looked round the restaurant, a cheerful place full of busy people, with a piano making very agreeable noises and a subdued hum of contented chatter, and sighed. 'We'll come back here afterwards, when it's all sorted out and we know you're clear. We'll have fun, hmm?'

'That's a date,' he said gratefully, waving for the bill. 'Ta for being so good to me, George.' He made a little gesture, flicking his thumb and forefinger at the invisible brim of the hat he was not wearing, and she could have wept, it was so brave.

In a way, she told herself when she got to the hospital next morning, it had been better that Gus had gone off to his own flat alone. Like him, she had needed to think about what she would do and how she would do it; and she had started by listing questions she would ask Mike Urquhart.

First, had he any idea what the CIB team were up to? Could he find out if he hadn't?

Second, were there any documents lying around in the big room where Gus had worked when he was at Ratcliffe Street, with Sergeant Salmon and the two DCs, Bannen and Lipman? She was proud of herself for remembering their names, and had written them carefully in the ring-binder notebook she prepared for her efforts on Gus's behalf. The first page had a list of all the police personnel who might have some knowledge of the case Gus had been working on. She was quite sure, she had told herself soon after Gus had gone, that the reason for this attempt to fit him up lay in the work he had been doing. She had suggested as much to him on the way back to her flat after supper and he'd produced a sort of grunt of assent.

'What other reason could there be?' he'd said, then lapsed into silence; and he was right. What other possible reason was there for someone gunning for Gus except the possibility that he was getting too close to something important?

She phoned the nick at nine-thirty sharp, hoping to catch Mike before he was sent out on some case or other, but giving him time to get in late. He'd put in a lot of overtime recently and might in consequence be indulging himself a little in the mornings. She'd planned it right and that made her absurdly pleased with herself.

'Hello, Dr B.,' he said, his voice subdued.

'You've heard, then?' she said.

'The place is alive with it,' he said. 'It's gone round like a brush fire. Is the Guv all right?'

'He's coping,' she said. 'Mike, I need some help.'

He sounded alarmed. 'Again?'

'It's all right. I told Gus I'd be asking you.'

'Oh.'

'So will you help me? Not me, really. It's Gus. I have to try to find out what I can about what's going on, who's accusing him, and what for, so that we can get some sort of defence together.'

There was a little silence and then he said uncomfortably, 'I'm no' sure this is a good time to talk. Or the right place.'

'No,' she said. 'You're probably right. Look, maybe – Let's see the list of today's – Yes, I thought I saw one. There was a hit and run yesterday and there's some argument about whether the victim was hit from the front or the side. It makes a difference to the statement of the driver, it seems. Are you able to come and represent the police when I do the PM?'

'A hit and run? What's the name?'

'Um . . . Leopardi, Vittorio Leopardi. Man of seventy.'

'I'll look. Hold on.'

When he came back he sounded a little more cheerful. 'It's supposed to be Morley but he hates PMs. So I've told him I'll do it for him, if he takes on a pile of phone calls I'm supposed to do. He thinks I'm mad, but that's all right. What time?'

'Ten-fifteen,' she said. 'Get here as early as you can so that we can talk properly.'

'Right away, is it?' he said, speaking a little more loudly. 'Right, if that's the way it is, Dr B., I'll be on my way. Sorry to delay you.' And the phone rattled in her ear. She grinned. A good man, Urquhart. Setting up his alibis as neatly as may be for the benefit of possible listeners; though who would know better how to do it, after all? She went hurriedly to speak to Sheila about the day's work before taking herself down to the mortuary where Danny was sorting out the PM room ready for the hit-and-run victim.

Mike arrived before she had changed. She came out of her cubicle, her rubber apron flapping against her legs in a comfortingly familiar way, to find him outside. She smiled at him warmly.

'Bless you for coming so quickly, Mike. We can talk in Danny's cubby hole till ten-fifteen. I can't start before then because Harold Constant's down to attend this one too for the coroner's office and he'll not understand if I'm half finished when he gets here. I take it you had an audience when you spoke to me?'

'Only at the end,' he assured her. 'The Inspector came by.'

'Oh, him,' she said darkly, then shook her head. 'Gus thinks very highly of him.'

'We all do, really,' Mike said. 'He's a bad-tempered bloke and you could shake him, sometimes, but he's all right.'

'Well, we'll see,' she said, dismissing Rupert Dudley from her thoughts. 'Mike, tell me, what's the word on the street? What are they saying round the nick?'

He looked gloomy. 'It's all over the place that the Guv's in the crap and it's growing with every word you hear. As I understand it, there was a complaint laid that he had taken money after threatening someone he'd put 'em away.'

'But why would he do that? Doesn't everyone know he's got all the money he needs, or, more to the point, wants?'

'I said that, but, as some of the others are saying, money does strange things to people.' He shook his head sagely. 'The more they get the more they want. It's like an addiction.'

'That's crap,' George said loudly, 'as far as Gus is concerned.'

'So I said, as did a lot of the others. But some of them — Look, you asked me what people are saying. It's no use arguin' wi' me when you dinna like what I tell you!'

She simmered down at once. 'Sorry. So what leads have you got on it?'

'Well, according to Molly Ledger — she's one of the civilian clerks who works with the Guv and she's been doing some work with his team as well as with the CIB fellas — according to her, the informants include a policeman.'

She stared at him, aghast. 'A police — but how? Who?'

'That's what I asked when she told me. She says she doesn't know who. It was on one of the statements. The letter that came in said that the Guv, in the presence of another officer, had taken the money from the informant after warning him that he could be prosecuted for breaking rules regarding his premises. Something to do with safety on the site. Also that he'd shut his eyes to some dirty business to do with a load of goods that had been hi-jacked. It's very complicated, anyway, Molly said, and it was made even harder to understand because she just had to put some corrections into the report that was already on the computer. She hadn't much time to do it in and she was supervised all through by the head of the civilian clerks, so she couldn't read the rest of it the way she usually would have done, but she did pick up that much. After that I did some checking on my own account. I couldna discover the name of the policeman, but did find out – well, anyway, I did some checking. But it was no' easy. Everyone's pretty burned up about it. I mean, who would behave like that from our lot? If someone went bad and mucked in with someone else who was bending the rules, I'd understand that. But to pretend to join in and then shop your mate –'

She felt cold suddenly. 'Is that what they're saying?'

'Some of them.'

'So they believe Gus has gone bad?'

He looked very unhappy. 'There're always people who want to think the worst of everyone. Especially someone who's popular. And rich. And he's got a sharp tongue on him, the Guv. He's made a few people smart, I can tell you, and they're the ones who're enjoyin' all this the most and saying things about smoke and fire. You know how folks are.'

'I know how they are,' she said grimly. 'Listen, Mike, let me tell you what I need and you tell me if you can get it. I know you've already tried to find out, but I really have to know who the civilian informant is.'

'Och, I can tell you that,' he said surprisingly.

She stared and shook her head. 'You can? How? I thought you said –'

'I said I couldna find out the name of the policeman who was fingering him. But I did find out who the civilian was. He's called Lenny Greeson.'

'Lenny – Good God! It can't be!'

It was his turn to look startled. 'You know him?'

'I know his name, but he couldn't have made a complaint. It was he who gave Gus the money, sure, but –'

Mike actually changed colour. 'Are you saying this man did give the Guv – Jesus!'

'It's all right,' she said impatiently. 'There's a perfectly good reason.' And she explained it. He listened with great concentration and then very slowly shook his head.

'It sounds a bit, well, far-fetched,' he said. 'Or it would to anyone who didn't know the Guv.'

'Precisely. Knowing him as I do, it's exactly what the crazy bastard would do – lend someone the money to prove he's got a business that will cost more to Gus when he buys it from him. It's bad business, of course it is, but it's the sort of decent thing Gus would do, especially as he's known the guy's family for ever. And now you say Greeson insists the money was got from him with menaces? And that there was a policeman involved too? It's the craziest thing I've ever heard!'

'Well, there it is on the charge sheet. I've seen what I wasna supposed to. But I went prowling. It's not that difficult to find out what you want to know if you're sensible about it.'

'I'm going to talk to that man,' she said, very determinedly. 'But I can't till after he's been interviewed by the CIB. I imagine he will be? Can you find out for me when they've been there?'

'This morning,' Mike said. 'They were going this morning. I heard them talking before they left the nick. I – we – I was in the next office. And –'

'If you stand with your ear to the wall you can hear?' she said, her eyes glinting with laughter.

Mike was very dignified. 'Something like that. Anyway, they were going this morning.'

'Then it's OK for me to go this afternoon,' she said and got to her feet. 'I'll need an address.'

'I'll get it for you,' he promised. 'Anything else?'

She stood thinking and then nodded. 'Get me what information you can about the people who've been working with Gus, will you? The Sergeant: Salmon, Bob Salmon. And Bannen, he was another. Doug, I think?'

'I think so, yeah.'

'And Lipman. I can't remember his first name.'

'Peter,' Mike said. 'They're all right, I reckon. I've shared lunch and so forth with 'em a few times. Seem all right to me. Gil Morley was a trainee with Bannen, he says he's a good chap. And some of the others say they remember Lipman from Hammersmith when he was working there.'

'Does anyone know Salmon?'

Mike shook his head. 'He's older than average,' he said. 'He doesna fit in with any of the sets we've got at Ratcliffe Street. Keeps himself to himself a good deal. Anyway, I'll get what I can. Is that all?'

'I doubt it, but I'll let you know.' She was on her way to the door, looking up at the clock. It was getting late and she could hear Harold Constant's voice out in the corridor. She stopped and came back. 'Yes, there is one more thing,' she said slowly.

'Anyone I know?'

'Mmm.' She looked at him thoughtfully. 'That man Gus was meeting at the pub in Poplar. Gus said he knows everyone and everyone knows him. Well, that might come in useful. And I don't suppose the CIB lot'll know about him, or if they do, they won't think of talking to him because he won't seem to have any links with this charge. But he may be useful. So let me have his address too, will you? Do you know it?'

He laughed. 'No, I don't. But I know a man who does.'

'Great. Come on. We'll cut up this guy waiting for me now, and then you be on your way, and get me that stuff as fast as you can.'

'How fast?' He was strolling along the corridor beside her.

'Oh, half past one'll do,' she said. 'I can get away this afternoon at two, so I want to have both addresses by then at the very latest, but half past one'd be better. Then I can plan it more easily, maybe make a phone appointment.'

'Half past one? In three hours' time? Do me a favour, Dr B.'

'Oh, all right,' she said. 'I won't rush you. I can hang on till half past two, if I must, I suppose. But no later!'

And she led the way into the post-mortem room, leaving him to follow her as best he could as he scribbled the notes of what she wanted in his pocket book. Working with George, he realized, could be quite an experience.

18

'It's called the Chargeable Chippy,' Mike said when he phoned her with the full address at two thirty-five. 'Because of where it is. You'll see. And I've done remarkably well to get that much.'

'Have the CIB people been already? Is there any risk they'll still be there?'

'I don't know if they've been there,' he said. 'I know they went off to see Lenny Greeson, but not necessarily at the chip shop. It's not possible to find out everything.'

'Shit,' she muttered under her breath, but then as Mike asked, 'What?' said more loudly, 'Nothing. I suppose I'll just have to take a chance. Gus was worried that I might be seen to be interfering with police work.'

'If they find you're digging around, you can be sure they would say that,' Mike said.

'You're a great comfort. Here, I've an idea. What sort of car are they using?'

'Eh? Oh, a Volvo. Estate. They carry a lot of their gear around with 'em, by the look of it. Their own laptops and portable faxes. It's an amazin' amount o' stuff.'

'What sort? Colour and so forth?'

'Hold on. I'll find out.' The phone clattered as he dropped the handset and she waited impatiently.

'It's a metallic grey,' he reported when he came back. '330 XOY, a G reg.'

'Not a police car, then.'

'It might be. They're not all black and white with blue lights, you know.'

'Well, I'll look out for it. If it's there, I'm away. If not, I'll risk it. Thanks, Mike. Leave any other info on my answer-phone, OK? I'll go over there now. Er . . . Mike?'

'Uhuh?'

'Wish me luck.'

'You're going to need it,' he said and hung up.

The shop, when she found it, was surprising. Used as she was to Gus's rather handsome establishments, glittering with chrome and engraved glass windows, this one was decidedly shabby. The outside displayed peeling plum-coloured paint with lettering picked out in a particularly bilious green, and the windows were steamed and streaked with grease. No handsome extractors to keep the atmosphere sweet inside here, she thought. The name of the place made sense when she saw where it was, a few doors up from the corner of Chargeable Lane in Barking Road, a bare fifteen minutes drive from the hospital, even in thick traffic, through the new tunnel. She sat looking at the place, sitting quietly at the steering wheel of her little car, watching.

It was now almost three in the afternoon but the shop was still open and dealing with lunchtime trade. It smelled rather pleasant and she thought, it doesn't look that good but the food may be OK, and was suddenly aware that she hadn't lunched. She slid the car into gear and drove round the corner into Chargeable Lane to park.

There was no sign of a metallic-grey Volvo Estate in the main road, and she scrutinized every car she passed in the tangle of streets that lay behind Chargeable Lane. By the time she had assured herself she was safe from any prying eyes, parked neatly behind a sizeable van, and walked back, the door of the shop was closed. She swore under her breath. Had she missed her chance? But there was someone behind the high fronted counter, and he looked up as she rattled the door appealingly and nodded and came round to open it.

'Am I too late?' she asked innocently. 'I was just passing and I thought . . .'

'I gotta bitta cod left. Nice tail bit. An' a few chips, ya? I fix?'

He was a round man in every respect: his belly, his shoulders, his face, his eyes. He was dark-skinned, dark-eyed and dark-haired and his accent was heavily Greek Cypriot.

As he bustled around behind his counter, shovelling the fish into a split paper bag and then putting a couple of scoops of rather sad-looking chips on top of it, she studied the place. Inside was a little more prepossessing than outside. There were a row of stools and a long shelf, covered in red plastic, on the far wall, where obviously those who preferred to eat on the premises could perch, a computer game which hummed and pinged to itself frenetically in a corner, and posters everywhere. Pictures of fish jostled with advertisements for Tizer and White's Lemonade and lists of the foods available: *Fried Cod, Fried Haddock, Fried Plaice, Fried Skate, Fried Saveloys, Fried Chicken* ... on and on in a litany of artery-clogging specialities ending in a bleak *Pickled Onions fifty pence*. She wouldn't have been surprised to find that they were fried too.

Behind the counter with its row of fryers and its hot glass-sided display unit in which the remains of the day's fry waited listlessly, the tiled walls and shelves offered vividly coloured tins and bottles of drink and packets of tartare sauce in nasty little plastic envelopes, while the counter itself bore bottles of watery vinegar and large battered aluminium salt shakers. Above all of it was a hand-drawn and rather wobbly image of a mermaid, against which someone had scribbled: *Vital statistics, thirty-eight, twenty-six, seven-and-six a pound.*

'That's cute.' She pointed at it and the man, who was now wrapping her lunch in a large sheet of yellowish paper, looked over his shoulder.

'We get rid soon. Next week, you come back, all clean and nice.' He sniffed. 'Not so nice now. Next week you see, we make good.'

'Oh?' She lingered as he slapped the parcel, which was already showing patches of grease on it, on to the high counter ready for her. 'Is Lenny going to get the place redecorated, then?'

'Oo?' He looked at her suspiciously, then said, 'That'll be two-ninety.'

'Lenny,' she said and began to rifle through her shoulder bag for her purse, deliberately not finding it. 'Lenny Greeson. The owner.'

'Oh. Not owner. My mamma's the owner.'

She looked at him with her brows creased. 'I was told that it was Lenny Greeson?'

'No such person 'ere,' he announced. 'Two-ninety, pliz. You got change? If not, I got change.' He held out a large red hand and glared at her.

She opened her mouth to speak and then turned sharply as a thin voice behind her said, 'Can I help you?'

The woman who stood there was as round as the man behind the counter, but looked considerably older. Her eyes were sharp and watchful and she had a filled tooth that glittered a little on the left-hand side of her mouth when she spoke. 'You lookin' for someone?'

'Well ...' George set three pound coins down on the counter. The man snatched them with a sort of relief and rang up the till. 'It's not important. I mean, I just thought ... A friend of mine told me about this place. Said it was the best fish and chips for miles around, and I was just passing. My friend said that the man who owned it was a friend of his. I should say hello.'

'You're an American,' the little woman said accusingly.

'Well, yes.' George smiled disarmingly. 'My friend isn't though. He's English.'

'Me, I lived in America. Pittsburgh. Learned to speak English good there.' And indeed the woman did have a tinge of a familiar accent. 'Your friend is wrong. This place belongs to me and my son. Nick, my son. Me, I'm Agape. My family, they call me Eppy. Not Nicky. He calls me Mamma.'

George blinked. It seemed unnecessary information to give to a passing customer, she thought somewhere at the back of her mind. I wonder why? Because she's anxious, her mind answered her, and she felt stronger.

'Oh? Well, very nice,' she said and looked at the parcel of

fish and chips. Suddenly she wasn't so hungry any more. What had seemed an agreeable smell when she first noticed it had become thick and cloying.

'So, you tell your friend, the owners here is us. We make it all very handsome, we do. We paint next week, we got new equipment coming, big fryers, not rubbish like this.' She banged on the top of the hot display unit contemptuously. 'Soon we really have the best fish in all the East End. Not some of your rubbish like the other stuff you see.' She sniffed. 'Big place, glass fronts, very fancy, lousy fish.'

George, who knew at once the sort of shop to which the woman referred, felt a great wave of loyalty arise and almost swamp her. 'Oh, I don't know,' she said shortly. 'I've had fish from a place at Aldgate which is just fabulous, to die for.'

The woman stared and then cackled. 'To die for? Yeah, to die for. Belly-ache it gives you, to die for!'

George opened her mouth to argue and then closed it. This wasn't, after all, the purpose of her visit.

'So, when did you take over from Lenny?' she said casually, looking at Nick. She didn't turn her back on Eppy, but was certainly smiling at Nick when she said it, and it seemed to affect him. He had been staring at her; she knew all too well the sort of glint he had in his eyes while he did so, and capitalised on it.

'Two weeks,' he said without thinking. 'Two weeks. Is good, yeah? Next we make it good lookin', make it smart.'

'Nicky, shut up,' the woman said. She glared at George. 'What for you askin' questions? You the police or what?'

George looked at her and raised her brows. 'Oh, have they already been here?' she said with an air of innocence.

'For why should they come here?' the woman said. She seemed to expand the way George had seen angry frogs enlarge when she had disturbed them during childhood fishing trips. 'Nothing wrong here, I told them, nothing here.'

'Then tell me where Lenny's gone,' George said, choosing the direct approach. The pussyfooting was getting her nowhere but thoroughly irritated. 'My friend asked me to give him a message if I was passing and I'm passing. Where do I find him?'

'Dunno,' said Nick, for she was looking at him again, at the same time as his mother said loudly, 'He don't want to be found!'

'Oh?' George turned back to her. 'He told you that?'

'I know.' Eppy smote herself hard on the breast in a way that made George want to wince, and looked even more puffed up. 'He sold, he gone, is finished. You take your fish, you go, you're finished,'

'I don't think so,' George said. 'I don't think that fish looks very fresh.' She began to improvise a little wildly. 'I'm from the Council, actually, you see. That was why I was passing. I have to check on food hygiene. I don't think this fish is very hygienic. I think maybe I should go back to the Council and see to it they send their inspector round. The one who charges the fines.'

The woman was now almost goggle-eyed with rage. 'Me, not hygienic? Me, what buys six bottles bleach and disinfectant every week? Me, what works my fingers to the bone like a dog? You say my fish not hygienic?'

'We had a few complaints a while ago,' George said. 'Let me remember. Would it be . . . three weeks ago?'

'Then not us,' Eppy said. Her eyes lost some of their panic. 'Not us. That was the one before.'

'Ah? So it was Lenny then? He sold to you?' George smiled benevolently at the woman, who stared back, somewhat nonplussed, and then seemed to lose interest in the whole conversation. She shrugged.

'We come here two weeks ago. There was a debt owed us and it was paid two weeks ago. So, we come here, take over, and next week we –'

'I know. Clean up. Decorate,' George said. 'So, where did the man you bought from go to?'

'Oh, we don't –' Nicky began behind the counter but his mother bristled at him.

'What do you know, idiot?' she shrieked and then burst into a flood of Greek at which Nicky began to shout back equally

174

incomprehensibly, but clearly in self-defence. George put her hands to her ears and then shouted herself into the hubbub. It worked. They turned to her.

'So, we don't know nothin'. Like Nicky said. We don't know nothin'. The man isn't here when we come. We get the key, come in, take over, the customers not even see any difference, except the food is better. And next week, when we –'

'Decorate. Yes.' George cut in. 'So, you don't have any information about anything? OK, OK, I believe you. Where did you get the key from? Who is the person who deals with the money and the lease and the rest of it?'

Eppy shrugged, her eyes now hooded as she kept her eyelids down and her chin up, staring at George from beneath her lashes. 'Me, I'm just a simple woman, a fish fryer, what do I know of such things? I got the key in the post. We do all that we have to do with letters, with faxes, with phone calls. And it's none of your business. The police, it can be theirs, but I told them I didn't know and they went away this morning happy. I didn't know nothing. If they can believe me, why can't the Council believe me?'

'The police were here this morning, then? I thought so,' George said and nodded in satisfaction. 'And you told them the same things you've told me?'

Eppy scowled. 'I tell them how it is. I tell you how it is. Now go, huh? Enough. You go.'

'In a moment,' George said. She stood there thinking and the two of them watched her warily. After a while she said, 'I think you'll remember soon who it was you bought this place from. Or rented it from, or whatever. I think maybe you need to think about why you can't tell me, hmm? I think maybe a little money will help you think. What do you say to that?'

'Money?' the old woman said. 'How much money?'

'Enough,' George said and did some rough additions in her head. She had about fifty pounds in her purse, no more. Would it be regarded as bribing witnesses to give them money to get information? How could it? She wasn't bribing them to tell her. Just helping them think, and remember a few facts.

Fifty pounds was a lot to lose, but Gus would make sure it was all right. Gus didn't have money problems. And then she thought, but I can't let him pay for this investigation. It could criminalize him or something. Shit. It's going to cost me, all on my own. And I haven't paid the car costs this month yet. Oh, *shit*.

'Enough to you ain't the same enough for me,' Eppy said after a while. 'Show me.'

George sighed and got out her purse. She pulled out the four ten-pound notes and the couple of creased fivers and set them neatly on the counter. 'Fifty,' she said. 'Just for the name of the man you got this place from.'

The woman looked at it and then at Nick and he looked back. It was as though they were talking to each other. George looked from one to the other, trying to get hold of some vestige of the conversation, but failed utterly. And then Eppy reached for the money and slid it off the counter in one smooth movement. George didn't see where it was after that. It just seemed to disappear.

'Estate agent,' she muttered. 'Docking Berths. In Millwall. Now I gotta go. Work to do.' And she turned and scuttled away, much like one of the crabs on the poster above her head, to disappear behind a bead curtain at the back of the shop.

'Me too,' Nick said hurriedly as George turned to him, her mouth open to speak, and he vanished as quickly as his mother had, leaving just the swinging bead curtain behind to remind George he had ever been there.

She sighed and turned to go, leaving the packet of fish and chips on the counter. That was the last thing she wanted after standing there smelling it for so long. It would be cold by now, anyway.

'Chargeable Chippy?' the young man behind the desk said. 'Oh, yes. Freehold. Very nice to get a freehold these days. Even in Canning Town. Well, as near as makes no matter to Barking. Very nice.'

'Worth much?' George said casually.

He looked judicious. 'Not over the top. Good services, nice position if a bit, well, not top drawer, but for the purpose it's used for, very suitable. Oh, around a hundred and fifty K.'

'Hmm,' George said, trying to look as judicious as though she really were looking for a shop with a flat over it. 'But hardly the place for a shop that specializes in dried flower arrangements? My partner does them,' she added swiftly as he showed interest and opened his mouth to ask questions. 'I'm just the dogsbody, you know. Checking up on available premises and so forth.'

'You ought to go further west,' the young man said earnestly. 'A lot further back west into the real Docklands. Near the newspaper offices. They'll love a place that does dried flowers. All those fashion pages, you know. And presents for the missus when they've been working late, slaving all day over a hot secretary.' He glanced up at her, saw the absence of admiration for his wit, and moved swiftly on. 'I could do you a lovely little place in Tobacco Dock or down here – Look.' He had a map out and was thudding it with a short nail-bitten finger. 'Not enormous premises, but for very little more than a hundred K or so, you'll get something worth *having*. Peppercorn rent for the leasehold, believe me, peppercorn, considering the money you'd make out of your business.'

'I'll think about it,' George said, and smiled, thinking, lying bastard, as she did so. Do I look such a fool? Remember, though, you're pretending to be one. Stop being so silly. 'Tell me, how come this place' – she pointed to the part of the map that took in Chargeable Lane – 'is available freehold? You said that was rare.'

He shook his head sadly. 'It's a leftover from the old days. People used to buy their premises and hand 'em on down a family. This place was a family business, fish and chips, you know? Very old East End that is. Not the new Docklands set-up at all.'

'Hmm. And they own it still? I wonder why they're selling.' She opened her eyes widely at him, looking innocent and enquiring and as American as she knew how. Estate agents, in her experience, were good at despising foreigners.

He fell for it, and became expansive, leaning back in his chair and tucking his fingers into a garish copy of an Albert watch chain that was stretched across his meagre front. 'I wish I knew,' he said. 'It's a puzzle, this one. It's been bought in for management by a company who got it from the people that used to own the freehold. We're to let and administer it. They brought the first tenants with them.'

'Wasn't that an odd thing to do?'

He shrugged, 'Well, some owners are! I think we'd have got them better tenants, but maybe they thought they'd do better. If they'd come to us first, of course – but there you go. They didn't. Never mind. We'll collect the rent for them, watch over the place, and eventually they'll see the error of their ways and let us deal with the property as it should be dealt with.' He seemed to stretch with pride. 'And then they'll see some selling going on! Times have been hard for us but the recession's bottoming out. Everyone says so, and we at Docking Berths'll show everyone else the way to make the best of it.'

'Well,' she said. 'All this is very interesting but I suppose I'd better be on my way.'

'Don't forget your details.' He was all eagerness at once. 'There're some lovely properties there, really lovely. We'll be ready and willing and more than able to negotiate for you when you've chosen. Just pop in any time or call me – here's my card, mobile number on it too, of course – and I'll be here waiting to jump at yours and your partner's bidding!'

'My partner?' George said blankly, forgetting her cover for a moment.

'The girl with the dried flowers?' He looked perplexed, but she laughed merrily.

'Of course. My partner. That partner. I thought you meant my boyfriend.' She simpered sickeningly and turned to go. At the door she stopped and smiled at him. 'By the way, who are the company that own the Chargeable Chippy property?'

He was already back at his desk, thinking of something else. 'Mmm?' he said vaguely. 'Oh, that's Copper's. Copper's

Properties Limited.' He frowned and looked at her sharply. 'Why do you want to know?'

'Oh, I don't know,' she said, still smiling sweetly at him. 'I just wondered.' And she went, closing the office door smartly behind her.

19

'So, how do I track down a company which isn't listed in the phone books? I know it isn't, because I've looked,' she said, reaching over and putting some more mashed potatoes on his plate. He seemed not to notice. He was sitting staring at the opposite wall of his little kitchen with unfocused eyes. 'Gus?'

'Mmm?'

'I said, I have to track down this company. The people who own Lenny's property now. They might be able to give me a lead on where he is. But they're not listed anywhere.'

'I don't understand it,' Gus said with a childish fretfulness that made him seem very vulnerable. She put down her own fork and went round the table to stand behind him and rub the back of his neck. It was tightly knotted under her fingers and it took some effort to help him relax.

'I know you don't. Neither do I. Yet,' she said. 'Nor will we till we get the facts somehow, and then –'

'I mean, *Lenny*. Of all people to shop me. Lenny! It's not possible. I'm bloody scared for him, you know that?' The muscles tightened again as he turned and looked up at her. 'Do you hear what I'm saying, George? Lenny's in such big trouble, I feel it in every bone of my body. He'd never do such a thing to me. Not to Alf Hathaway's son! It's just not possible.'

'You think Mike got it wrong?' she said quietly, and he shook his head miserably.

'I don't see how he could have. He's a sensible fella, Mike

Urquhart. Not the sort to make cock-ups from not checking his facts. If he says Lenny was the informant then he bloody was. Anyway, he got the right address, didn't he?'

'Yes,' George said. 'He did.'

'And these Cypriot people you talked to had been there . . .'

'Only a week or two.'

'Yes. So . . . Oh, shit, it's true all right. Someone's pushed Lenny out of his business and his home and there's no way he'd have gone of his own free will. He's in some sort of trouble. He's got to be.'

'Gus, don't get annoyed if I suggest something?' She said it carefully, knowing how close he was to the edge. 'Let me just make a few suggestions?'

'Why should that annoy me? Isn't it what we're both trying to do? Make suggestions about how to climb out of this hellpit I'm in?' He sounded savage and she ached to hold him, but knew he wouldn't tolerate that.

'OK. So, Lenny was desperately short of money for himself, for his debtors, for his brother –'

'I'd got that sorted,' Gus snapped. 'I told you all that. Why the hell else am I in such a mess now?'

'Perhaps it wasn't sorted. Perhaps he was . . . Well, I saw the place. It's not like yours, all inviting and glittering. It's a real . . .' She hesitated.

'I know. Greasy spoon. But people in these parts have more sense than to just use their eyes. They know quality when they meet it, and Lenny was good. I'd offered him a job often enough as a manager and head fryer for me, but he was always bloody independent. Wanted to have his own place like his Dad before him. Wouldn't work for other buggers, he always said.'

'Well, all right. He had his regulars. But to make the sort of money he was paying back to you, surely he'd have needed more than a few regulars? A lot more? I went there at lunchtime and there was no sign of a crowd.'

'Then the word had gone round that Lenny's not there any more.' Gus was stubborn. 'They've started going someplace else.'

She sighed. 'Let me go on trying, Gus. Suppose you're wrong and the shop wasn't taking that much money. He had paid off his debts but now he was in hock to you –'

'Well, suppose he was?' Gus interrupted truculently. 'I wasn't going to dun him. I wasn't even expecting any interest, for Chrissakes! He didn't have any cause to worry about me.'

'But he was an independent-minded sort of guy,' she said. 'You said that. Anyway, we're only supposing. Let me finish supposing, huh? Suppose someone came along who told him that he'd solve all his problems. Or, wait a minute . . .' She sat up more straight. 'I'm thinking on my feet so bear with me. Suppose someone came along and *threatened* him? I don't know what with or how, but suppose – and the only way he could resist them was to hand over his business and –'

'No,' Gus said flatly. 'He'd never just hand over his business. If he'd been like that, he'd have handed it over to Don. Or me, even. He was trying to *sell*, remember? At a good price. That's why he borrowed. All that mattered to him was to get out on his own. He has this notion he could build up a chain like mine, only south of the water. There's no way he'd just hand over his main asset, George. I keep telling you that's why he borrowed from me, for Gawd's sake! To maximize his assets. You're barking up a hell of a wrong tree.'

'But Gus, there must be something in his life he'd put in front of all that! A wife? Children?'

'Lenny isn't the marrying sort,' Gus said shortly. 'And he never had any regular blokes, either. So that's out.'

'Other relations maybe? This brother, is he married? Does he have children?'

'Don's straight,' Gus said. 'He never married but he's straight. I've never heard of any children – or none he admitted to.'

'Well, anyway, he cares about his brother, doesn't he? Lenny, I mean. Wouldn't a threat to Don be enough to make Lenny cave in?'

'What sort of threat?' Gus was listening more carefully now.

She shrugged. 'I don't know! But suppose you were getting too close to someone in this investigation you've been on –'

'I was getting more and more information,' he said. 'I had no idea who was in the middle of it all, but there was no doubt in my mind that I was dealing with one hell of a big organization. We've never had the mob here the way they do in the States, all those Godfathers and so forth, but we've had our villains who like to control everything – the Krays and their kind. And it was clear to me that we had that sort of American set-up here on the patch.' He scowled. 'And now I'm off my own bleedin' case and those three'll never sort it out on their own. The whole bloody lot'll clear up the evidence we'd collected, smooth it all over and we won't have a shred of anything to take them to court on.'

'Which is why they needed to get rid of you,' she said triumphantly. 'Can't you see it? The best way to get you out of their hair is to trump up some sort of charge against you. With you fitted up and out of the frame then they can do their tidying in peace. And they chose Lenny to get to you. They found out somehow that you'd be a – that you'd respond to an appeal from him. Doesn't it make sense?'

He looked at her for a long time. 'I suppose it does,' he said at last. 'I told you. I'm scared for Lenny. Because these sort of people have as much – well, they'll do what they want to anyone. And if they did find a way to fit up Lenny so he laid this complaint against me, they'd have to get him out of the way before anyone could question him.'

'Which is why he's vanished. And to find out where he's vanished to, the best way is to talk to the people who own the business now. Like I was saying. So, how do I find out who owns a set-up like this Copper's Properties?'

'Companies House,' he said. 'In the City.' He was clearly abstracted, thinking hard. 'Has anyone else tried to find Don, do you know?'

'The brother?' George said. 'Not me, nor Mike, to my knowledge. I can't say what the CIB people are doing. Why should they? Do they know about him – the CIB guys?'

'Who knows? Maybe. If I was one of 'em, I'd have found out by now, but I'm not, and who knows if they're any good?' He looked sombre then. 'Though I s'pose they are. They usually choose the best blokes for jobs like that.'

'Well, we don't know if they know, but *we* do. How do we find him to see if he knows where Lenny is?'

'It shouldn't be that hard. You check the betting shops on the patch and the race meetings around the country and put someone on to going after him,' Gus said. 'Tell Mike to do that –' He scowled. 'You can't.'

'I know I can't,' she said. 'Nor can you. I'm right, aren't I? While the CIB are doing their job you have to keep out of the way, and so does everyone else.'

'Oh, God,' he said violently. 'I think I'll go out of my mind if this goes on!'

She risked putting her arms about him but he shrugged her off.

'No time for canoodlin',' he said. 'Got to think. Look, I'll go to Companies House –'

'But Gus, if you're found out –'

'Even if they know I've gone there, they won't be able to do anything. I've got my own company, remember? I've got a business to run while all this crap is going on. I've as much right as anyone else to be there. Leave that to me. At least it's something I can do. And …' He hesitated. 'Forget the bit about looking for Don Greeson. We'll see first what we can get out of this company.'

'But I could try the betting shops,' she said, 'couldn't I?'

'No!' He said it very loudly. 'You go around betting shops looking and the whole world'll know something's up. You're not precisely the sort they usually see in places like that. Anyway, it mightn't be necessary. Once we've talked to this company. What sort of company is it? Did the estate agent say?'

'Only that it's called Copper's Properties.'

'Hmm,' Gus said. 'An interesting name. Well, I'll get on with that, then.' He was out of the kitchen and reaching for his jacket, which he'd left on his bed, by the time she caught up with him.

'But Gus, for heaven's sake. It's half past eight in the

evening! They surely don't work there at this time of night! A City set-up?'

'I wasn't going straight there!' he said. 'I'm going to talk to a few other people on the patch about 'em first. See what I can get out of the local gossip. It's just as valuable as the stuff that's listed officially.'

'You can't,' she said. 'You know that could be misconstrued as interfering in the investigation. It'll have to wait till you can do it the legal way. You know that.'

He stared at her blearily, and then very slowly dropped his jacket on the bed.

'Yes,' he said. 'Yes, I suppose so.'

She had a lousy night. He refused to let her stay at his flat, telling her he was rotten company and was damned if he was going to drag her down with him into the miseries, and no matter how she argued that she'd be even more miserable on her own, he was determined. So she had driven home and spent the evening ostensibly watching television but actually turning over and over in her mind all the possibilities, and had gone to bed early.

Only to dream that Gus had set out to solve his own case and to watch helplessly as he was chased by blank-faced figures with knives and ropes in their hands – which were newly dissected ones from her own mortuary, with blood dripping from the fingertips – while she stood clinging to a shelf high above the scene, which was a town with streets laid out like a maze, and could not reach him to help. She had woken at last with a violent start and the dull sick feeling that comes with the hangover of ugly dreams. She had to go out to walk off her discomfort if she could.

The streets were already stirring, with people walking as purposefully as she was and a few joggers looking solemn and self-absorbed as they sweated their way past her, glazed eyes fixed ahead on some impossible goal. She envied them their single-mindedness. If only she had nothing better to do with her time than to run in silly clothes in that pointless fashion, how pleasant life would be. As it was she hunched her shoulders against the early sunshine, already hard and hot on her back, and walked on towards the hospital, thinking hard about Gus and what she might be able to do for him.

She had to face a thought that had been uncovered by her ugly dream and deal with it. The people who had set up Gus with this charge were capable, she feared, of doing more than just ruining his career. If, as she was now quite certain, all this had happened to Gus because someone somewhere wanted to protect himself against Gus's investigation, surely he wouldn't stop at destroying only a career? She felt cold and sick as she let the thought form completely. Could they, these shadowy someones she was seeking, could they – or he – attack Gus? Kill him even? Could he be found in a charred bed with his face burned off and –

She stopped quite still in the middle of the pavement and stared sightlessly ahead. That, she told herself, was an absurd thought to have come into her mind. She had told Mike she suspected there might be a serial killer involved in those two deaths by fire – and it seemed a long time now since her only concern had been to get hold of Gus and persuade him to take on those cases – but those deaths had been very similar. Both young women, both prostitutes – or at least earning their livings on the fringes of prostitution, and good livings at that – both living in expensive well-furnished homes.

But Gus wasn't a bit like them. If there was a serial killer at work, he would go for the same sort of victim and use the same MO. That was what gave such people the label of serial killer. Even if Gus were to be – hurt, was the only word she could bear to let into her mind now – even if Gus were to be hurt, it would be totally unconnected with those two cases.

And yet she had thought of them as part of this present mess. She frowned hard against the glitter that was increasing with the strength of the morning sun as she tried to sort out her feelings. If she had learned one thing in the last big cases she had worked on with Gus, it had been not to ignore the value of her own gut reactions. And this morning her gut had told her there was a link between the two deaths by fire and the charge against Gus that had been laid by Lenny. She didn't know why she had made the connection but she'd done so, and though she wouldn't talk to anyone about it – least of all to Gus himself, who always wanted evidence – she wouldn't forget it. She wouldn't be able to, she thought, with another frisson of fear. Risk to Gus's life was too painful to contemplate.

She began to walk again, a little more purposefully. There was much work to be done on the case, and done soon, and she chewed her lower lip as she thought about the lab and what was on the schedule there today. Tuesday: a busy day always, with specialist clinics like cardiology and endocrinology, which put a heavy pressure on the department for immediate assays and tests of various kinds. Yet somehow she had to get some time to herself. And then as the solution came to her she began to run towards the bus stop. The sooner she got over the river to the hospital, the better. She'd be waiting on Ellen's doorstep as soon as she got there. That she told herself wryly, remembering her long-ago days in the school operatic society, would provide a little corroborative detail to add verisimilitude to an otherwise bald and unconvincing narrative.

'How long for?' Ellen said. 'It won't be easy, you know. Alan hasn't been with us long, and –'

'Ellen, I really don't know.' She lied with all the fervour of total candour. 'All I can tell you is that she's my dearest friend and I really can't let her down. I've never sought compassionate time, ever, since I've been here, have I? Only been off sick once, that time a couple of years ago when I had a needle-stick injury in my hand that went bad. Surely you can give me a few days now.'

'I'll have to talk to the Professor,' Ellen said.

'You know as well as I do he won't argue. You're the Business Manager and you do more to run this directorate than the clinical people do.'

'And Mr Herne –'

'None of his business. We're running the lab – he runs his own job. As long as all the work is done, he's happy.'

'You think Alan can cope?'

'I'm sure he can,' George said, crossing mental fingers. 'It'll be good for him. And anyway, he won't be alone. He's got Sheila, who can be tiresome, I know, but is the heart and soul of the lab. There's nothing she doesn't know about what's going on and how to deal with it. And Jerry, of course.'

'Yes,' Ellen said dryly. 'There's always Jerry.'

'He's a great guy!' George said quickly. 'Really one of the best. Just a bit . . .'

'Bloody-minded,' Ellen said sweetly. 'Look, Dr Barnabas, if you must you must. And I do know that post-partum depression is hellish. My own sister had it. Cried for weeks.'

'This is more a post-partum psychosis,' George said. 'Her husband was in despair when he called me. She's threatening to kill her baby, the whole thing.'

'Shouldn't she be in hospital then?' Ellen looked at her sharply.

'Possibly. But I can't know till I get there and see for myself.'

'Yes . . . Well, all right. But please, leave a phone number so that we can reach you.'

'I'd rather not. It might cause disturbance to an already upset household if you ring at a difficult time. I'll – er – I'll call in regularly for any messages and problems.'

'But in emergencies, how will you know we need to talk to you?' Ellen said. 'I'll lend you a bleep, I think. Yes, that's the best thing. Not your usual one, but one of those outside ones we use for the district midwives. I'll get one out of the Human Resources people as soon as they get in. Can you hold on till then?'

George looked at her watch. 'I guess I'll have to,' she said. 'Anyway, I have to talk to the people in the lab and explain to them.' She was beginning to feel guilty about this tissue of complicated lies she was building up, but her guilt was well controlled by her gratitude that the scam was working so well. 'But I'll have to be on my way no later than nine.'

'Whereabouts in the country do they live?' Ellen was reaching into her desk drawer for a folder and not looking at her, which was just as well, because George hadn't thought about such a question and found herself scrabbling for an answer.

'Um – er – Chislehurst,' she said plucking the name out of some recess of her mind after a long moment, long enough to make Ellen look up at her in some surprise. 'That's it. Chislehurst.' She smiled widely at Ellen. 'I can never remember some of these English place names, even after a dozen years here.'

'I'd have thought it was as easy to remember Chislehurst as it was Poughkeepsie or Peoria,' Ellen said a little dryly, and for a dreadful moment George thought she had been caught out. But Ellen went on smoothly enough. 'Before you head for Kent, though, let me give you a quick update on the St Dymphna's situation.'

George, relieved, said quickly, 'Please do. I'm really concerned about that.'

And indeed she was. The thought of having the lab closed down was almost insupportable. But she was so used up worrying about Gus that she barely had the energy to worry about that too. She looked hopefully at Ellen. 'A reprieve?'

'Not precisely,' Ellen said. 'But definitely a stay of execution. It's gone to a sub-committee to consider – there are two people from St Dymphna's, one from the Region and two of our NEDs: Mickey Harlow and Lewis McCann. They'll need a few months before they come back with anything, especially as it's high summer and they'll all be sloping off on holiday any minute now. So there's time on our side. But the battle's still to win.'

'And we'll win it,' George said with a confidence she didn't feel. 'Thanks for being so understanding, Ellen.' She escaped, to hurry across the courtyard towards the lab, ashamed and exhilarated in equal measure. To have lied so successfully was part of her excitement, but most important of all was the fact that now she would be free to be a full-time battler on Gus's behalf. She'd get this bloody mess sorted, to use Gus's own language, if it killed her. And somewhere at the back of her mind a quiet little voice murmured: do you know, George, it just might at that? But she ignored it.

20

Before she left the lab, after making sure that Alan and Sheila knew all they needed to know to enable them to cope for the next week or so on their own (and Sheila swelled like an excited puffer fish at the thought of so long a time in which to bully everyone and get extra close to Alan Short) she called Mike Urquhart.

He listened in silence as she told him her plan as succinctly as she could, then continued to be silent as he digested it.

'I'm no' sure it's a great idea,' he said eventually. 'You're no' precisely experienced in such things, are you? And anyway –'

'Well then, you do it!'

'I canna possibly,' he said. 'I've got my own work. Inspector Dudley'd be down on me like a load o' manure if he thought I wasna busy about what he sent me to do. I'm interviewin' every Tom for miles around for leads on the burnings.'

'So, there you are. Someone has to. You can't. Gus can't. I must.'

'I canna see the compulsion,' he said a touch sharply. George made an exasperated sound through her teeth.

'Of course I must. I can't let these CIB people have it all their own way. They'll be looking for evidence against Gus, remember. I won't.'

'I know, but all the same –'

'I'm doing it,' she interrupted. 'Listen, I need that address, remember? Monty Ledbetter.'

'Oh, that, sure. I got it here. He's on the register. He's over at Gidea Park.'

He dictated it and George wrote it down. Then she asked, 'What register?'

'Eh?'

'You said, "he's on the register". What register?'

'Oh. They keep a list here of informers. People you can get a bit of guidance from, you know? That's all.'

'Oh.' She wasn't surprised. Gus had said Ledbetter knew everyone there was, so everyone knew him. 'So I should get a good deal of help from him. Thanks, Mike.'

'You're welcome,' he said. 'But for God's sake keep yourself out of trouble. If you need any back-up, call me.'

'Gladly. How?'

'You've got a point there. Look, I've got a portable phone of my own. I'll carry it as well as my usual communication stuff.' He recited the number at her and then said. 'Can I reach you?'

She gave him the number he'd need to put a message on her bleep and he noted it. 'I can't use my mobile phone, it's out of order. But the bleep'll work well enough.'

'All right. But take care – and good luck.'

'I need all of that I can get,' she said and rang off. Then she stood, thinking. Should she go straight from the hospital? She looked down at herself, at her neat pleated cotton skirt and polo shirt in dark blue, the ideal clothes to wear in summer under a white coat, and shook her head. She'd look like a cabbage in a rose garden dressed that way. It would have to be home first.

While she was changing – and it wasn't easy to find precisely the right gear for a day as hot as this was, and yet which sent the right messages – her phone rang. She left it, leaving it to the answering machine. If Ellen was checking up on her, she wasn't going to be caught. She grimaced at herself for reacting like a schoolkid playing truant, even though that was precisely what she was doing.

But it was Gus. She flew to the phone to intercept him as he began to leave a terse message and was just in time to stop him hanging up. 'Gus!' she said. 'I've taken the week off.'

'Eh? What are you up to?' He was immediately suspicious.

'No need to get paranoid! It's just that trying to work at Old East and deal with all this is too much. Old East has to do without my magical presence.' She wanted to get some sort of response from him that would show a glimmer of the old happy wicked Gus who laughed and joked his way through the most dire of experiences, but clearly he was too deeply sunk in anxiety. All he did was grunt.

'So, what are you going to do with all this free time?'

'Oh, this and that,' she said, suddenly aware of the pit she had dug for her own feet. 'I just want to be available to do anything that's useful. You tell me.'

To her gratitude he was diverted. 'Well, there is something, I suppose. You could get in touch with Monty Ledbetter for me. I'd call him myself but he's listed as one of my contacts at the nick and it might seem ... Well, it's better if I'm not seen to be going to him. If he talks to you, though, it might be OK. Will you do that for me?'

'Of course,' she said. 'I was going to talk to him anyway.'

'You what?' he said sharply. 'How do you mean?'

'I remembered you telling me he knew everyone so I thought he'd be useful. And I also thought the CIB blokes wouldn't know about him, so wouldn't talk to him, but –'

'But you were wrong. It's my guess they'll check on all my registered informants and talk to every bloody last one of them. Look, you'd better not call Monty after all. It was a bad idea of mine. You won't be able to prevent yourself getting too deeply involved, and I don't want to risk that. It could add to the mess. So lay off. I'll have to cope on my own somehow. I can't risk it.'

'But surely *I* could.'

'No!' He said it loudly and with a good deal of violence, but now she knew it for what it was; a form of panic, and certainly not anger directed at her. It was rage at the frustration of being caught in an iron network and unable to break free at any turn. It must feel to him, she thought suddenly, like being a character in one of those computer games, constantly being knocked back.

'All right.' she said peaceably. 'I'll do nothing to make problems for you, Gus.'

There was silence for a moment and then he sighed. 'I know, doll,' he said. 'Jesus, I know. Where would I be without you? Maybe what we ought to do is say to hell with all this. I'll leave the job and sell the business and you dump Old East and we'll retire to the South Seas, just you and me. We'll sit in the sun all day and make love all night.'

She wanted to weep again at his bravery. 'Sounds like hard work to me,' she said. 'When would I get my toenails painted?'

He managed the ghost of a laugh. 'Let that be the least of your worries, doll.' But then he sighed again. 'I'm going to Companies House, the way I promised I would, but –'

'No buts,' she said. 'I'll be waiting to hear from you. Take care, Gus.' She let her voice show her anxiety for him. It seemed to help because he sounded rather more like his old self when he responded.

'I'll look both ways when I cross the road and I won't take sweeties from any strangers, OK?'

'OK,' she said gratefully. She stood listening to the burr of the phone after he hung up, thinking. Was she doing the right thing in going against his wishes? Could it lead to more trouble for him? But she replaced the hand set and shook her head firmly at it. 'What else can I do?' she said aloud and went back to getting dressed.

She chose to start in the area where Lenny's shop was. She'd seen a betting shop almost opposite when she'd gone there, and there had to be more of them around. They were as common as pubs in this part of London, and heaven knew there were enough of those.

When she had plucked up the courage to pass the curtain that hung over the entrance she stopped by the door. She felt a frisson of unease as she looked round. It was a very alien sort of place for her to be in, for she had never had any interest in gambling. This place seemed to be the dreariest advertisement for it she'd ever seen. The walls were painted a dull cream and adorned with handwritten blackboards which carried information she didn't comprehend in the least, together with half a dozen TV screens, wall mounted, all blank. There were shelves round the walls with pens attached to the edges at intervals by short chains. There were burn marks from cigarettes along the edges of the shelves that gave them a scalloped look, and the place reeked of dead, sour tobacco. At the far end there was a counter set behind a grille pierced with speaking holes, and behind one of them she could see a humped figure. Looking braver than she felt she walked up to the counter.

'Hi there,' she said brightly.

'You're a bit early,' the humped figure said accusingly. 'First race today ain't till two o'clock at –'

'I'm not here to make a bet,' George said hastily.

The woman looked up at her doubtfully. She was about forty, tall and bulky, and had her dark hair pulled back into an incongruously girlish pony-tail. There was something vaguely familiar about her, but George couldn't quite think what it was. 'What do you want then?'

George took a deep breath and launched herself on her prepared tale, very aware at the back of her mind of how fluent a liar she had become.

'My name's Bridget Connors, you know, and I, like, work for an American company? I'm the London representative. We're based in Las Vegas and we deal with the casinos there, but I work here. My job is to recruit people who understand the British way of betting, you know, and especially how the horse-racing system works. So I advertised and I'd collected a lot of good people to interview, and the best of them were all listed on a floppy disk on my office computer, you know? And that goddamned computer just went down and I lost the lot! I mean the whole goddamn shebang. If the company finds out they'll fire me as sure as eggs and I'll never get another job here on account of I don't have a work permit for a British firm. And I have a friend here. I just couldn't bear to leave. I can't advertise again – the company'd find out, and I'd be in deep do-do. I just *have* to find the people. So I have this list of names and I thought, like, seeing they're into gambling, maybe you knew some of the people on it? That way I can pick up where we left off and interview them properly and maybe give them jobs.'

She smiled winsomely. 'We need some British talent real bad. My company is really hot, too, great jobs on offer. I sure hope you can help. It would just about break my heart if I got fired.'

She smiled again and prayed deep inside her head that the woman, who had sat lumpishly staring at her all through her breathless spiel without showing any reaction at all, would believe her. She had found her accent slipping into a highly stagey Southern drawl as she went on, and could only cross her fingers in the hope that the woman wouldn't know one American accent from another.

The woman still sat and stared at her and then sniffed. 'I know all there is to know about British betting,' she said. 'Gotta job for me?'

George hadn't expected that, foolishly, and had to think fast. 'Well, sure, maybe! Let me tell you about the job. It's well paid, but we have to ask our people to put in the hours, you know? Lot of hours. The gambling starts at eight a.m. and goes on till around three in the morning. And our company always has the same people all through to watch for cheats. They reckon they pay the rates so they can get folk to do that. You get to live in a dormitory, top of the hotel, with the others. It gets a touch hot in the summer, but folks get so tired they don't even notice. And it pays good.'

The woman sniffed again and said, 'Yeah, well, let me know how much, an' all that, and I'll think about it. Send me over an application form.'

'I most certainly will,' gushed George. She looked at the sheet of paper in her hand. 'I'll do it the second I get back to the offices. So meanwhile could I ask you about these folk I have listed here? I reckoned this'd be the best sort of place to find guys who say they regularly bet. Let me see now . . .'

She reeled off the list of names, most of them filched from the phone book, but with first and surnames carefully mixed up, and dropped Don Greeson's name in towards the end of it. She read it a little more slowly and with a hint more emphasis than the others and looked up casually at the woman as she read the last of the names on the list.

The woman clearly reacted to Don's name. She'd been dully looking at the list in George's hand as it was read to her, but when Don's name was spoken she lifted her eyes to look at George.

'Everyone knows one o' 'em,' she said. 'That Don, he's been in an' out of here since the day we opened back in the seventies.'

'Oh, that's great,' George said, trying to sound casual and relaxed. 'Would he be likely to be in today, do you think?'

The woman sniffed richly. 'Can't say. He hasn't been in in a month or more.'

'But you said he was in and out all the time?'

'Sure. When he's around. But he goes off to the races and stuff, don't he? You don't think a serious gambler does all his business in a shop like this, do you? He's in and out all the time when he's here.' She said it as though she were speaking to a half-wit. 'Like when he stays with his brother what used to have the chippie over the way.'

George lifted her brows. 'Used to? You mean his brother isn't there any more?'

'Nah.' The woman looked a shade animated for the first time. 'We were all really pissed off over that. One day he's here, the next it's those bleedin' Greeks. Can't fry fish to save their lives. It's all soggy and greasy, and as for chips – they don't know nothin' about chips. They gotta have a bit of crisp about them, know what I mean? Not all broke up and greasy.'

'So he's gone and you haven't seen this man – which one did you say? Mr Greeson?' She peered at her list in a slightly exaggerated way. 'Yes, Mr Don Greeson. You haven't seen him either for a long time?'

' 'S right. Not for a month or more. But he'll be back, I dare say. He always is. Hope old Lenny comes back an' all. Can't get a decent bit o' grub now he's gone.'

'Maybe I could go to his house?' George said. 'Do you have his address?'

The woman stared at her in contempt. 'Didn't I tell you, or

didn't you listen? I can see 'ow you got your stuff all lost if you don't listen. I told you, he lives over the road with his brother.'

George reddened, allowing herself to be annoyed. 'You said when he *stays* with his brother.'

'Tha's right. When he's in London 'e stays with his brother. When he goes travelling to the races and that he stops in places. Hotels when he's flush and boarding houses when he ain't. But in London he lives over there with his brother. Likes to see his dog, you see.'

George sharpened. 'His what?'

'He's got a dog,' the woman said again with the exaggerated patience required for a stupid listener. 'Bloody great black thing. Mostly he takes it with him when he goes away, but sometimes he can't. Gets all upset – he's potty about the thing. If he can't take it, it stays with Lenny, over the road.'

'And that's not been around for a month either . . .' George said slowly.

'I *told* you!'

'Yeah, you told me. Well . . .' George stowed the list in a pocket. 'OK, I'll be on my way, then. If he should come in –'

'Who shall I say called, moddom?' the woman said, leering at her. 'And where do I go to get this great job you're on about? And who do you think you're kiddin', eh?'

George blinked. 'Excuse me?'

'I said who do you think you're kidding? Do you think I don't know a private dick when I see one? What's up? Has he dumped some woman again? He's always doing that. You snoopers is always coming round after him. They go looking for him and much good it does 'em! You tell whoever she is she's wasting her money. Specially using a detective like you what sticks out a mile and don't have a sensible cover story.'

'Oh, shit,' George said. She turned and scuttled out. And laughed all the way to the next betting shop. Gus would enjoy that story, once she was able to tell him, that was.

When she got there, much the same thing happened, except that the boy behind the counter swallowed her story eagerly and wrote down the fictitious company name and phone number she gave him to seek a job for himself, as did several of the other customers in the place (for his shop, unlike the first, was doing brisk business, even so early in the day). He told her the same thing. Yes, they knew Don Greeson, no they hadn't seen him for a month or so, and yes he had a big black dog. She found out this time it was called Meff ('Short for some fancy name for the devil,' the boy behind the counter told her) and had a bad temper and nasty teeth on it ('Ought not to be allowed!' according to an old woman in the corner).

At the next two betting shops she found she drew blanks, but at the fifth she gleaned one extra piece of information.

This place was rather more handsomely turned out than the others and showed signs of being run with a certain amount of attention to decor and ambience. The chairs were not broken down bentwoods but well-made hi-tech chrome ones, and there were tables on which customers could write out their slips, rather than shabby shelves round the sides. There was a small tea bar and the counter where transactions were carried out was shielded by glass rather than wire meshing. There were no blackboards; only the TV monitors showing lists of runners and prices. The clerk here was a very pretty girl in the tightest of short skirts George had ever seen, even this summer, which was easy to see because she was perched on a high stool that ensured every inch of her amazing legs could be seen.

She swallowed the software-loss story without blinking, and talked eagerly about Don Greeson.

'Well; I must say his ship really has come home, hasn't it?' She had a high-pitched nasal voice which emerged from a perfectly painted pair of pouting lips and a tendency to toss her head so that her tumbling mane of blonde hair behaved just as hair did in the commercials for shampoo. 'First the big money job and now this!'

'What big money job?' George said, leaning on the edge of the counter in a confidential all-girls-together mode.

'Oh, it was wonderful! He likes betting in a few different places, you know. Like he says, if he puts all his business in the same places with the same bookies, everyone else would know as much of his business as he does. He likes to put himself about a bit, does Don, and why not, good-lookin' fella like him, and a *very* snappy dresser. Well, last time he was in – that'll be the beginning of June, yeah, that's right – or no, middle, now I think of it, on account it was just after my Mum's birthday and that's on June nineteenth, well he told me that he'd been given this great opportunity. He wouldn't say what it was, but it was big. And as soon as he gets back he thought he might have to go abroad for a while. He even took his dog with him – he loves his dog, a really beautiful one, it is, a sweet thing. So he was over the moon about that, and as soon as he gets back, like I said, he's taking me out for a real slap-up dinner up west. And a bit more, maybe.' Again she tossed the mane of hair which was beginning to look to George as though it had been spun out of polyester and viscose. 'As soon as he gets in touch, I'll tell him you was looking for him, all right? Just give me the number what he's got to call.'

George gave her the fictitious number she'd given the rest of them, hoping the unfortunate person whose number it really was wouldn't get too apoplectic at being called by so many wannabe croupiers, and went.

There was no need to go to any more betting shops, she decided. She was pretty sure that although she didn't precisely know what had happened to Don Greeson or his dog, there was enough reason to speak of him in the past tense.

21

Kitty slapped the plate down in front of Gus and said sharply, 'If you don't eat that, I'll tell all the other customers it was on account of we gave you a bad bit o' fish.'

'You wouldn't bloody dare,' Gus said, but there was little spirit in his voice. 'And I don't want –'

'I bloody would and I don't care what you want. You look as though you haven't eaten for a week, and it's not good enough. You tell him, Dr B. I swear to you if you don't eat I'll raise such a fuss half your bleedin' customers'll get out and never come back. It's up to you.' And she flounced off in her tight cotton dress, the apron flaps bouncing against her round bottom.

George grinned at Gus. 'You might as well give in,' she said. 'You know she means it.'

He made a face but he picked up his fork and began to eat. It was clearly not with any appetite but he did shovel the food in, and she was grateful to Kitty. There was no doubt that Gus had lost weight. It might be only three days since the bombshell that had shattered his world had been thrown at him but he had shrunk in that time. His square shoulders had lost their swagger and his cheeks had a flattened look that, while it suited him, for it made him even craggier, told her that he was not looking after himself at all.

After a while his metabolism, however, did take over and he ate the second half of the fried halibut with some evidence of liking it. George leaned back in her own chair and watched him, her own meal almost untouched.

Around them the restaurant was its usual glittering self, with the light of the big central lamps bouncing off the chrome of the chairs and the white of tablecloths and the rich smell of good food well cooked wreathing around the ceiling in an almost visible haze. People looked comfortable and relaxed and she glanced at them and thought: will we ever again be as comfortable as they are? It seemed an eternity since the last time they had sat here in the Aldgate branch of Gus's fish-and-chip empire to laugh and tease their way through a meal. Would it be another eternity before they did so again?

'Well,' he said abruptly and put down his fork. 'I've eaten it, all right?'

'All right,' she said. 'That'll keep Kitty off your back. So, how did it go today? Did you get anything?'

'Not a lot,' he said and scowled. 'It takes forever there. They must go out of their way to get the most weary willies they can for their staff. They've got three speeds: slow, dead slow and stop. A few of 'em seem to go backwards. Still, I got what I needed in the end.' He made a face. 'It makes a difference being just a punter. Usually when I do this sort of thing I flash my ID and that's it, I'm in. But today – well, it took time.'

'And what did you get?'

'Copper's Properties is part of a network of companies. It deals not only in property but in metals. That's why it's called Copper's, I suppose. I thought at first it might be some sort of bad joke tied up with the police, but that's really getting paranoid, ain't it? Anyway, there's a list of directors and so forth. None of them names I know, and mostly giving addresses that turn out to be other companies. I spent all day going from one to another and I finish up with an address for the managing director, OK?'

He reached into his breast pocket, took out his wallet and out of that a slip of yellow paper and pushed it over to her. 'Here you are.'

She looked, excited for a moment, then bent her head closer to look again. 'But that's the address of Lenny's shop.'

'You noticed! Great lady. Yeah, that's the address of Lenny's shop. And that is all I could get. After a whole day in the horrible place, I just came full circle. Whoever Copper's boss is, he's very clever.'

There was a silence and she said tentatively, 'So, now what?'

He shrugged. 'I'm up a gum tree. Wherever I turn there's the CIB. If they go where I've already been they'll think I'm involved in a cover-up. But since I can't find out where they're going, I can't go there afterwards. It's like walking over a floor covered in glue.'

'I could, though. Why not let me —'

'No,' he said. 'Don't drive me crazy, George. I won't have you doing things that are dangerous. And the more I think about what's going on the more I believe there's danger in it.'

'I do too,' she said soberly and caught her tongue between her teeth. Could she tell him what she had done this morning? Would he be impossibly angry? Would it make him feel worse about his helpless situation or better because someone was doing something on his behalf, even if he couldn't himself?

She had a thought then and contemplated it. After a while she decided to put it into action. 'I need you to tell me what to do.'

'Eh?'

'I want you to choose a colour. Green or blue?'

'What for?'

'It's a thing I used to do with my mother years ago. If I couldn't make up my mind what to do, I'd ask her to choose a colour. And the one she chose told me what to do.'

'Why not toss a coin?'

'That's simply chance. This way involves you, and it's about something to do with you. I have to make a decision. It's the way the questions I had used to involve Ma. So, choose a colour.'

He quirked his head and laughed. It was the first relaxed and unaffected laugh she'd heard from him since the whole affair had begun and it made her feel warm all the way through to her middle. He wasn't, after all, completely destroyed by what was happening.

'You are a daft object, you know,' he said fondly. 'But I like you ...' He leered horribly and she tossed her head at him, rather like the girl in the last betting shop.

'I've seen that Dick Emery imitation too often. Choose a colour.'

'OK. Blue.'

'Oh, shit,' she said. 'I was hoping you wouldn't. I think.'

'Why?'

'Because I'm now going to make you mad.'

'How?'

'Telling you I've done something I said I wouldn't.'

He sat up very straight and pushed his plate to one side so that he could lean forwards to glare at her. 'What? Just what have you done, you – you – what have you done?'

'The betting shops. This morning.'

'Oh, Christ.' He closed his eyes. 'That's just peachy, that is. Peaches and cream and a bit of banana thrown in. You silly old bag! Suppose the CIB get the same idea and start looking for Lenny via Don? If they find out you've been asking questions at those places –'

'But George Barnabas hasn't been asking questions,' she broke in. 'It was Bridget Connors who did. I hope she forgives me for it too. Next time I call home I'll confess and get her absolution. I was Bridget Connors, employee of a casino company in Las Vegas who's dumb as it's possible to be and who let her computer go down with some important addresses on it. And she's looking for them. That's who went round the betting shops.'

'Dumb? You're off your bleedin' trolley!' he bawled and Kitty, who was at the next table, looked up and grinned happily. That was more like the Guv'nor. 'What did you think you'd get, you daft –'

She sobered. 'I got a lot, in fact. Gus, listen.' She dropped her voice a little. 'I found three places where they knew Don Greeson. They all told me the same things. He hasn't been seen for a month or thereabouts – I couldn't get any actual dates out of them except for one girl, and she wasn't quite sure, but they all said a month or so. They all also said he had a dog – a big ugly thing, a lovely dog, a good fighting dog, depending on who was doing the telling. And one of them, the girl, told me that a piece of luck had come his way and he'd told her he might be going abroad, because he'd been given his great opportunity and when he came back they'd splash out on the proceeds. Only he hasn't come back.'

Gus was silent, sitting and staring at her. Then he said simply, 'Oh!' and leaned back.

'Yes,' she said after a while. 'I think all I can say is, "Oh!"'

'No more than that?' He looked at her hopefully. 'More facts?'

'Isn't that enough? But there's something else you mightn't know about.' She hesitated. 'You'll remember the severed leg we found on the foreshore?'

'Yes. And I've been thinking about it, don't think I haven't.'

'It was well dressed. Expensive shoe. Silk sock. Manicured foot and so forth.'

'Yeah.'

'Does that fit Don Greeson?'

He said it unwillingly. 'He was always dapper. Well turned out, if that's what you're asking.'

'I confess I am. I guessed he might be. I asked the girl in the last place I went to. She said as much. Always looked good, she said. A snappy dresser.'

'You think it could have been Don's leg?'

'That's not all. There was something a few days later.' And she told him about the dog's carcase. He sat and listened, watching his own fingers playing with the crumbs of his bread roll on the tablecloth and saying nothing.

There was a long silence between them when she'd finished and then he stirred and nodded. 'It's a theory, I grant you, it's a theory. Whoever it was wanted to fit me up did it through Lenny and somehow Don got to know about it. Maybe he got Lenny in? It's very likely. And then for his pains . . .'

'Yes. And the dog was always with him when he was in London. No matter what, he had his dog with him. It was his –

his trademark. And if they hurt Don, whoever they were, the dog wouldn't have liked it. So they dealt with the dog too.'

'Oh, Christ,' he said softly. 'Lenny. That poor bastard. What's happened to him, George? What's happened to him?'

'I'm sorry, Gus.' She longed to reach out and hug him but couldn't, not here. 'But I think we have to face the possibility. He could have been dealt with the same way Don was. Not that we know for sure about Don, of course.'

'It's all too horribly likely, isn't it? Though ...' His face puckered. 'How the hell did just one leg land on the foreshore? Where's the rest of him? And of the dog come to that. It wasn't the whole body, was it?'

'No. It was a skinned section of the trunk.'

'Skinned? How –'

'Horrible. Yes, it is a horrible thing. It's odd, too. Why should they bother?'

'I can't imagine. Until I know just who did it, I can't begin to guess, either.'

They sat for a long time, smiling vaguely at Kitty's bright scolding chatter when she brought them cups of coffee, saying nothing to each other. Then George moved abruptly and said, 'I'm going to go and see Monty Ledbetter, Gus. I know you don't want me to, but I must. I can't think of any other step to take and I sure as hell won't stand still. So I'm not asking you to choose a colour, I'm just going.'

He said nothing, just drank his coffee and looked at her. After a while he nodded.

'You don't mind?' she ventured.

'I mind like hell, but I know I can't stop you. So why waste breath?'

'At last. You're being sensible.'

'No, I'm not. I'm defeated.'

Filled with compunction, she reached out and touched his face. 'I'm sorry. I didn't mean to – Let's go home, Gus. To me or you. You need a lot of hugging.'

'No,' he said, and then, at the sight of her stricken face, said quickly, 'Don't take that personally.'

'I can't help but take it personally,' she said, and indeed she had. Her eyes were hot and tight with unshed tears of anger at his refusal to let her take care of him. 'It's not as though it'll do you any harm.'

'But you're wrong there,' he said quickly, then shook his head as she lifted her chin sharply to look at him.

'What do you mean?'

He was quiet for a long moment and then said, 'Choose a colour!'

'What?'

'Choose a colour.'

'Blue.'

'It's hell, this. You get stuck with what you'd rather not say.'

'Too bad. Blue.'

'OK. I'm being watched,' he said. 'If there's one thing a copper knows it's when someone's stalking him. It's been going on the last two days and I – well, I don't want you part of it. It's OK that we came here separately, OK if you leave on your own. But I won't have you labelled in any way, not by anyone. So I won't go home to you and you can't come home to me. Not till this whole stinkin' mess is cleared up.'

'I don't give a damn if they label me in any way they want to! They can call me the Whore of Babylon if they like. Why the hell should I worry if –'

'Oh, George, give me a rest!' he said. 'I don't know if – I don't know who the tail is, all right? And that's why I can't let you be part of this. When it's over, OK? Now go home. On your own.' He leaned over and kissed her briefly. 'I love you. Now go *home*. And' – he managed a grin of sorts – 'be careful with Monty. He fancies ladies with long legs.'

'He should be so lucky,' she managed to say. And went. And let the tears run down her frightened cheeks all the way home.

22

She drove off eastwards, negotiating the heavy traffic through Barking and out on to the Eastern Avenue, map open on the seat beside her, too concerned with finding her way to worry unduly about what she might say when she got there. It took her almost an hour because of the inevitable rash of roadworks, and when at last she turned into the leafy road she had been looking for, she pulled over to the kerbside to sit and think about how she would deal with Monty Ledbetter.

There could be no question of telling him the sort of nonsense tale she had used in her dealings with her contacts so far; tales about Las Vegas casinos or flower-drying partners would get her nowhere. He knew she was a doctor, knew her name, knew she was a friend of Gus's. That being so, she thought bleakly, it will have to be the truth. What was it Edgar Allan Poe said? Or was it Sherlock Holmes? When everything probable has been eliminated all that is left is the impossible. Well, something like that, and with a strong suspicion she'd got the quotation quite wrong, she released the brake and moved on, peering along the side of the road for the Ledbetter house.

It was a wide road lined with plane trees, with houses on her right and an open tree-scattered green space on the left. Gidea Park itself? she wondered. Probably. The houses were big, handsome and clearly expensive; many of them had fancy names rather than numbers and she grinned a little at an artfully engraved pseudo-rustic board outside one of them which read *Green Badge Towers*. A taxi driver, she told herself. This, she had been told by Gus, was where inner-London taxi drivers aspired to live. Clearly here was one who had succeeded.

The house she was looking for was called *The Better Place* and sat foursquare and smug behind a wide paved carriage drive and a couple of round flower-beds filled with carefully barbered grass and neat shrubs. There were unconvincing and absurdly white pillars holding up a canopy over the front door and on each side of the broad doorstep a pair of heraldic lions, equally snowy, displayed large blank shields. The bricks walls were perfectly pointed, there were a number of brass-trimmed carriage lamps, windows carefully fitted with security mesh behind which ruffled net curtains flounced (which means that even Monty, powerful though he's supposed to be, isn't immune from the attentions of would-be burglars, she thought as she looked at the glitter of the metal) and flowering baskets hanging from each window-frame. It looked, George decided, like the cover of a catalogue of a really cheap and nasty build-your-own-furniture kit warehouse.

I'm getting to be as snobby as the Brits, she thought as she pressed the doorbell. Making judgements about other people's taste this way; I should be ashamed.

Within the house there was a tinkle of 'Greensleeves' played on chimes and then she heard footsteps. The door was opened by a girl with very long legs encased in tight scarlet leggings, topped with an almost see-through black silk shirt, beneath which she was clearly wearing nothing at all, and with yellow hair frizzed into a wild Afro mop.

'Yes?' she said in a bored drawl and stared. George managed a bright smile.

'I wonder if I could speak with Mr Ledbetter?' she asked. Mr Monty Ledbetter? If he's at home.'

'Who wants him?' the girl said, leaning on the doorframe so that George couldn't see into the house, even if she had been trying to. She hadn't, not yet.

'My name is Barnabas. Dr Barnabas,' George said, beginning to be irritable. This child was barely sixteen, if that, and had a patronizing air that was remarkably annoying. 'Mr Ledbetter will remember me, I'm sure. A friend of Detective Chief Inspector Hathaway of Ratcliffe Street Police.'

'Really? That's nice for you,' the girl said, staring even more offensively.

'Isn't it?' George said with gritted-teeth charm, managing to smile back. 'So, if you would ask your father –'

'Uncle,' the girl said contemptuously. 'He's busy. I dare say you could phone.'

'But I don't want to phone,' George said with the same poisonous sweetness. 'I do want to speak to him, however. And I am here.'

'Well ...' the girl began, but then someone behind her pulled the door open and peered out over her head. It was Monty Ledbetter and George managed to prevent herself sighing with relief. She just smiled even more widely, if that were possible.

'Mr Ledbetter, I do hope you remember me. We met –'

'With Gus. Yes, I remember,' Monty said and pushed aside his niece (if that is who she really is, George thought fleetingly) with a finger's pressure on the side of her head. 'Why didn't you call me, Jade?'

'You said to see who it was and get rid of them.' The girl was less sneering but still very much in command of herself. 'So I attempted to do so. Simple obedience.'

'Well, that's as may be. But I never meant it for someone like the doctor here, now did I? You ought to use a bit o' common, my girl. Your fancy school and your GCSEs don't count for fourpence if you don't use your common.' He held the door open widely in a gesture of invitation. 'Bright as they come, this one, doctor. School talks very highly of her. Goin' to do an A level in Sociology, they say. Now do come on in. It's a privilege to see you in my home. You're very welcome.'

Jade went hipping away with a return of her original insolence, her hair bouncing on her shoulders, and Monty Ledbetter, looming huge above George, chuckled admiringly.

'Just look at her, will you? I spend a fortune on that girl's schooling, just like the rest of 'em, and all she can do is turn out like that. But there you go, that's modern kids for you. Do come into the lounge.'

The hallway in which they were standing was floored with highly polished blonde parquet on which lay a couple of clearly expensive Persian rugs, and was lined with matching wood panels, within which strips of mirror created an illusion of crowded space, full of her own multiple image. It made her a little giddy, and he smiled benignly as he pushed on one of the mirror panels which showed itself to be a door leading to the right-hand side of the house.

The room into which he led her was massive, running from back to front of the whole house, and the big net-shrouded windows at the front were matched by french windows, minus the nets, at the back. The french windows were open to the heat of the afternoon and beyond them George could see a garden stretching well back to what looked like a sizeable pool. The garden was full of shrubs and vividly coloured roses and a lawn which bore the perfect stripes of a mower so that the whole space looked just as much like a catalogue as the exterior, but this time for a seedsman.

The room itself, George registered, was even more expensive than the hall: thick carpets; deep sofas and armchairs in white leather; a stone fireplace in which logs were piled; and, clearly because it was summer, an elaborate arrangement of dried flowers. Everywhere there was the glitter of silver and chrome and glass from low tables and wall fittings and a drinks bar that dominated one corner. The overall colours of the room were pink and peach, pale green and lilac, so that George felt she was in a bowl full of sugared almonds. As she blinked around at it she remembered oddly that the last time she had seen a room furnished like this, with maximum expense and minimal taste, it had been a bedroom and there had been the body of a murdered man in the middle of it. But in this room were live breathing people and she straightened her shoulders, preparing herself for what could, clearly, be a difficult time ahead.

She thought at first the place was full of people, but once again it was illusion, because, as in the hall, there was an abundance of mirrors. There were, in fact, no more than a dozen people there, including herself and Monty. A large woman in a black silk dress rather too short for her chubby knees sat in the armchair to the right of the dead fireplace, a large trolley in front of her which was laden with silver teapots, hot-water jugs, a kettle on a spirit stove and cream and sugar pots. There were also a number of very delicate china cups and saucers and plates of cakes and biscuits and very small sandwiches on lace doilies. It all looked almost agonizingly pretty, George thought.

'You're just in time,' Monty Ledbetter said heartily. 'We'll need another cup, Mother!'

The woman by the fireplace stared at him and then nodded and got to her feet. She didn't look at George but went to a door at the french-window end of the room and vanished.

'Now, let me introduce you,' Monty said. 'Just a few family members, you know. A little celebration.'

'Oh, I'm so sorry,' George said, mortified. She should have phoned first, dammit, even at the risk of being refused an appointment to talk to him, as she had first feared. This was dreadful. 'I didn't mean to intrude. It was just that it –'

'It's no intrusion. We're used to it. There's always someone turning up on my doorstep, doctor. There always has been and there always will be. I don't want any of the usual ones today, mind you – that was why I sent Jade out to answer the bell – but you're different. A colleague, like, eh? Do let me introduce my nephew Philip. Dr Cobbett, Dr Barnabas!' He beamed from one to the other, clearly deeply gratified to make such an introduction between people of high academic and medical achievement.

She looked at the other man as she held out her hand. 'Hi,' she said. 'Good to meet you.' He was tall, though next to his uncle he looked rather weedy. Over six feet, George estimated, and with a bony look that seemed artificial, as though he'd been born to be solid but had starved and exercised his way to a fashionable thinness. His hair was fair, though not as light as Monty's, and elegantly cut. His clothes, like his uncle's, were equally elegant, although he was in an Italian suit of very costly cloth and a wide silk tie while Monty was studiedly casual in linen slacks and silky sports shirt.

'We're by way of celebrating,' Monty said. 'It's my wife's birthday and we always get together to wish her well no matter what day of the week it happens to fall on. Philip here has come up from Harley Street especially.' He seemed to smirk as he said it. 'And here are my other nieces and nephews.' He took her elbow and led her round the room, introducing her to people who looked at her blankly and nodded and murmured and went back to their private conversations, and she felt more wretched by the moment.

'You have a lot of nieces and nephews,' she said at length as he led the way back to the tea trolley at which his wife was once again settled, giving out tea with great fuss. 'It must have been nice for your children, growing up with so many cousins.'

'Oh, Mother and me, we don't have no children,' Monty said. His wife didn't look up, keeping her head well down over her teapot. 'The Good Lord didn't see his way clear. But I had seven brothers and sisters, and they had children. God, how they had children!' He laughed and stared round his big room and its inhabitants with obvious pride. 'So, I took them on instead, eh? Didn't I?'

There was a murmur of agreement, and the tea drinkers moved away from the trolley, scattering to their corners again, eating and drinking and gossiping with the intensity that is only possible between people who spend a lot of their time together. Monty settled George at his wife's side on a low pouffe and then lowered himself into the facing armchair. Mrs Ledbetter, still silent, gave George tea and offered her a plate of highly coloured iced cakes. She didn't dare refuse one and it sat on the plate on her knee, ignored, as Monty talked at her.

That it was at her and not to her was undoubted. He spoke of his commitment to his family, his concern they should all do well and the fact that he expected nothing in return for all he spent on their education and homes and wellbeing; 'Only that they should be happy and successful,' he boomed, beaming at George. 'It's all I ask of them. They should always be happy and successful, that's all.'

What a burden, George thought, very aware of the fact that, even though they all still seemed to be talking together, the others were listening to Monty (how could they not when his voice was as big as he was?). What a dreadful burden to put on people. To be always happy as well as successful. That was to ask them for the moon as a reward. Whatever he might have spent on them such demands for recompense were excessive.

'But that's enough about our affairs, my dear,' he said and beamed yet again. 'You haven't said why —?' He stopped with an elephantine delicacy and cocked his almost invisible eyebrows at her; she looked over her shoulder and felt her belly sink. To explain in front of all these people . . .

He seemed to understand and got to his feet. 'Come into my study. We can be quiet there. Mother?' He looked down at his wife. 'Will you excuse us?'

'Yes,' she said, and George realized that this was the first time she'd heard her speak. Her voice was rough and deep. 'It's all right with me. If it's all right with you.' And she looked at George. Her eyes were red-rimmed and tired.

'Oh, yes,' George said and then, aware that it would sound like an afterthought, 'Many happy returns of the day.'

'Thanks.' She made a little grimace. 'Not that it's a day I want reminding of. Sixty-seven, it's a dead liberty, 'n't it? I feel the same as I ever did and here I am a pensioner!' Now that she was speaking, she had lost the heavy sour look she had seemed to carry and George smiled at her, almost in relief.

'You don't look it,' she said truthfully. 'I wouldn't have given you more than — oh — ten years younger than you are. If that.'

'There, you see, Mother?' Monty said. 'And that's from someone who knows!'

'Well, that's as may be,' his wife retorted. 'You don't hear Philip saying it. And he —'

'What does a boy know?' Monty began and then laughed.

'Of course he doesn't say such things. Fancies getting his hands on you with his knife, eh, Philip?'

Across the room the elegant man with the sleek fair hair looked up, nodded at the girl he had been talking to and came across to join them.

'What's that?'

'I'm saying you wouldn't say nice things to your aunt about how young she looks, not when you could chop her about a bit and get a nice fat fee for it.'

The young man went a sudden blotchy red around his neck. 'As if I would dream of either charging – or saying –' he began and then stopped. 'Really, that wasn't funny.' For the old man was laughing uproariously now, enjoying himself hugely. 'You shouldn't say such things even as jokes.'

George looked at Philip Cobbett, mystified, and his neck seemed to flush even more.

'I'm a plastic surgeon,' he mumbled in response to the query on her face. 'Uncle Monty likes to tease me about it.'

'And why shouldn't I?' demanded Monty. 'Haven't I the right?' Philip looked at them and managed a grin of sorts.

'Of course you have. You paid the bills for Harley Street, isn't that what you mean? It's just that I think you look great, Auntie Maureen. I wouldn't change an atom of you.' He bent and kissed her with real affection and she put up her arms and hugged him. It was a sudden sweet moment and George found herself wondering why she had ever thought Maureen Ledbetter sour or miserable. She was looking now as radiant as a woman could look.

'You see what I mean, Dr Barnabas?' Monty said. 'What man could ask for more reward than this, hey? Not only successful and happy but lovely to his old relatives as well. We're fortunate people, all of us. Me to have the wherewithal to do what has to be done for the young and the young for having me to do it, and all of us having each other.' He beamed once more, a familiar wide toothy grin, and the others murmured back at him as he set a meaty arm across George's shoulders and led her to the door.

'Me and Dr Barnabas here have to talk business,' he said,

revelling in his importance again. 'Don't hurry away, now. I won't be long, eh, Dr Barnabas?'

'No,' she said hastily. 'Not at all.' How quickly can I explain the situation to a man like this? she wondered as he opened the door and led her out into the hall again.

The room he took her to was aggressively masculine. Leather sofas and chairs again, in deep-buttoned dark green this time, with heavy oak furniture and wood panelled walls and books everywhere. 'Bought by the yard,' George thought and then scolded herself for snobbery again. But it was clear that the handsome leather-bound volumes on the shelves had never been opened.

'Sit down now, sit down.' He fussed over her, settling her in a chair that was as uncomfortable as it was costly; the leather was slippery and the deep buttoning seemed to push her upwards and outwards, as though the chair was trying to spit her out. 'What can I do for you? A charity thing for the hospital, is it? It usually is. I spend a fortune on these places, a fortune. First the kids, poor little objects, and now you, hmm? What is it, then?'

'No, it's not charity,' she said. 'It's a bit more complicated than that. It's Gus.'

'Gus? Is he giving you trouble?' He frowned. 'I'd not have thought it of Gus, not ever. But you never know. The women who've sat in that chair like you and told me tales of the way their men behave, well, you wouldn't credit it. But I always tell them it takes a weak man to raise his hand to a woman and a strong one to –'

'It's nothing like that!' she said, horrified. 'Not at all! Oh, perhaps Gus was right. I shouldn't have come.'

He frowned again and looked at her sharply, his pale lashes making his eyes, large as they were, look somewhat piggy. 'I thought you'd come on your own account. But if Gus sent you, that's different. What's the trouble? I'll fix it. I can fix almost anything, you know. Yes. Tell me what it is, that's all you have to do.'

23

'Lenny Greeson,' Monty said ruminatively. 'I know who you mean. Not much of a fella, is he?'

'I don't know,' George said. 'I've never met him. He's Gus's friend.'

'Yeah. Well, his dad knew Lenny's dad. Stands to reason he'd say he was a friend, doesn't it? But he's not much of a fella, from all accounts. If he had been he wouldn't be in this mess now, would he?' He shook his head ponderously, oozing disapproval from every pore. 'Borrowing money to pay debts ... Gus should have had more sense than to agree to it.'

George's jaw tightened. 'I really can't say,' she began. 'I only know –'

'Mind you, I'd ha' thought the less of him if he'd not done it, seeing how it was between his dad and Lenny's dad. It's one of those devil and deep blue sea jobs. Yes ...' Again he sank into rumination.

George, wishing more and more that she hadn't come, stirred in her chair. 'Well, if you can't help –'

'Who said I couldn't help? Course I can. I can find out anything that's to be found out on this patch, and I'll find out for you what's happened to Lenny. And Don.' He cocked one of his almost invisible eyebrows at her sharply. 'You think something's happened to him, don't you?'

She hesitated and then said, 'Yes.'

'Well, it wouldn't surprise me. That one really is a bleedin' fool. Calls himself a gambler and what's he got to show for it?

The clothes on his back and that's about it. Lives off his brother, always sponging from him, can't even pay for his own dog food. A real professional gambler, now, he makes a living, has a place to call his own.' He waved a meaty hand comprehensively to take in not only the room they were sitting in but the whole house. 'A man needs a place to call his own, a place he can take pride in.'

She tilted her head and stared back at him very directly. 'Is that how you made your fortune?'

He chuckled fatly. 'Well, now, that'd be telling, wouldn't it? And I didn't get where I am today by telling all and sundry about my business. No. But I'll tell you this much. I've forgotten more about the dogs and horses than Don Greeson'll ever know. There ain't a dog that runs in the whole East End, or a horse in the whole country, what I don't understand and know about. It's as simple as that. But don't you worry, my dear. There's a lot more to know and all. I'll find out what's happened to young Lenny and his brother and I'll be in touch.'

Clearly the conversation was at an end. George bit her lip, wanting to say more but feeling it might be a mistake.

'I'll send word to you then, eh? Not to Gus. Don't want to go falling over no nosy coppers, do we? No.' He laughed his big laugh again. 'That'd never do. So, where's your gaff?'

George blinked, aware of a sudden urge to keep her own address secret. There was no need to be afraid of this man; he was Gus's contact and Gus had assured her he was safe. All the same, the thought of this bulky figure standing inside her little flat made her feel cold. But she pushed away her doubts and gave him her address and phone number.

'I'll be in touch then,' he said again, tucking away the little notebook into which he had written the information. 'Don't you fret. You go back to your hospital and stop worrying. If there's any dirty work going on, I'll uncover it. I'll find your Lenny.'

He was halfway to the door by now and she followed him, eager to get out of this house, yet aware of a sense of dissatisfaction. His soothing words had done nothing to reassure her; at bottom she was convinced the visit had been pointless.

Outside in the hall, the front door was open and there was a little flurry on the doorstep as some of the nieces and nephews kissed Maureen Ledbetter goodbye. At the sight of Monty they turned back and started their goodbyes all over again and George hung back, waiting for the fuss to die down before taking her own leave.

She looked round the hall again as she stood there, wanting to see if her first impression had been accurate, and this time saw at one side a pile of cardboard boxes. The girl Jade was crouching beside them, turning over their contents. Curious, George craned her neck and then moved casually to see what it was.

The boxes seemed to be full of old clothes and, as George watched, Jade pulled out a coat, shook it, and held it against herself.

'Auntie Maureen,' she called, ignoring the fact that her aunt was talking to someone else. 'Auntie Maureen, what's this made of?'

Maureen looked over her shoulder and peered. 'Oh, Jade, do leave those alone! They're for the shop!'

'I know that. But this looks interesting. What is it?'

Maureen finished her goodbyes and, leaving Monty to deal with the rest, came back through the hall to Jade's side. 'It's – um – I don't know. Some skin or other. It's one of the ones I got from Connie.'

'Oh!' Jade dropped it with a disdainful twist of her fingers. 'Then it's a real skin, not a fake? That's disgusting.'

'Of course it's real!' Maureen sounded indignant. 'He wouldn't give me rubbish, you know! He cares as much as I do about the shop. He gives me good gear so that I can make the best money I can.'

'But real skins ...' Jade turned up her nose. 'How can you wear an animal's body on your own? I thought it might be simulated. If it were I'd have taken it, but I wouldn't touch it with a bargepole now.'

'And who said you could have it anyway, my girl?' This was Monty joining them. 'Don't I buy you enough as it is?'

'Yes, well, this is different, Uncle Monty. It's cool to wear old gear. Everyone does. But no one wears furs. They're gross, and skins are the same.'

'Like your leather jacket? The one I gave seven hundred for?' Monty said and winked at George with great good humour. 'These kids with their fads and their fancies, eh? Not ashamed to wear seven-hundred-pound leather jackets but wouldn't wear a coat made of bullskin.'

'I thought it was ponyskin,' Maureen said. 'I was going to label it that way.'

Monty picked up the garment and peered at it more closely. It was a dark brownish-black in colour, a short sleek garment, simply made and rather dull, except for the sheen on the surface. He made a face at it.

'Ponyskin, bullskin, dog or cat or moleskin, what's the odds? Once they're dead you might as well use up the bits and pieces. It says that in the Bible, don't it? Man having dominion over the animals and so forth.'

'Well, the Bible's got it wrong,' Jade snapped. 'It's revolting for people to wear dead animals. I won't do it.'

'No one asked you to,' Monty said. 'Now go home. Your dad'll be wondering where you are and I don't want him breathing down my neck. Be a good girl, come here and give me a kiss.' He was reaching into his breast pocket as he spoke and the girl saw the movement from the corner of her eye. She came over to him, her brows raised in the same supercilious curve but eagerly enough, and George watched as he pulled a handful of notes from his wallet and pushed them into her hand.

'Jade,' Maureen Ledbetter said as the girl turned to head for the front door. 'Could you come over tomorrow and give me a hand? I have to take all this up to the shop and there's some stuff there that has to be taken over to Connie's, and then I need to take the money into the office at the hospital. I thought you could drive me?'

'Car's up the spout, Auntie Maureen,' the girl said, looking sideways at Monty. 'I won't get it back till Friday. If I could drive the Merc?'

'Not on your bloody Nelly,' Monty roared. 'What have you done to yours? Pranged it again?'

'Some nerd ran into me,' Jade said. 'It wasn't my fault. These days you're not safe out with the sort of people who drive –'

'Like you,' Monty interrupted. 'I've seen you. The nerd who pranged it was you, and don't you deny it. I suppose you're expecting me to pay for it.'

'Dad is,' Jade said sulkily. 'I wasn't even going to tell you. If Auntie Maureen hadn't asked me to take her somewhere I wouldn't have.'

'That is not the point,' Monty began wrathfully, and suddenly George couldn't stand it any more. She had hovered at the edge of this family squabble long enough and wanted to be out of it. But until she heard the words coming out of her own mouth she didn't know what she was going to say to arrange that.

'I'll drive you, Mrs Ledbetter,' she said. 'I'm free tomorrow and I'll be glad to help. Charity work – so useful.'

There was a little silence as they all stared at her and then Jade said, 'OK then. That's settled. I'll be off. 'Bye, all.' She went sliding out of the door almost, but not quite, slamming it behind her.

'Well that's very kind of you, I'm sure,' Maureen said doubtfully. 'But it's asking a lot. I mean –'

'It's no trouble,' George said wretchedly, hating her own impulsiveness for dropping her into this, wasting precious time she needed to help Gus. 'What time shall I collect you?'

'Well, about nine would be nice, if that isn't too early,' Maureen began to brighten. 'Connie has to be away by eleven, I know, and I promised not to be late.'

George felt better. 'Then it's just the morning?'

'Pretty well. Though we could have lunch at the hospital.'

'The hospital?' George shook her head. 'Oh, no. That's not possible. We don't have any arrangements at Old East for –'

Maureen laughed. 'I don't mean Old East. I raise money for St Dymphna's. The Psychiatric Unit, you know? It's a lovely little hospital and so – well, it's one I care about. We could have lunch there.'

'Oh.' George smiled brilliantly. 'That's very kind of you, Mrs Ledbetter. I'll be glad to help. Nine o'clock, you say? I'll be in good time, I promise.' And she went at last, leaving them both on their doorstep waving her goodbye.

Someone somewhere had been on her side, she decided, when they prompted her into offering her services. There could be some value in going to St Dymphna's, from her own professional point of view. And getting into Maureen Ledbetter's good books could be one way of persuading her husband to make even more efforts for Gus. Taking it all round, her visit to Gidea Park had been a profitable one.

Repeating the journey to Gidea Park next morning was much quicker; she knew the route, which helped, but she drove quickly too, partly because she was rather annoyed with herself. What had seemed a reasonable idea yesterday now seemed a waste of time. To be carrying stuff for Maureen Ledbetter? What could that do to help Gus, after all?

But once she was there, and found Maureen waiting anxiously for her, surrounded by boxes, her irritation melted. There was no harm in doing something for someone else, even if there were no benefit to herself or Gus in it. She loaded the boxes in her little car as quickly as she could, and then settled Maureen in the front passenger seat.

'You'll have to direct me,' she said. 'I've no idea where your shop is, I'm afraid.'

'Barking,' Maureen said. 'I know it doesn't sound a very interesting area, but you'd be surprised how many regular customers I have. When times are as hard as they are these days, people aren't as fussy as they used to be about buying secondhand.'

'I've often wondered about charity shops,' George said, as much to make conversation as anything else. 'Where do you get your stock?'

'Oh, that's not a problem – right here – I ask people around here in Gidea Park where they've got a lot of money for their cast-off stuff. They're glad enough to let me have it. Then they can nag their husbands for more money because they've got nothing to wear.'

George laughed. 'It sounds a good wheeze, I guess. And that gives you enough stock?'

'Oh, no, I buy some cheap things in and sell them at a small profit. It doesn't get me much but it makes the shop more interesting. And then I get a certain amount from Connie.'

'You mentioned that name yesterday,' George said. 'Do I go straight on here?'

'Yes, right down to the next roundabout and then follow the signs for Barking. Connie? Oh, yes, he's part and parcel of the shop, as much as I am, really.'

'He?' George was amused. 'Here am I with a man's name and there's a he with a girl's name?'

'Constantine. He's called Constantine Georgiopoulis. Greek, you know. Lovely chap. Can't do too much for St Dymphna's. Really.'

'St Dymphna's,' George said casually. 'You know a lot about it?'

'Oh, yes,' Maureen said, and there was a tension in her voice that made George glance at her. She was staring ahead out of the windscreen, her expression bleak. 'Oh, yes.'

George had been a pathologist for the greater part of her professional career, but in her early medical days she had worked with live patients as well as dead ones, and some of her expertise with them lingered still. She could certainly recognize emotional distress when she met it, and she responded as she had been trained to do.

'Would you like to talk about it?' she said quietly.

There was a little silence and then Maureen said, 'I used to be there every day, you know. They said it made no difference, that she never knew me and never would, but all the same . . . Every day.'

'Yes?' George said gently when the silence had gone on long enough. She was driving carefully, watching out for the signs so she could find her own way without distracting Maureen.

'And then what?'

'Well, she died, didn't she?' Maureen said. 'I knew she would. They told me she would the day she was born and she did better than they'd said. I mean, she wasn't quite two and they said she'd never make it to a year old, so she did well. But she went and then … Well, it was still there, wasn't it? St Dymphna's? She wasn't but the place was and I was used to it. So I went on going every day. It was –' She stopped then. 'I went every day. And they gave me things to do like being one of the Friends, you know, and then I started the shop.'

She smiled widely and leaned forwards so that she could look at George directly, distracting her from her attention to the road. 'It was the best thing that could have happened really. It's made all the difference to me. The shop.'

Once again it was intuition, whatever that might be and wherever it came from, that gave George her next question. 'And did you name the shop after her?' she said.

'Of course. I couldn't call it anything else, could I? We've made getting on for half a million, you know, since we started. Built the swimming pool in the basement out of it, they did, and the gymnasium where they do the exercises – the physios – and all sorts of stuff like that. And now they need more for the new units they're building. I dare say we'll be helping with that too.' She produced a broad grin of great satisfaction. 'Maybe they'd call part of it after her, too. I'd like that.'

'I hope they will,' George said, and then after a moment, 'That was a lot of money to have made just from the shop, wasn't it? Selling just old clothes and so forth?'

'It's good, isn't it?' Maureen was plump with satisfaction. 'It's been pretty steady, right from the start. In the last few years the recession's been a bit of a problem, of course, and in the beginning money wasn't so – well, prices were lower. But on average we've made about two hundred and fifty pounds a week over the years. Less at the beginning, not so much now, lots in the middle, know what I mean? It all adds up.'

'It does indeed,' George said abstractedly, trying to do the arithmetic in her head. How long does it take to convert two hundred and fifty pounds a week into half a million? Say that's a thousand a month, twelve thousand a year: the sums wobbled in her head but she managed it. Forty years. No, longer. For the past forty years or so, this woman at her side had been sorting through old worn clothes and buying and selling cheap oddments to help her hold on to her grief for a dead child. A child who had died before she was two, who had never recognized her mother – or so it appeared from what Maureen had said. That had been the spring of a vast sum of money for the hospital that had taken care of her. For the first time George was glad she was helping Maureen Ledbetter, not because she wanted to get anything out of her; but because it was worth being with her just for her own sake; and she at last brought the car, under Maureen's directions, to a halt in front of the shop proudly displaying its name: *Carolynn's Charity Shoppe.*

24

It was surprising how much fun it was to play shops, George thought. She helped Maureen and a little bustling woman in a pink overall, one of the regular volunteers who acted as saleswoman, hang the new stuff they had brought on the rails, while another helper, who looked much the same as her colleague but wore a blue overall, busied herself writing price tags. Maureen kept up a steady chatter of explanation.

'Ah, these will sell fast, Dr Barnabas. They always do, these new things. Connie gets them for me, and we're so grateful. I don't know for sure where he gets it all from. I suspect he uses new material, you know, and gets some of his contacts to make the things up for us. Isn't that kind? Then there's the cabbage, of course.'

'Cabbage?' George was diverted. 'I thought you just sold clothes and books and knick-knacks. Do you sell food as well?' She looked round the shop, which showed no signs of any such items.

Maureen laughed merrily. 'Oh, no, not vegetable cabbage! It's what the people who get cloth from big firms to make up into coats and dresses and so forth call the leftovers. The big firms can't do all their work so they get these little local firms to do it.'

'Ah,' said George. 'Sweatshops?'

Maureen looked vague. 'I'm never sure what that means. Anyway, it's called CMT work in these parts. Cut, make and trim. If they're clever, they can get as many as a dozen extra

225

dresses or coats out of the material they've been allowed for making a hundred garments, say, and then they can sell the dozen for what they can get. Well, Connie buys up cabbage and then lets me have it. He's so good to us and to St Dymphna's.'

'Did he have –' George began and then stopped, but Maureen wasn't fooled.

'No. He does it out of the sheer goodness of his heart. He's not married, so he's got no children.'

George almost smiled. There was something very sweet about Maureen's naïvety.

'I tell him to put a move on or he'll be too late but that's a joke. Monty thinks ... well ...' She stopped and then made a little face. 'Monty said I ought to introduce Connie to a nice girl, but I like to keep Connie to myself, to tell the truth. He really is a great friend to me. Look at this.' She held out the skin coat that had so incensed Jade. 'That's new, you know. I sometimes get cleaned-up leather and suede jackets Connie's rescued from the stuff that comes to him, but this one looks new to me. Doesn't it to you?'

George looked at it and had to agree it did. It had a garish red lining in very new rayon and there was the faint smell of tailor's soap about it that bespoke an unworn garment.

'I wonder if it is bullskin,' she said, handing it back to Maureen who hung it on the rail. 'My mother had a bullskin coat once.'

'Dogskin,' the little woman in the pink overall said unexpectedly. 'I used to live on Tenerife when my husband was alive, and they were always selling them there. People used to say it wasn't fair on a dog to keep one, especially a big one. They used to steal them for their skins when they couldn't get any bullskin. It was for the cruise ships, you know. They used to come in with all those Americans and ...'

But George wasn't listening. She was staring at the dark brownish-black short-haired skin coat hanging on the rail and hearing in memory the voice of the woman in the betting shop. *He's got a dog. Bloody great black thing* ...

She reached out a finger to touch and then let her hand fall without doing so. There was something so hideous in the thought that she couldn't bring herself to make the contact. She frowned as she thought and Maureen went on burbling away.

'. . . there now, that's all that done. Dolly, have you got the stuff that's to go back to Connie? You see, Dr Barnabas, we can't always sell everything we get so what we can't, we take to Connie and he buys it back, just like he does everyone else's.'

'Mmm?' George said.

'He does it for most of the charity shops in London, and the junk shops, and jumble sales. Wherever they get old clothes. Buys them in, sorts them, sells them on, and so forth. That way everyone benefits. It's ever so ecological, too.' She beamed her satisfaction at being so very up-to-date.

'I'd like to see this man's place,' George said abruptly. Maureen stopped and stared at her, a little startled by the sharpness of her voice.

'Well, we're going there,' she said. 'At least, we are if it's still all right with you. You did say . . .'

'Oh, yes.' George managed a smile, sounding as casual as she could though now she was itching to get away and see this man Connie and his establishment. 'That was what I meant. What can I carry out?'

Again the car was filled with boxes, and sacks too this time, all bulging with clothes, some of which had the slightly sour smell of old wardrobes. Unobtrusively George opened her car window a little to keep the fresh air flowing through. Once more Maureen was quicker than she expected her to be.

'It does whiff a bit, doesn't it? It's amazing to me that there isn't a bad smell at Connie's, seeing how stuff like this can reek a bit, but he's very fussy. The place smells more like a hospital than a hospital does these days.' Again she produced that cheerful laugh of hers. 'He uses lysol and carbolic and all those unfashionable things, to keep the mice and rats away, he said. Mind you, he's got the cats for that.'

'Yes,' George said, not really concentrating on what she was saying. 'Maureen, do tell me – left here? Oh, I see.' She swung the wheel and Maureen hung on to her seat belt as the car hurtled round a corner. 'Tell me how the place works. So that I don't seem too ignorant when I'm there. I hate to seem a complete fool.'

'Oh, I do know what you mean,' Maureen said in heartfelt tones. 'Well, let me see. The stuff comes in the front of the warehouse. You'll see – it's piled up, miles high. They do the first rough sorting there. He has ordinary workers for that. The homeless do a stint sometimes, just to get a few bob, though they wouldn't do it full time. Well, no one would really, though he's got some who don't seem to mind. Anyway, they throw all the shoes on one pile and all the handbags on another and the odds and ends somewhere else, you know the sort of thing. Then all the clothes, they're thrown on the conveyor belt. You should see it! Ever so big it is. Well, you will see it, won't you?' Again that tinkling giggle. 'That's when it gets really tricky. The people who work on it, they have sort of bins beside them, big things on wheels, great big dustbins really, and they pick out the stuff that's right for their section.' She shook her head admiringly. 'Connie's ever so clever, you see. He discovered that what goes in one country won't go in another. So he gets people from all different countries to come and do the sorting for him. He's got a regular United Nations there.'

'You mean he uses immigrants?'

'You've got it. Students and so forth. It's all on shifts, you see, so they fit in what hours they can. And they know how to sort. There're the East Africans: they'll take high-heeled shoes and really bright-coloured stuff that the Nigerians won't look at, and there're things he can sell to Taiwan that they wouldn't touch in Hong Kong and so on. You'll see. Just turn here, into those double gates. That's it. If you'll pull over right by those double doors the unloading will be easier.'

Obediently George brought the car to a stop beside the huge doors that stood open to the morning sun of the court-yard, a wide expanse filled with vans and lorries, some of which were piled high with great knotted bales of what looked like greyish gauze. There were men moving around tying loads into place and checking clipboarded lists; the whole yard had an air of purpose.

'Here we are then!' Maureen had extracted herself from the car and George was a little amused. When her husband and family were about she needed to be helped. Now she was much more spry. 'Good morning, Bert. Is Connie about?'

The old man in the dark blue stores coat she had spoken to nodded at her. He lifted his head and bawled, 'Connie!' at the top of his voice. From somewhere inside the big building, a space which seemed to be filled with shadow beyond the double doors, someone bawled back incomprehensibly.

'It's me, Connie!' Maureen produced a high fluting sound which was remarkably penetrating. There was a rumble of more shouting from inside the building and then a man came out. He was tall, wearing dark trousers and a shirt of so perfect and blinding a white beneath bright red braces that it made George blink. He had crisp dark hair, huge, very dark eyes with the longest lashes George had ever seen on a man, and the most melting of smiles.

'This is Dr Barnabas,' Maureen said with great formality, clearly pleased as punch to be showing off her friend, to whom she was now clinging, one hand tucked into his elbow. 'She came just to help me, wasn't that nice of her? I do hope you can find a moment to show her things. She's ever so interested, aren't you, Dr Barnabas?'

'Oh? Oh, yes,' George smiled. She was indeed desperately interested, but that was not the thing she wanted this man to know. He would expect of her no more than the sort of polite interest newcomers to his establishment showed out of good manners, so that was all she tried to display.

She must have succeeded, because he smiled. His teeth were as George had suspected they would be, a very bright and glittering mouthful, and she understood with a little stab of admiration just why Maureen was so happy to count him as a friend. Any woman would be: he really was a most attractive creature. His age was an indeterminate forty or so – she could now see in the brilliance of the sunshine a few grey hairs beginning to appear at his temples – and was altogether a pleasure to look at.

'You want to see the way round my rags?' His voice was pleasant too, though deep and a little loud, with a North country accent, which startled her. He grinned as he saw the expression on her face. 'You thought I'd talk like a stage Greek, didn't you? Well, I was born and brought up in Newcastle. So there you go!'

'I can't tell one English accent from another,' George lied. 'Seeing I'm a foreigner myself. I'd love to see your ragheap. Maureen's been explaining and made it sound real interesting.'

'Oh, it is,' he said, and turned his head. 'Bert? Unload this stuff, and check if I've anything to go back to Mrs Ledbetter. Put it in the boot if there is. You'll find a pile in the office. Come on then, I'll show you round.'

He turned, Maureen still on his arm, and made for the dark doorway, not stopping to see whether George followed him or not. Inside it was amazing. Once her eyes were used to the change in the light levels she could see easily. A pile of old shoes was the first thing that caught her attention. It had to be at least fifteen feet high at its peak and its base was spread widely across the floor. She wouldn't have thought there could be that many old shoes in London. On the mountain's other side was a smaller heap, which was almost as impressive, of hats: men's hats, women's hats, children's baseball caps, all sorts. She blinked at it. Who wore hats any more?

He laughed beside her, clearly reading her thoughts. 'It is amazing, isn't it? People do wear hats, though. In the old days, when my dad was in this business in Gateshead, there were more hats than shoes. But there're still a lot. The other bits of leather are over there.'

He pointed and she stared at the pile of handbags and suitcases that lay further inside the warehouse, and opened her mouth to speak; but he was already moving away, and after a moment she closed it, feeling cold inside. The sight had triggered a memory in her, a memory that was hateful; and she followed him silently, as Maureen, still clinging to his arm, started chattering again. The last time she had seen a sight like that, George thought, it had been on a TV screen showing a film of Hitler's labour camps where people's possessions were processed much as the people themselves had been. Wasting nothing, the Germans had made piles of items like this too; and George could have shuddered. The people who had worn these clothes here hadn't been liquidated, of course they hadn't, but the mountains of possessions looked the same and it sickened her.

So much that she hardly noticed what came next, until they were standing halfway up a long aisle into which Connie and Maureen had led her.

'See, Dr Barnabas?' Maureen said excitedly. 'See? There they all are, the people I told you about, sorting all the stuff that lands on the conveyor belt, fast as they can go.'

The belt was indeed a huge one, trundling noisily and fairly slowly towards the far side of the building. George glanced ahead and estimated it ran about seventy feet, and it was piled high with old clothes. Standing a few feet apart along its length were the workers, men and women, some in turbans, some in saris, some wearing masks over their faces (to keep out the dust, George guessed) though others seemed content to breathe in whatever was there, their eyes fixed on the things passing in front of them. They picked over the items in front of them at amazing speed, pulling out dresses and coats, blouses and skirts, trousers and shirts and tossing them into the great bins at their sides. Between them all a couple of boys were darting about, taking away full bins, replacing them with empty ones which were swiftly filled.

'There you see?' Maureen pointed. 'On the side.' Obediently George looked at the side of the bin that had just been delivered to the man behind whom she was standing and she saw the stencilled lettering. *Caribbean.*

'You see, Dr Barnabas?' Maureen shouted, above the rumble of the belt. 'It's all so –'

The man at the conveyor belt jerked his head round. He was tall, and very black, with a woolly Rastafarian hat pulled down over his dreadlocks. He grinned widely at George.

'Well, doctor, fancy seeing you here,' he said and immediately turned back to his conveyor belt, reaching out, pulling at items, throwing them into the basket or discarding them to go on to the next picker in the line. 'You turn up everywhere!'

She stared at the back of his head and then peered round to look into his face. 'Do I know you?' she said.

'Oh, Gawd, don't it make you feel good?' the man said to his neighbour, a tall black woman in a turban who nudged him without for a moment losing track of the items going by on the belt. 'You think they'll know you and they never do. Mind you, you can't blame them. I can't tell *them* apart, neither.'

George laughed gratefully as suddenly the memory slid into her mind. 'Mangoes,' she said.

'At last! I wouldn't have told you, not after you didn't know me last time neither.'

'You're out of context!' George protested. 'You see a guy in the market, you don't expect to see him here as well.'

'A man has to make his gold where he can!' The woolly hat bobbed as he broke into a song, turning the words into a sort of rap. 'A man got to work, pay his debts when he can, every man got to work, eat his dinner where he can . . .'

'Dr Barnabas!' It was Maureen. She and Connie had moved further down the conveyor belt, and George saw that Connie had vanished. She touched the man's shoulder and said quickly, 'You'll hate me, but I've forgotten your name too. I guess I'm getting past it.'

'That's OK, doctor! You meet a lotta guys like me, I know that. I'm Gregory, Gregory St Clair.'

'Hi,' she said gratefully. 'I'll never forget again. I'll come back and talk to you later.' She moved away. 'Sorry I was so dumb.' And she hurried down the line to Maureen.

'Connie had to take a phone call or something,' Maureen said and again she sounded important. 'Said I was to show you the rest. So, here you are . . .' She launched herself into a great tide of explanations, clearly entranced to be doing so, Remembering the subdued woman who had sat serving tea in her own living room in Gidea Park, George marvelled a little. Did Monty Ledbetter know this wife as well as he knew his usual one? She seemed to have dropped ten years from her age, she was so animated.

She talked on and on about the different places the various workers came from. Indeed they made a remarkable sight; some of them were in their national dress, especially the Indians and Pakistanis, others in tight jeans or leggings and shirts. But George let her mind wander. Gregory St Clair; what was he doing here? He had his stall; did he need to do work like this? That it was unpleasant was clear; the air was thick with dust which smelled sour and tired, it was disagreeably hot. And noisy. She could feel inside herself the vibrations from the heavy rumble of the conveyor belt and the thudding of a great press which was pushing the clothes into the huge bales she had seen outside, before wrapping them in the sheets of cheesecloth that gave them their uniform colour.

'Washed coverings from the cheeses they import from Canada,' Maureen said, noticing the way George's glance was directed. 'Neat, isn't it?' At that moment another noise began, and George caught her breath. It was amazingly loud, crunching and shuddering, and seemed to shake the floor beneath her feet. She put her hands to her ears in self-defence.

Maureen grinned and nodded at her. 'I'll explain that,' she bawled, 'when it stops. Have you seen enough of this?'

'I think so,' George shouted back. She turned and followed Maureen as she made her way back up the conveyor-belt line. George wanted very much to talk to Gregory though she couldn't see quite how she could in this din; then it stopped as suddenly as it had started. The residual noise of the presser and baler and the conveyor belt seemed pleasantly quiet in comparison.

'There, that's better,' Maureen said. 'I expect it's gone wrong again. It's always doing that. We really ought to get back, if we're to be at the hospital in time for lunch.'

Deliberately George stopped just behind Gregory. 'Why does it go wrong? And what is it?' she asked. She didn't really care all that much but she did want to remain near enough to Gregory to start another conversation with him if she could.

She didn't know why she needed to, she was simply certain that his presence in this place was important to her.

It was Gregory who answered her. Another tall Afro-Caribbean man had come strolling up the aisle to take Gregory's place at the belt, and Gregory stretched, stepped back and turned to George.

'That there was the old macerator,' he said. 'It's for chopping up the leftovers into rags. Ain't that right, Mrs Maureen?'

'So I've been told.' Maureen sounded fussed now, as though she was uncomfortable talking to Gregory. 'Connie'll tell you if you like. I was going to explain to you, but I don't really know much about it.'

'I'd like to see,' George said. 'Could you ask Connie to show me?' And she waited, in the hope that Maureen would go away and fetch Connie, leaving her to talk to Gregory.

After a moment's hesitation, Maureen did. She went plodding away up the aisle, calling over her shoulder, 'Once you've seen, we'll have to be on our way.'

'I'll show you the macerator,' Gregory said. He was no longer wearing the tight black shorts George remembered from the market, but a pair of very expensive-looking black jeans under a crimson shirt. He straightened his cuffs as he moved away from the belt to lead her back to the doorway end of the aisle.

'Like my jeans?' he said, stroking his thighs lingeringly as he walked, looking over his shoulder wickedly. 'Not so good as the legs, but nice, hey? You find good gear on the belt and old Connie, he doesn't mind if you have the odd bit, as long as you don't get greedy.'

'He's a nice man,' George said almost as a question, and Gregory nodded vigorously.

'Oh, he's a good guy. One of the best. Lets a man pick up what he can while he pays his debts,' he said. 'It ain't so bad when you walk out with a pair o' good jeans after a long day here and no cash.'

'No cash?' George was puzzled. 'Doesn't Connie pay you?'

'Oh, sure he pays! Only he don't pay me. He pays the man direct, doesn't he? It's to be sure the debts get sorted. Me, I'm a bad man, bad, baaad man!' He laughed, a fat happy sound deep in his throat. 'Give me the cash and won't I just go and put it on the horses someplace else? The old man, he don't like that, so Connie pays him direct. And me, I get some jeans. So! Here we are. The machine that makes the noise. Only now it looks all broke down again, hey, man?'

He stood to one side, peering down a narrow spiral staircase in the corner of the huge warehouse, beneath which there was another floor, some machinery and several men standing about looking disconsolate. George could see all there was to see through the slats in the iron steps: a vast oily machine with a hopper in front and great balers behind, and huge glittering blades, set in a massive corkscrew pattern, at its heart. And as she stared into the space she knew quite certainly what had happened to Don Greeson and his dog. And, perhaps, to Lenny Greeson too.

25

George was proud of herself. She showed no visible sign of the way her pulses were thumping with excitement, making her chest feel tight; nor did she show any undue curiosity. She just stood and stared down into the basement and said casually, 'Would they let me go down and take a look? It's one hell of a machine, that!'

'Oh, they fuss a bit,' Gregory said. 'Don't reckon it's safe, you know? Big knives. But you're a doctor. You're different. Go on down, see what happens! Me, I'm going to get coffee and a pattie.'

She was torn. 'Oh. I wanted to talk to you.'

'At your service, doctor, that's me!' Gregory said cheerfully. 'Talk away.'

She looked over her shoulder to see if Maureen was coming back with Connie and since they weren't, said hurriedly, 'I was just wondering how it was you were here. I mean, this isn't at all what I'd have thought you'd do. Don't you own that stall in the market?'

'Own it?' Gregory said judiciously. 'Not to say *own*. But it's mine all right. You know how it is with the money and all that, doctor. It kinda drifts away. A bit of this, a bit of that ...' He winked and sniffed, turning up his nose at her.

Deliberately George ignored the hint. His bit of this or that, whatever it was — pot, crack? — was none of her affair. He seemed a happy and healthy enough young man, and she had no right to be censorious. 'But why work here? Can't you do better than this? It doesn't look very pleasant.'

'It's disgusting,' Gregory said with some force, but then shrugged. 'Still, the man said it was the work he wanted done, so I just said, great, I'll do it. And I get the jeans, don't I?'

'What man?' George asked. He looked at her sideways, his eyes glinting.

'What's it to you?'

'It's a lot to me,' George said a little desperately now. 'I'm trying to find out about — There's a guy I'm trying to help, and someone's treated him bad on this patch. And I think maybe — I don't know, I just have a feeling that this place here has something to do with it. So I wanted to know why you were here, anything I can find out about the place.'

'Hmm,' Gregory said. He looked over her shoulder too. 'Well, I'm off to my coffee and pattie. See you in the market sometime, doctor!' And he went, just as Connie and Maureen arrived at her side.

'So you're interested in my macerator?' Connie said and smiled at her, his teeth gleaming in the shaft of sunlight coming in through the big double doors. 'It's only a big machine. You like machines, doctor?'

'I love them,' George said fervently as Gregory vanished. 'It looks a really great one. My grandfather was an engineer, you know? He'd have loved to see this.' She smiled brightly as the lie embellished itself easily. 'He used to work with the textile factories, and I guess he'd have had to use a machine like this, huh? To chop up the incoming stuff? I know they used to make a lot of yarn out of rags.'

'Ah, that's not the same as this. They used to make cotton scrim and so forth out of cotton waste. I know that. But this machine takes whatever comes. We don't sort it out, see. Just anything that can't be sold on — about an eighth of what comes in here — I chop into rags, sell to India. They like it for' — he shrugged — 'all sorts of things. Stuffed into furniture, maybe, who knows? I don't really care. All that matters to me is that they pay a reasonable price. But they won't take it till it's chopped, so I chop it. Well, it's been a pleasure to have you here, doctor. Sorry I had to pop away. Had a business meeting in my office. But Maureen here will have looked after you ...' He put his arm across Maureen Ledbetter's shoulders and hugged her and she beamed happily at George from the crook of his arm.

'Oh, it's been great. But I really would love to see that machine,' she said and deliberately turned and began to walk down the spiral staircase, moving carefully. The iron was cold and slippery and the turns very sharp.

'Well, I'm not sure that –' Connie began, then seemed to accept the inevitable and let her go. After a moment he followed her.

'I'm not going down there,' Maureen called down. 'I'll just see the stuff is put in your car, Dr Barnabas. Is that all right?'

'A pleasure!' George called back heartily as she arrived at the foot of the staircase. 'I'll just have a quick peek.' She went towards the machine across the floor, which was made of stone and covered with a thick soft layer of what looked like pinkish snow. George could see clearly, however, that it was the multi-coloured fibrous dust left by the fabrics that were piled in the hopper of the machine.

A man was peering into the bowels of the great thing as she came up to it, and Connie said loudly behind her, 'What is it this time, Allen?'

The man looked up, shrugged and shook his head. 'It's happened again. I don't understand it,' he said fretfully. 'I clean it, get it well oiled and then not twenty-four hours later there it is again, all choked up with sludge and all the oil gone. I've checked it right through the drains, and cleared the lot. They were thick again. We'll have to get new filters fixed. I keep telling you that.'

'We put new filters in a few months ago,' Connie said. 'Allen, this is Dr Barnabas. She's interested in our machine.'

The man nodded, but he was clearly uninterested in her; he wanted to get on with his tinkering. George turned to Connie and said brightly, 'Why do you have to chop it all up so small? Can't you send it out the way it is?' She pointed to the big hopper at the front of the machine, which was filled with jackets and trousers and various other garments, all of them looking very battered.

He shook his head. 'Indian Government rules,' he said shortly. 'I told you. They won't let it be imported unless it's chopped as fine as we can get it. If you'll forgive me, I think we ought to leave Allen to –'

But she had moved around the machine to the other side, carefully not hearing him. 'And this is where the chopped stuff comes out? Yes, I see.'

There was a platform on the other side which was surrounded by bolted-on sheets of metal and she could see at once how it worked. The hopper at the front fed the garments into the great blades and what came out on the other side was unrecognizable. It was extremely finely chopped; there was no way of telling what the garment had been originally. She looked over her shoulder and said to Connie, her eyes wide with admiration, 'It's a very powerful machine, isn't it?'

'One of the best in the world,' he said with a sort of unwilling pride. 'We can get tons of stuff through that in a day, tons and tons. Very effective.'

'I guess the clothes have to be carefully picked over, and buttons and zippers and so forth taken off? They'd spoil the blades, wouldn't they?'

He laughed, almost contemptuously. 'Zippers? I could put sheet iron through those blades, and it'd come out like wire wool! That set of blades'd chop anything. Anything at all. I save zippers for resale, o' course – they're worth good money – but not to protect the machine. Now, I think Maureen'll be waiting and –'

But again she was absorbed in what she was looking at. 'And this here? This gully? Is that for – what is that for?'

'That's the drain that takes the cooling water,' he said. 'Generates a lot of heat, a machine like this. There has to be water going through and it drains there.'

'Into the river?' George said brightly, looking at him directly now. He shrugged.

'I don't know! I leave that to the men whose job it is. Now, if you'd like to –'

It was the man Allen who helped her then. He had come round the machine to check one of the inspection points on that side and looked up at her question.

'Nothing goes into the river but water,' he said firmly. 'I know what you're thinking, that we pollute the river. Well, we don't. That drain is filtered and protected and all is as it should be. Nothing can get to the river except when the guards are taken off and they never are.'

'So it does go down to the river then? The gully?' George said, sounding as relaxed as she could. 'I thought it might, you're so close here, after all. It makes sense that a cooling system'd use the river. It couldn't be polluting, obviously. Not just warm water. It's a lovely design.'

Allen seemed to preen. 'Isn't it though? It ought to run sweet as a nut. That's why I get so mad when it acts up this way. It's like it gets all bunged up. Must be a lot of oil and dressing in those clothes.' He looked a little accusingly at Connie. 'The stuff I clean out all the time would amaze you. Stinks, it does.'

'I told you to use the disinfectant,' Connie said. 'These are soiled garments, for God's sake. Of course they carry a bit of grease and what have you. That's what brings the rats. If you use plenty of the strong stuff that'll get rid of it. And the rats.'

George nodded. She had noticed the reek of carbolic and heavy pine disinfectant when they had arrived at the warehouse, but not commented on it, since Maureen had mentioned it anyway. Now, she thought grimly, I know why it matters so much to Connie. It isn't rats he's bothered about. Not the usual sort, anyway.

She began to feel a sort of nausea; not because of the way she knew this machine had been used – and it *was* knowledge. It wasn't a guess, of that she was completely certain. She *knew* – but because of something else. Physical humanity, in any form, she could handle; it was the minds of some people that sickened her. She moved abruptly and made her way back towards the foot of the spiral staircase.

'Well, thanks a lot for showing me, Allen. It's been really interesting. I wish my grandpa were still alive so I could tell him about it. Thanks, Connie, for letting me look round. I hope you don't mind me calling you that? The way everyone else does?'

'Not at all, not at all,' Connie said genially, clearly relieved that she was ready to go. 'Up you go then, and I'll see you to your car. It's been a pleasure to have you here, doctor. And thanks for helping Maureen. She does so much for that hospital, and it's my pet charity too, so any help that's given her is given me too. I thank you for it.'

'Only too pleased,' George murmured. She dusted her hands off as she reached the top of the spiral stair. 'And I do congratulate you. All very – ecological. Splendid.' Connie beamed and took her elbow to lead her to her car. He was making sure that nothing would stop her departure this time, George thought. Much good may it do him.

George drove to lunch ignoring Maureen's busy chatter except for her instructions about the route, and thought furiously all the way. It was a hellish way to kill a man, but an incredibly efficient way to get rid of a body. That wide gully with its removable guard – it had to be removable to let the maintenance people clean it – offered a direct route for getting rid of the evidence of a crime, and it was big enough to let a leg through. And a chunk of canine carcase. She shivered inside at the picture that rose in her mind: someone pushing a body towards the blades on that great machine. But then her questions took over and disposed of the shudders.

Why was a leg left behind? If the machine could chop a human frame into such minute pieces that it could be literally poured out from a bucket into the gully and so delivered to the river to become part of the mess on the river-bed, why wasn't the whole of it put through?

Because the machine broke down, her mind retorted. It's doing that all the time. It may be able to take a human body, it may be able to cope with great chunks of tissue, but it gets sludged up after a while. There's a lot of fat and blood and gloop in a human body. That leg must have been left behind by a breakdown and they couldn't get rid of it any other way, so they took a chance and dropped it in the river too. Thought it would sink. But it didn't . . .

Who were the 'they' though? She tried to imagine Connie standing there at the foot of his spiral staircase, pushing a man through the blades of his macerator, and then collecting the resulting – whatever – at the other side. (What in? Buckets? Hardly, too small. One of the great bins on wheels they used at the conveyor belts? Perhaps. Who could know?) Somehow, though, the image wouldn't stick. She could only see him standing there fastidiously dusting down his trousers, pulling on his shirt-cuffs to neaten them. But he must have known his machine was being used for that purpose. Why else had he been so anxious, indeed so eager to get rid of her? What other reason could he have had for that uneasiness?

'And here we are!' Maureen said triumphantly. 'St Dymphna's. Isn't it a nice-looking place, Dr Barnabas?'

George looked out at the building appearing round the curve of the driveway that had led up to it. It was squat, built of turn-of-the-century yellow brick with darker bricks used to pick out patterns over the windows and round the doors. George thought it hideous. Efforts had been made to improve the building's appearance with plants; cotoneasters grew up the lower levels of the walls and Virginia creeper over the upper parts, and in front flower-beds were dotted among the gravel patches that made up the drive. It looked, George found herself thinking, as though it would smell inside of boiled cabbage and watery stewed mince.

'Lovely,' she said. 'May I park here?'

'Right here,' Maureen said. 'I have a special place.' As she preened again, George found herself warming even more to this woman. There was a deep pathos about her, but she had courage and a gift for making the most of very little. She leaned over to Maureen as she switched off the engine and said quickly, 'Thank you so much for letting me come with you today. It's been a real privilege.'

Maureen flushed, blinked, opened her mouth to speak and then closed it again. She smiled and got out of the car and as George joined her said breathlessly, 'It's been so nice of you to come out with me like this. The family, they don't understand the way I feel. Not even Monty. So it's nice to have someone interested.'

'It's been fascinating,' George said, a little grimly, glad Maureen couldn't know – could she? – just how interesting it had been. She followed the dumpy figure into the main doorway.

The place did smell, but not of cabbage and mince. Instead it was rich with old-fashioned beeswax polish – the floor was made of ancient deeply shiny parquet – and flowers from the bowls which had been put on every available surface. One wall bore a massive brass plaque with names of benefactors engraved on it, another a large white marble statue of a man in Victorian dress beaming benignly if a shade sternly, while a man in a head porter's uniform, well buttoned in brass, sat in a small sentry-box arrangement just inside the entrance.

He greeted Maureen effusively, nodded at George when he was introduced, then led the way to the lift, which was hidden behind the big curving staircase that adorned the far wall, and pressed the button for them before going magisterially back to his sentry box.

'I know it looks old-fashioned and all that,' Maureen said a little breathlessly, 'but really it's very up-to-date in its treatments. Very. The wards are lovely. Would you like to see?'

George opened her mouth to say she didn't really have the time and heard herself accepting graciously. As the lift arrived to carry them up to the top of the building, she cursed silently. She needed to get back to Gus as soon as possible, to tell him of all she had seen and of her new ideas. She didn't want to waste time here.

But the tour was interesting. The wards were indeed well appointed and clean, gleaming with colour and comfort. The patients, most of them clearly profoundly mentally handicapped, and several more severely physically disabled too, looked well cared for, and the staff, though all rather on the elderly side, seemed cheerful and friendly enough. But she was irritable with herself as she toiled after Maureen who

nattered on and on about the various comforts and embellish-
ments her fund-raising efforts had provided. She was aching to
get away, to think more about the new direction her investigations were taking. It was all very well to have found where the
bodies were disposed of, and how the leg and the dog had got
into the river, but she still didn't know for sure whose leg it
was, who had put it there and above all why. And what was
the connection with the fires, if there was one? There had to
be something that tied all of the mess together and made
sense, but what?

Could the women killed in the fires be a totally separate
affair? It was possible, she had to allow, but in all her experience it was very rare – to the point of never happening – to
have two separate murderers roaming the same small area at
the same time. All her instincts told her that there had to be a
connection between the deaths of those women and the findings she had made at Connie's rag factory this morning. But
what? She couldn't find a loose end in either puzzle that fitted
into the other.

And she couldn't think clearly about it all anyway, as
Maureen Ledbetter took her through ward after ward and
department after department, chattering about so many
things that really didn't matter except, of course, to
Maureen.

George was just about to point out as tactfully as she could
that time was getting on and she wouldn't be able to stay for
lunch after all, when they turned into a corridor and Maureen
said brightly, 'This is the part of the hospital that will interest
you, doctor, I'm sure. This is our laboratory. It's a bit over-
crowded, they tell me, but it's very nice.' She pushed open
the door at the far end and held it wide, inviting George to
enter.

She did, and found herself in the familiar atmosphere of a
biochemistry lab; the smell of the reagents, the sound of the
equipment, the faint hiss from the refrigerators, all were
deeply comfortable to be with. But she didn't expect what she
saw.

Which was Mickey Harlow, sitting perched on a tall stool

that was too small for him, alongside Lewis McCann who was standing leaning against the lab work counter, his hands in his pockets and a faint sneer on his face. And behind them both Reggie Lester was leaning silently against the window.

26

'Oh!' George said. She could find no other words, looking from one to the other of them, nonplussed.

'Well, well, look who's here,' Mickey Harlow said easily. 'You do take your work seriously, don't you, doctor?'

'Pardon me?' George said. She couldn't think of anything else she could say.

'I know you're not keen on the idea of our sending Old East's path. work here, but all the same, coming to check up on it . . .' He laughed, a cheerful sound in the big room. 'And who's to say you mightn't get the top job here anyway, as and when it happens? You might be worrying over nothing.'

She realized then why they were there, and managed a bright smile. 'I'm not just worrying about my own job, Mr Harlow,' she said. 'It's Old East and the patients I'm concerned about. I guess I could get myself a new job anywhere I chose if it came to it. I'm not precisely at the bottom of the employment heap, you know!'

McCann snickered at that and Harlow threw him a sharp glance which he ignored. Lester said nothing, just watched them all. 'I don't suppose Harlow here meant to suggest you were,' he said. 'For my part I'm very gratified you take the needs of Old East so seriously you've made time to come and see for yourself. It can't be easy to get away from the pressure of your work in your own lab to spend time here.'

The smile George had pinned to her face began to fade as she remembered that she was supposed to be away nursing a sick friend. Was there any chance that either of these two would meet Ellen, and casually mention they'd seen her here? That could really start a fuss.

'This is coincidental,' she said quickly, looking over her shoulder. Happily for her, Maureen had moved away and was talking to one of the lab people, and George was able to move a little closer to the two men and drop her voice. No need to let Maureen hear her embark on one of her elaborate tales.

'I have a sick friend – I'm actually on leave at present taking care of her – and I need some path. work done on her. I don't want to take it back to Old East – being off duty, you see – so I dropped in here as she lives quite close. I thought they'd help me out.' She smiled widely, praying deep inside that her luck would hold, and immediately slid off on another tack. 'I wouldn't have expected to see you here, either. You're not on the Board here as well, are you?'

'No way,' said Harlow. 'Got enough to do watching over Old East, take it from me. But we have to keep an eye on everything Old East's Trust Board does, don't we? I wouldn't let them transfer the Path. Department here unless they'd all seen it. So that's why we're here. I'm showing my colleagues the set-up.'

'So,' George said, looking round. 'Is it enough of a department to swallow up mine?' In all her preoccupation with Gus's predicament she'd stopped thinking about her own professional problems. If there was an opportunity here to resurrect one of them, why not?

'Not as it stands, of course,' McCann said. 'But it wouldn't be as it stands, would it?'

'No, it wouldn't,' Harlow said, and it was clear he was returning to a line of argument which she had interrupted. 'I told you, the building wouldn't be any big deal. I can promise you we'd have no problems with the planners.' He glanced sideways at George for a moment, a swift appraising look, and then back at McCann. 'I won't bore you with details now, Lewis, but take it from me, the building contracts won't be a problem. The land's there and –'

'The land's there all right,' McCann said with an odd emphasis. 'But that doesn't mean to say it's available for your building contracts, however easy they might be to organize, does it?'

Lester moved then, straightening up and leaving the window

to come forwards. 'Oh, I doubt there's any need to worry about that. It's the quality of the service that matters, and everyone involved – *everyone* – is, I'm sure, willing and eager to do the best thing.' His agreeable, carefully controlled voice seemed to make Harlow more tense, rather than less.

'Well, that's something we have to talk about more. So, shall we be on our way? Mustn't get in Dr Barnabas's way, must we? No. Good afternoon to you, doctor. It's been a pleasure to see you.' And he almost hustled McCann away, with Lester following quietly at his own pace, leaving George staring after them, her brows a little creased. Ideas and thoughts were stirring deep in her mind that would need lifting out into bright daylight and inspecting. She let some vague yet possibly relevant memories swirl around: Monty talking to Gus, *I won't work with no lemons, and they know it*; *Poor little kids ... only elevenpence ha'penny to the bob*; and Gus, talking on the same occasion: *I'll keep a well-open eye and ear on the contracts inside.*

Was this the connection? Maureen spent most of her waking life thinking about St Dymphna's. It wouldn't be strange if her husband, the Universal Fixer and Sorter-Out of Other People's Problems, was involved in it as well. Was there some scheme going on that might benefit St Dymphna's at Old East's expense, into which McCann and Harlow had been recruited? And was there any connection with Connie, another warm supporter of St Dymphna's, via Maureen? And –

'Well, lunch now, yes?' Maureen said brightly, dragging George out of her glazed-eyed reverie. 'Sandwiches is all there is, I'm afraid, but they'll be nice ones, I promise. Come along.'

George came along willingly. There was even more she might dredge out of Maureen's artless chatter that could be useful. All sorts of notions were crawling around in her head now. The only place where she could not see a link was between the fires and the women who had died in them and the St Dymphna's/Connie's factory axis. But it had to be there. Somewhere.

When she got back to her flat at last, Gus wasn't there. He'd left a curt note. *Gone back to Companies House. Might be able to get a bit more info. See you later. G.* So she sat in her living room, staring out of the window and trying to think what to do next.

The conversation with Maureen hadn't been particularly illuminating – at first. She had chattered about their lunch – smoked salmon sandwiches and miniature crab vol-au-vents – apologizing for it, quite unnecessarily, as George told her, and then slid away to talk of her work at the shop, much of it very dull. George had sat and listened, chewing her sandwiches and trying to look interested. But it wasn't easy.

When Maureen's talk drifted on to her family, it wasn't quite so hard to concentrate. Jade, it transpired, was everyone's biggest worry.

'Her mum, you see, ran off with another man when Jade was three, and her dad – well, he's been all over Jade ever since to make up for it. My Monty's the same. I think they've spoiled her, but who listens to me? Like one of the others said, what do I know? I've never had to bring up a child.' She had brooded for a moment and then brightened a little. 'Mind you, the boys are nice to me.'

'The boys?'

'Oh, Philip, you know, and Patrick.' She seemed to swell a little. 'Dr Cobbett. Or I should say Mr Cobbett, shouldn't I? Seeing he's a surgeon.'

'Oh, yes,' George said. She put down her plate. 'Do tell me about them.' She remembered the tall weedy man with the fair hair and the bony look and the very expensive clothes. He'd seemed rather aloof from his cousins, who had favoured rather sparkier clothes to adorn their stocky bodies, and displayed a taste for heavy gold identification bracelets. His wrists had been innocent of anything apart from, as she now remembered, a rather expensive-looking watch. A Rolex? She thought so. Perhaps the cousins weren't so different, after all.

Maureen needed little encouragement. She talked enthusiastically and at length about the young man who was clearly her favourite nephew.

'He's so sweet to me. The others tease like anything. They say he just wants to operate on me and give me a new face because he doesn't like the one I've got, but I know it's not true and that he loves me as I am. Still, he gets upset when they go on about it, the others. They say he might make me worse than I am already, and that's why I won't let him do it, and of course that upsets him. He's very proud of his work.'

'I'm sure he is,' George said. 'Which is his hospital?'

'Oh, he's in Harley Street,' Maureen said, looking at George almost pityingly. 'He isn't a *hospital* doctor.'

George managed to hide her combination of amusement and irritation. 'Well, yes, but the best specialists always have a hospital appointment too. It's their NHS hospital which gives them their specialist status, you see, not where they have their private consulting rooms.'

But Maureen wasn't listening. 'No, he went to Harley Street very early on. No messing about, Monty said. He was to be the best, and have the best. So – Well, no need for details.' She looked a little flustered for a moment. 'I shouldn't be gossiping like this. Family stuff.'

'Oh, it's not gossip,' George said reassuringly. 'It's natural family pride. Very commendable.'

Maureen looked happier. 'Well, I am so proud of him. Monty is too. He said to him, when he set him up in Harley Street, you just make yourself a name, and that'll be that. I don't want nothing paid back. Just to be proud of you, that's enough. He's very good, is Monty. But he does spoil Jade.'

'It's natural enough,' George had said diplomatically, looking surreptitiously at her watch. If Maureen was going to start talking about Jade again she just couldn't cope; and there was no time to waste anyway. Talk to Gus, that's what I've got to do, she thought and turned a bewitching smile on Maureen.

'It's been really lovely being with you,' she said. 'I've had a fascinating morning. Thank you so much for letting me come.'

'Oh, no, thank *you*.' Maureen surged to her feet in a flurry of gratitude. 'I'd never have managed on my own, and you've been ever so kind to me. It's so nice having help with it all. If you're ever free again –'

'I'll call you,' George promised hurriedly, mentally crossing her fingers. 'Right now I really must be on my way. No, it's all right. I can find my own way out, truly I can.'

Now, sitting in her living room, she felt flat, yet restless. The morning and the new ideas it had brought to her were buzzing away in her head, and here she was with no one with whom to share them. She needed to be able to bounce her ideas off someone who would help her see them more clearly.

She did it almost without thinking. She went over to her little desk and pushed all the stuff on the working area – the pile of *Lancet*s and *British Medical Journals* and *Pathology* journals – on to the floor and pulled out a big sheet of paper and her mug of coloured pencils. She'd do what she'd done before when she'd been in such a state. Make some sort of list.

She made a heading without hesitation. CONNECTIONS, she printed in large capitals on the top of the page. And then stopped to think. She sat staring at the window for some time, her eyes glazed but her mind twisting and turning, dredging memories and sorting ideas; then, slowly, she began. She wrote in different parts of her sheet of paper the various things that had happened in the past few weeks, and then looked at them.

What she found herself looking at when she'd done that made scant sense.

CONNECTIONS

GUS
Investigates local
network of villains.

GUS
Informer says he has
demanded money
with menaces. Is
suspended. Reason:
misunderstanding of
Lenny Greeson
loan.

CONNIE
Owns factory with
a macerator to chop
fabrics which could
chop bodies, often
out of order. Gets
gunged up.

GREESON
Lenny, Don and
dog all disappear.

Some of the items connected. Some didn't. But she thought she might as well put in what connections she could. So she did.

CONNECTIONS

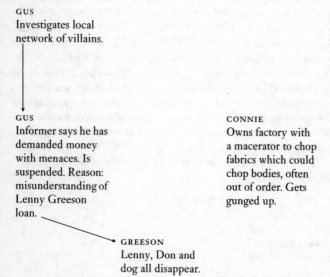

GUS
Investigates local
network of villains.

GUS
Informer says he has
demanded money
with menaces. Is
suspended. Reason:
misunderstanding of
Lenny Greeson
loan.

CONNIE
Owns factory with
a macerator to chop
fabrics which could
chop bodies, often
out of order. Gets
gunged up.

GREESON
Lenny, Don and
dog all disappear.

Two arrows neatly connected up the left-hand side and middle of her page. That was fine as far as it went, she decided, but it clearly didn't go far enough. There were other odd events that had to be fitted in: the leg, for example, and the dog carcase. And the multitude of fibres found in them when they were examined in the morgue. So after a moment she made more headings on her paper, and another arrow. She looked again, and then tentatively added yet another arrow with a question mark. As far as she was concerned the machine at Connie's had to be the way the job had been done, but she couldn't be really certain, could she? Hence the question mark.

CONNECTIONS

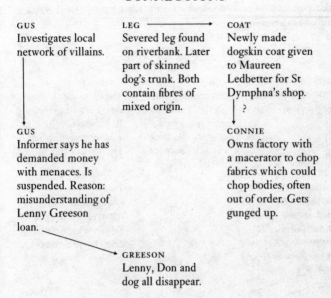

GUS
Investigates local network of villains.

LEG ⟶
Severed leg found on riverbank. Later part of skinned dog's trunk. Both contain fibres of mixed origin.

COAT
Newly made dogskin coat given to Maureen Ledbetter for St Dymphna's shop.
?

GUS
Informer says he has demanded money with menaces. Is suspended. Reason: misunderstanding of Lenny Greeson loan.

CONNIE
Owns factory with a macerator to chop fabrics which could chop bodies, often out of order. Gets gunged up.

GREESON
Lenny, Don and dog all disappear.

Is any of this leading me anywhere? she asked herself. If all the items connected up it would be different. As it was, they just seemed to dangle in mid air. Perhaps she hadn't put in all the possible elements that could be part of the equation?

Again she looked at the window, letting her eyes glaze a little. It was a vividly bright afternoon, and the sun was slanting in through the panes to lift the room to a rich glow. She could see her own reflection clearly in the glass as it shimmered slightly, so that her face seemed distorted by her relaxed unfocused gaze.

And then it happened. Sitting there, a little distracted by the heat, her mind did what it had done for her in the past – left her behind, set to work on its own and made its own connections. Distorted faces . . .

She found another idea had slipped to the top of her consciousness. She looked down at her page again, picked up the pen and after a moment's hesitation found herself writing another two items.

CONNECTIONS

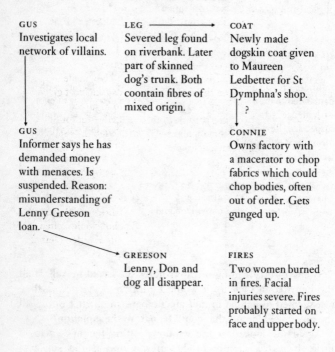

GUS
Investigates local network of villains.

LEG ⟶
Severed leg found on riverbank. Later part of skinned dog's trunk. Both coontain fibres of mixed origin.

COAT
Newly made dogskin coat given to Maureen Ledbetter for St Dymphna's shop.
?

GUS
Informer says he has demanded money with menaces. Is suspended. Reason: misunderstanding of Lenny Greeson loan.

CONNIE
Owns factory with a macerator to chop fabrics which could chop bodies, often out of order. Gets gunged up.

GREESON
Lenny, Don and dog all disappear.

FIRES
Two women burned in fires. Facial injuries severe. Fires probably started on face and upper body.

FACIAL INJURIES
Monty and Maureen Ledbetter's nephew, Philip Cobbett, is a plastic surgeon.

She sat trying to convince herself that her subliminal musings had cheated her. But hadn't the same idea come into her head once before? She had had that ugly dream which had had frightened her so, only to find herself convinced there was a connection between the two fire deaths and Gus's case. But wasn't she being hysterical? It was all too far-fetched, surely? And yet ... Slowly she picked up her pen again and made more arrows. Two of them she gave two ends to; it seemed a logical thing to do.

CONNECTIONS

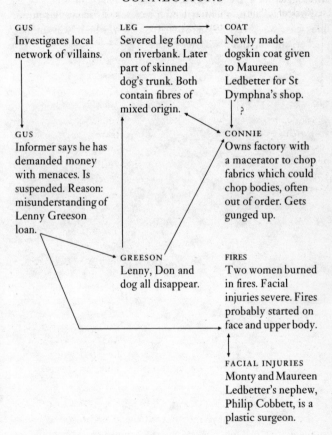

GUS
Investigates local network of villains.

LEG
Severed leg found on riverbank. Later part of skinned dog's trunk. Both contain fibres of mixed origin.

COAT
Newly made dogskin coat given to Maureen Ledbetter for St Dymphna's shop.

?

GUS
Informer says he has demanded money with menaces. Is suspended. Reason: misunderstanding of Lenny Greeson loan.

CONNIE
Owns factory with a macerator to chop fabrics which could chop bodies, often out of order. Gets gunged up.

GREESON
Lenny, Don and dog all disappear.

FIRES
Two women burned in fires. Facial injuries severe. Fires probably started on face and upper body.

FACIAL INJURIES
Monty and Maureen Ledbetter's nephew, Philip Cobbett, is a plastic surgeon.

She sat for a long time after that, studying her sheet of paper, uncertain whether she'd helped herself at all. That there were some logical connections here was undoubted; but the fires? Wasn't she stretching logic absurdly to think that Philip Cobbett had anything to do with all this? She'd only thought of him, surely, because Maureen had talked about him today. And she actually put out her hand for the bottle of Tipp-Ex to paint out that item on her sheet, but somehow couldn't bring herself to do it.

That was the moment at which two sounds made her jump; one was the bleep Ellen had given her, which was in her pocket; and the other was her phone.

27

She answered the phone first, obviously. It was Monty Ledbetter and he greeted her with an avuncular tone that grated a little.

'Dr Barnabas? Well, how are you? Bloomin', I trust. I do want to thank you for being so helpful to my Maureen. She's just been telling me about how kind you was this morning. It's much appreciated. She needs this little job of hers; keeps her contented, you know, and having someone like you take an interest cheers her up no end.'

'It was a pleasure, Mr Ledbetter,' she said, too aware of the bleep, which she had taken from her pocket to stop its noise, to be as irritated as she might have been by his tone of voice. She could see the message on the little strip of screen. *Phone M. U.* it said. *Urgent.* She was itching to get this call ended and dial the number of Michael Urquhart's mobile phone. She couldn't quite remember where she'd put it; somewhere secure, she thought. I wrote it on a scrap of paper and put it somewhere safe and sensible, but oh God, where? She couldn't remember. She let Monty burble on about how happy Maureen had been made by her efforts, saying nothing as she dug into the pockets of the shirt she was wearing, even though she knew she'd been wearing a different one when Mike had told her his number, and wanting to swear aloud at her own incompetence.

'So, I said to her, no need to be shy. Dr Barnabas is like our Philip, like all good doctors, just wants to help people. It makes her feel good to help people, no need to be so worried about making use of her, I said. She'll be glad to help any time, I said, and I'm sure I'm right, hey?'

'Mmm?' said George abstractedly. 'Oh, yes, any time. Er – if you'll forgive me now, I have to –'

'Now, about the little matter you asked me to look into.' His voice had changed; had become a little deeper and softer, as though he was being confidential. Silly, a part of her mind registered, to be hushed over the telephone. Unless he had a listener at his end, of course. That was possible. He was a man who liked people to know how powerful he was, how much clout he had. Maybe he did have an audience at that.

'The chap you was enquiring about. The one that – um – isn't at home just now.' He spoke even more softly then. 'The one that has a brother, where there's what you might call a ditto situation.'

She would have laughed if she hadn't been so agitated about the need to call Mike as well as the need to hear what Monty might have to say.

'The Greesons,' she said. 'Lenny and Don.'

'Now you be careful what you say, especially on the phone,' he advised sharply. 'Remember all that about Squidgy and so forth. Anyone could be listening and probably is.'

'Hardly,' she said a shade tartly. 'I'm no princess and you're not exactly – Well, anyway, what about them?'

'You've no need to fret over either of 'em.' He sounded pleased with himself. 'I've got it on the highest authority – the *high*-est auth-or-it-y – as they're all right.'

'What authority?' she asked bluntly.

'You can't ask me to tell you all my ways, doctor.' He sounded quite shocked. 'Just you take my word for it. One of 'em – with his dog – has gone overseas. Middle East. A really good job, and very happy he is about it, I'm told. By the –'

'Yes, the highest authority,' she said. 'But can you be sure that it's true? How high is the authority?'

'Believe me, I know the things I know. He's gone overseas, and glad to do it.'

She thought for a moment and then said, 'And the other one?'

'Same thing!' Monty sounded pleased with himself. 'Not abroad, mind you. Oh, no. Here in good old England. Brighton, to be precise.'

'Bright – What's he doing there?'

'I'm told, a job of work,' Monty said, sounding a touch frosty now. He had expected fulsome gratitude, clearly, and all he was getting was a catechism, and he didn't like it. 'It's his business, I imagine.'

'He's just walked out of his business! I have it on another high authority that he wouldn't have done that easily.'

'Not easily, no. But he got a price, didn't he? A price he couldn't say no to. From all counts he'd have had to be stark raving bonkers to have turned it down. Part of the deal was to go right away from this part of the world for a while so the new people could get established on the premises. He'll come back to London I dare say, in a while, but right now he's sitting pretty in Brighton.'

'I don't believe it,' George said, more to herself than to him, and he spluttered at the other end of the phone.

'You don't – Well, I never thought – Why shouldn't you believe it? I'm not in the habit of lying, you know, or of –'

'Oh, I'm sorry, Mr Ledbetter. I didn't mean I didn't believe *you*. I just can't imagine how Lenny could – I mean, just *vanish* like that! Gus has been looking for him – other people – the police have been looking for him because he's Gus's answer to these charges, and he's only gone to Brighton, you say, and they haven't been able to find him? It can't be. I mean, if he knew Gus was in trouble on his account, he'd be back like a shot, surely?'

'Well, that's as may be. I told you he wasn't much of a fella. Easy to push around, Lenny, always was. People don't change.'

'But all the same, a guy, a very old friend, has helped him out with a loan and all he has to do is tell the truth and the guy's out of trouble! No one could be such a nerd that he wouldn't do that!'

'Don't you believe it. People have ways of getting what they want, and if there's someone wants to push this fella around, well, he'll be pushed. And that's all there is to it. I'd keep out of this if I was you. Not a lot you can do, see. Not a lot anyone can do. Look, I've been around long enough to understand the types on this manor. I don't know all the ins and outs of their business, and I'll tell you frankly, I don't *want* to know. The less I'm involved, the better off I am. These people are hard cases, you hear what I'm saying? Just take my word for it, Lenny's all right, in Brighton. Leave it at that.'

Her voice sharpened. 'You mean there are people in whose interest it is that Lenny stays quiet? That's why they've taken him away and –'

'I'm not saying anything. I'm just saying that the blokes you was asking about are all right. Leave it at that. Gus'll sort out his own business well enough. You tell him what I told you and leave it to him. You go on stickin' your oar in and you could make things a lot worse. Remember I told you that.'

She became even sharper. 'Are you warning me off?'

Now he sounded as usual, comfortably pleased with himself and his own power. 'Now, have I done any such thing? I just gave you a bit of fatherly advice, that's all. It's good you want to help Gus, but like I've told my Maureen many a time, the best way to help your fella is to keep out of his affairs when they don't concern you, and keep him warm and happy and well fed. Believe me, that'll be the best thing for you to do. It's up to you, o' course, but I can tell you these blokes are all right. So, ta again for your help to my Maureen. G'bye, doctor.' The phone clicked in her ear and settled to the steady buzz of the dialling tone.

She shoved the handset back in place and went scuttling for her bedroom to dig out the clothes she had worn the last time she had spoken to Mike and search for the missing phone number. She tried to hang on to all Ledbetter had said so that she could think about it later, and, of course, she thought (as at last she found the number precisely where she'd put it, which was in the flap of her change purse, the last place, naturally, she'd looked), to pass it all on to Mike. Maybe he could make a search in Brighton and see if what Monty had said was true?

Mike answered after a couple of rings and she had to struggle to hear him. He was clearly out of the nick and somewhere where reception on the radiophone network was not all it should be. She strained her ears to listen.

'Hello, Dr B.! Is the Guv there?'

'Mike? Where are you?'

'Shadwell. Doing routine checks. Still talking to the working girls. We're no further forward than we were, dammit. The Guv'nor – Inspector Dudley – isn't happy.'

'Nor am I,' she said. 'If he'd let me help, maybe I could give him some leads. Well, never mind. I'll go on my own way and tell him when I've got there, wherever it is.'

'What?' he shouted. 'I didna catch that. Say again?'

'Not important,' she shouted back. 'Listen, why did you call?'

He managed to hear that. 'I've got a bit of news. I've got a bit of news that the Guv – Gus ought to hear,' he bawled. 'He won't like it but he'd better hear it.'

'Oh, hell,' she said. 'What is it? I hope to see him later today and I'll tell him –'

'I can't talk about it on the phone. I'll come round. When will he be there?'

'Oh, Gawd. I can't say. He's not exactly keeping office hours. Can't you tell me?'

'Phone's risky,' he said. 'You never know these days who –'

'Yeah,' she said. 'Squidgy. Well, I'll take the chance and pass on something to you. The man Gus got the money from, remember?'

'The fish-shop owner.' The thin voice faded and crackled and then came back more strongly. 'What about him?'

'I've had a tip-off that he's in Brighton, working there.'

'Is he, by God! Where?'

'If I knew I'd be off there now to find him,' she said, suddenly irritated. 'For crying out loud, Mike, isn't it enough I got the *place*? With your contacts surely you can find him?'

'If he's using his own name, if he's doing his old job, then you may be right,' Mike said. Even through the bad reception she could hear the acid in his tone. 'If the man's gone to ground there, then it'll no' be that easy. But I'll see what I can do. There's a couple of ex-Met chaps on the patch, I seem to remember. Tell Gus I have to speak to him, will you?'

'I will,' she promised. 'And Mike?'

'Yes?'

'Sorry if I was snappy, I didn't mean to be.'

'It's all right. It's a strain, all this. You're doin' a grand job, Dr B. Just hold on to your hat, now.'

'I will,' she said, and suddenly wished he was there. It would be a great comfort to have his bulk standing beside her, making her feel a little less alone and frightened. Because she had to admit she was very frightened. It all seemed to be more and more confusing. In spite of my careful chart-making I'm no further forward than I was when it all started, she told herself as she cradled the phone again and stood staring blearily at the window. Now what do I do?

What she decided to do in the end was to go to Watney Street Market. There was no reason to be certain Gregory St Clair would be there, of course; he'd been working at Connie's factory this morning and perhaps by now he'd feel he'd done enough of a day's work. But she couldn't think of any other way to fill her time and there was still no sign of Gus. If he had, as he had said in his note, gone to Companies House again he would stay till they threw him out, which meant he wouldn't be here at the flat till . . . She tried to work it out but she gave up. Late, anyway, and she couldn't just sit here like the sort of woman Monty Ledbetter admired, just waiting for her fella to make sure he was warm and well fed when he got home. Bugger that for a game of soldiers, she thought, using one of Gus's favourite phrases. I've got to be up and doing. *Something*.

The market was buzzing when she got there. The afternoon had settled to the rich sweating heat that Londoners were beginning to take for granted this summer, and the crowds around the stalls jostled and shouted at each other busily, filling their bags with fruit and vegetables and cut-down jeans and half-price trainers (probably fallen off the back of someone's shop, thought George, seeing the brave display that filled one stall) and generally spending money few of them could afford. It was an invigorating and cheerful sight and George's spirits rose. Whatever happened, they would sort this out, she and Gus, and life would go on as it had. She bought herself a half-pound of cherries from the first stall that had any and strolled through the market, wolfing them and spitting the stones into the gutter like everyone else.

Gregory was nowhere in sight when she reached the stall where she'd bought her mango and she felt a stab of disappointment; but then mentally shrugged. She hadn't any right to expect he'd be here, after all, in spite of what he'd said at Connie's place, which she had understood to be an invitation. She'd just have to kill the time till Gus got back. There was little else she could do; and she tried not to think of her Connections chart waiting at home on her desk. If she kept her mind clear now, maybe when she came back to it, fresh and alert, she'd see something she'd missed before. It often happened like that.

By the time she'd been round the market twice, the combination of the heat and the vigorous sweating she, like everyone else around her, was experiencing, together with the sweetness of the cherries that lingered in her mouth, had given her a raging thirst. She looked about for somewhere to quench it, and went purposefully across to a little café in the far corner. Its battered fascia no longer told passers-by anything about the place's name, but its cheerful front window was full of advertisements for Coca-Cola and Fanta and the promise of *Jamaica Patties, sizzling hot!*

The place was almost full and she had to push past people to get to the counter. She asked for a club soda, forgetting for a moment that she meant Perrier water. (However long she lived in London, traces of her American life still lingered.) When she was given the bottle and a straw by a cheerful woman with a vast bosom straining under a red T-shirt, which read in undulating lines *You Don't Get Many of These to the Pound!*, she turned around to lean on the counter on one elbow. As she sucked up the water she looked about her.

Someone came up behind her and laughed softly into her ear. 'Hey, doctor, we can't go on meeting like this. Folks are goin' to talk!'

She turned her head and blinked. 'I came down here to look for you!' she said delightedly. 'It's a hell of a coincidence to have found you just like that.'

'Coincidence? Just like that? Nothin' of the sort! I been watching you ever since you got down the market. Sweet cherries for a sweet lady, huh? I knew you was looking for me.'

'Why didn't you speak to me then?' she said and he laughed.

'You must think me so stupid! I don't go talkin' where folks can see what I'm doin' and who I'm with! It don't do. I'd ha' followed you outa the market if you'd gone, but there, I guessed you'd come in here. It's a hot and thirsty day, and there's nowhere else you could go. So, how do you like Connie's place?'

'Why is it all right to talk to me in here, when it wasn't outside?' she said. He laughed again.

'Look around you, pretty lady. Who's here that'd make trouble for a good boy like me?'

She looked, puzzled. No one seemed to be aware of her scrutiny; pretty girls with their hair plaited into corn rows; men in the current uniform of tight spandex shorts and loose T-shirts sat with their heads together, busy about their own affairs. She had just realized what he was trying to tell her when he said softly, 'Not a honky in sight, 'cepting for you, doctor! There ain't no one here'll take notice of who I talk to. Out there it's different.' And he jerked his head towards the street beyond the poster-filled window. So poster-filled that no one could easily see in.

She caught her breath. 'What is it you can tell me?'

'What do you want to know?' He was looking at her sideways, his eyes very watchful. He would not miss the least

264

change of expression on her face, she realized. Whatever she felt it had to be true and honest, or he'd know it. And suddenly it mattered to her, mattered a great deal, that he should think well of her, and her truthfulness. So she would be as true and honest as she could.

'My fella's in trouble,' she said. 'Someone is trying to fit him up. And I think someone's been killed and I think they used the machine – that chopping machine at your friend Connie's place – to do it with.'

'He's no friend of mine,' Gregory said softly after a long pause.

'Well, the man you work for.'

'I work for me, not him. He just pays off some debts for me.'

'Oh, Gregory, stop playing games with me, will you?' she snapped suddenly. 'I'm hot and I'm tired and things aren't going right for me, one bit. Just talk straight, for heaven's sake!'

He looked at her for a long moment and then nodded. 'I guess you are at that. Come and sit down, doctor. Another bottle, Melissa, for the lady,' he said over his shoulder as he led George to a corner table that only a moment before had had a couple of people sitting at it. It was almost as though he'd willed them away so that they could sit down.

The big woman appeared behind her with another bottle of Perrier, and added a plastic beaker this time for her to pour it into. George wanted to laugh. Clearly being with Gregory gave her high status.

'All right,' Gregory leaned closer to her. 'You been good to me and mine, you and the hospital. All that work you do there for the babies with the sickle cell, you know? We're glad of it. Very glad of it. There's not enough who care for the pain we get or the misery of it. They send babies home from hospital screaming with it, sometimes; blame their mothers for being stupid. Not at your Old East though, and I'm glad of it, you hear me? So I'll tell you – only I warn you, I tell you and no one else. I go into no honky courts, tell no honky cops what I know. I tell *you*. If you can get it sorted out, great. I'm not evidence for you, though, and that has to be clear. Is it clear?'

She thought for a moment, looking at him. His eyes were wide and the white areas had a bloodshot look; he hadn't been getting much sleep lately, she thought. He probably worked all night at Connie's. His skin shone ebony in the softened light of the café and the shading of green and purple tones gave it a gloss of such beauty that somewhere deep in her mind she thought, I wish I were a painter. But she shook that away and said, 'How will I know you're telling me the truth?'

He laughed. 'You won't. You just got to trust me or not. Anyway, what'd be in it for me to tell you lies? I told you, I get good vibes about Old East. So, it's up to you. I'll tell you what I pick up around the place – and we talk to each other, you know, us brothers – and you can do what you like with it. So, you say what you want. I ain't evidence for no one, but I got the story. You want it or not?'

She took a deep breath. 'I want it.'

'OK, so here it is. There's a guy down this part of the world that is doing very bad things around your hospital. He's using it to get stuff to Connie, see? And then Connie sells it on. To India. I'll bet he got very bothered when you wanted to see his machine, hmm? His baling machine down there? Because he puts the stuff inside the bales, and that's how they get it out. No sweat. No one looks till it's unpacked in Calcutta and who in Indian Customs wants to dig around in stinking rags without a nice bit of cash on the side for his trouble? No one. And there ain't no one cares enough to pay the cash. So it gets through, no questions asked, and Connie and the man make a lot of money. A *lot* of money – and they intend to go on making it. I've heard them talk. I got good ears and a very long nose. I like to know what's going on. And this has been going on for a long time, and'll keep on for a long time yet.'

There was a long silence and then George, deeply puzzled and not ashamed to show it, said, 'But smuggling what? Stuff stolen from the hospital? People are always taking stuff, but

266

not enough to smuggle in bales that size. I mean, what are they sending out?'

'Drugs,' Gregory said.

'Drugs?' George shook her head. 'But they grow opium and cannabis there, maybe even coca. Why should they –'

'Not my sort of drugs,' Gregory said almost contemptuously, and laughed softly. 'Your sort. Steroids and antibiotics – the new kinds – and the special stuff for cancer. That's the sort. Lots of it.'

28

_____

Gus sat and stared out of the window as though there were something there worth looking at. His plate of pasta was ignored in front of him, but she said nothing. He'd eaten the melon and Parma ham and she was grateful he'd managed that much.

She hadn't had to ask him how his day at Companies House had gone. It had been, he told her shortly without any prompting, a total frost.

'I've got no more than I got last time I went. A circle of companies feeding back into each other, shell inside shell. It takes a greater expert in these things than I am to untangle it all.' He'd thrown the sheaf of papers tucked inside a plastic envelope on to her sofa in disgust and left it lying there. She hadn't picked it up to look for herself. There seemed little point, for she was no better at comprehending business structure than he was – a great deal less capable, in fact – and looking for herself would just have annoyed him. So she left it lying there, a forlorn limp thing among her cushions.

She had told him of the result of her own day; of the visit to Connie's as well as to St Dymphna's – though there hadn't been much there that was of any use to him – and of her conversation with Gregory. But he'd shown little reaction. He'd just listened and nodded and said nothing, and she'd been too bitterly disappointed by his reaction even to mention her efforts to plot a chart that would show how the disparate events linked together and affected his situation. She had just swallowed her hurt to let it lie, undigested and hot and painful, somewhere between her lower ribs and her belly.

'Mike has some information for you,' she ventured when the silence had gone on so long it seemed unbearable to her. 'He was on his mobile, didn't want to say on that what it was.'

'So I should bloody think,' Gus grunted. 'You might as well go to the BBC and read it out to the whole bleedin' world as do that.'

'I told him to come over later. That I hoped you'd be here.' She was uncertain about talking about Mike to him; did he still have any lingering resentment? This was hardly the time to find out, she thought; but he seemed unmoved, just shrugging an acknowledgement.

'Are you sure that what Monty told me –' she began but he shook his head irritably.

'I told you I'm not sure of anything, but I'm bloody extra unsure that he's right this time. He can be a great help, knows everyone and everyone knows him, but this time he's come a cropper. If Lenny had been in Brighton we'd know by now. There's a good relationship between the Met and the local force. They'd have seen to it we were tipped off there was a local villain of ours turned up on their patch.'

She frowned. 'Is Lenny a villain?' she said. 'You've never said so before.'

He made a little grimace. 'No more'n most round here. Been done for a bit of receiving now and again. Fish from the market, some vegetable oil fell off the back of a Soho restaurant – nothing all that terrible. But enough to have him listed at the nick. Enough for one of the Bill in Brighton to have let us know if he'd suddenly fetched up there and settled in. So I don't think Monty's got it right this time.'

'But suppose he's using another name?' George persisted. Somehow she had believed Monty. There had been a certainty about him that would have been hard to simulate. 'Suppose he's hiding from you and –'

'Oh, George, do stop and think, woman,' he snapped. 'Lenny's got no need to hide from me! Yeah, sure, I'm pissed off with him. I'd give him a hell of a tongue lashing. But I wouldn't *hurt* him, whatever he's done to me! He knows that perfectly well. He'd paid off his bloody debt. Even if he hadn't he'd have no call to run away, not from me. And however daft he can be, he's surely not daft enough not to know that. There'd be no reason for Lenny to play any such stupid tricks as using a cover name. I just can't believe it. He doesn't have the – the –' He stopped.

'According to Monty, he's a nerd.'

'Monty said that?'

'Well, not the word exactly. Just that he wasn't much of a fella.'

'He's right there. He wouldn't have the wit to use a cover, take it from me. If he had, he'd never have got his form. Whenever he's been caught taking a bit of stolen gear, he's done it in such a stupid fashion he's bloody nearly called us out to witness it happening.'

'You don't believe the bribe story either? That he was made an offer he couldn't refuse?'

'Mafia stuff? I know they're trying to organize themselves along those lines but it's not established here or anything like it. Sure, Lenny might be a bit worried about who set him up for this, but all this stuff from Monty! I don't believe a word of it!'

'But –'

It was a relief when the phone rang. Gus was sunk deeper than ever in despair and arguing with him seemed to be making him worse; yet surely she couldn't let it go so easily? Monty had come up with information that she believed. Why couldn't Gus? Because it might help him? It was almost, she thought as she reached for the phone, as though he wants to be found guilty. I've never seen him so miserable.

It was Mike, checking Gus was there, and promising to push himself as fast as he could from the other side of Canning Town to come to see him. She hung up and quietly took away Gus's plate and fetched coffee instead. He drank it absentmindedly and she pushed a plate of amaretti biscuits closer to him in the hope he would equally absentmindedly eat them too. He didn't.

It was beginning to get dark at nine-thirty as Mike's ring at the bell made them both jump. She let him in with a bounce in her step and an eagerness to see him that she didn't bother to hide, but regretted when she returned with him to the living room and saw Gus's scowl.

'News,' she said briefly, leaving Mike to stand in the middle of the room as she went and sat on the sofa. Whatever she said or did, she thought sourly, Gus would find fault tonight.

'Hello, Guv,' Mike said.

Gus grunted.

'It's not good, I'm afraid.' Mike sounded gruff. 'Can I sit down?'

'Of course, you fool!' Gus snapped. Mike seemed to wince at the harshness in his voice, and suddenly it was all too much for George. She'd bottled it all up, the fear and the anger and the frustration, and now it was not possible to contain it any longer.

'Gus, shut up!' she snapped. She jumped to her feet and came round the sofa to stand with her elbows sharp at her sides and her fists on her hips. 'I've had just about enough!'

'Eh?' Gus blinked and stared up at her, clearly startled.

'You've been impossible and bloody selfish all evening,' she shouted. 'Carrying on as though you're the only one who's miserable about what's happening to you. Indulging yourself in the most abysmal miseries, paddling in self-pity, turning yourself into a snivelling heap of –'

'Hey, hey!' Mike cried, coming forward to stand on Gus's other side. 'Dr B., will you stop that! You've no right to speak to the Guv so!'

George was startled now, taken aback by this opposition from someone she had actually been trying to protect; but she was not startled for long. 'I've got every right when he's behaving like a spoiled child who's lost his little kiddy-cart,' she blazed. 'I'm sick of walking on eggshells because the poor little darling can't cope with a teensy-weensy bit of pain, sick of . . .'

Mike shouted back, but she didn't give him a chance; she just roared above his attempts to make her listen, letting out all her frustration and disappointment and confusion in a great wave of noise, and Mike gave her as good as he got.

They clearly would have gone on and on, neither paying any attention at all to the other, if it hadn't been for Gus. He sat and looked up at the two of them, one on each side, turning his head as they spoke – or rather shouted – at each other like a spectator at a tennis match, and suddenly he started to laugh. It was real laughter, not the forced sound of someone trying to put a good face on a bad scene, and the laughter grew loud enough almost to rival the roars that Mike and George were producing, and went on for some time. Then he leaned forwards, his head in his arms, his shoulders shaking as he rested on the table in front of him.

Mike stopped yelling first and leaned over to shake Gus's shoulder, alarmed. Slowly Gus sat up, to face George, who was red in the face and had a trickle of sweat finding its way down one cheek, and began to start laughing again.

She couldn't help it. She had never been violent, never had felt the need to hit anyone, but this was more than she could bear. Rage lifted in her, like the fury of a frustrated, bewildered child, and she had to give it expression. Almost before she realized it was happening she brought her right arm back and delivered a slap to his face so loud that all three of them were shocked into silence. Her hand tingled and she stared in horror at Gus as he stood with one hand across his cheek staring back at her in blank amazement.

'Wow,' he said after a long moment. 'That was – wow!'

'Oh, shit!' George cried. She turned and, slamming the living-room door behind her, hurtled into her bedroom slamming the door there too before she leaned against it in a flood of tears that made her shake and feel sick.

Eventually the tears eased, slowed, and began to dry up. She crept across her room to lie on her bed, curled up and miserable. She could hear the soft buzz of voices from the living room and tried not to listen, but she couldn't stop herself. She lay there with her head turned so that both her ears were free to pick up the sounds, and registered that they were talking, not shouting, and once even they laughed.

At that her rage was huge again; she actually sat up and stared at the door, almost ready to go rushing out to pummel them into silence. How dare they sit in her living room and laugh when she felt so godawful lousy? When she had actually hit out physically like some sort of half-witted, half-mad –

Even in her thoughts the words failed her. She lay down again on her damp pillow and snivelled a little to herself, enjoying the self-pity. Outside she heard footsteps as the pair of them walked along her minuscule hallway to the front door, heard it open, more speech and then a click as the door closed.

She knew only one of them had gone out: Mike. She buried her head in the pillow now, carefully covering both her ears this time. She wouldn't listen, she wouldn't, no matter what.

She felt him come in and sit down on the bed beside her and became rigid, her back tightening against his touch. He hadn't tried to touch her yet, but heaven help him when he did.

'I'm so sorry, George,' he said. His voice came to her muffled because of the pillows and she moved a little, so slightly that he wouldn't notice, in order to listen more easily.

There was a silence and then he said more loudly, 'George, I'm truly so sorry. I behaved disgustingly and I do beg your pardon. I've apologised to Mike and he's forgiven me. Please will you do the same?'

'Oh, you bastard,' she howled, banging her head under the pillow. 'Not even giving me the chance to tell you what I – Oh, you're a *bastard*.'

'So you said.' He spoke with an air of humility but she could hear the hint of laughter in him. 'Honestly, I am sorry, George, and you can say anything you like and I'll listen to every sodding word, I promise. Everything you say, for always. I won't just listen, I'll take it in and I'll agree with you, and –'

She whirled on the bed and stared at him from hot red-rimmed eyes above damp flushed cheeks, her hair tumbled over the pillow. 'What good is that, for God's sake? I don't want a man who sits there and just takes what I say, any more than I want one who expects me to do it! I just want someone who'll – who'll –'

'Stop being so selfish and stupid and who'll make an effort not to take out his miseries on other people. To be honest, George ...' He hesitated and peered down at her in the half-dark of the unlit room, illuminated only by the spill of light coming in from the hallway. 'To be honest you've shown me what I thought I wanted. I thought I knew, but I didn't. Please, George, isn't it time we got married?'

'Such a ridiculous way to plan your life,' she said dreamily, and stirred against his shoulder. 'Stupid, really stupid. Dumb. Crazy. *Stupid.*'

'Who's planning?' he said drowsily. 'I'm not.'

'Hmm,' she said and then took a deep breath. 'It's not even as though we – well, did we?'

'Did we what?'

'You know perfectly well.'

'Made love?' asked Gus.

'Silly word. British word.'

'Beats "fooling around". Isn't that what your lot say?'

George tried to sound dignified. 'But it's not as though we did. Did we?'

'No,' he said gravely. 'We didn't.' His hand was warm on her shoulder and she fitted her head into the curve of his neck. 'Does that matter?'

'No,' she said and yawned. 'Not in the least. Who's got the energy? Fighting takes it out of you. In fact it makes it –'

'I know. Better. More, well, *serious.*'

'Mmm.'

'Anyway ...' He snickered softly in the darkness.

'Mmm,' she said again and thought for a while. 'I always thought if and when I got the proposal I wanted to accept – well, I thought it'd be different.'

'How different?'

'Not after a fight,' she said. 'Never after a fight.'

'It takes a fight to show you what you couldn't see, sometimes.'

'Mmm,' she said.

There was a long silence. When she spoke again he moved

beneath her head so she knew he'd been on the verge of falling asleep. 'Gus, if you have to give up the job, will you be –'

'Impossible,' he said. 'I'll be impossible. For at least a week. Then we'll be like we are tonight and there'll be no nookie, but I'll love you to bits, and feel better. Can't be bad, hmm?'

'Seriously for a moment, please. Will you be happy?'

He was silent for a long time and then said, 'Honestly, I don't know. It doesn't matter as much as it did. There's you now, and – well, it just doesn't matter so much. But whether I can be properly happy all over, you know? I can't say. I love you but –'

'It's all right, you fool,' she said softly. 'I'll be going on with work, so why shouldn't you? I love you too, but I do need other things as well.'

'I've got the business,' he said. 'All that fish to fry. You won't have to –'

'If you say I don't have to work I'll take my word back and you can go and marry a doormat somewhere else,' she said.

'Shut up. I was going to say you won't have to worry about taking any job you don't like. You can be choosier; leave Old East if you want to.'

She contemplated that. 'But I like it there.'

'Then stay there.'

There was another silence. 'But the best bits are doing cases with you. Maybe I won't like it if you're not at Ratcliffe Street nick any more.'

'Then go somewhere else.'

Again she was silent for a while and then said softly, 'I've got a better idea. We'll sort out this stupid business and get you back to work. At Ratcliffe Street. How does that sound?'

'Almost as good as getting hitched to you. Shall we have a fancy job or a little send-off? Cockney do with jellied eels and "Knees Up Mother Brown", or posh affair with champagne and crooked pinkie fingers?'

'I'll let you know.' She sat up. 'First we've got to get you back to work.'

'I was just coming round to the idea that I don't give a

damn about work,' he said and then wrinkled his face and threw up his hands as she reached across him and switched on the bedside light. 'Ouch. Turn that off! It's blinding me.'

'You look a mess,' she said dispassionately, looking down at his rumpled shirt and hair and general air of dishevelment.

'Take a gander at yourself, lady. You're like the Witch of Endor.' He squinted up at her. 'It's a good thing I'm marrying you. No one else'd have you for fourpence in a jumble sale.'

'Phooey.' She got off the bed. 'Come on. I'm hungry and so are you. I'll make some coffee and we'll see where we go from there. I've got some work I've done I want to show you and I want to hear what Mike had to say.'

He sat up and passed both hands over his untidy head before swinging his legs to the floor. 'He told me who the copper was who framed me,' he said after a moment. She sat down beside him, her knees giving way beneath her. He sounded suddenly grim again and she found herself thinking, to her own amazement, Roop. Don't let it be Roop. That'd break his heart.

'Salmon,' he said. 'Bob Salmon, it seems. Says he's got a lead from someone else and watched me and saw the handover. He must have misunderstood. He can't have been deliberately – I mean, can he? He might have thought – I should have explained to him, but I never thought – Well, it's my own fault if he did. He must have, mustn't he?'

She put her arms across his shoulders and hugged him gently. 'Honey, I don't know. We'll have to find out.'

'I suppose so. It's not true, George, really it –'

'Say that again and I'll have to hit you again,' she said softly. 'Of course it isn't true. I know that perfectly well. So where do we go from here?'

He lifted his head and looked at her. 'Oh, George,' he said. 'You really –'

'Shut up. Or rather, don't. Tell me where we go from here.'

'Mike's gone to Brighton,' he said and she lifted her chin in amazement at that.

'What did you say? Brighton? But I thought you didn't believe Monty when he –'

276

'I didn't want to believe it,' he said, standing up. 'I was just so – I've known Lenny all my life, nearly. It just didn't seem – Well, anyway, Mike's gone to look around. He knows him by sight as well as I do, so he'll see what he can see. He's a good fella, Mike. It's his day off tomorrow and he's doing this for me. A good fella.'

'A lot of people are,' she said. She put up her hands to hold his shoulders. 'I'm a good fella too. Come on and see what I did this afternoon. I've been doing some thinking, and we can go through the evidence of it together. When we've had some supper.' And she took him out to the kitchen.

29

It was as though they'd already been married for years. They woke when her alarm clock called them at eight and shared the bathroom, dodging each other carefully, communicating only in monosyllables as he shaved (using her silly little Ladyshave) and she scrubbed her teeth. It was the same when they had breakfast; she gave him cereal and coffee and he wolfed it in silence and then went and pulled on his jacket and made for the front door.

'I'll try and call you some time,' he muttered and she nodded.

'OK. I'll leave the answerphone on. I might go out. I've a couple of ideas that could be worth looking into.'

'Like what?' He looked at her sharply and she shook her head at him.

'I don't know yet! I've got things to think about. I'll look again at that chart I worked out. It might lead me somewhere. I'm certainly not going to sit here and just wait till –'

'No,' he said a little more peaceably. 'Nor am I. I'll see if I can find out when the hearing will be and then get some sort of defence notes written out.' He stopped when he reached the door and came back. 'I'm not being very – Well, I'm never at my best in the morning. Sorry.'

She managed a faint grin. 'I've noticed. Not to worry. Me too. It takes time to get your head together.'

'I'm not sorry, though.'

'Sorry about what?'

'That we're getting married. In fact, I'm – I'm . . .'

The grin widened. 'Yes?'

'I don't know!' He shook his head. 'I think I'm just trying to say I'm happy. It mightn't look like it at the moment, but I've a lot to think about and I won't be able to concentrate on anything else till all the mess is sorted out. Does that make sense?'

'It makes total sense,' she said. She went over, kissed him and smoothed her hand over his hair to tidy it, because he'd rubbed it into peaks as he tried to explain. 'All the sense I need, anyway. Go on, be about your business. I'll see you when I see you.'

'Yes,' he said gratefully and went.

She finished her own breakfast then, sitting and staring out of the kitchen window at what was clearly going to be another scorching day. Shouldn't she feel different? Excited, pleased, *different*? The last time she'd accepted an offer of marriage – Ian, she thought, Ian in Scotland, and couldn't even remember his face – the last time she'd been full of tearing excitement, cock-a-hoop, really. She'd bounced around the day after he'd proposed – all proper and pretty over dinner, an actual candlelit dinner in the most expensive hotel in Inverness – as though she'd had rubber feet. Now, there was no bounce, no sense of achievement, just a comfortable certainty that this was as right as it could possibly be and what was there to be excited about? It was almost as though any actual wedding would be an irrelevance. They were as much a pair as they could be, she and Gus. Certainly more than she had ever been with Ian; and again she tried to remember his face and failed. Interesting, that, considering the sort of memory she had that rarely let her down.

She shook herself back into action as she caught sight of her wrist-watch and got purposefully to her feet. Nine o'clock. Quite what she was to do today she hadn't in fact decided, but she certainly wasn't going to spend it slopping about like this, and she went to work purposefully, cleaning her little kitchen and then making the bed, tidying the bathroom, making space in the bathroom cupboard for his gear, as well as in her wardrobe, for surely he'd be bringing some of his stuff over here now, and then setting to work on the living room. There were a few dead flowers to dispose of and last night's detritus to clear up.

She picked up the plastic folder Gus had dropped on the sofa and which had migrated behind a cushion and frowned. Would he want it this morning? He'd said he was going to organize his defence for the hearing; maybe there were things in here he'd need? He'd been very dispirited about his attempts to track down the people who had taken over Lenny's shop. Maybe there was in fact nothing here that mattered. But before she got worried about his forgetting it, it would make sense to look at it. And, anyway, it might add something to her own information bank. There was always a chance.

The folder contained several sheets of paper on which he had scribbled in his familiar spiky handwriting, using his own special shorthand. As long as she'd known him she'd failed to follow the thought processes that led him to make the notes he did. She'd often looked at pages like these, covered with cryptic comments, question marks set against names and dates, and been lost within moments. Even where she could read the words he'd written they made little sense.

These pages were the same; there were amongst them, however, photocopied pages from some sort of register, and she looked at them first. They might give her some sense of what was on the handwritten sheets.

They were lists, no more. Names of companies and the directors of the Boards which ran them, together with columns of figures which made no sense to her at all. She ran her eye down them, one after the other – there were about twelve of the pages in the folder – and shook her head. Incomprehensible. What did Franklin Holdings plc and Jennings P. J. Ltd Iron Factors and Ludlow and Sons Ltd Import/Export mean to her or to their investigation? Nothing at all. She flipped over to another page and then another. They all looked the same and she sighed as she let the names slide past her eyes. Olaf Jensen Timber Importers; N. H. Blasi Spice Dealers Ltd, L. E. T. Hakim and Sons (Metals) plc; M. R. H. Market

Traders Ltd, Ashgar and Mamouli Fabrics Ltd, David Gellings plc.

She stopped and looked back, aware that her attention had been caught by something and not sure what it was. There had been something in that list, surely, that meant something to her? And she looked down more carefully, observing addresses as well this time.

Olaf Jensen Timber Importers, in Ipswich. N. H. Blasi, the spice firm, in Shadwell. Not far away at all, she thought. Was that what I noticed? Their address? It seemed a bit tenuous, so she looked on. L. E. T. Hakim and Sons (Metals) Ltd were at Tilbury, well down the river. M. R. H. Market Traders had an address in Bond Street. A bit fashionable for a market trader, she thought, and went on. Ashgar and Mamouli . . . And realized all at once what it was she had noticed and went back to stare at it.

M. R. H. Market Traders Ltd. She closed her eyes to listen to the memory of what had been said to her on the day of the Trust Board Meeting, what Ellen had told her, and what she had heard at St Dymphna's, then began to search furiously through the drawers of the little desk for the booklet about the new Trust that had been sent round to all the staff when the NHS reforms had taken over at Old East.

She found it and scrabbled through the pages furiously. She stopped, her fingers on one entry, staring down at it. The list of new non-executive Trust directors.

Michael Roderick Harlow, she read. M. R. H. The market trader in a big way of business. He had more market stalls and market sites than she could count, he had told her. What was the name of his company – and she was quite certain it was his – doing among those Gus had collected in his search for the owners of Copper's Properties who had taken over Lenny Greeson's shop and who, perhaps – and it wasn't too far-fetched a connection – had for reasons of their own disposed of Don Greeson and his dog in Connie's macerating machine?

Now excitement did begin to bubble in her. She settled down to go through the papers in Gus's plastic folder more carefully. There might be information here that would make the links even more clear.

It took her a while but eventually she saw what it was he had been trying to do. Each of the companies on the Companies House Register had to list their directors. Gus had been looking for companies where directors overlapped; where the same name appeared on more than one Board. He'd found several, but none of them made any sense to George. There were names after names and she'd never heard of any of them. On M. R. H. Market Traders' list of Board members there were no names that meant anything at all to her, though some were obviously there to do as they were told. J. R. Harlow and L. F. N. Harlow were clearly members of Mickey's family and as such likely to be obedient to his demands. The other two names meant nothing. One of them, however, the innocuous sounding E. Pike, also appeared on the list of Board members of three other companies on Gus's lists, and those also had members on different Boards elsewhere. By linking from one to another she at last found a track that meandered between Copper's Properties and M. R. H. Market Traders, but it involved five companies and many names, and she could not believe that each and every one of these people, whoever they were, were ciphers who just did as they were told. Perhaps they were, but was it likely? It seemed highly improbable, the more she thought about it. And anyway, even if they were ciphers, would they all collude in murder? And if so, why? Why was Don Greeson murdered at all? Why should Mickey Harlow want him murdered, which would appear to be the logical outcome of her musings, and why . . .

Her head was spinning now. There was clearly much more going on here than she had realized. She had seen her searches as first of all involving just a severed leg and perhaps a couple of burned women, which were of course bad enough, but in her terms, understandable. Now it seemed she had stumbled into a morass of City-type wheeling and dealing that mystified her. Digging around in dead bodies I'm good at, she thought forlornly. Coping with live money dealers foxes me completely.

Money dealers, she thought then. Money, and murder. What was it Gregory had told her? That Connie was a smuggler of medicines to India, and that they were being obtained via Old East? She leaned back in her chair and stared sightlessly at the window again.

Connie was, according to Gregory, making money as a smuggler of Old East's property. Nonsense. If sufficient Old East stuff had been stolen for Connie to make much out of it, she'd have known. The whole damned hospital would have known. They could never have kept such a thing quiet. She remembered what had happened a couple of years ago when there'd been a rash of pilfering; there hadn't been a soul in the place who hadn't suspected everyone else, who didn't watch his or her fellows with slitted-eye concentration. And anyway, even if someone had been successful in silent theft, once the robberies had been discovered the thefts would surely have been stopped. Yet Connie, again according to Gregory, saw his smuggling as an on-going activity.

Slowly her eyes lost their glazed look, focused and became sharp. There would have to be some digging around done; but how? She herself couldn't just turn up at the hospital, not while she was officially on compassionate leave, and start nosing about. Anyway, she wouldn't have access to the places she would need to investigate.

She thought hard, letting her mind move as it wished, knowing that to be the most fruitful sort of thinking she could do. Memories attached themselves to ideas, pleated into them, made new forms; memories of her family's business talk, so boring, so incomprehensible in childhood, now making a curious sort of sense. She saw in her mind's eye the range of vans with their names painted on them in Connie's yard, and then, slowly, she reached for the phone. A pattern had formed deep in her mind and emerged into daylight, fresh now and very seductive. If she'd got it right, it was the answer. Or, of course, it was just so much moonshine. There was only one way to find out. It was a gamble, but it might work.

'I'm glad she's so much better.' Ellen's voice was a touch sardonic at the other end of the phone. 'Does that mean you'll be back soon?'

'As soon as I can be, Ellen,' George said. 'How are things working in the lab?'

'I hate to tell you this, but absolutely fine. Alan's coping nicely, got Sheila eating out of his hand, and there haven't been any nasty episodes at all. I gather you arranged for any forensic work to go to the other police lab.'

'Well, I did let them know I was off work,' George admitted. 'I thought they might do that. You don't mind, I hope?'

'We're glad of it,' Ellen said. 'It means we can concentrate solely on hospital work while you're away. When you get back and can take over the forensic, that'll be soon enough to change the arrangements.'

'OK.' George hesitated. 'Ellen, sitting here with my friend – she sleeps a lot, you know? – I've had time to think. I'm ... Hell, I'm not sure how to explain this.'

'Try from the start,' Ellen said, her voice suddenly eager. 'What is it?'

'Well,' George said. 'It's sort of to do with St Dymphna's.'

'Oh?' Ellen sounded sharper than ever.

'Mmm. I – er, I managed to get a free day in the week – my friend's neighbour took the day off work, so I used it to visit St Dymphna's.'

There was a little silence. 'You came all the way from Chislehurst for that and didn't come in here?'

'I know.' George began to feel wretched. Her usual propensity for lying was letting her down. Perhaps there was too much truth in what she was saying? She hurried on. 'I just got to thinking about the Board and what they're trying to do – Listen, Ellen, I overheard something and – Well, there was someone there who, er, wanted to help Old East, you know? I can't go into details.' (Glory be, I can't, the back of her mind thought feverishly. This lie is getting very complicated. I can't imagine a lot more that won't make Ellen see right through it all.) 'But let me explain. It seems possible ...' She hesitated. 'It seems possible that someone has been stealing drugs from Old East. In large quantities. Not narcotic drugs,' she said that hastily, hearing Ellen's sharp intake of breath. 'Steroids, antibiotics, anti-cancer stuff. Expensive mainline therapies.'

There was a blank silence and then Ellen said, 'Good God!'

'The thing is, I'm not sure – well, let's put it this way. If such thefts were happening, I think we'd all know, wouldn't we?'

'You're damned right we would,' Ellen said firmly. 'There's no way stuff could be disappearing from here more than the usual pilfering quantities without us knowing it. We all, the business managers, you know, watch our budgets like fury. And Pharmacy is on *my* patch and I'm here to tell you that there is no way this side of the millennium that I'm being ripped off. Not me.'

'I know,' George said. 'And I've had the craziest thought. I wondered if you could look into it.'

'Well?'

'A bit of explanation first. How are orders placed and filled for pharmaceuticals?'

'How? We fill out order forms and send them to the manufacturers. How else?'

'Not to intermediaries, or wholesalers?'

'No. We buy direct. We're a big hospital, so we get direct sales and the discounts that go with them.'

'I hoped that was how it would be.' George caught her breath as excitement began to grow inside her. 'OK. How is it done?'

'What? Oh, well, the order forms are made out in my office. Monthly. I collate the demands from the whole hospital, wards and departments, and make up the orders. Then they're checked by the Purchasing people in Accounts. They're sent the forms.'

'And then?'

'In due course we get a delivery notice confirming the address and the name of the person responsible for accepting the delivery and checking it for accuracy. The goods arrive a while later and a statement comes with them. Then the firms send an invoice. I check the goods received against it; if it's all right, I pass the invoice to Accounts who pay it. That's all.'

George took a deep shaky breath. 'Listen, Ellen. Suppose someone sent off orders in Old East's name, but when the delivery notice comes authorized delivery to a different address?'

'It would be sent there,' Ellen said, mystified. 'That happens sometimes. We've got a branch unit, a sort of spoke to our hub, out in Sussex, remember? And there are some outreach clinics. The orders are written to go there directly.'

'I knew it! And when the invoices are sent, do they go to you or to the place the stuff was delivered to?'

'The place it was delivered to,' Ellen said. 'Then they check their orders against records, send us the invoice and we arrange payment.'

'Then that's how it's done,' George said almost to herself.

Ellen said, 'What?' and when George didn't reply at once said it again, louder. 'What are you talking about?'

'It's all right, Ellen. I'm so sorry,' George said. 'It was such a puzzle, you see. I knew no one could buy listed therapies just for the asking. It has to be proper hospitals or doctors. I just couldn't see how the orders were made in the first place. Then it's a doddle just to embezzle on the payments, isn't it?'

'Is it?' Ellen said.

'Here I was thinking I had no head for this sort of thing. But I do, don't I?'

'I can't tell till I know *what's* in your head,' Ellen said tartly. 'You're not talking sense! If you could just –'

'I'm sorry!' George was jubilant. 'Listen, the – er the person at St Dymphna's who told me that we were being robbed didn't have it quite right. We aren't being robbed at all. But someone else is – the manufacturers. I'm not sure what the scam is but there is one. Orders are sent out, seeming to come from Old East, so no one at the pharmaceuticals firm queries them – we *are* Old East, after all! – and when they send out the delivery notes, someone there at the hospital intercepts them and arranges to have the deliveries sent to – somewhere else. Then some sort of arrangement is made about the payment – I don't know what. But I'll bet there's a crooked accountant or bookkeeper or someone at the firms supplying the goods who lets them go through in some way without payment. To the company, that is. I dare say they get paid

286

handsomely enough for what they do. And there it is. Quantities of drugs ready to be sold abroad for vast sums, after they're smuggled out. It's a hell of a business!'

'It sounds crazy to me,' Ellen said. 'How could anyone —'

'I know it does. But I also know it's happening. Oh, you'd be amazed at how clever thieves can be! I'm sure I'm right. It makes total sense. Mind you, it doesn't explain the burned women. There has to be a connection there! If only I can find it.'

'What burned women?' Ellen sounded despairing now. 'George, are you sure you're not ill yourself? You're talking an awful lot of, well, odd things.'

'It's all right, Ellen,' George cried jubilantly. 'It actually makes sense, believe me. I'll be back soon, I hope. Next week, maybe. See what you can discover there to back me up, will you? You'll see I'm right. Bless you for your help.' And she hung up the phone with a little clatter and then stretched her arms above her head and shouted her elation at the ceiling.

30

After that it seemed impossible to sit still. She wandered about the flat, tweaking at already perfectly neat cushions and straightening pictures so that they hung crooked instead, generally prowling. Not to have Gus here to explain to him what had happened, the way she'd worked out the Old East/ Connie connection, was agony. And then, as suddenly as she had been swept up into euphoria, she was thrown into gloom.

None of this helped Gus in his dealings with the CIB in the least. To get him out of the hole he was in with them they would have to find Lenny Greeson. And they hadn't. Would Mike manage it there in Brighton? Her spirits nosedived even more. Could she phone him? Find out?

But it was too early. She looked at her watch and knew he could barely have arrived in Brighton, let alone had any success in his searches. She would have to find something else to do. Something *useful*.

She thought again about Gus's folder. Could she take it over to him at his flat? After all, he might need it. Maybe he wasn't there any more, though. He'd said he was going to Ratcliffe Street nick as arranged with the Super there to work on his defence notes. But she phoned his flat all the same and, as she'd expected, got the answerphone. There was no point in leaving any message.

She picked up the notes again to look at the lists of companies and knew suddenly the only thing she could do now; there was no point in trying to use Gus's notes. She'd have to follow her own path of investigation, and at present there was only one that was open to her. She ran to get her bag and a loose linen jacket to throw over her slacks and short-sleeved shirt, because she ought to look tidy at least, she thought, and ran for her car, hoping against hope she could remember precisely where the place was.

She remembered after a couple of false starts, once she got into Barking, and parked about fifty yards from the shop, finding a vacant meter just as she needed one. That was a good omen, she told herself as she fed it with coins, knowing she was being absurd. And then turned and strolled towards Carolynn's Charity Shoppe.

'It's lovely to see you!' Maureen fluted excitedly. 'Who'd have thought you'd come back again so soon!'

'I was just so fascinated by it all,' George said. 'The way you run things here and the amount of money you make. It's very impressive.' It was nice to be honest for a little while, she thought. It made a pleasant change from her usual elaborate deceptions.

'Oh, you are sweet to me!' Maureen said. 'Isn't she, girls?'

The girls, three iron-haired women well into their sixties and wearing the same sort of sugared-almond-coloured overalls that yesterday's pair had worn, beamed and nodded. One of them scuttled off on Maureen's command to make tea.

'Anyway, I thought I might be useful,' George said. 'I could see there was a lot of work to get through.' She waved her hand vaguely. 'All this stuff to be sorted and hung up and priced and so forth.'

'Everyone's so kind to me.' Maureen looked round the shop a little helplessly. 'I'm not sure what I could ask you ... I mean, pricing the clothes is tricky. You have to have a bit of experience.' She looked hopefully at George, who immediately denied having any knowledge of the art of valuing secondhand clothing. 'I thought as much. Well, let me see ...' She looked around again and then produced a delighted smile. 'Of course! I know just the thing for you, all your education and all. I was wondering how to work out a price for these.'

She hurried over to a cardboard box in the corner of the shop. 'Here they are.' She hefted the box on to the counter and pulled a tall stool closer. 'Do sit down and have a look. They're books. I have no idea in the world how much to charge for them. I understand about novels and so forth, you know, love stories, but these are special.' She produced one of the most satisfied of her smiles. 'Philip sent them, you know. Isn't he sweet to me? He cleaned out his library, he told me, and wanted me to have them.' She looked a little worried for a moment. 'He's thinking of making some changes, it seems. Anyway, here they are. What do you think? They look very good to me.'

Obediently George reached into the box, wondering what she had let herself in for. The books were large, glossy, wrapped in heavily coloured printed covers; clearly they had been very costly when new, but now they had a well-thumbed look. They were all about beauty, hair styling, make-up, clothes, jewellery, manicures and pedicures, aromatherapy, reflexology, and every other kind of fashionable quack notion. George looked through them with amusement, at page after page of pictures of models with scrawny bodies, sulky expressions, pouting heavily lipped mouths and incredibly small noses, mostly tip-tilted.

'They do look odd,' she murmured, more to herself than to Maureen. 'Their noses are all out of proportion, aren't they? I suppose they've all had them bobbed. Silly, isn't it?' And then she remembered and caught her breath. She looked up at Maureen with her lower lip caught between her teeth. 'Oh, Mrs Ledbetter, I didn't mean to be rude. About Philip, I mean. I know a lot of the work plastic surgeons do is very important – people with facial injuries and so on. I didn't mean to criticize in any way.'

'Oh, that's all right,' Maureen said. She lowered her voice confidentially. 'Actually, Philip would agree with you. He's told me as much. He talks to me, you know, more than to anyone else. He says I'm the best friend he could possibly have.' She flushed a little, her cheeks mottling. 'Isn't that sweet of him?'

'Yes,' George said, smiling at her, relieved not to have hurt the woman's feelings. Her private views on Harley Street plastic surgeons would hardly be of interest to Maureen, and it would be sheer self-indulgence on her part to express them.

'Actually, he's told me – he's thinking of giving it up and going into something else. Dermatology, maybe. It's a very good speciality, he said, and one he thinks he could do well. You don't have to operate so much and though Monty's keen he should be a surgeon, Philip says he just isn't cut out for the work.' She giggled. 'Isn't that a funny thing to say? Not cut out to be a surgeon. Anyway, he's going to think about it. Maybe he'll go down the brain drain to America – only I got so upset when he said that that he promised he wouldn't.' Her face had crumpled at the mere idea. 'I told him, Monty'll be all right whatever you do as long as you do it well, and I'm sure you would. Well, of course he would, he's so clever. I told him, Monty'll come round to you being a dermatologist, if that's what you really want. Just don't tell him right now. Anyway, he's already trying to change things, Philip says. No more face operations.' She pushed at the book in George's hands with a dismissive forefinger. 'That's why he wants to get rid of the books. His patients used to look at them, you see, to choose what sort of look they wanted. So if you could price them for me, I'd be really grateful.'

It was ridiculous. Quite absurd, George told herself as Maureen went away to see what had happened to the tea, leaving her staring down at the books and the pictures of wide-eyed vapid perfection. It's the most absurd idea I've ever had, and to hell with intuition. I'm getting too full of myself, having these notions and always thinking they have to be right. This has to be quite –

Right. Absolutely and totally right, her inner mind whispered to her. You're right, you are, you are. What other reason could there be apart from the one that just leaped into your mind? Think about how they looked. The way the fire spread. The way the damage to the tissues showed itself. What other reason could there be?

Maureen's assistant came over with the tea, and she took it

291

with a vague thank you and sat there sipping it and thinking. It made a horrible logical sense. Here was a young, recently qualified doctor with the most limited of surgical skills, and an overwhelming relative determined to see him at the top of the professional tree, immediately. Not for this relative the years of sweat and struggle, of learning the craft and the art and the skills of the specialist. He had to have success for his boy right away, and thought, in the all-too-common way of lay people, that what made a man a specialist was where he did his work rather than the work he did.

So the pushy relative sets the young doctor up in a fancy set of consulting rooms and boasts about him everywhere among his friends. 'My nephew, the Harley Street specialist.' It would take a strong young doctor to resist that, especially if, as was very likely, that same relative had paid all his expenses during his training years. The relative would think the six years basic training was more than enough to turn out a specialist. So would the rest of the family, most particularly the young doctor's beloved aunt. I wonder, George asked herself, which influenced Philip most in giving in to their fantasy? His uncle's demand for gratitude and success or his adoring aunt's utter certainty he was the most clever and the most successful doctor there could possibly be anywhere? The latter, George told herself, watching Maureen as she bustled about her little empire, blissfully happy, and she thought of how Maureen had been when she was at home; subdued, quiet, plain, dull. And Philip loved her.

She gave herself a mental shake. This was no time to be sentimental. Think it through. How had it worked? Monty had given young Philip the cash to be a Harley Street man. The next step would have been to get himself patients. How had he done that? With no hospital appointment to bring him renown, no track record to persuade general practitioners to refer their patients to him, how would he build himself a practice?

No problem, she thought. Uncle Monty. She could see him as clearly as if she had actually been present; Monty sitting in the corner of a favourite pub, serenely affable as he dispensed his wisdom, revelling in his role as local guru, fountain of all knowledge, guide, philosopher and friend to all and sundry in this patch of London. She could see him talking to the sort of women who would be most interested in plastic surgery, and who could afford to pay for it, women who relied heavily on their looks and the illusion of youthfulness. Professional women. Working girls. Toms.

Young Philip Cobbett had taken them to some private hospital, somewhere that wasn't too fussy about to whom it rented its operating theatres and consulting rooms, to try his hand at improving those ageing faces. And botched it badly. Perhaps they'd been left with lopsided faces – that could happen to experienced plastic surgeons, let alone novices – nerve damage that left them with dragging muscles and sagging eyelids or drooping mouth corners. She watched the action inside her own head: the angry disappointed patients going back to him, raging at him, threatening to sue him for massive damages, young Philip aghast, thinking of how his uncle would react to it all, especially the publicity, but even more about the effect on his loving aunt.

She shook her head. Maybe she was right; but even if she were, did it follow that his reaction would have been to have got rid of them as they had been got rid of? She tried to imagine Philip Cobbett creeping up to that block of flats, to that little house, breaking in, pouring inflammable fluid over the pillows of the sleeping women, setting light to it, adding more fuel to their faces, so that all the evidence of his ineptitude vanished and with it the threat of exposure. It was impossible. For a start, she couldn't see him doing it, not frightened edgy Philip, and secondly she couldn't see how the women could have lain still long enough to let it happen. No one just lies quietly in bed while third-degree burns of the most horrendous sort are inflicted.

It had to be someone else who had done it. Someone who had Philip's advice, maybe, on how to render the victims comatose, someone who had Philip to provide the prescription that did it. She tightened her eyes as she imagined it: seeing him writing the prescriptions; giving the women the drugs that – and then the images shivered and changed. He didn't give them prescriptions, of course he didn't. He told them he had a new treatment that involved putting a special material in their operation sites or some tale of that sort. That he would rather do it in their own homes, so that they could easily sleep off the effects of the minor tranquillizer he would use to make the treatment comfortable. She could see him telling them he was doing it to make it easier for *them*, to save *them* money; see them tucked into their beds; imagined them trusting him, lying there obediently so that he could give his injections. And knowing that no evidence of his doing so would show at post-mortem because of the widespread tissue damage there would be. Whatever he had used on them to make them lie there so still and peaceful as they burned to death, she would never know, because there was no way she could find out. Philip would have left after he'd carried out his 'treatment' so that the ground was clear for whoever was going to finish the job for him. Whoever he had hired for it. Because he would never risk starting the fire himself, and failing to burn *all* the incriminating tissue. He'd have had to employ an expert; someone who would help him keep the truth of his failure a secret, who would protect him from an avidly reported court case and massive damages – because he'd be sure to lose – by destroying not only the evidence of his original surgery, but the evidence of his involvement in the women's deaths.

The more she thought about it, the more seductive a theory it became. She felt a deep certainty that she'd got it right. But there was only one way to be sure she had, she told herself as she stared down sightlessly at the book on her lap. And that was to ask him. Directly.

A wave of panic rose in her at the very idea and she remained very still, working at controlling the anxiety. How silly to be so scared. All she had to do was find some way of spending time with Philip and then embarking on one of her elaborate tales. They rarely let her down, after all; she'd find a way to get some sort of evidence out of him. Wouldn't she?

And perhaps also the attentions of whoever it was who had

helped him murder those two women. Why should they do it? What was in it for whoever it was? Could Philip afford to pay some vast sum to a contract murderer? Possibly, but would he? Wouldn't that leave him in just as bad a situation as he was in already, with someone who knew things about him that would make him deeply vulnerable? No, that one won't work, she thought. There had to be another reason for Philip being able to find someone to get rid of his embarrassing patients for him. Someone who owed Philip a debt perhaps, that he was repaying this way? Someone who knew that because each owed the other so much, each could rely on the other's silence. That made a lot of sense, George thought, and felt her panic subside slowly. She'd have to be careful in her dealings with Philip, obviously.

The thing was, she realized, that she was quite sure of Philip's involvement. Was that reasonable? She ran the whole scenario over in her mind again, and the more she thought of it the more convinced she was that she had found another link in her Connections. Not the last one, but a very important one. If she could just work out who had helped Philip and why, her Connections chart would be complete.

Across the shop Maureen called loudly, 'How are you getting on with the books, doctor?'

George smiled and nodded and then saw that there were several customers wandering round now. She quirked her lips. Clearly Maureen had wanted to preen about the quality of her helpers; the emphasis she had put on the word 'doctor' had been very clear. It was easy to see how Philip must be beguiled by his aunt; she was so transparent a creature, finding her satisfaction in such small and unimportant things that she was very endearing. It would be all too easy, George thought as she reached in her pocket for a pen, to do all sorts of things to please Maureen Ledbetter. She had all the power of the weak and the helpless; and that, George thought bleakly, as images of her mother drifted into her mind, is a very great power indeed.

Without thinking about it much she began to scribble prices in the corners of the front pages of each of the books, ranging from five pounds to seven pounds fifty pence, and then carried the box over to Maureen who was sitting importantly by the cash desk, as her helpers wandered around the shop trying to use their creaking salesmanship to push secondhand vests and knickers on to pensioners who knew real value when they saw it and intended to pay only half the asking price anyway. Whatever it was.

'Done already?' Maureen said brightly and looked into some of the books at what George had written there. 'Ooh, isn't that rather expensive? I mean, around here people don't have a great deal of spare cash.'

'The sort of people who'll go for these will spend more,' George said with a conviction she did not feel. 'Anyway, you've got to have a high price to bargain from, haven't you? Whatever you ask for they'll offer lower, so start high and you've a chance of getting a bit more. Er . . . I think I'll have to be on my way now, after all. I've thought of something I have to do. Such a pity. I'd have loved to have stayed a little longer.' She picked up one of the books again casually. 'You say these came from Philip's consulting rooms?'

'That's right.' Maureen beamed. 'They're lovely rooms too. All freshly done up with lovely furniture and everything. The waiting room's really gorgeous. You ought to see it.'

'I'd love to,' George said and then looked up at Maureen innocently. 'I know a couple of people who might like to consult Philip. What's his address?'

Maureen flushed with pleasure. 'Well, he said he was stopping operating, doing this dermatology instead.'

'That's right.' George looked even more limpidly at her. 'That was what I had in mind. So if you'll just tell me the address in Harley Street and his phone number?'

'Oh, yes,' Maureen said eagerly and reached in her pocket. 'I always have some cards with me.' She had pulled out a small wallet and was scrabbling through it. Eventually she found a square of thick cream pasteboard. 'It's a nice card, isn't it? Really tasteful.'

It was not. The printing was in gold and looked very expensive. More like a brothel-keeper's card than a doctor's, George thought a touch waspishly.

'Monty designed and had it printed, a couple of thousand of them, just to start him off. Really nice, they are.'

'Yes,' George said non-committally and smiled. 'Well, it's been lovely to see you. I really have to be on my way now. And Maureen, whatever happens, I do wish you well.'

Guilt was rising in her. This woman adored her nephew and George was going to do all she could to expose him as a killer. My efforts are going to break this woman's heart, George thought, and somehow managed to smile again, said, 'Goodbye,' and after a moment leaned over and kissed the rather sagging moist cheek.

Maureen beamed and said happily, 'Oh, you are sweet to me!' and George almost ran out of the shop to avoid looking at her a moment longer.

31

For once she stopped to order her thoughts when she'd got
back to her car. Her impulse had been to go straight to Harley
Street and talk to Philip Cobbett; her commonsense now told
her that could be risky if he was, as she suspected, at the very
least an accomplice to murder. Deliberate red-hot murder,
done in ice-cold blood; as the image formed she tried to pull
herself back to a more sensible frame of mind. 'You're thinking
like a melodrama queen,' she murmured aloud as she tried to
think logically.

The intelligent thing to do would be to call on Gus to go
with her as an official policeman entitled to ask questions, and
also as a protector. But he was locked away with the Super at
Ratcliffe Street nick, so that wasn't an option. Mike, then.
Would he go with her? The thought made her brighten and
she switched on the engine and let in the clutch. She'd find
the nearest available phone box and call him. Maybe he'd
know of another man from Gus's team who could help her.
She couldn't ask Rupert Dudley, the obvious person to turn to
(or so Gus would say, she thought a touch sourly), so it would
have to be Mike.

It was a noisy phone box, on the corner of Cotton Street
and the East India Dock Road, and she stood there with one
finger stuffed into her other ear as she struggled to hear him.

'I was about to put a call on your bleep,' he said. 'You must
be psychic.'

'Something like that. Listen, Mike, I have to go to –'

He ran over her words, seeming not to hear her. 'It's worked, Dr B.! I've flushed him out!'

She shoved her finger into her ear even harder as a massive lorry rumbled by, and bawled, 'What? Lenny?'

'Right!' Mike was jubilant. 'I put it about the town that his brother was in trouble. It seemed to me the best way to get Lenny interested, and I was right. It got round really fast – they don't mess about, these fellas! It seems he's been working in a Kemp Town fish shop as a fryer, calling himself Lenny Barking. Not very imaginative, is he? Anyway, there were plenty of the fraternity in Brighton who knew where he came from and that he was keeping himself out of view and kept quiet about him. But they took him the message about Don and that worked.'

'Have you talked to him?' George was eager.

'Well, no.' Mike allowed some regret to come into his voice. 'He's cleared off. To London, according to the man he worked for. Said he was going to find his brother.' There was a little silence. 'He got a bit agitated, seemingly.'

'Where in London?' George demanded.

'He didn't say. Just that he was going after his brother. The guy at the fish shop said he imagined he was going home.'

'Except that he hasn't got a home in London any more, has he?' George cried bitterly. 'Oh, Mike, I thought you were going to find him yourself! It's one thing to get him to come out of hiding and quite another actually to get your hands on him! We have to get him to talk to the people at the nick, so that he can explain to them about Gus and the money. Now all you've done is made him up and rush off and disappear again. We're no better off than we were.'

'We are not!' said Mike, sounding pugnacious. 'I mean, we are. At least we know the man's alive and well and in this country! Anything could have happened to him and we none the wiser. As it is, we know there's a witness for Gus somewhere there in London. So –'

'Oh, I'm sorry, Mike,' George said and shifted the phone to the other side, for her ear was beginning to hurt from the pressure of her forefinger. Now she had to plug the other one.

'It's hell talking here! I can only just hear you. Listen, Mike, come back to London and –'

'I'm at the station waiting for a train,' Mike said. 'I know fine what I should be doing.'

'There I go again!' George said. 'Sorry, Mike, I didn't mean to complain. Tell me what you plan to do.'

'I'll check his old neighbourhood.' Mike sounded a little mollified, but only a little. 'Lenny's not the most imaginative man, as I said; he'll go back to Barking, I've no doubt, and start checking whether Don is in his usual places. And I'll go to the usual places too. Betting shops, and so forth.'

'I'm sure you'll find him!' she said as warmly as she could. 'I'm sorry I acted up, Mike. It's just that I'm so worried about Gus.'

Now Mike melted completely. 'Yeah. Well, I am too. If I knew where Lenny'd be most likely to go, then I'd be there before him. As it is . . .'

'I'll tell you what, Mike!' She was suddenly alert and excited. 'I know who will know.'

'You do?'

'Monty Ledbetter! He was the one who told me that Lenny was in Brighton in the first place.'

'You might be right.' He sounded dubious. 'But had it no' occurred to you that Ledbetter might be the man he was running away from? These local fellas who fix things for everyone else, they can throw their weight around a bit, you know. Even when the Guv was using him as a snout, I told him I didn't completely trust that man. And the Guv said I wasna all that wrong, but he knew what he was doing. So it's best to be careful. I'd no' like to upset any apple carts by going off half cocked, so to speak. For all we know, Ledbetter lied to you about Don when he told you he'd gone abroad. When a man knows more than other people know, maybe it's for the wrong reasons, if you get my meaning.'

'Monty!' George stared blankly at the speckled mirror over the phone, into which the local Toms had stuck their phone numbers on little printed cards. She didn't see them; all she could see was Monty's pallid face and piggy white-lashed

eyes. Monty? Could he be the man behind all that had
happened? Could it be he who – She shook her head as Mike's
voice sounded tinnily in her ear.

'Dr B.? Are you there, Dr B.? Are you still there?'

'Mmm, yes. I'm here. Are you suggesting that – Oh, no,
Mike, I don't think so.'

But even as she said it, her mind was whirling, fitting
Monty's name into the blanks in her Connections, seeing him
helping Philip kill the women. But if Monty helped Philip,
what happened to Philip's motive? She had imagined him
getting involved in the killing of his damaged patients as a
way of keeping the truth from his family. If the family already
knew, then why –

'Money,' she said aloud. To avoid the damages the court
would award the women and to let him stay on in practice.
He'd be struck off if he lost his case, and lose it he would. The
motive's still there. And it's a motive for Monty too, who
would probably have to pay the bills. 'Money,' she said again.

Mike's voice sounded more distant now. 'I can barely hear
you, Dr B. This line's awful. What did you say?'

'It's not important Mike,' she shouted. 'Look, get your train,
come back to London and see if you can find Lenny round the
betting shops or whatever. I've an idea of my own to follow
up. I'll call you again first chance I get, OK?'

'What?' he said but she didn't repeat it or say anything else.
There didn't seem any point; if she told him what she planned
to do, he'd get agitated over the risks she'd be taking. Well,
she'd been agitated herself, but she had to live with that.
There was no other way now but to take the chance.

The house was like all the others in the long handsome street;
it had two or three steps up from the railings, a heavy front
door painted in high gloss with a multiplicity of brass plates
on it, and discreetly shrouded windows. She wondered idly, as
she waited for a party of Arab women in full Middle Eastern
dress, complete with face-masks which made them look like
little beaked birds, to pack themselves into a large car ready to
be driven off, thus releasing a parking space for her, what

would happen if all the brass-plate owners turned up in the street on the same day. They'd have to set up their consultations in the corridors, the back gardens and the street itself. Her imagination conjured up a picture of desks and couches on every pavement, at which serious faced doctors plied their trade as taxis and vans inched past. And she was grimly amused. What these people were doing, she told herself rather self-righteously, was indeed acting as tradesmen rather than as real doctors of the sort she admired. Well, not all of them, she allowed, as at last the car, a very elderly and capacious Bentley, pulled its stately way out of the parking bay; some of the consultants at Old East have rooms here once or twice a week, and there are some pretty good doctors among them. But there are too many of the other kind, the Philip Cobbett kind, the so-called alternative kind, who have more hype than real experience to offer. They were the sort she despised.

It was as she locked the car and turned to walk along the pavement to the house where Philip had his rooms that she realized what she was doing in thinking so. Filling her mind with thoughts about the rights and wrongs of private Harley Street practice, instead of thinking of how the coming interview might go, was a ploy. She shouldn't be here alone, that was the truth of it. It was asking for trouble, not least of which would be Gus's rage. It was her own impatience that was driving her; that and the thought of Gus facing the discipline board at Tintagel House to hear whether they believed the evidence of his own past history as a superb policeman or the uncorroborated testimony of a much less senior officer. Gus getting the third degree, she thought, and blinked. 'Like the burned women,' she murmured aloud and then tightened her lips. This had to stop! She must concentrate on what she was here to do. She hurried on to the house where Cobbett had his rooms.

She paused on the top step, staring at Philip's plate. *Philip Cobbett*, it read. *MB, BSc, LRCP, LRCS*. It looked good, she imagined, to lay people who would assume these were high qualifications and didn't know they were in fact only the most basic, the ones you started out with after you trained in an

English medical school. She thought of her own string of letters, and most particularly of her FRC Path, the Fellowship of the Royal College of Pathologists which she'd worked so hard to earn, and smiled grimly. Would young Cobbett have been able to do as well? Had he even tried to gain further and more important qualifications?

'I don't have to be scared of him,' she whispered as she reached forward and pressed the brass bell. 'It's broad daylight, a busy house in a busy street. He can't harm me.'

The girl who answered the door looked, George thought, like an advertisement in an American magazine for haemorrhoid cream. She was wearing the crispest of white dresses, very snug about the waist and bust, white shoes and tights, and had a scrap of lace and starch perched on her carefully arranged blonde curls. She was blue-eyed, had a tip-tilted nose (though whether by birth or intervention George could not at this point be sure) and looked exactly as George supposed Philip Cobbett's patients wanted themselves to look. Certainly she bore little resemblance to the nurses George knew at Old East in their somewhat crumpled blue dresses, hardworn black shoes and tights, and capless heads. That's how real nurses look, she thought as she nodded at the girl and stepped inside the house, not waiting for an invitation. Not like this kewpie doll.

'Mr Cobbett,' she said. 'Please tell him Dr Barnabas is here.'

'Oh,' the girl said. 'Um – do you have an appointment?'

George contrived to look lofty and amused at the same time. 'Didn't you hear, my dear? I'm *Doctor* Barnabas.' Here's hoping she takes that seriously, George thought, and doesn't come on like a dragon guarding a gate.

She didn't. She just said, 'Oh!' looking somewhat flummoxed, and then turned and went away, leaving George standing in the hallway. It was big and bright and heavily scented with floor polish and flowers and just a hint of old-fashioned antiseptic. Clever, George thought. They've made it smell both welcoming and reassuringly hospitally. Salesmanship, or accident? She suspected the former.

The girl had vanished behind the white-painted staircase at

303

the end of the hallway, and George lifted her head to listen. Silence. No distant voices, no phones ringing, no lifts rattling. A quiet time in the house. No patients? She moved forwards a little gingerly, pushed open a door on the right-hand side and looked in. She heard Maureen's voice in her ears. *The waiting room's really gorgeous. You ought to see it.*

Wow, she thought. The walls had been clad in peach fabric and she reached out to touch. Wild silk, she thought. The windows had been shrouded in layers of peach-coloured net and everywhere there were mirrors, softly lit, again with peach lights. Even the furniture was mirrored; the huge centre table, which was laden with more of the books George had seen at Maureen's shop as well as piles of glossy magazines all reflected in the glitter, and the scatter of small tables that were set everywhere. There were sofas and armchairs too, upholstered in deep peach velvet and trimmed with gold braid. The floor was the same colour in a deeper tone, with carpet which looked to George to be inches thick. The whole place breathed extravagance and chill. Not physical cold; in the white marble fireplace that dominated the far wall piles of imitation logs flamed and hissed, even on this summer day, and there were discreet radiators everywhere. It was the fact that the room felt as though it was largely unused that gave it its sense of chill.

She had moved further into the room to look about, and was startled when the voice spoke behind her.

'Dr Barnabas?'

'Oh! Yes. Hello, I do hope you remember me?'

'Er, yes, of course.' He was watchful. His pale face looked even paler beneath the smooth fair hair and his eyes gave nothing away.

'At your uncle's house?'

He said nothing, just looked at her with brows raised in a question.

'Well,' she said and managed to let her shoulders relax so that she seemed at ease with him. It was far from easy to do. 'I do hope you don't mind me just turning up like this. Perhaps I should have phoned and asked to come and see you.'

He was staring at her still with those expressionless eyes, but now he seemed to reach a decision. He smiled. It made George's shoulders tighten again for a moment; it was so tense a grimace that it looked as though it hurt him. Still, it was meant to be a smile. 'Are you consulting me as a – as a doctor, or as a –'

She laughed then, making the most of it as a chance to ease her own tense muscles. 'Oh, not as a patient! I doubt you could do anything for me! Past redemption, I am.' And she found herself thinking, shut up! That's the most blatant of fishing trips. You should be ashamed of yourself.

He opened his mouth to respond, but she hurried on. 'No, it's purely professional.' She reached into her bag, which was looped over her shoulder, and, with her head bent, as though she were concentrating on finding the relevant page in the notebook she pulled out of it, said, 'I've been doing some checks on a couple of my jobs, and I thought you might be able to help.'

'Oh?' He looked at her more warily now. 'But I thought you – I mean, what's your – You're at Old East?'

'Well, now,' she said. 'How do you know that? I don't remember it being mentioned when we were introduced.'

'It wasn't,' he said. 'My aunt told me. She said you, er, have been very kind to her.'

'It's a pleasure to help someone so energetic and lively,' George said and smiled at him. Was it possible to make this man relax? He stood there woodenly, looking old, somehow. He couldn't be much more than thirty or so, yet standing there in that stuffy dark suit and with his fair hair so carefully smoothed over above that bony pale face, he could have been half as much again. 'I like your aunt a lot. There aren't enough Maureen Ledbetters in this world.'

'No,' he said. 'There aren't.' For the first time he seemed to relax a little and she pushed her advantage.

'Well, she's right, of course. I am at Old East. Did she tell you my job there?'

'Er, no. I don't think so.'

'Pathologist,' she said, watching him. He stared back, as still as ever. More still? More watchful? It was hard to be sure.

'It's a couple of my cases that I need your help with, Philip,' she went on easily. 'Perhaps we could go to your consulting room? You'll need to look at your records, I imagine, and anyone might walk in here at any moment.'

'I have no immediate appointments due,' he said. 'And as for my records, I have an excellent memory for my patients.'

Poor bastard, George thought, feeling, in spite of her conviction of his guilt, the doctors' camaraderie as she looked at him standing there beside the big mirrored table with his reflection peering up at him from its gleaming surface. I don't suppose he's had enough to forget any of them.

'Oh, well, fine then.' She looked down at her notebook again, but only briefly. She needed to watch his reactions. 'I have some path. work to add to their notes and I've been having some trouble tracing them. It seems they've both been patients of yours as well as Old East's, and I thought it might be of value to collate the records.'

If he believes that, the man's a fool,' she said to herself. Private and NHS records don't have to be collated, but he's so inexperienced, I doubt he'd know that.

'Well, if you'll tell me their names,' Philip said, and stood there waiting, his face as impassive as ever. She took a breath.

'Lisa Zizi and Shirley Candrell,' she said, fast and loud, and never took her eyes from him.

He stood there for a moment and then slowly shook his head. 'Oh dear,' he said. 'Those two. Poor things. What's happened to them now?'

32

She gaped, unable to speak for a moment, and he peered at her in the warm peach light and said, 'Dr Barnabas? Has something happened to those two? Or have they sorted it all out?'

She swallowed and managed to answer him, though her mouth was dry. 'I – actually they – they're dead.'

She hadn't meant to be so direct, but his reaction had so stunned her that she'd lost control of the situation. Now it was his turn to be startled.

'Dead? Both of them? Good God, why? What happened? Young women, both of them. Dead? It must have been –'

'Fire. They died in fires,' George said. She shook her head, as if that would clear it. 'Look, would you mind explaining how you know them?'

'With pleasure,' he said, and put out one hand towards her. He seemed much more relaxed now, as though her reaction had melted the frost with which he had protected himself. 'Look, shall we sit down? I'd take you to my consulting room but, to tell the truth, I've had so few appointments lately that I've sort of sublet it for a while to – um – a colleague. It all helps with the rent, you know, and – well, I can only see you in here.'

He was disarming in his little burst of honesty, and she began to feel more comfortable with him. 'Yes,' she said, and managed a smile. 'Of course.' She sat down with a little thump in one of the armchairs. He came and perched his rump on the table in front of her, folding his hands across his front as he contemplated her with that same flat, watchful expression on his face. Clearly it was natural to him and meant nothing special, she found herself thinking.

'Lisa and Shirley,' he said. 'I think they're – this is as between clinicians, of course, confidential – I think they're – they were prostitutes, you know.'

'Really,' she managed weakly. 'What makes you say that?'

He looked uncomfortable for a moment and then shrugged. 'Oh, I don't know. There was something about them both. A sort of way of talking. And sitting and moving. Studied, you know. Anyway, they'd been treated by a real quack – one of those collagen-injecting places. A friend had paid for them, they said. They didn't come to see me together, you understand, but they knew each other and had had the same experience. The first one I saw was Shirley. She told me what had happened. She turned up here in dark glasses and a scarf – you should have seen what those botchers had done! They'd tried to fill out the eyebags and the mouth lines with some sort of synthetic stuff and the mess was dreadful. Lumpy, discoloured skin where the material had leached through, a drooping mouth due to nerve compression. Shocking. I told her frankly she needed someone much more skilled than I am. I've not been doing this sort of work long and to tell the truth I'm strongly considering abandoning it altogether. It's not for me. I find skins much more interesting. Much. And more worthwhile. To deal with melanoma for example, that's real medicine, isn't it? Not like this vanity business. Anyway, I referred her on. And then the other one came a couple of days later. Zizi, odd name. Yes. Lisa Zizi. She told me a friend had suggested she come to me, and I told her the same thing. Her face wasn't quite so bad, but it wasn't a case I would have touched myself. So I referred her on too. And that was the last I saw of either of them. And now you tell me they're dead? In a fire? Poor things.'

'In separate fires,' George said steadily. 'Fires that seem centred on their faces.'

He frowned, and the watchful look deepened. 'Separate

fires? Their faces? Are you saying . . . Good God! Deliberately?'

'Something like that,' she said. And then added in a loud clear voice, 'I thought you might have had something to do with the fires.'

'I?' He gawped. 'I? How could I – Oh!' He went a sudden crimson as the tide of realization lifted through his pale skin and now at last he looked the very young man he was. 'Christ almighty, me? But how? I mean, why? For heaven's sake how could I –' He spluttered to an end and just sat there, staring at her.

'I worked out that you must have seen them,' she said. 'Your uncle knows everyone locally. Both these women lived in Wapping. And if someone on his patch needed plastic surgery advice who would they go to but you? He'd see to that.'

'Yes,' Philip said with a sharp note in his voice. 'I can't deny that. Dammit, this is embarrassing. All right, I let him set me up here in practice, even though I knew bloody well it wasn't for me. I'm nowhere near qualified enough. I did a couple of house jobs in facial reconstruction and so forth, but that wasn't enough. But Uncle Monty – he's a force of Nature, you know? Hard to say no to. I happened to say plastic surgery had interested me, and there was no stopping him. But I'm sorting it out now. I've been talking to the people at the Institute of Dermatology. I'll change the practice, build it myself and he'll settle down. He'll have to. I can't take much more of his – Well, he's a good old man but he really can't run my life.' He shook his head and primmed his mouth and was silent.

'I think I understand,' she said. 'Look, let's get this sorted out. I'm right then, and he arranged for you to see them?'

'Yes.'

'After they'd been treated at a clinic somewhere?'

'Yes.'

'Which one? Where?'

He shook his head. 'I did ask them but they said it was a condition put on them both not to make a complaint.'

'A condition?'

'I had the impression their fees were being paid by someone else,' he said. 'They certainly weren't on BUPA or anything of that sort.'

'Could your uncle have been paying for them?' George said.

He looked amazed. 'Why on earth should he?'

She thought for a while and then shook her head. 'Frankly, I don't know. I'm not sure of anything any more. I was sure you were involved, and now . . .'

'Well, I'm not. And I'd be amazed if Uncle Monty were. He's very good to his family, and very free with advice for outsiders, but he's never splashed his money on anyone but his own kith and kin.' He grinned briefly. 'Your real Cockney, believe me.'

'I have to,' she said. 'So, you referred Shirley and Lisa to another plastic surgeon.'

'Yes.'

'Did they go to him?'

'I've no idea. I heard no more.' He slid from the table. 'I suppose I could find out.'

'Please do,' she said. He nodded and went briskly out of the room, in search of a telephone, she assumed, and left her staring at the soft golden-pinky glow around her and trying to collect her confused thoughts.

The whole edifice of her theory had tumbled about her head, she thought mournfully. If neither Monty nor Philip were involved in the women's deaths, who was, and why? And had they any connection with what had happened to Don and Lenny Greeson? And via them with Gus's predicament? She no longer knew. In her mind she took the pages of her Connections chart and tore them into shreds.

He seemed a long time coming back and she began to be restless. She wandered out into the hall to see where he was, just as he reappeared from the space behind the stairs.

'Oh,' she said and went a little pink. 'I was just –'

'I'm sorry I took so long,' he said. 'I was just going to get you his phone number – it's here' – he held out a sheet of paper on which he'd written a name and address – 'but I took a chance and phoned him. He was there. And he said he never saw them. Neither of them made an appointment with him.'

She frowned. 'Never? I wonder why not? If they were so damaged that they came to see you, why didn't they take the next step? What put them off?'

'I can't possibly know,' he said. 'I'm sorry.'

'Could they have gone back to your uncle? Asked him about this chap you referred them to?'

He shook his head firmly. 'No. He'd already asked me what had happened with them. I told him I had to refer them on – I said they needed a different sort of specialist. It's easier to tell him lies than to make him understand my situation – and he was quite happy with that; as long as they'd been helped, and he'd been the first person they'd gone to, he was content. Never gave them another thought. Neither did I, till you came here today.'

She nodded and looked at the sheet of paper in her hand and then said, 'When did they come to see you? Can you remember?'

'Yes, I can.' He looked embarrassed again. 'I haven't had that many referrals, you see. I saw Shirley Candrell on the morning of 21 June and Lisa Zizi a couple of days later, in the afternoon.'

She had been leafing through her notebook, but now her gaze sharpened as she looked up at him. 'A couple of days? Can you be more specific?'

'Um, yes. It would have been – let me see.' He squinted into his memory. 'It would have been the Thursday, 23 June. I remember because it was the day before my rent was due – I pay quarterly. And I knew I'd have to go to Uncle Monty again. I wasn't feeling good about that, and here I was having to turn patients away because I couldn't take their cases. That was really the point at which I knew it was all going to have to change. I'd been thinking of going to the States, but I knew then it had to be better than that, and got in touch with the Institute of Dermatology about more training. Oh, yes, I remember the date.'

She looked up at him, her forehead creased. 'That was the night that the fire happened. The first one. The one that killed Lisa Zizi.'

There was a long silence as he looked at her and then he said in a tight voice, 'I think I need to sit down.'

He led the way back into the waiting room, clearly very shaken. She stood beside him as he sat perched on the arm of one of his peach armchairs, and waited till he felt better.

'I'm sorry,' he said after a while, his voice a little husky. 'It's just that – God, I feel so responsible.'

'That's crazy!' she said. 'How can you possibly be responsible?'

'If I'd been able to offer the right sort of help, maybe – As it was, I sent her on to someone else. She must have thought she was beyond help. People do strange things when they're in despair.'

'Suicide?' She almost laughed. 'Are you suggesting it was suicide? With that sort of method? Come on! You can't be for real! I know doctors like to take on the responsibility for their patients, but this is way out of line!'

He looked up at her, his face bleak. 'Do you really think so?'

'I know so,' she said firmly. 'Both of them died in bed, lying still. They made no attempt to save themselves, even though the seat of the fire was their own bodies. It would have been impossible for anyone to have lain still enough to die like that unless they were heavily sedated. And they must have been. I did the post-mortems and couldn't find any evidence of systemic drugs, though the bodies were so badly damaged there was no way I could have done. But believe me, someone did this to those two women. It was never self-inflicted. They were knocked out, somehow, and then were anointed with something flammable and –'

He went even more pale, so that his skin had a chalky greyness, and she pushed his head forwards and down so that he could recover.

'Sorry to upset you with the details, but there it is. They didn't kill themselves. Now, take a few deep breaths, that's it. You'll be OK in a moment.'

He was, and slowly straightened up. He still looked drawn, but his colour was a little better.

'Thanks,' he said. 'I'm sorry to be so – I'm really the last person who should be doing medicine, I can't handle this sort of thing at all.'

'And you with surgical ambitions,' she said lightly, and he shook his head.

'It's my uncle who has those,' he said with a return of his bitterness. 'Well, he'll have to settle for boasting about his nephew the skin man. Look, is there anything I can do to help you? I gather you're trying to investigate these deaths? Do pathologists usually do that? I thought that after the medical examinations were over the police took charge.'

'Um,' she said. 'Well, yes. They do. But I take a special interest, and anyway ...' She hesitated. She had been about to blurt out that it was because of Gus that she was taking a special interest in the dead women, but stopped herself in time. She barely knew the man and until a little while ago had been convinced he was a murderer. Though all he had said and done since had shown her that this was highly unlikely, there was always the possibility that she had been right the first time and that his reactions had been those not of an innocent man but of a brilliant and remarkably cool-headed actor. She looked at him now and tried to judge just how truthful he had been. All her instincts told her that he was incapable of maintaining such a collected front as long as he had; but all the same she wasn't going to take a chance.

'Anyway, I'm interested. It's a long, complicated business – there are other cases linked with the women – and I'd like to sort this out for myself. Look, may I use your phone?'

'Oh, yes, by all means.' He looked at his watch. 'Can you give it a couple of minutes? My colleague should be finished with his patient very soon and I'll be able to get into my office. If you can spare the time?'

'I'm not sure ...' she began but even as she opened her mouth there was a sound down the corridor and he lifted his head.

'Good,' he said with satisfaction. 'There she goes now. Just a minute.' He made for the door, George following closely.

The haemorrhoid cream advertisement was hipping her

way along the corridor, a drooping woman wandering behind her with a faintly bemused expression on her face. 'If you'll just come into the office, Mrs Henderson,' the advertisement fluted, 'I'll sort out the bill. Will it be cash or credit card? Dr Agula much prefers the former, if it's possible.'

Philip's office down in the basement was as handsome as his waiting room. Here the walls were a clinical cream and there was a good deal of chrome and glittering glass about to give it a surgical air, but there were also soft chairs and a wide modern desk in pale wood in front of the big window that looked out to the area, above which the railings that fronted Harley Street showed glimpses of passing feet. The man sitting at the desk was wearing a white coat that buttoned across one shoulder, which made him look like an advertisement too, this time for something even more intimate than haemorrhoid cream, George thought, and was writing up some notes.

'All right with you if I check my files for something, Agula? I need a couple of things. And my, er, friend here needs to use the phone. Dr Barnabas, Dr Agula.'

'With pleasure,' Agula said. He had a rich deep voice that matched his large dark eyes and a soulful expression. George wondered what sort of consultant he was, and didn't like to ask. But he led the way.

'How d'ye do, Dr Barnabas. Go ahead, Cobbett. We have to talk. Mrs Henderson made appointments for treatments for the next six months,' he said in high satisfaction.

'We'll discuss it,' Philip said vaguely, looking uneasily at George. 'Not now. Rather pushed.'

'What sort of treatments?' George said innocently, as one doctor to another, and Agula winked.

'High colonic lavage,' he said. 'They love it, these uptight sorts. Does 'em a world of good too. Well, I must be going. Have to be in the King's Road in fifteen minutes. We'll talk on the phone about future arrangements, then, Cobbett?'

'Oh, yes, absolutely,' Philip said, his head down over a drawer he had pulled from a filing cabinet in the far corner. Agula nodded cheerfully at George and went, and she took his place at the desk and reached for the phone.

'High colonic lavage?' she murmured.

Philip looked at her sideways. 'He was the only one who answered my ad,' he said. 'And if some people like it, who am I to interfere?'

'I suppose so. But doesn't it sicken you? These people who make money out of colluding with patients' nastier fantasies?'

'I try not to make judgements,' Philip said, and George felt herself wince in embarrassment.

'I suppose I can be a bit censorious sometimes. OK. No more about Agula. Let's stick to what we're here for.' She picked up the phone and dialled Mike's number.

It was engaged and she hung up and bit her lip. Now what? Call the nick? Maybe by now Gus would have finished there? It was well into the afternoon and surely it wouldn't be wrong to try to reach him? But she held back still. The embarrassment he'd suffer if she talked to the wrong person would be considerable. And by 'wrong person', she knew she meant Rupert Dudley.

Philip emerged from his filing cabinet with a couple of folders in his hand. 'I thought I'd see if there was anything else in their notes that might be useful to you,' he said. 'But I doubt there's anything here I haven't already told you.' He read aloud, 'Lisa Zizi, number seven Ropemakers' Fields House, Wapping. Age thirty-seven. No, I've told you all about her – nothing else in this one. And here's Shirley Candrell. This'll be the same, I'm sure. Address, eleven to seventeen St Saviour's Yard, Bermondsey. Age twenty-four. Her complaint was of a . . .'

He murmured on, but George wasn't listening now. She was staring at him, her face creased in a frown.

'What did you say?'

'What?' He looked up at her. 'Oh, swelling in the left orbital fossa –'

'No. Before that. Her address.'

'Eleven to seventeen, St Saviour's Yard,' he said. 'And she was just twenty-four. Very young.'

'But she didn't live there! She lived near Lisa. In Wapping. That's where –' She stopped and caught her breath, and sat very still.

After a moment he said, 'Perhaps that was her work place? Sometimes patients do prefer not to give home addresses, don't they?'

'Maybe she did do some work there,' George said a little dryly. 'Prostitutes work in all sorts of places.'

'I'd forgotten about that.' Philip went a little pink. 'Silly of me. Well, maybe it was a friend's place? Or an accommodation address.'

'No,' George said. 'It was neither of those. I know just what it was. That's Connie's place.'

'Who?' Philip said, now completely lost.

'It doesn't matter.' George was jubilant suddenly. 'Oh, Michael, Michael get off the phone!' She redialled his number, praying the line would be clear. It wasn't.

She rubbed both hands through her hair in an agony of indecision. That she had to go to Connie's and find out all she could about why Shirley Candrell had given Connie's yard as her address was undoubted. She was itching to go right now, but she had to tell Mike what she was doing. Such common-sense as had not been stifled by her impatience told her she shouldn't go there till she'd told him and asked him to come too. There could be dangerous people there. After all, Lisa and Shirley were dead. And so was the owner of that leg, who was, she was certain, Don Greeson. But leave it much longer, she thought as she glanced at her watch, and the day would be gone and maybe Connie would have left. She had to go, and go *now*.

She looked up to see Philip gazing at her owlishly and at once knew the answer.

'Listen,' she said. 'This phone has a last number redial facility?'

'What? Oh, yes.'

'Then keep on trying the number I dialled, will you? And when Mr Urquhart answers, tell him I have an urgent message for him. That I've gone to St Saviour's Yard – give him that address in Shirley's file – and ask him to come as soon as he can. Tell him I'm sure the answer to everything is there at Connie's. Got that?'

'Connie's,' he repeated like a child with a lesson book, 'got that,' and she jumped to her feet, reached for her bag and fled as fast as she could go.

33

The combination of Friday afternoon as the start of the weekend and the continuing hot spell that had left London tarmac soft and everybody irritable and sweaty had clotted the traffic almost to a standstill. She took over ten minutes just to get round the one-way system from Harley Street back to the Marylebone Road so that she could turn east and head for the City and ultimately Tower Bridge, and by the time she at last slotted herself into the almost static huddle of cars and vans and buses on the Marylebone Road she was a wreck. Her shirt was wet with sweat and her hair was clinging in damp tendrils to her forehead. But there was no way she was going to give up. No matter how long it took her, she'd get to Connie's, and prayed that there would be someone still there so that she could get into the building, look about, see what she could find.

There were, she told herself, at least two good reasons for seeing the place as the focus of her investigation. One was the macerating machine; another was Mike's news that he had flushed Lenny out of Brighton in a search for his brother. It would have to be to Connie's Lenny would go to ultimately, George told herself, convinced as she was that that was where Don had died. There had to be a connection between Don and Connie that she didn't yet know of, but which Lenny did. She hung on to that notion determinedly, even though equally firmly held beliefs about this case had been shattered: like the role Philip Cobbett had played.

But even if I'm wrong, she thought when at last the traffic began to move and she reached the approach to the Euston Road underpass, the fact that Shirley Candrell gave Connie's yard as her address is a good enough reason, all on its own, for me to go there to look for answers. And somehow I've got to get there soon.

She abandoned her original planned route and turned south at the corner of Euston Road to push her way along Kingsway to the Adelphi, and on down to Waterloo Bridge. Maybe the going would be easier on the south side of the water, she thought, and for a moment was diverted by her own behaviour. In just a few years she had become the complete Londoner, learning by heart the complicated map of her adopted city, picking up all the tricks of London drivers who knew how to duck and dive through the metropolis and prizing every minute shaved off a journey time as a major achievement. As indeed it was.

By the time she reached Jamaica Road it was past seven o'clock and the traffic had thinned a little, and as she made the plunge into the tangle of narrow streets that led towards the riverside and Connie's yard, she felt a prickle of apprehension run down the back of her neck. Perhaps coming here on her own had been wrong, dangerous even? But she'd done all she could to get a message to Mike, and she was sure that once he got it, he'd turn out to meet her there. That in itself was a protection. Perhaps she could consider calling Gus? But she quailed at that. Even if she managed to reach him he would be furious with her for trying to do this at all. His advice – which would be forcibly expressed – would be to leave the job to the professionals: himself and his colleagues.

And I can't do that, she whispered to the windscreen as she peered through it for the turning to Connie's yard. Because he's suspended right now, and has no power at all.

The yard was full of vans and lorries, just as it had been the last time she came here, but there was no bustle around them. They were all locked up, it seemed, and put away for the weekend; and she frowned, trying to remember what Gregory St Clair had told her. Had he said they worked shifts here?

That there were people who worked at night as well as during the day? Even if they did, though, perhaps the weekends were different, with no shifts at night on Fridays and Saturdays? She couldn't remember, however hard she tried, and decided the safest thing to do was to assume the place was occupied.

She had paused at the entrance to the yard to peer in and now, instead of turning in and parking there – and there were spaces where she could – she moved on, taking the car round the next corner to park it tidily between a battered old Ford Capri and an elderly white van which smelled strongly of fish. I'll be safer if it's here, she thought, locking it, and then was annoyed with herself. It didn't make the slightest difference to her safety where she parked the car, for heaven's sake! She was safe anywhere. Broad daylight in a big city like this? Silly to fuss.

She pulled her linen coat around herself more snugly and pushed the shoulder strap of her bag further on to her shoulder so that she could hold it firmly under her arm. That made her feel safer too, and she turned and walked casually – neither too quickly, nor too slowly – to the yard. Without hesitation, she turned into it. There was no need to skulk or be anything other than what she was: an enquirer. Anyway. Connie had given her an open invitation to come and look round again if she wanted to, hadn't he? Well, here she was, accepting it.

She walked steadily across the yard to the entrance through which she and Maureen had gone the other morning. Now the great double doors were closed and there was a padlock across the handles; but set into one of the doors was a smaller one, and tentatively she tried the handle. It turned, gave way, and the door opened.

She had to stand quietly inside for a moment to get her eyes accustomed to the low light levels. It didn't take too long. Somewhere ahead there were lights burning, and there was a faint glow along the walkways beside the conveyor belt, but the belt was still and there was much less noise than when she had come here last time. No rattle and buzz from the belt; no clatter and thudding from other machines; no chatter of voices. Only a faint hum of electrical activity somewhere; or was that a sort of tinnitus in her own ears? She set her fingers into her ears for a moment to test them and knew her first impression had been the right one. There was something electrical switched on somewhere in the bowels of the place.

After a moment's hesitation she pulled the small door closed behind her. She wasn't trying to be deceitful and hide, dear me no, she thought. But there was no need actually to advertise her presence, either. Maybe she would find what she wanted – whatever that was, and right now she had not the least idea – before Connie even knew she was here. That would be really great.

She waited another few seconds as the darkness increased with the small door's closure, and then lightened again as her eyes became used to the new levels, and she moved forwards. She was wearing soft summer shoes that were blessedly quiet, and she moved across the messy stone floor easily and silently towards the walkway that led alongside the great conveyor belt.

The smell was strong in her nostrils now. The space was hot and heavy with the day's sunshine and, indeed, the stored heat of many preceding days of the heatwave; and the smell of old fabric and human bodies and the sweetish odour of decaying organic matter that was part of it all seeped into her. It's as bad as the mortuary on a busy day, she thought, shifting her bag to the other shoulder, so that she could more easily move alongside the conveyor belt.

It was still strewn with clothes, and the work-stations where, the last time she had been here, busy people had stood pawing through the unsavoury items on the belt had a forlorn look. There were stools beside some of them, with tied-on rags to pad the seats, and above the belt, in some places, people had pinned little markers of their own. A picture of grinning happy faces from Sierra Leone, as the script said clearly at the foot of the card; pin-ups from aggressively white magazines of breasty women with unfeasibly long legs and pouting lips like pillows; snapshots of family members; curly-edged birthday cards. There was something deeply touching

321

about them, George thought as she slipped past, something so human and so very lonely. She felt a twinge of pity, but didn't know quite why, or for whom.

The light was getting steadily stronger as she reached the end of the conveyor belt and she stopped when she got there and peered round it. At the far side of the vast warehouse, so far away that it looked like a toy, a door stood open, and a beam of light was thrown out on to the littered wooden floor. She stood and listened hard.

She thought she could hear a voice now, but it was hard to be sure. It was a long way across from where she stood to the doorway – as much as 120 feet, maybe more, she estimated; this really was a massive place. When she'd been here before she hadn't realized just how wide a spread it had, though it was comparatively narrow in the other dimension, fitting neatly as it did between the road that led into the yard and the river beyond. That would be only about fifty feet, she hazarded. Possibly less. Not too far for the gully that ran from the macerator in the basement to the river and its running water . . .

She would not think about that now; she had to concentrate on what to do next. She decided to walk across the big expanse and knock on the door and see who was there. She had no reason not to be here, after all. She'd broken down no doors to get in.

But all the same she moved as softly as she could, so that she wouldn't be heard as she made her way across the dark space to the open door.

The hum of the electricity diminished and she thought, wherever that's coming from, it's not up here. Down in the basement, perhaps. She looked around, peering into the darkness, and could see there was no access to the floor below here, unlike the other side of the conveyor belt, where there was a hole in the floor through which the spiral staircase made its way down. The macerator, switched on and ready to operate? Perhaps, and again the idea made her shiver a little, and she pulled her collar against her neck as she refused to think about that horrible machine. It was nice to be cool, she told herself defiantly, but knew she wasn't. It was as hot and heavy on this side of the warehouse as it had been on the other. She was plain scared, that was the truth of it.

Now she could hear voices. There was little doubt of it. A faint murmur, steady and soft, without emphasis or any rise and fall in inflection. She stopped for a moment, trying to hear properly, but there was no way she could tell who it was. There was nothing in the sounds that stirred any memory in her, and she moved on, until she was standing no more than a few feet from the door, a little to one side of it.

This was the point at which she should have knocked on the door, stepped in and announced herself. Asked for Connie; said she'd come back as invited. But what would be the point of that? she asked herself now. He's not going to answer any questions. Indeed, a part of her mind jeered at her, what's the point of being here at all? What do you think you're going to find out? And she had to admit she didn't know. She just had a deep conviction that the answer to everything lay in this space, and that those answers would free Gus from his trap. She didn't know what she was looking for, but she knew she'd as sure as hell recognize it the moment she saw it.

'So how should we know?' The voice was suddenly a little louder; not very much so, but enough to be comprehensible, and she stood very still. Was it familiar? Or did she imagine that it was because she so much wanted it to be? She could not be sure. Nor could she move, and certainly couldn't knock. 'All we did was arrange a job for him. That's all, no more, no less. He was happy, so why aren't you?'

''E 'asn't phoned nor written.' This voice was very different and though she had never heard it before, George was sure, immediately, of its identity. Lenny Greeson. There was a whine in it, a sort of miserable pleading that matched everything she'd heard about the man. She moved a little, needing to be closer, to hear more. See, even.

She had moved somewhat sideways and now she could see into the room via the crack in the open door; a long sliver of light, broken in places, and as she concentrated she could see that she had the back view of someone who was sitting at a desk. There was something about the head, she thought, that was familiar, and she frowned again, trying to recognize it. Connie? No. His hair was thick and curly and dark. This head was very sparsely covered, with little more than a mousy fringe at the back. Again it was vaguely familiar, but she could not place it. There was another person there too, throwing a shadow across the desk, but she couldn't see who. Just that it was a large person, with heavy shoulders.

"E always keeps in touch wiv me,' the whine said. 'Always. I never knew 'im not to. An' it's bin all this time and never a murmur. I don't like it, and so I tells yer.'

There was a truculent note to the whine now and it made George uneasy. It was so irritating and so silly a sound that it made her impatient, and she thought, whoever he's talking to won't take kindly to that. It will make him angry. And I fear that anger.

'Are you his mother or his brother?' the other man said. There was a cold sneer in his voice which was now clearly audible. I was right, George thought with a moment of triumph. It *is* Lenny. And this other man is angry. I was right.

'But I don't like people to be anxious,' the man said then, and now his voice was back as it had been, low, almost impossible to hear, and uninflected. 'We'll see what we can do for you.'

'I'd be 'appier,' Lenny said eagerly.

I wish I could see him, George thought. I must know what he looks like. I know that's who it is. It has to be.

'I mean there's only me an' Don left, see? An' I get upset, like, when I don't know what 'e's up to, 'e's bin in trouble a lot, see. Always was a bit of a lad, even when we was nippers, and I've always bin the one what's looked after 'im.'

'Yes.' The other man spoke so softly it sounded like a breath and then the light coming to George from the crack in the open door changed and shifted its shadows and she realized that the man sitting at the desk had got to his feet. Now, she thought. Now I must step forward and tell them I'm here.

What she actually did was slide sideways and to the right, so that she could press herself against the wall in the area where she estimated the shadow of the door would fall once it was fully open. Oh, God, she thought. I pray my jacket's not lighter than the wall, please don't let my jacket be lighter than the wall . . .

She need not have prayed so hard. No one looked back to see her. The door was pushed open and two people came out, a tall man following a thin scuttling shape that was obviously Lenny Greeson. This second man was wearing jeans, which seemed to emphasize his overall bigness and rather heavy legs, and a short-sleeved aertex shirt, which showed his arms were heavily muscled, rather than just fat. George couldn't see his face, because only his back was illuminated and that for only a brief time as he caught up with Lenny, who was walking just in front of him. He hurried Lenny forwards.

The glimpse George had was very quick, but she was sure she'd got it right and felt as though she'd been knocked down by a horse and left breathless. She stood gazing blankly into the darkness as she tried to digest the information.

Salmon? Detective Sergeant Bob Salmon, for pity's sake? How could he be here? Had he found the connections already? Was he trying to solve the problem too? And even as she thought it she knew she couldn't be more wrong.

Bob Salmon, who had supported Lenny's complaint against Gus. Bob Salmon, who had been put in Gus's team to break up the local criminals who had been working too closely together for the police peace of mind. Bob Salmon, big, strong, up to his ears in the whole business, in a position to know all there was to know. Her rage was so sudden and so powerful she had to bite her tongue to distract herself from the urge to rush out, hit him, scream abuse and hatred at him. But she controlled it, and caught her breath as he disappeared into the dimness.

She was about to step forwards to follow them when the door moved again and the last man came out. She stood very still, staring at the door to see who it was. Had she recognized his voice, or had she imagined she had? But he turned off the light as the door moved and she could see no more than a shadow; a shadow which closed the door behind it and then walked confidently into the darkness behind the others. Connie? Perhaps.

She stood there for a long moment and then, with a deep and quiet breath, followed them, walking very softly now as they went back to the conveyor belt walkway and alongside it. The hum of the distant electrical equipment became louder again; and as she reached the halfway point along the walkway herself, a bright light sprang up ahead and left her standing, terror-stricken, as still as an animal caught in the glare of a predator's gaze.

The light had been switched on in the basement. She could see the brilliance pouring up in a great cone above the hole in the floor through which the spiral staircase passed, and in the centre of the cone the shadow of the staircase, curling like a caricature of a helix. And saw against that the moving shadows of three figures going downwards. They did not stop or show any signs that they had seen her behind them.

The shadows disappeared but the light remained; then suddenly the place seemed to erupt into din. She yelped aloud in her acute fear and was frozen with the conviction she had given herself away. But nothing could be heard above the din and now she knew she was safe from being heard, as she recognized that the noise came from the maceration machine being switched into full action, she sprinted for the hole in the floor and peered down.

The three foreshortened figures were there: Bob Salmon standing close beside the machine; and in front of it, apparently staring at it with his shoulders tense and his back expressing a shrinking uncertainty, the man George was sure was Lenny Greeson.

She moved forwards, wanting to see the other figure more clearly. As she did so, it came into view, almost directly beneath her and behind Lenny.

She could see the right hand with something held in it, covered with the fingers of the other hand, and that frightened her. She leaned further over still for an even better view; and her bag, which had been hanging from her shoulder, swung forwards, slid off the smooth fabric of her jacket and down her arm to swing wildly over the head of the man standing behind Lenny.

He looked up as its shadow tracked across the space and she knew she was clearly visible. The light from the floor below was too strong to have left her unseen, and anyway she could feel the heat of it on her face. He could see her as easily as she could see him and she stared at him in amazement, a sense of blazing triumph filling her. She'd been right. She had heard that voice before. Those even, elegant tones that she had always found so surprising. Now all she could do was smile widely at him, her fear quite banished by pride in her success at tracking him down.

'Hello, Mr Lester. Mr Reggie Lester. Did you take any bets on me being here?'

34

She was never to forget the speed of his reaction. He reached up and with a sort of half-jump grabbed for her bag and pulled hard on it. Instinctively she held on, and used her other hand to keep herself from being pulled head first down the spiral staircase; by which time Bob Salmon had registered what was happening and had leaped for the staircase and was halfway up it, reaching for her.

That was the point at which she let go of her bag at last and scrambled back, but her feet slid on a piece of rag on the floor and she fell over. By the time she was on her feet again, Salmon had reached the top of the staircase and was stretching out a hand towards her.

But at last she was up and running, cursing herself as she went, because stupidly she had gone the wrong way; back up the walkway by the conveyor belt in the bowels of the great warehouse, instead of towards the double doors and the way out. Once she was through the little door and into the street, she knew she could get away; there would perhaps be other people . . .

But she ran headlong into the darkness, leaving behind the cone of light from the basement, wincing as she went, terrified of both the man pounding after her and the looming invisibilities ahead of her, of machinery and stools and bins and baskets. At one point she ran into a wheeled bin, and nearly fell but managed to get round it, giving it a push behind her as she did so. It careered back and caught her pursuer. She heard him grunt and swear as it hit him and that cheered her, made it possible to run even faster, especially as the darkness was getting friendlier now that she was away from the light and her eyes had again become accustomed to dimness.

She dodged round the head of the conveyor belt and ran back down the other side. All she had to do now was go round the great press at the far end – and she had a woolly memory of how that had looked and precisely where it was from her previous visit to the place, when the doors had been open and the light burning brightly overhead – all she had to do, she told herself as her lower teeth began to ache with the effort of breathing so fast, all she had to do was dodge round it and reach the little door set into the double doors, and she'd be out and away – all she had to do –

She had forgotten Lester, until she found herself sliding awkwardly on another pile of rags and fell clumsily. He had, she realized, run the other way, around the head of the conveyor belt, to cut her off on that side, but in the darkness missed her and ran past, nearly colliding with Salmon, behind her. She heard them both shout something loud and furious, but what she couldn't tell, for the row of the maceration machine was still going on. She doubled herself up and rolled, so that she disappeared, she hoped, beneath the overhang of the pressing machine's baling platform. She pulled her head down so that it was shielded by her bent arms, making herself as foetal as she could; and prayed silently with all the desperation of a terrified child that she was invisible.

She wasn't. She knew she wasn't as she heard the voices of the two men who had been running after her; they had realized what had happened and were coming back towards her, together, bending low, sweeping their arms in wide arcs as they reached under the conveyor belt, and it would be, she knew, only seconds before they reached the baling press and touched her. She couldn't move without being seen, and the bulk of the great press stopped her from escaping to the side or rear. She tightened her eyelids until her vision exploded into coloured dazzle and tensed herself against the hands she knew would grab her at any second; but then there was another sound. She twisted her head round to hear it more clearly, then rolled out of her hiding place to reach for the legs of whoever was nearest to her and pull on them.

'You bleedin' bugger!' a thin whining voice had shrieked, so high in tone and so loudly that it was clear even above the roar of the machinery. 'You bleedin' bastards, I'll kill you. I'll kill you, I'll kill you –'

Lenny had come up from the basement to join in the hubbub and hurled himself at the two men. As George came out of her hiding place, she blinked, realizing there was more light in the building now; the small door had been opened and the late afternoon sunshine was pouring in in a long wide tranche, and, amazingly, the two men had been caught in it.

They went down together under Lenny's frantic impact, crashing loudly as they hit the ground, and she pulled on the only leg she could reach, as hard as she could, and had the grim satisfaction of hearing a shriek of pain; but whether it was pain she had inflicted or Lenny had, she did not know.

Because she didn't stop to find out. She was up on her feet and running for the open door as fast as she could. There was someone standing there, peering in, and as she reached it he spoke loudly and truculently in an attempt to hide his obvious fear.

'What the 'ell are you doin' in there? This place is supposed to be shut up! Who's bin meddlin' with the machinery? I could 'ear it clean acrorst the street.'

'Police,' she managed to gasp. 'For Christ's sake get the police.' She stood holding on to the doorframe struggling for breath, for suddenly her body refused to do another thing she asked of it. She couldn't walk, could barely stand, certainly couldn't run; it was all she could do to get the words out. But when the man did nothing but stand and gape at her – she could see who it was now, the old man, Bert, the foreman, who had checked in Maureen's goods the first time George had come to this place – she managed to find a last blast of energy to speak again.

'Get the police, you idiot!' she shrieked. 'Police!' And then tumbled out through the door to lean against the wall in the sunshine, sobbing for breath and resting her head back with her eyes tightly shut. Even if Salmon and Lester came out of the door now, looking for her, reaching for her, she wouldn't be able to move, she thought in a confused way. I'd just stand here and let them do what they liked. It's like being paralysed. Oh, God, let me *breathe* . . .

Out across the yard sounds reached her. After a long moment she managed to open her eyes to squint into the brightness of the sun and see what was happening. There by the entrance gate two or three people were standing and looking in; passers-by attracted by the noise she had made, she thought blurrily, and as she looked at them and then around her, she realized Bert had vanished. Inside the building? There was nowhere else he could have gone in the time and she managed to call in a croak, 'Someone get the police.'

One of the people at the gate, a thin boy pushing a bike, leaned the machine against the ironwork and came across the yard towards her. 'Someone's rung 999,' he said, his eyes wide with fear and self-importance, as he peered over her shoulder in through the open door. 'They run off to do it as soon as you – Oh.' He glanced over his shoulder. 'There, you see? You only 'as to ask.'

The blue light revolving hysterically on the roof of the car was, George decided as she closed her eyes again, the most beautiful sight she had ever seen.

They went belting into the building almost before the car had stopped, leaving just one uniformed man outside with her. 'Where?' one of them had called to her and she had managed to jerk her head over her shoulder. Now she made a conscious effort to breathe more normally and opened her eyes to look at the policeman who was standing with one hand on her shoulder as he talked into his intercom.

'Ambulance on the way,' he said as he shoved it back into its shoulder holder. 'You don't look too good and they'll sort you out!' He peered down at her. 'Here, don't I know you?'

'You might,' she said huskily. 'Pathologist. Listen, is –'

The noise stopped her from saying more. Sirens blaring,

331

two more cars arrived and pulled right into the yard. Out of the first of them came Mike and she lifted her chin at the sight of him and to her own rage burst into tears. The constable standing beside her made a clucking sound and took her firmly by the elbow and led her to Mike's car.

'You'd better sit down, Miss,' he said. 'Doctor, I mean. You don't look right at all. What's going on in there? Can you tell me?'

'Mike,' George said. She managed to sniff hard and stop crying. 'Sorry. Listen, Lenny's in there and they're after him and they tried to get me, but I ran for it when Lenny came up as well and –'

'No need to explain,' Mike said. 'They won't be in there much longer. Got the world and his wife here now.'

She looked over his shoulder and then at last was able to take a deep breath instead of panting and felt her legs dissolve into jelly beneath her. She sat down hard on the back seat of Mike's car as more policemen arrived and went running into the building. Mike crouched on the tarmac in front of her and looked up into her face.

'Will ye be all right if I'm away to see what's happening?' he said 'I'll not leave you if –'

'Oh, for God's sake, go in and get the sons of bitches!' she cried. 'And take care of Lenny. I think they were going to push him through that godawful machine too.'

'I'll no' be long,' he said and was gone. She found a little section of her mind with which to be amused. He was like a small boy at a party, aching to get in there with all the others. She leaned her head against the side of the car waiting to feel better. This adrenaline reaction will wear off soon, her medical self lectured her jelly-legged one. Just be patient. Soon.

Perhaps she dozed off for a second or two in the middle of all the hubbub; for now even more cars had arrived so that the whole yard seemed to be full of them. She couldn't be sure. All she knew was that she opened her eyes and there he was, in front of her, crouching on the tarmac just as Mike had done and peering up at her with his dark eyes glittering with anxiety. She reached out and held on tightly.

'Oh, Gus,' she said. 'Oh, Gus, I think I've managed to finish my Connections chart!'

35

By the time they had taken the two men in custody, gone through the ritual of cautions, interviews, statements and all the rest of it, and got the warrants for the arrests of the others – Mickey Harlow and Connie, and the woman in the pharmacy at St Dymphna's – it was almost one in the morning. Bob Salmon, in the hope of getting off more lightly if he turned Queen's evidence, had been only too happy to name the woman as the inside partner in the obtaining of medical drugs for smuggling, as well as their source of sedating drugs for the people Lester had killed; 'and it was all down to Lester,' Salmon had cried, literally, with tears running down his cheeks. 'Lester did all the killing, not me. I was just forced to watch him, the bastard.' ('He has a great line in acting,' Gus told her disgustedly.)

George came out of Ratcliffe Street nick and stood on the steps staring up into the night sky, aware of a deep weariness but also of an even deeper sense of self-satisfaction.

I've done it, she thought, staring dreamily at the only star that was able to show itself against the glow of London lights in the blackness of the night. I made the connections and I got Gus off. Come Monday, when they hear the case, they'll have to apologize to him. I did it, I did it . . .

Gus came out and stood beside her, sliding one hand into her elbow in a companionable fashion. 'He's singing like a bloody nightingale,' he said even more disgustedly. 'There's not a detail he hasn't given us. Spilt every inch of gut he's got.

334

It's enough to make you sick. I know he's hoping to get off with a bit less time, but all the same . . .'

'Why complain?' George said comfortably, well aware of how Salmon, from the moment Mike had clamped his big hands on him at St Saviour's Yard and rattled off the usual caution, had fallen over himself to answer every possible question in great detail. 'Isn't he making your life easier?'

'Oh, yes, of course he is. But it makes me want to puke all the same. Bad enough him being as bent a copper as a ha'penny nail, without being a bent villain as well. Lester's fit to be tied.' He laughed. 'He's done his best to keep his mouth shut and leave it all to his brief, and there's Salmon laying it out with a trim of roses and honeysuckle. You could almost feel sorry for Lester. They collect all this stuff from Salmon and then trot round to the other interview room where they're working on Lester, and tell him all the stuff they've got and Lester's face is a study!'

She stretched. 'I got it all right, then?' she said, looking at him wickedly under half-closed lashes.

'It all depends on what you mean by right,' he said. 'If you're saying you solved this one on your own –'

'Well, why shouldn't I?' she said, firing up immediately. 'I was the one who spotted the link between Philip and the women who were burned, even if I did go a bit further in my assumptions than I needed, and then the way the drugs were got for Connie's smuggling when Gregory St Clair trusted me. Lester's smuggling, that is. *And* I was the one who worked out what happened to that leg we found – the fibres and the clean cut – it had to be that hellish machine of Connie's. And I was the one who –'

'No one's arguing,' he said. 'You did a great job.' He bent and kissed the back of her neck. 'I'm very grateful.'

'Oh,' she said, nonplussed. 'I'm – Well, all right then. I mean, I'm glad. I mean –'

'I always give credit where it's due,' he said with a sententious air, grinning down at her. 'I hope you can do the same.'

'Oh? Like where?' She lifted her chin at him, and he laughed.

'Like I'd worked out the tricks that Harlow and Lester were trying to make work, using Copper's Properties as their front, with a phoney Board registered at Companies House, using that fella E. Pike – remember? – as a tool on all the Boards. They manipulated the value of the chunk of land Harlow owns behind St Dymphna's by getting Monty to push for planning consent on it from his Committee. They flattered the old idiot till he was blue – he never did know what they were up to, believe it or not. Meanwhile they tried to get Old East to commit to sending their path. work there. That could have netted the two of them around a million, you know? A lot of cash. I was as close as dammit to getting them on that until Lester set Lenny and Salmon on to me and got me suspended. Lester's been using Salmon as a private inside copper for years. Some sort of blackmail, from way back. And Salmon managed to fix it so that the whole investigation into Lester and his doings was folded up.'

'You knew it was Lester you were after?' she said. 'You never mentioned his name to me. Though you did mention a bookmaker.'

'There were a lot of names I never mentioned to you. Any more than you *told* me of the St Dymphna's–Old East pathology business. If you had, I might have worked it all out sooner! So don't complain because I didn't tell you all there was to tell. Why should I? I was running my case, and I couldn't see any connection between what I was doing and your severed leg and those burnings. Why should I have done? It was a very tangled connection, after all!'

'Oh, I don't know.' She began to move, walking slowly down the steps to the street. Linked with her as he was, he had to fall into step alongside. 'You said it was a network thing. That you had so many assorted villains involved you weren't sure what or who was going to be part of it next. But when I told you I wanted you to take over my leg and the burnings, you didn't want to know. If you had agreed to talk to me about them, I might have got round to telling you all that *I* knew! But you wouldn't listen when I said you should be dealing with those killings. Left it all to Roop!'

'I wish you wouldn't call him that,' he said. 'It drives him potty. It's all right when I do it, but it sort of gets to him when you do.'

'I know,' she said. 'It's one of the reasons I do it. Stop ducking the issue, Gus. Admit you were wrong. If you'd listened to me, you'd have solved the whole thing sooner. You'd have realized that Lester and his companies had taken over Lenny's property, because that was the address they used. You'd have worked out it was Lester's people who were tailing you to make sure you didn't get too close to the action. You'd have found out that Lester had been using Don Greeson as a bully boy, Don being hard up for betting cash as usual, and willing to do anything to earn it, and then when he got greedy, killed him in Connie's machine.'

'How do you know that?' Gus demanded. 'We've only just got that out of Connie.'

'I was talking to Mike,' she said and looked sideways at him in the darkness. 'He knows who he owes his tip-offs to, if you don't. If I hadn't got Philip Cobbett to call him he'd never have been in on the arrests at Connie's place, and wouldn't have found out –'

'Pax,' Gus said. He stopped walking. 'Do me a favour, doll. Let's not try to add up scores on this one. Let's just say it was a big nasty tangle and we sorted it out. We. Us. Both together.'

'Didn't we just,' she said dreamily. 'Just let me see if I've got it all straight in my head. I've picked up a good deal from talking to Mike, but not everything.'

'I'll bet you've been talking to Mike!'

She ignored that. 'First of all we have Reggie Lester who's a greedy man, after all he can get his hands on. He owns this rag factory and puts Connie in as a sort of front. Connie agrees because –'

'Because he owes Lester so much money he has no choice. Lester's been lending around the patch for years, wicked rates of interest too. It was that side I first started to investigate.'

'You said we wouldn't be totting up scores. So don't.' George said firmly. 'OK, Lester's the start of it all. He finds out there's a market in India for expensive Western medicines, and uses his inside know-how, as a member of the Trust Board – and Heaven alone knows how he got *that* little plum of an appointment! – to get his hands on the goods. It was only him, by the way, never McCann or Harlow. They were just caught up in Lester's schemes. They've done nothing they shouldn't except be conned by Lester. Anyway, Lester puts pressure on Connie who owes him a fortune from failed betting, and uses him as a front for selling his drugs to India, stuff he gets on a scam using St Dymphna's as well as Old East. He made use of Monty to get in there, poor old Monty.'

'Yes,' Gus said and sounded sober. 'Poor devil never did a really wicked thing in his life. Just likes to show off and be the big Mr Fixit and look where it gets him. He never could resist being asked to do a favour. However powerful he is, however much he gets, he just loves to be the swaggering I-can-do-anything geezer. Like that fella – the millionaire whose wife worked for a film company, remember? Last year, in all the papers. He agreed to help someone make a lot of money out of insider share dealing when the company was taken over, and he got the office from his wife. There was nothing in it for him. Just showing off. Like Monty!'

'Yes, I remember,' George said. 'I thought that guy was a real nerd, and I still do. But I know Monty, and it does make a sort of sense. Will he be in trouble over this?'

'Of course he will. You can't go around being the Chairman of an important Local Authority Committee and let yourself be used in wangles like Reggie's, even if you weren't rewarded for it and only did it to be seen as a powerhouse. It's not allowed. Monty'll probably get to do some porridge for it. And it'll be his poor fool of a wife who'll suffer as much as he does when he goes inside.'

'Oh, I don't know,' George said. 'There's more to Maureen than you might think. She's the sort who can always find someone to look after her.' She smiled into the darkness, remembering. 'Everyone is always so sweet and kind to her, you see.'

'Well, if you say so,' but he sounded dubious.

'OK,' George said. 'So how far have we got? Oh, yes. Lester

338

uses Connie's place as a front for everything – including murder when it suits him. But why the fires? The way they were done, burning their faces . . .'

'Ah, I have the answer to that,' Gus said. 'Connie knew that. Lester owned the clinic where the two women had their collagen treatments.'

'Oh!' George said blankly and then, after thinking for a while, nodded. 'It makes sense, I suppose. They suffer damage, set out to find someone else to put it right . . .'

'And Lester is afraid of an expensive legal case against his clinic,' Gus said. 'It's cheaper to kill the women. And Lester has no problems about killing people. He's sitting there now looking furious that he's been caught and that Salmon's digging the biggest hole for him and filling it with shit to drop him in, but any signs of regret? Forget it!'

'But why did Shirley give Connie's place as her address? That was the detail that really broke this case, you know. If she hadn't, I'd not have gone to check there.' George shook her head and sighed. 'Poor creature. What a horrible way to die. I've seen third-degree burns before, but never quite as bad as those.'

'Yes.' Gus was solemn. 'Very horrible. But Lester didn't seem to worry about such things. He gave them injections of sedatives from the stock he'd collected for India, and used methylated spirits to start the fires. Like a barbecue, Salmon said. Swore he was a helpless bystander when Lester did it, and couldn't stop him. We'll have to go into that claim, though. It's my guess Salmon's lying and *was* directly involved, both times. He knows so much about what happened, he had to be. Whatever he says, he's an accessory after the fact – if not before as well.'

'I wonder why Lester didn't put them through that horrible machine?' George said. 'It would have been just as effective as the fires.'

'Getting them to go to the place might have been a problem,' Gus said. 'If they didn't usually go there.'

'So why did Shirley give it as her address then?' George peered at him in the darkness. 'That makes no sense.'

'Yes, it does. She knew it as *Lester's* place. He was paying the bills, and she wanted an accommodation address. She *never* gave her own for anything. Very hot on personal privacy, was Shirley. So she used Lester's. Or so Salmon says.'

'Salmon.' She shook her head and started walking again. 'What a bastard.'

'What a bastard indeed. And Lester, as cold a killer as I've ever met.'

'He killed' – she counted on her fingers – 'Lisa Zizi and Shirley Candrell, Don Greeson, and was all set to kill Lenny too.'

'Yes. Poor old Don, stupid bugger that he always was. He'd do anything for folding money to bet with. He let himself get hooked up with Lester and when he tried to get out, maybe because he didn't like what he saw . . .'

'He was chopped up for his pains,' George said soberly.

'Yes.'

There was a little pause and then Gus said, 'If the machine hadn't broken down that night, so that they were left with just a leg, maybe Lester'd have got away with it. How many people do you suppose he's killed that way? According to Salmon it's one hell of a list. All sorts of awkward bods ended up in the river.'

She shuddered slightly. 'It makes me feel sick,' she said. 'It's a horrible thing to do.' She was silent for a while, and then said thoughtfully, 'Though I have to say it's incredibly efficient. Just turning a body into sludge. It would have been so finely chopped that –'

'Spare me the details,' Gus said hastily. 'Is there anything else you want to sort out?'

'Yes,' she said. 'The dog. Why kill that?'

'It made such a row when they killed Don, they had to,' Gus said.

'Oh.' She was silent for a while and then said, 'I wonder whether Connie did make a coat out of its skin? It did seem possible.'

'I'll ask him,' Gus said. 'If it matters.'

'I don't think I want to know.' George shivered. 'Anyway,

what are they going to charge Connie with? I'm almost sorry for him. He just did his rag-picking and went home and left the place to Lester and his people. Why should he –'

'Accessory,' Gus said. 'He might have tried to keep out of it, but he knew perfectly well there was something going on. Like the way the machine kept breaking down, and the smell, and the rats. But it suited him to play blind. It doesn't wash, that. If they're caught, he is too.'

'Well,' George said after another little while as they went on their slow walking pace, covering the grey streets easily, heading towards Tower Bridge and the way home. 'That's another one over and done with. Now what? Have I only got my battle to keep my Path. Department going at Old East to keep me happy? Chances are the St Dymphna's idea'll shrivel up and die now, anyway. So, as I said, now what?'

He looked down at her sideways. 'Well, I've got my superintendent selection to think of, after Monday when the CIB at Tintagel House agrees I'm well and truly off the hook, which Salmon now occupies in my place.'

'Yes,' she said with great satisfaction. 'And I hope he wriggles and suffers and – *chokes* on it.'

He sounded genuinely surprised. 'That's not like you, George. Whatever people do, you're not usually so vindictive.'

'You don't know what you looked like while you were suspended,' she said and pulled him a little closer to her side. 'You don't remember how miserable you were. I'm allowed to be vindictive towards the man who did that to you.'

He tightened his arm so that they were even closer. 'Oh yes, I do remember,' he said quietly. 'I remember perfectly well.'

'You were even miserable enough to suggest we got married,' George said, not looking at him. 'I mean, how miserable can a man get, I ask myself?'

'Hmm.' He squinted out across the road towards Tower Bridge which they had at last reached. The traffic lights winked their lollipop colours across the blackness of the empty pavements and the skein of lights along the roads glittered in the warm, still, river-scented air. 'Yes. That's a good question. We'll have to talk about that, won't we?'

And he marched her across the road towards Tower Bridge. And home.

Read on for a taste of the latest volume
of Claire Rayner's outstanding thriller series,
featuring Dr George Barnabas

FOURTH ATTEMPT

Out now from
Michael Joseph

The gossip spread around Old East like oil on a marble slab, oozing into every corner of the hospital until not only were the staff talking about it, so were the patients.

'I said to Sister when she was doing my dressing this morning, I said, "Well, Sister, what's going on here then? And who'll be the next? Is there anything worrying *you*?"' The rather fat woman in the peach chenille dressing gown, sitting awkwardly festooned with drainage tubes and IV lines in the shabby dayroom on Annie Zunz Ward, shook with pleasure at her own wit and then grimaced as her operation site gave her a twinge of pain. 'Ooh, you take your life in your hands when you laugh, don't you? Still, you've got to laugh, haven't you? It's the best medicine, I always say.'

The woman sitting on the other side of the dayroom, who had heard enough of Peach Chenille's opinions on everything upon which it was possible to hold an opinion, forebore to answer, but later, when she went back to her own bed, she too spoke to her immediate neighbour about it all, wondering what was going on at Old East and who might be next.

'Three suicides in as many days, so they're saying,' she said. 'If it was the patients, you'd understand, what with worrying about yourself the way you do, but the staff... Well, it makes you think about there being something wrong in the place, doesn't it? You read a lot in the papers about morale being low in the NHS and all that, but this is really too much.'

Her neighbour, who knew herself to be dying of her liver disease and was already detaching her mind from other people's interests in consequence, managed a faint smile. 'People don't choose to die because of the way everyone feels,' she murmured. 'It's always because

344

of something personal.' She closed her eyes and wondered if it wouldn't be easier to die now herself rather than a few weeks down the line. She'd always promised herself she'd choose when to go; but since she no longer had the strength either emotionally or physically to take action on any decision she made, she wisely chose not to think at all any more.

But others did: most of all, the staff. They, after all, were most affected. If people they worked with were choosing to hurl themselves prematurely and to an extent violently out of life at Old East, didn't that mean they should look a little more closely at what life in the hospital entailed? As the patient in Annie Zunz had surmised, morale was indeed low, and the implication that you might be driven to commit suicide at any moment did nothing to raise it.

Sheila Keen, the senior technician in the path. lab and famous throughout Old East for her passion (and great gift) for gossip, seemed excited rather than depressed by what was going on. She was displaying a bright-eyed relish for it all that irritated her colleagues immensely, not least her boss Dr George Barnabas. George had been sitting in her cubby hole of an office, looking over the notes that had been sent down with Pamela Frean's body and the post-mortem request, when Sheila came in, bearing a tray with a pot of freshly made coffee and biscuits. Since Sheila was often loudly on record as not being part of Old East's staff in order to make coffee, the sight of her made George scowl.

'What are you after, Sheila?' she said bluntly. 'And try not to be so obvious about it, for Pete's sake. I'd prefer you to come right out with it and ask instead of all this buttering-up stuff.'

Sheila's fixed smile became a little more brittle but didn't falter. 'Oh, Dr B.,' she said indulgently 'you did get out of the bed on the wrong side this morning , didn't you?'

'I did not,' George said, managing not to clench her teeth. 'What do you want?'

Sheila opened her eyes wide. 'I just thought I'd see if there was anything special you wanted done. I could take your PM notes for you maybe? Just to take some of the weight off you?'

'Oh, balls!' said George. 'Who do you think you're kidding? You just want to be there when I do it.'

'Well, why not?' Sheila dropped her air of innocence and looked avid. 'You can't blame me, Dr B.! I mean, what a carry on! Three suicides among the staff and –'

'Who says they're suicides?' George snapped. 'I don't believe I made any such suggestion about the last two. And as I recall,' she added with heavy sarcasm, 'I think I did do the PMs, didn't I? Not you?'

'Oh, Dr B., come on! They can't just be accidents. Not three times in a row. You might as well expect your lottery tickets to come up as that.'

'The first two *were* accidents. I can't say what this one is. Not till I do the PM. And I don't ned your help with it, thank you. I can cope perfectly well with Danny's assistance.'

George went down to the PM room, clutching the notes and swearing inaudibly at letting Sheila rile her so much. Sheila had always been the most difficult member of the staff while at the same time being the most expert at her job. If only she didn't have to be so hard to get on with, George thought as she dumped the notes and made for her dressing room to get into her greens. A taste for gossip shouldn't madden me so much, I like gossip myself. But she really is the end . . .

By the time George was ready, her hair tied up in a tight cap, rubber-aproned and with her feet tucked into the oversized boots that protected her from the water Danny always sent splashing so enthusiastically over the slabs, she had managed to push Sheila and her irritating ways to the back of her mind. She had a job to do and she had to concentrate on it.

But all the same, as she and Danny prepared to start, she couldn't help mentally reviewing the previous two cases involving members of Old East's staff on which she had worked in the past few days: Tony Mendez, the theatre porter who had died of alcoholic poisoning; and Lally Lamark, from the Medical Records department, who had been diabetic and who had died in an insulin coma. Both had clearly been accidental, she thought, yet all over the hospital there had been this rush of gossip that they had been suicides. No wonder Sheila had been so eager to come and find out what had happened to Pam Frean.

George looked down at the body on the slab and felt the twinge of pity that she still experienced whenever the subject for a PM was young. But this was being silly, even sentimental, she told herself. 'Right, Danny,' she said briskly. 'Let's get going.'